THE
Masterpiece

MaryAnn Minatra

HARVEST HOUSE PUBLISHERS
Eugene, Oregon 97402

Scripture references are taken from the King James Version of the Bible.

THE MASTERPIECE

Copyright © 1994 by Harvest House Publishers
Eugene, Oregon 97402

Library of Congress Cataloging-in-Publication Data

Minatra, MaryAnn, 1959-
  The masterpiece / MaryAnn Minatra.
    p.   cm.
  ISBN 1-56507-172-7
  1. Family—United States—Fiction.   I. Title.
PS3563.I4634M37   1993   93-27042
813′.54—dc20   CIP

This is a tribute,
no matter how inadequate or imperfect
to the one who prayed for me,
to the one who said,
"No one can make me laugh like you can"
. . . to my brother, Jim.
1955–1979

Mississippi, 1914

♦♦ ♦♦ ♦♦

*S*he knew her brother and sister didn't understand her interest in the past. What could be so all-absorbing about things that happened decades ago to people long in their graves? Wasn't the present exciting enough? Who had time to read faded newspaper clippings or yellowed letters or stroll between moss-covered headstones? Those were generations past, dim and distant. Wasn't their hold on today fragile and tenuous?

She didn't think so. It didn't matter that the others didn't understand. No, not at all. She clutched her little leather-bound journal and kept walking. She knew where the stone was. She had been here before. It was drawing on late afternoon when she found what she was looking for. She bent down and brushed away the leaves across the headstone.

She was a young girl of 18, blue-eyed, with short, curly red-blonde hair. Some in her family said she reminded them of her paternal grandmother. That pleased her. Her grandmother had always been a favorite with her, never tiring of telling her the "old" stories. It thrilled her that the gracious old lady had been a nurse in the Civil War. It had stirred her sense of romance and adventure. If only she could have half the excitement her grandmother had had.

She stood up, smoothing her light linen skirt and adjusting her broad straw hat. She opened her diary, pulled the pencil from her purse, and scratched down the last line written on the headstone before her. Someday Kate would know the whole story...

She drove a little buggy that stood in the shade of two giant cypress trees. The mare looked up at her with devoted brown eyes and went back to cropping the grass. The girl climbed in, frowning a moment at the newspaper her brother had left on the floorboard. It didn't belong in an afternoon like this, golden with memories. Its black banner was a bold intruder: GERMANY DECLARES WAR!

They all found that so exciting at home. Even at school the teacher had included it in his history lecture. A far-off place with an unpronounceable name, Sarajevo. An assassination of an archduke and his wife. She could barely find the places on the globe. What did this obscure little war have to do with America anyway?

She sighed. What about our own past? She thought of the line she'd written in her diary—the last line carved in stone. She had heard of it before of course, but she always wanted more details.

She rolled it off her tongue, enjoying the sound of it, *Magnolia Remembrance...*

Part I

The Palette

Chapter 1

Chisolm Crossing, Mississippi, 1885

♦♦ ♦♦ ♦♦

*M*icah Jefferson was born shortly before sunset. He came into the world with a piercing cry and his little dimpled brown hands drawn up into fists. His grandmother predicted he would be a fighter. She couldn't have been more wrong. The little infant would grow into a sturdy lad with a quick laugh and an even, sunny disposition.

His mother, despite her extreme exhaustion, sat up in bed and examined him. He was the most beautiful baby she had ever seen, and she promptly fell in love with him.

"Oh, Granny, isn't he just wonderful?" she asked her mother-in-law in a raptured voice.

"I reckon he's just another black boy, that's all," the old woman replied crisply.

The new mother turned away from the old, wrinkled face to gaze again at the new, smooth one. Never mind what Granny said—this was no time to argue. She breathed in deeply, pulling him closer, laying her cheek against his, closing her eyes.

"Go on now and quit foolin' over him, girl. Let him suckle," the old woman commanded. She had leaned over the bed, her beady eyes trying to find a flaw in her daughter-in-law's mothering skills.

"I will, Granny, I will..."

But she didn't. The babe lay so quiet and content in the crook of her arm that she hated to disturb him. Besides, she wanted to wait for her man. He had missed the birthing; she didn't want him to miss any other special thing with their first child. She wouldn't try to explain it to Granny. She wouldn't understand.

She glanced over at the old woman who now sat in the rocker by the fire, mumbling and chewing a stick dipped in tobacco. She was desperately thirsty, but she didn't dare ask her for a drink. It would only release another tirade of sarcasm and complaints.

Then the little cabin door flew open, and a tall, lean black man was framed in the doorway. His handsome face was etched in fear and anxiety. He had been around the cabin years ago when his little sisters had been born. He knew the terrible agony a woman could go through to bring new life into the world. The young woman could see the tall white man standing just behind him. She smiled—he had brought the doctor.

Her man was on his knees at the bedside in an instant.

"Ah, Viney darlin', are you all right?" he gasped.

"She's fine, of course! No need for him," his mother snipped, pointing at the doctor with a knobby finger.

The black man ignored her and leaned closer. "Viney?"

Viney smiled up at him, laying a warm hand on his cheek.

"I'm fine, Seth. Just fine."

His voice and face were still in distress.

"Viney, I came runnin' just as soon as I saw Tom come to the shop. I just knew. But, gal, why didn't you send for me so much sooner?"

Again his mother cackled from the chair across the room.

"As if your own mother wasn't good enough for the birthin'!"

Seth didn't bother to turn around. "Ma, I told you I wanted to be here with Viney. I ... told you." His voice was tight.

The old woman snorted. "You is as foolish as they come, even if you is my son. Menfolk is nothin' but trouble at birthin's. And white doctors are about as useless too."

The young doctor smiled. Viney's voice fell to a whisper.

"It all happened so fast, Seth. When I felt the first pains come on ... well ... Granny said first time it could go on for days and not to bother you. I wanted to send for you."

When she saw the anger rising up in her husband she knew it was good that she did not tell him that she had begged his mother to send for him. She laid a hand on his arm, willing him to stay calm.

The old woman seemed to hear their whisperings.

"She didn't birth like she's supposed to. Went too fast."

Viney wished her mother-in-law was living with another child just then. She wished she had Seth all alone to show him their son.

"Seth, it doesn't matter. I'm all right. Look!" She pushed aside the blanket to show him the baby.

His eyes grew wide and filled with tears.

"Well ..." He could say nothing more.

"Isn't he beautiful?" Viney asked.

Seth nodded. "He's ... fine ... He'd fetch a blue ribbon at the fair, I bet!" They both laughed, and Seth reached out a trembling finger to touch the child.

"Hello, Dr. Browning," Viney said.

"Good evenin', Viney. Looks like Granny was right. You didn't need any of us. He's a handsome boy. Mind if I have a better look at him?"

The old woman resumed her mumbling, but they ignored her. The new parents were in their own little world.

Later Seth lay sleeping soundly at his wife's side, spent from the hard work and excitement of the day. But Viney Jefferson couldn't sleep. All she could think about was her new son.

What would life be like for the son of a poor black laborer? There were things she wanted for him. Things that money couldn't buy even if they had it. Things like a sense of humor and good, honest character. She sighed to herself. Perhaps she was just being silly, thinking so far into the future.

Yet there was one thing she had always wanted for herself, wanted for Seth. Now she would be wanting it for their son.

To read.

Viney Jefferson wanted her son to read. Granny Jefferson would certainly snort at the idea. But it was an unchanging dream the young woman had. Somewhere...sometime...someday her son must have a teacher, have a school to go to like white children. *Someday*...

Tanglewood, Mississippi, 1890

In some ways he felt he had been alone all his life, never close to or understood by anybody. Perhaps that would change now. Today was his wedding day.

His mother had been a socialite of gentle Southern society, more concerned with lawn parties and new hats, operas, and afternoons at the racetrack than she had been with nurturing her two children. She had loved them in a distant and distracted sort of way. When the war between the states ended, his mother could not absorb or become accustomed to the sweeping changes in the South. She was confused and clung to the old ways. When she realized they were gone forever, her mind faded quickly.

Patrick Cash rolled his chair closer to the large picture window, memories filling his mind. He could see himself, tense and reluctant as he left home to join the Confederate Army of Northern Virginia. He was 30 years old.

He hadn't any desire or inclination to go off to war. He had gone because his family wanted it. He had gone to please his father, a father most difficult to please. His father had wanted him to be strong and aggressive, an eager heir to the prosperous cotton plantation he would someday inherit. But he had loved horses, and literature, and painting, not facts and figures. It wasn't that he wasn't capable in business. He just wasn't interested in running a plantation, overseeing hundreds of slaves. He had tried to be aloof and remote toward slavery, quietly neutral. But slavery was needed to make his father's plantation a success. He knew in his heart that he was a disappointment to his father.

His father felt all respectable Southern sons should shoulder a rifle and fight for the honor and glory of the Confederacy. So he had gone off to fight the Yanks for four long years.

Perversely, his father felt little pride when, late in the war, his only son was carried home with a bullet wound in his spine. Deathly pale,

Patrick Cash was tormented at night with terrible dreams. The father died six months later, leaving a huge plantation devastated and in debt—a broken legacy falling to an equally broken man.

Cash smiled bitterly now. No, his father hadn't had much faith in him. But he had recovered. His quick mind had grasped what so many other ruined Southerners couldn't—or wouldn't. They must change. They must change in order to survive, and perhaps succeed again. He had not been unwilling to do business with men from the North. He had invested with them in textile mills built in the heart of Dixie. Now he owned mills for his own cotton and lumber. He had seen that the South must industrialize, merge its agrarian roots with the future in order to have any place of influence in the Union.

He leaned forward in his chair, gazing out at the well-manicured garden in front of him. It was a beautiful garden of roses and magnolias. The plantation looked so different than it had 25 years ago. He had renamed it Tanglewood shortly after his father died. It had been like that—neglected and in near ruin, wild and grown over, its fields barren and empty. Only the house had stood, an empty shell, looted of its former glory.

It had taken 20 years to rebuild. Twenty years to restore the Cash name and become one of the wealthiest families in western Mississippi. Now it was simply himself and a handful of servants in a big, lonely house. The grandeur had been restored. He had exceeded even what his father could have done or imagined. But there was no mother or father to be proud of him. The name Tanglewood remained even if it no longer applied. He thought it an important, indeed bitter, reminder of the past.

He had sold a portion of his land for a handsome profit and delegated business investments to appointed associates. Though he had grown more enfeebled of late, he was now free to do what he really liked—raising fine thoroughbreds and painting.

He sighed and shook his head, imagining the smiles and comments from his neighbors and business partners. A man of 58 getting married! And very nearly a cripple at that!

But his bride would surely bring laughter and freshness to Tanglewood, dispel the creeping loneliness he felt more and more these days. He had known her for years. He knew how she thought, how she appreciated beauty as he did. He knew he could speak to her from his heart, from the long years spent alone, of his hurts and his dreams. He felt that with her he would finally find someone who understood him.

He rubbed his chin thoughtfully. She was a special woman, and he hoped with all he was that he could make her happy. He looked down at the quilt that covered his lap. Make her happy . . . Was that possible in a marriage such as theirs? A marriage of convenience . . .

Greenville, Mississippi

She had been waiting tables at the hotel since six in the morning. Greenville had been wrapped in a dingy yellow fog when she had put the coffee on. She could hear the creaking of the ships half a block away where they rocked in their berths. It was an ominous sound to her. But this would be the last morning she would have to hear it. Tomorrow she would be safe...

At eight that evening, she took off her apron. She was too tired to eat, too tired to count the half pocket of coins she had made in tips. She had just enough energy to climb the creaky wooden stairs to the bedroom she shared with three other girls who worked at the hotel. She held a hope, a vain hope she admitted with a frown, that her roommates would be as exhausted as she was and in no mood to gab. She could hear them laughing from the bottom step.

They threw rice at her as she opened the door.

"You wouldn't invite us to the wedding," one of the girls laughed, "so we brought the wedding to you!"

She smiled. It was kind of them, yet all she wanted to do was sleep. She didn't want to look like an unkempt, bleary-eyed hag tomorrow. Her groom certainly deserved better than that!

They kept her up for another hour with their little party. They gave her little tissue-wrapped gifts that were dear to her because she knew what it had cost them to give. Those gifts had come from stacks of dirty plates, and unmade beds, and aching feet that had walked miles between the kitchen and dining room—and smiles toward dock workers who didn't know much about respecting a woman.

She had been sincere. "Thank you, girls, for all of this. You've been so nice to me."

One of the girls had chuckled, a throaty laugh.

"Our things will look like rags next to all the fine things you're coming into, Amy."

Amy winced. She did hate to hear the change that was coming to her life referred to like that—as if her marriage was just an acquiring of wealth. It was that, yes, but more, wasn't it? She didn't want to talk about it to the girls. They wouldn't understand. She had tried to keep her plans from them. But when she gave her notice, she had to tell them. They deserved to know. They had been so kind when she came looking for a job with only a small bag and the clothes she wore.

"What do you think *he* will do when he finds out, Amy?"

The question cast an instant shadow on the party. Everyone looked to Amy with concern. This was obviously not a reference to the prospective groom.

She must give them a quick answer, satisfy them, then hopefully she could go to bed.

"I don't know. But it doesn't matter. What I do...it doesn't matter what he thinks."

"It's a good thing he's in Natchez. He'll be mighty upset with you, Amy, when he hears you've gone and got yourself married."

"It doesn't matter," Amy asserted again, this time more firmly.

"Don't be so gloomy on Amy's weddin' eve, Lizzie!" another girl chirped up.

Finally the lamps were blown out and Amy listened as each girl fell into rhythmic slumber. Tomorrow was a day of new beginnings, and she must not think of what *he* could do when he found out.

Chisolm Crossing, Mississippi

Young Dr. Browning held the slender wrist, feeling the pulse, feeling the beat of life that was growing fainter and fainter. He was not really a good-looking man, but a smile could do wonders to soften his features. The doctor did not smile often.

The patient stirred on the corn-shuck mattress.

"Can you even feel it, Doc?" he whispered.

"It's running, Harris, like that timepiece you showed me once when I was a boy."

The old face was as wrinkled as a sunbaked apple. But the eyes were still bright, the mouth still often curved into a toothless grin.

"I showed you a timepiece once? When?"

"When I was about eight or nine. You came over to help my father on our house. Said you knew all about layin' rock."

"Now that was surely a long time ago. Your pa always said you had hands to be a doctor. Said you nursed him like...since you two were—"

The doctor's voice was unusually sharp. "Don't talk, Harris."

But the old man could not hear him. "Fine hands for healin', your pa always said. Said you were everything to him."

Unwillingly, the doctor was moved to the past. His voice grew gentle as he remembered. "My father prayed over my hands once...when I was small," he mused.

The old man drifted off to sleep, but the young man kept vigil beside him. He had always liked this old patriarch. As a boy he had admired the smooth, chocolate-brown skin that never freckled or burned or blemished, and the cap of tight white curls that reminded him of a perfect cotton bowl. Now he was staying with him, hoping to comfort him in some small way as the old man made this final journey.

The old man spoke up suddenly.

"Seen Sherman and his men march through Georgia. That was the spring of '64. Never forget that...never. His men were a burnin' and a bustin' every living thing they could see and lay hands on."

"Yankees," the doctor muttered tersely. But the old man did not hear.

"I ran out there to them a marchin' past, and I shamed 'em for what they was doing. Acting like a bunch of... of soulless Canaanites! One soldier boy stepped out and slapped me. Said to hush old man, they was doing it all for me. I says it's my back that's gonna have to build back up what you tore down!"

"*Soulless Canaanites...*" The doctor was amused. "For Yankees, that's a fitting term, Harris. Now you settle down. Look how your talking is making you cough."

"You don't have to stay up with me, Doc. Why you stayin' up with a dried-up old black man? Don't you know I can die all by myself?"

Then the doctor smiled.

"I like you, Harris. You know that. We've been friends for a long time."

"You lonely, Doc? I lived through four wives!" the old man beamed proudly.

"I'd say you're hard on women," the doctor attempted playfully.

A raspy chuckle came from the bed. "No, sir, I says I'm... irresistible to womenfolk!" He fell back on the bed gasping.

"Take it easy, Harris."

The medical man could do nothing professionally, nor could he act professional any longer. He leaned closer and stroked the wrinkled brow. It never got any easier to watch this ageless drama unfold.

The vapor of life, steady for 103 years, slowly faded. Tears formed in the clear gray eyes of the young man. He held the hand a few minutes longer.

He stood up then, feeling the burning outrage of cramped muscles in his neck and back. He went to the cabin door and looked out on the morning sun beginning its steady, golden climb.

"Are you lonely, Doc?" he whispered. Then the face of a woman flashed into his mind. A face that always brought pain...

New Orleans, 1891

When Andy Alcott heard the back of his shirt rip, he remembered the letter. Rather than throw another punch or even fend one off, his hand went quickly to his shirtfront pocket. With satisfaction, and some disappointment that he had forgotten it until now, he felt the smooth crispness of the envelope. Funny how he was able to detach himself from the violence around him for just a moment and remember his family.

But that instant of remembering was too long and too costly. A mighty hand spun him around with a curse and slammed a heavy fist into his face. The punch glanced off the bridge of his nose, landing with full impact on his cheek. He felt as if the bone had been crushed. Blood gushed from his nose, and he knew that the letter had probably been splattered with his blood.

Now he was on his back, feeling the shards of broken glass on his skin and the blinding hot pain in his face. His opponent was standing over him, cursing and smiling with twisted pleasure. With the same detachment, Andy was able to look at the man a moment, to look at him closely.

The man above him was neither big nor incredibly strong. His infamous fighting abilities came from his own inner brutality and love of destruction, of defeating an enemy quickly and thoroughly. The patchwork of scars across his face and upper torso testified that he had been about violence most of his life. Andy studied the network of tiny broken blood vessels across the man's bulbous nose. It reminded him of a map of rivers. Another time, under vastly different circumstances, he might have pointed his observations out to the owner. He thought of the writer of the letter in his pocket; she would have had some funny comment about the man's interesting nose.

Andy refocused. The man was boiling with rage.

"I've had enough of your interfering ways, Alcott! Enough! I told ya to leave Lilly alone!"

His hands went into a circular grip and Andy realized he was about to be choked to death. There was nothing he could do. The pain and the exhaustion were too much. He glanced aside to see that his partner, Ben, was still slumped in the corner, unconscious. The man's hands tightened on his neck now, slowly, ever so slowly increasing their pressure. Andy closed his eyes. It would be better to die not having to look up into this man's face.

Suddenly there was a thud, the sound of breaking glass, a groan from the man above him. Andy was showered with blood and wine as the man's body collapsed across him. Sometimes it could be like that—one heave of the ax, and the mighty tree will topple. Andy gasped for air as he looked up into the surprised face of Lilly O'Hara.

"I suppose I should have used an empty wine bottle," she said, apologizing to Andy with a smile. "You're a mess!"

"Lilly. Get him...off me!"

The young woman needed all her strength to push the unconscious man over onto the floor.

"There!" She wiped her hands on her dress, as though touching the brutal man had been offensive.

Andy had closed his eyes again, his breathing labored, his body racked with pain.

"Andy." Lilly was shaking him now. "Andy, you've got to get up! He'll be stirrin' anytime now. Andy!"

"Aw, Lilly, my whole face," he groaned.

She began pulling him into a sitting position. Andy swayed with dizziness.

"Andy, you've got to get up! We've got to get out of here. Don't you know what he'll be like when he wakes up? What he'll do...to me?"

Andy's eyes cleared as he took in Lilly's words. If the man woke up, Andy would be in no condition to protect Lilly. The man would kill them all.

"Go see about Ben. Get him up too. Hurry," he responded.

She left him and went across the room. Andy got to his knees, then stood up. Suddenly there was an incredible pain in his foot.

"Lilly!" he panted.

She was there beside him, along with Ben.

"Andy, you all right?" Ben asked.

"My foot! I think it must be broken."

Ben put his arm around Andy's shoulders, supporting him.

"Come on," he said, glancing nervously at the form on the floor. "You know what a wounded grizzly's like. We got to get out of here. I'll carry you. Come on, Lil."

Captain Angus Treadle stood with his arms crossed over his massive chest, peering critically over the surgeon's shoulder. He was very angry. His first mate lay stretched in front of him with a smashed face and a badly broken foot. For all his gruffness, Treadle did hate to see a man in pain. And if the truth be known, he had a grudging respect and affection for Andy Alcott.

The surgeon tossed down an instrument.

"Just short of the foot being totally crushed, it's about as bad as I've seen. Broken across the toes and just below the heel."

Turn-of-the-century New Orleans was a rowdy, boisterous city. The waterfront could brag of at least one ship under flag from nearly every country—and a fistfight in any nationality or tongue. The doc saw the fine results of brawls every day; it made up the majority of his cases. He saw more bruised, battered, dying human life than he did the birthing of innocent, fresh, new life.

He turned to Ben, who hovered nearby.

"What did you say he was hit with?"

Ben's voice was squeaky. "A lead pipe. Hawk heaved it on him with all his strength just before Lilly hit him."

Captain Treadle muttered something between a curse and a snarl.

"What about his face? It's pretty messy."

"No broken bones that I can determine. Just 'messy' like you say," the doctor agreed.

Andy groaned.

"And the foot?" Treadle prodded irritably.

The surgeon stood up, gathering his tools into his bag. "Well, I should think a rather lengthy recovery for that foot. He'll have a limp at the very least."

"Just how lengthy a recovery?" the captain snapped.

"Treadle, that foot is more of a mess than his face. I'm a doctor, not a miracle worker. He'll need to stay off it for six weeks—"

"Six weeks!" Treadle exploded.

"And then take it easy for at least three or four months. It's a hard thing to predict." The doctor looked down at Andy without emotion. "Consider him a cripple for a while. Here's the laudanum for the pain. I'll be back in the morning. Good evening, folks."

The ship cabin was quiet. Treadle began to pace as was his habit when greatly agitated. He stopped in front of Andy occasionally to glare at him, then continued his pacing. Finally he stopped and pulled up a stool to Andy's bed.

"Well?" he demanded.

Andy shrugged and gave him a weak smile.

"Did you hear what the doctor said? Did you? A fine thing! A cripple he called you!"

"I heard what he said," Andy replied wearily.

"How in . . . how did this happen, Andy Alcott? Answer me that, will ya?"

Andy sighed deeply. "Ben told you."

"I heard what he said! But how in the world did you get mixed up with a character like Maxwell Hawk? I mean, I can take care of myself, but even I know to steer away from a bad egg like that!"

"I didn't steer into him on purpose, Treadle."

"So I'd like to know how this happened then. Of all the men in my crew, I'd not expect you or Ben anywhere near his territory. What put you in his way?"

There was a discreet cough from the corner, and Treadle swung around.

It had not been easy to get Lilly O'Hara on board *Ivanhoe's Dream*, but even in his weakened condition Andy had insisted. It was the safest place for her. So despite Treadle's resident rule that no women were ever allowed on board, Lilly O'Hara was there. In the course of the surgeon's work, she had been temporarily forgotten. Treadle gave her a withering and thoroughly accusing look.

"So." He looked at Ben for an answer, but the young man looked away guiltily. "Ben, take Miss—"

"O'Hara," Andy interrupted.

"Take Miss O'Hara to my cabin. Get her some tea. I want to talk to Andy alone."

Lilly came up to the bedside, leaning over it, her eyes brimming with tears. "Perhaps your captain will let me help take care of you. Oh, Andy, I'm so sorry for the trouble I've caused you. If only you—"

Andy reached up and took her hand. "Lilly, you're safe now, and you're saved now. Hawk's working me over is a small price really. Everything's going to be all right. Don't worry."

Treadle cleared his throat in a clear warning gesture, and Ben quietly led Lilly from the cabin.

"How did you get involved with this woman, Andy?" Treadle asked curtly.

"Now, Treadle? Do we have to talk now?"

Treadle was too frustrated to be kind.

"Now. Any other sailor I wouldn't have to ask. But you! She's one of Hawk's girls, correct?"

"*Was* one of his girls," Andy answered tiredly.

"You mean? Oh, Andy, you didn't steal a girl from one of the biggest pimps in New Orleans, did you? I'll be lucky if he doesn't burn this boat down to get both of you!"

"Ben and I were at St. Charles Park in the Old Square about a month ago, talking with people," Andy explained.

"Preaching!"

"Talking. We saw Lilly sitting off by herself, obviously afraid and upset. We went over and started talking to her. She came back every day after that. She...she's hurting, Treadle."

"You converted one of Maxwell Hawk's prostitutes, and she's left him! I see it all now."

Maxwell Hawk ruled his waterfront territory and "subjects" with the ferocity his surname implied. To tangle with one of New Orleans' foremost sellers of flesh was to dig yourself a watery grave.

"She's only 18 years old, not much younger than my little sister, Treadle," Andy said in a quiet voice.

"I've never objected to your preaching before, Andy. Not since you came aboard eight years ago. I've tolerated your religion."

"And for eight years I've been telling you I'm not religious." Andy's voice had grown hoarse. "It's my faith. Treadle, you remember that spring we were off the coast of Jamaica and found that wounded seal? You spent four days trying to nurse it back to health."

Treadle's face clouded, and his fists clenched. He did not like to be reminded of his gentler side.

"It cost you to take care of that seal. Now, isn't a soul a lot more valuable?" Andy asked softly.

Treadle stopped pacing and studied Andy. He would have been amused if he hadn't been so agitated. For eight years Andy had worked for him. For eight years they had wrangled over issues of faith and morals, and Treadle had loved every minute of it. Loyal and capable, Andy was one of the best seamen Treadle had come across in his own 35 years on the water. He'd taken Andy aboard when he had only his eagerness to recommend him. The young man should have been coarse and proud, but he did not fit the sailor's mold. Andy was sensitive and held tenaciously to his faith. Treadle waved an impatient hand, wanting to change the subject, needing to give full vent to his frustration.

"You know we were to set sail at the end of the week. Now what do I do for a first mate? Answer me that!"

"I'm really sorry, Treadle."

Andy's weak voice softened the captain. He cleared his throat, running an agitated hand through his coarse red hair.

"Hawk will know you're here on board. I'll have to post a guard."

"Lilly will have to stay too. She's in more danger than me."

Treadle started to protest but thought better of it.

"All right then. What do I do with you? You can't go on the voyage; you need weeks of medical attention. New Orleans isn't safe. And what do we do with Miss O'Hara?"

"I don't know. I have to think." Andy wished he could slip into the safe and painless oblivion of sleep. His eyes closed, and Treadle came to stand over him, his face momentarily softened.

Treadle's voice dropped to a mumble. "A hold full of problems, that's what I've got. And no first mate."

Andy was moved under the cover of darkness to a small boarding house in a remote part of the French quarter of New Orleans. Treadle arranged it all. The French woman who owned the house understood Treadle's directions perfectly. She would keep quiet about her guest and his "sister" who attended him. The doctor could now care for Andy's foot more closely, carefully resetting the bones if necessary.

Treadle's departure was brief and typically brusque.

"Try to stay out of trouble. I'll be back in September."

"Will I still have my job when you get back?" Andy asked from his bed with a smile.

Treadle snorted and ignored the question. "I'd have left Ben with you, but since I'm having to break in a new first mate..."

"Well, when I'm up and about, I'll find a part-time job while I wait for you," Andy continued.

"Not in New Orleans!" Treadle bellowed. "You may be forgiving, but Max Hawk doesn't know the meaning of the word. Go to Natchez for a while, or go home."

Andy shrugged. "Don't worry; I'll be fine."

Treadle studied the bruised and swollen face, then nodded. He wanted to linger, to say something that would tell Andy that he would miss him. But he only coughed awkwardly. "Well..."

"Goodbye, Ben."

The lanky, tow-headed youth had been one of Andy's "converts." Still pimple-faced and self-conscious, he had a skill and love of the ocean that matched his mentor's.

"Goodbye, Andy. I'll miss ya...and I'll be prayin' for ya."

Later that afternoon, Andy lay in the quiet room trying to ignore the throbbing in his foot and the soreness in his face. The laudanum could only do so much, only hold the pain to a nearly tolerable level. Andy hated taking it and was determined not to become too dependent on it.

He gazed out the window, knowing that in a few hours *Ivanhoe's Dream* would weigh anchor. The wind would fill the gigantic sails as the prow sliced the waters in a blue foam. He wouldn't be going, wouldn't be barking out Treadle's orders to the men below him, wouldn't feel the exciting rush as a new voyage began.

He idly wondered whether he would have been on board, his life going on as usual, if he had been a better fighter. It made him think of his younger brother Matthew. Matt could use his fists when he had to. He was built like their father, tall and broad shouldered. Andy was slim and lithe. He had never liked fighting, not even the rough-and-tumble wrestling between brothers. Now as he tenderly ran his fingers across his face, he half wished he had liked it.

Treadle called his talking with folks "preaching." He could never be a preacher, not in the stand-behind-the-pulpit sense like his Uncle Henri. But he was like his uncle in the desire to live the truth of the gospel in his daily life. So really, all he'd been doing was sharing his faith with Lilly O'Hara. "Thrown her a lifeline" she had told him on their second conversation. That made him feel good. Most of the crew of *Ivanhoe's Dream* did not share Lilly's appreciation for the first mate's faith. Andy often thought he talked to the wind that pushed the clipper, or to men with hearts of stone and seawater between their ears.

Thinking of his uncle brought back memories. He saw himself at 12 years old, stretched out on the grassy, shady banks of Peppercreek, a pole lazily crossed over his leg. He cared nothing for fishing, but Uncle Henri did, so he tagged along.

They had talked of all kinds of things that autumn afternoon when Henri told him the story about Jesus and his fishermen friends.

"'And I will make you fishers of men!' Jesus declared." Henri repeated the commission in his most dramatic voice, yet a voice full of joy.

Being a circuit rider, then preacher to a country church for over 30 years, Henri, Andy knew, had been a fisherman.

"That's what you do," Andy said quietly.

Henri smiled broadly and tousled Andy's hair.

"Try to," he replied simply.

Andy couldn't remember the rest of their conversation that afternoon, whether the catch was good or not. But he'd never forget that evening after his family had gone to bed. He'd slipped from the quilt-covered iron bed he shared with his younger brother Matt and crept downstairs. Moonlight streamed in the front window of the living room, helping him to put his hand on the volume he was looking for. It was beside the mammoth family Bible that reigned from the oak beam mantel. He took the little book to the kitchen where his mother kept her writing desk and lit a lamp.

In his own shy way, he did not want to be discovered, or questioned. It was too personal, too fresh in his heart right now to say the words to his parents. Carefully, almost reverently, he opened the slim little book.

This was his father's journal.

"You can read it when you're a man grown," his father had said. "Then you'll understand it better."

The first page was creamy white, smooth, penned in the flowing hand of his mother: *The Alcott Legacy.*

It was like a family tree, like the kind most often recorded in the family Bible. But his father Ethan had wanted more space to write. This record would be more than just a testimonial of births, deaths, and marriages. This was a registry of eternal births, his father had explained, for all the Alcott generations who cared to sign it.

William O'Dell m. Rebecca Cash

Their children,
Wyeth, Louisa, Elizabeth (Libby), Ethan Alcott

Ethan Alcott m. Sara James

Their children,
Andy, Matthew, Margarett (Meg), Daniel

Each name was also signed in a personal signature if the owner had made Jesus his or her Lord and Savior. Each name had been signed until his generation. He would be the first.

He dipped his pen and wrote in the steadiest script of a 12-year-old. He paused, still shy, yet proud in his boy's heart. Three more words. He hoped his family wouldn't mind his original flourish.

Andrew William Alcott, fisher of men!

A wave of loneliness for his family brought him back to the present. He was grateful when he heard a timid knock. The door opened. It was Lilly.

"Up to company?" she asked.

"Sure, come on in."

She pulled up a chair to his bedside, smoothing her dress. Andy smiled, noting the fresh beauty of her face, no longer matted with heavy makeup. Her eyes were clear and bright.

Lilly O'Hara was prettier than Andy had first noted. He had first seen her as she sat listlessly feeding the ducks from a park bench. She wore a cheap-looking, dark silk dress. No one went out in the morning dressed like that—unless it was your complete wardrobe. Her jewelry was as gaudy as her face makeup.

Ben had seen her across the park too. He had nudged Andy and said untactfully, "Looks like she's been playin' in her mama's dress-up things."

Her clothes were an obvious advertisement, the body underneath them the bait. Andy watched as women hurried their children past her, whispering and shaking their heads. No one had shared the bench with her. Finally one woman had hissed, loud enough to be heard to the farthest perimeter of the park grounds.

"Why are *you* here? This is a respectable park!"

Andy winced at the words and stood up. He had seen enough.

The young woman had had enough. She stood up also. When Andy approached her, she stopped. Their eyes locked, probing. He could see her stiffen. He knew what she was waiting for, the line in some variation that she'd probably heard a thousand times before.

"Good morning. I . . ." Andy wasn't quite sure how to assure her, to put her at ease. "It's a beautiful morning . . . to feed ducks, isn't it? Ducks are greedy, aren't they?" He nodded toward the birds that were squawking around Lilly's skirt. "Feed them once, they won't leave you alone."

In a moment, Lilly O'Hara had understood he was nervous. She knew he hadn't walked up to her to flatter her, then buy her. How could he be like that with such kind, almost laughing, blue eyes? He was a grown man, yet looking boyish.

"Well . . . I'm from Illinois. Where are you from?"

"Around," she replied. She must test him, not give him her confidence too soon. Men can be imposters, she had painfully learned.

"My friend Ben here and I—we come here to talk to folks about Jesus Christ. Do you know Him, Miss?"

It had been a long time since anyone had called her Miss.

"I know something about the Bible, if that's what you mean," she returned spiritedly.

"No, I mean do you know Jesus?"

"I've heard of him. Everyone's heard of . . . of God!"

Years later they would laugh together over this remark. But he leaned forward then, taking her hand unconsciously.

"No, ma'am, that isn't the same. Knowing *about* Him isn't *knowing* Him. Can I tell you?"

She smiled—they would be friends for a long time.

Her future was as uncertain as Andy's. She was still in danger from Max Hawk if she ventured abroad the streets of the city. Yet she had found faith—and she was free.

"Madame Mourier has been after me all morning about going to an early Mardi Gras dance with her nephew Louis. She declares I need a break from nursing my poor brother."

"That's very considerate of her," Andy replied.

Lilly tossed her dark red curls and smiled.

"Well, actually I think it's more concern for poor Louis. From what she has said, I think he must be more than a little awkward with women."

"Ah."

"Of course, if she knew about me..." Lilly laughed, not amused at the sin of her former life, but at the thought of the little French woman's horrified face if she had known the truth about Lilly O'Hara.

"So I've been declining, saying I can't leave my brother, thank you."

She began to tidy up Andy's bed as she talked. It was a wonderful thing, she thought, being able to be close to a man without him grabbing or gawking or cursing her. Of course, Andy was hardly able to do much of anything. She smiled to herself. He was a normal, healthy man, but he respected her. And he had his faith.

Her eyes swept over his face in concern. She knew he was in great pain. Andy was a good-looking man, and she hoped his face wouldn't be scarred or disfigured. Despite his assurances and kind words, she knew he had taken the terrible beating for her. She chewed her lip, thinking of his foot. Possibly a cripple, the doctor had said. Lilly couldn't bear the thought of that.

Andy suddenly snapped his fingers, bringing her out of her reverie. "That's it! I remember now!"

"What, Andy?"

"A letter. In my pocket, the night of the fight. Can you find that shirt for me, Lilly?"

She found the shirt wadded up in a ball in the bottom of Andy's trunk. She held it gingerly and with a grimace on her face. The garment was ripped, bloodstained, and smelly.

"Here it is," she said as she pulled out the envelope. "Oh, Andy, it's—"

"Just a little dried blood and wine. Never mind it. Open the letter up and read it, will you, Lilly? I can't believe I've forgotten it this long."

She hesitated. "Important, hmm? From a woman?"

He matched her slyness. "Yep, a gal as pretty as you."

"Oh?"

"My sister, Meg," he laughed. He pulled himself up, and Lilly did not miss the eagerness in his eyes. Carefully she unfolded the pages.

"Dear Andy..."

Peppercreek, Illinois

Meg Alcott pulled the turkey-red sweater closer to her throat, smoothing her hair with her other hand. Her auburn-rich hair was pulled up in a fashionable pompadour, the style of the day, thanks to magazine illustrator Charles Dana Gibson. His "Gibson girl" was a lovely young American woman, fresh, intelligent, brimming with vigorous good health. Thousands of women were fashioning themselves after this delightful image. What had begun as an advertising gimmick had turned into a sweeping fad.

Meg Alcott fit the image in many ways—except that her pompadour was loose and lopsided, and during the long, cold Illinois winters her health was often fragile, never hearty.

She'd been outside, playing tag with her students. It made her feel "brimming with good health," the rush of piercing cold air making her eyes water and her lungs burn. Now she was coughing that racking cough that always came in November and stayed through February. She regretted that it would make her parents so concerned for her. Yet she had been like this since she was a little girl.

Now she was a young woman of 20 and playing tag! It was a wonder that she hadn't tripped on her skirt and pitched headlong onto the hard-packed schoolyard. How the little scholars would have hooted over that! She shook her head. She hadn't been very dignified—certainly not for a cultured Gibson girl.

She glanced around the building with a grudging affection. She had been teaching here for nearly three years, been a schoolgirl here as well. Her father had learned his Latin here. Her grandfather Will O'Dell had helped lay the cornerstones nearly 50 years ago. It was a sturdy building, she would grant it that—a building full of family memories sitting out on the prairie oblivious to the changes a soon-to-be new century was bringing with it.

Pulling herself closer to the sputtering coal stove, she sat down to wait. Someone from home would be coming soon to pick her up. She flipped through a *Ladies Home Journal,* letting it take her into a world far removed from her little rural schoolhouse. Schoolhouses were brick in the bigger cities, and certainly had more than one room. They had all kinds of "educational equipment" that she could only read about.

The magazine said these were modern days, and the phrase "gay nineties" was now used to describe the times in which she lived. Somehow she felt the magazine described life on another planet. Life at Peppercreek, Illinois, seemed neither modern nor gay to a young schoolmarm. The dawn of the twentieth century was not so far off, but Meg Alcott felt she had been left behind. Maybe it was her youth—she didn't know—but the roots of discontent with her present life were growing strong within her.

She reminded herself that it would probably be her father coming to pick her up. She looked down at her cold, chapped hands. Just six months ago there had been a ring on her left hand, a simple gold band. Now it was gone. She hugged herself tighter, willing herself not to cry, knowing her father would notice her red-rimmed eyes. He'd feel awkward trying to think of a way to comfort her. But they both knew he couldn't.

She had been engaged six months ago, and very happy. She would still have been living in unimaginative, unmodern Peppercreek, but she would have belonged to someone and had her own home. Her family had been happy for her too. The only shadow had been that her oldest brother wasn't home. He was off on a long voyage. She couldn't bear the thought of getting married without him being there for the grand day. They had always been so close. She told her fiancé they must wait till spring. A short interval, really.

That was the beginning. He didn't want to wait. Within a month she could sense his heart pulling away from her. She was powerless to stop it. Then came the moonlit evening when he politely asked for the ring back. He said he had found someone else. Meg Alcott wondered if she would ever get over this enormous, strangling feeling of rejection. The fierce indignation of her family and friends was bittersweet, but it did nothing to assuage the pain.

She took the letter that she'd read earlier from her pocket. It would help draw her mind away from the hurt awhile. She smiled as she looked at the careful, precise handwriting. She would know it anywhere—Andy had always won the penmanship awards in this very schoolroom. She read again, learning that he was on his way to Greenville, Mississippi, to see their second cousin, Patrick Cash. He told her all about his foot, and about Lilly O'Hara and Hawk. She laughed with delight as he described the man's nose. She felt she had read something out of a dime novel.

Granted her seafaring brother sailed to exotic ports, but this misadventure was out of character. She knew him well enough to know that his courage to save Lilly O'Hara came not from romantic love, but from a brotherly love, a love for the girl's soul. She knew the letter to her parents had not contained every detail as hers had. It gave her a warm pleasure that Andy trusted her.

She gathered up her things as she heard a team of horses enter the yard. Tucking the letter back into her pocket, she wondered if both she and her brother were destined for singleness. It was not difficult to imagine.

Chapter 2

The French Quarter, New Orleans

◆◆ ◆◆ ◆◆

*L*illy O'Hara had always loved to play parts—it was a way of escaping reality for a short time, of stepping out of your own troubled life into a different, safer identity. Of course, she really didn't understand those motives as a little girl. She just knew she loved to pretend that faded aprons and flour-sack dresses were the gossamer stuff that princesses wore. Old hats could be transformed into helmets and crowns or anything the vision of Lilly O'Hara could make them.

But pretending couldn't last forever. There came a gnawing, hungry stomach that could not be ignored, and a thin dress that was no defense against the winter wind, and long hours of work—and bruises from when Mama drank too much from the dark brown bottle. It was a hard and loveless life for a child.

For nearly 16 years Lilly lived that life, with fleeting moments of imagination and pretend. She could keep the neighbor kids spellbound with any recitation she had memorized from a ragged schoolbook. Advertisements, a piece of amateur poetry, Lilly could dramatize anything. Pretend worlds, faraway kingdoms—they belonged to Lilly. And for so many of her poor little friends, she was their escape too.

At 16 Lilly could not live like that any longer. The dark side of life was too dark—and too intolerable. Now there were men friends her mother brought home for a drink in the evenings. It was time to make it on her own. One final beating, one final threat, and she was gone.

Since her play-acting had always brought her pleasure and such applause from her humble crowd of critics, becoming an actress seemed like a natural pursuit. New Orleans had theaters, she had heard. So New Orleans became her destination.

Never mind its French elegance, its international sophistication, its gracious parks and fine homes, New Orleans was a tough town, and no place for a redheaded girl of 16 with nothing but her country good looks for a reference.

Lilly found out quickly there seemed to be only one profession she could apply for. She held out until she nearly starved. One of Maxwell Hawk's friends kept a vigilant eye for recruits, for women clothed in desperation. She had an eye for them. She found Lilly weak, pale, cold. She provided a warm bath, a hot meal, and a clean, warm bed. It was all Lilly wanted.

Lilly took the bait. She rested; she ate her fill. She swept the hallways and made beds in the Charlotte "Hotel." For six months it was what kept her alive. Then Max Hawk made his proposition. She must go into "service." It was a simple proposition, as old and as evil as the pit it came from.

One year. She could work long enough to save a few dollars. Then she could approach the theaters looking qualified, not dirty and starving. One audition was all she would need. Surely they would see the talent that her grimy-faced friends had seen. One year—a year in a yawning grave.

Then one afternoon she'd slipped away for the fresh air and beauty of St. Charles Park. There was Andy—and the steps from the grave began an upward spiral.

Lilly stood looking at the night sky over the French quarter. It was a sheet of violet with great black blobs of clouds. It reminded Lilly of ink, as if a giant bottle of it had been spilled in the heavens. A storm was brewing over the Louisiana coast. Yet a thousand gas lamps from the street corners, and lamps on the handsome cabs and carriages, and the lights from the restaurants and ships at harbor testified that New Orleans never slept. No storm could put the lights of the city out, for it was a city forever in a party mood.

And it was a city of music. Lilly could hear the thin strains of half a dozen melodies. It made her think of singing on stage and acting. She had left home, and now she had run away from the grasp of Max Hawk. His demands were gone, but so were his provisions. What now?

"What are you so deep in thought about, Miss O'Hara?" Andy asked from his bed.

She turned from the window with a smile.

"Do you know how to two-step, Andy? One of the girls said it's the new dance craze."

"Nope. We don't have much time to waltz aboard the *Ivanhoe,* Lilly," Andy replied, laughing.

"Waltz! Oh Andy, not waltzing, that's too old. I'm telling you it's the two-step."

"Is that what you were thinking about, Lil? Dancing?"

She smiled. She liked to be called Lil. It made her feel as if she belonged to somebody.

"Well, no . . . it's . . . well, Andy, what am I going to do after you can walk again? I mean . . . my future?"

"You can't stay in New Orleans. I'm sure Hawk has people looking everywhere for you."

Lilly shuddered. "I know."

"What would you like your future to be, Lil?"

"I like to sing, Andy. I think I have a decent voice. And..." She stopped, suddenly feeling shy.

"And?"

"I like to become other people. I like to act. Like on a stage some-where."

"You want to be a singer and an actress."

She nodded her head.

"Hmm...How do you become an actress or singer? Do you go to a school or something?" he asked.

"I'm not sure, Andy. Remember I'm just a backwoods girl from northern Louisiana. How did you become a sailor?"

"Well, I just went up to Captain Treadle and said I wanted to sail, and that I would work hard at it. Where would you learn about acting if it wasn't in New Orleans?"

Lilly's eyes grew bright. "That's easy. New York. All the famous plays and productions come from New York... Is my dream too big, Andy?"

"No dream is too big, Lil."

If only Lilly could go to New York. Andy puzzled on this as he lay in bed, trying to divert his mind from the pain in his foot. He could save Lilly from Max Hawk, but there were Max Hawks everywhere. And in a huge city like New York... Was Lilly strong enough to resist the slide back into that life again if times became hard?

Andy had something to return to after he recovered. What did Lilly have? How could he secure a future for her? One thing was clear. He could not leave her until she had something.

The thought of his father came into his mind. His father seemed so wise, always seemed to know how to meet a need.

"What would you do, Papa?" he murmured. "What would you do?"

Andy's concern was that Lilly know the truth of the gospel, that she become strong in it. Whatever her future, she must be prepared, and she must know the Shepherd walked with her. They began to read the Gospels together. A body healing and a spirit as well.

And in those hours when they laughed and learned and prayed together, they became friends that Andy's oceans and Lilly's success would never change.

There were tiny beads of sweat on Andy's forehead, like a suddenly appearing row of blisters. He was pale and trembling as he took steps across his room. Lilly watched him, chewing her lip to keep back the tears. He was in such pain, but the doctor had insisted he begin this therapy on his foot. Slowly and carefully, one tiny step at a time.

"How ... am I ... doing ... Lil? I feel like an old man!"

"Oh, Andy." She came to stand beside him. She had never expressed her feelings so openly. "It's my fault you're in such pain."

He put his arm around her. "Never mind, Lil. Here, I want to tell you something."

He eased himself back into the bed with a groan.

"I've been thinking and thinking about how to get you to New York to study voice and acting. I just couldn't let you go up there with no connections or not knowing anyone. New York is a lot bigger than New Orleans. Then I thought of my sister's last letter. She mentioned that our cousin was beginning a year-long project at Columbia University."

"Your cousin?"

"My cousin Caleb. I've told you about my Uncle Henri and Aunt Wyeth. He's their only son. Sort of the scholar of the family. Anyway, I wrote him about you."

Lilly could not help but wonder if this man would be as kind as his cousin was. No one could ever be like Andy ...

"He called me last night," Andy continued.

"I heard you in the hall. Madame Mourier and I were trying very hard not to eavesdrop. It was a great temptation."

Andy laughed. "Well, he has great news. He works with a city mission a couple of nights a week and he says they need an extra helper. Cooking and cleaning. Caleb says they're fine people, and I trust his judgment. You would have a small salary plus room and board. You'd also have free time to take your lessons. You can start in two weeks. Caleb can meet you at Grand Central."

Lilly felt overwhelmed. "Did they make this place for me, Andy?" she asked quietly.

He smiled and shrugged. "It's yours if you want it, Miss O'Hara."

But Miss O'Hara could not speak. She sat beside him and cried on his shoulder. No one had ever been so good to her ...

New Orleans

Lilly cleared her throat nervously. "Well, I suppose I'd better go ahead and get on board. Get a good seat by the window."

Andy looked at the long train and shook his head soberly.

"I reckon some people feel about trains like I do about ships, but I can't understand it. Trains are such ... monsters! I hate to see you on one, Lilly. Wish you could have gone up-river instead."

She laughed and squeezed his arm. "You're a true man of the sea, Andy Alcott. Will it always be your home, your life?"

She had asked the question in innocent fun, yet it caused Andy to look closely at her. Another time, another place ... could they have been more than good friends? The question hung between them now, for just an instant.

Lilly shook her head to break the spell. Andy was so kind. She envied the woman that would someday stir his heart to more than brotherly love.

Andy smiled, thinking how nice it would have been to have felt more for Lilly O'Hara than he did.

"You'll write me as soon as you get to New York?" he asked finally.

She nodded, not trusting her voice.

"You'll be a great actress," he continued. "You have the looks, the voice, a great stage name. What else do you need?"

They both laughed.

"A little luck perhaps?" she asked.

Andy took her hands and smiled. "Let the Lord help you find your dream, Lilly. Don't give into anything but His best for you."

She leaned forward, looking up into his eyes, the deepest blue eyes she had ever seen. She thought the beard he had grown during his convalescence suited him well. Somehow it seemed to add even more sensitivity to his face. He leaned heavily on his crutches as he placed his arm around her.

"Andy, how can I thank you for . . . everything?"

He stood back to look at her. "We'll meet again someday, Lilly O'Hara, and we'll be able to laugh at my run-in with Maxwell Hawk."

She was crying openly now as she placed her hand gently on his cheek. "God bless you, Andy."

She turned and boarded the train for New York.

Andy felt a comfort as he watched the train pull away, a comfort that Lilly knew the Lord now. He also felt a strange, comforting conviction that he would see her again someday.

The Mississippi River

Andy was on the water again. He felt at home, even if it wasn't the Gulf or the Caribbean. He eased himself down on a bench on the stern end of the deck as the *Governor's Lady* pulled away from the wharf. He leaned forward and scanned the river for a glimpse of other steamboats. There were only three within his view this particular morning. He shook his head sadly.

The proud day of the steamboat was over, gone now nearly 40 years. The coming of the railroad had ushered in a new age of travel and commerce. The roaring, smoke-belching iron horse had stolen away the glory of the steamboat. Now America's Main Street, the mighty Mississippi, was not so congested with riverboat traffic, so vital to linking

North and South. Towns like Natchez, Memphis, Louisville, St. Louis, even New Orleans, that had profited from the steamboat and the river highway now had to acclimate to railroad traffic and transport. Some towns had adjusted well; others were dying a lingering death.

The middle of the 1800s had seen hundreds of steamboats chugging up and down the miles of muddy water, their plumes of smoke reaching high above the trees, their piercing whistles shrill at the landings. Now the plumes of gray and clarion calls came from the countryside where tracks spiraled through hundreds of miles of forest and flatland. The steamboat had antiquated the river keelboat, log raft, and flatboat. Now, the railroad was muscling aside the steamboat. Many Americans vaguely wondered if invention hadn't surely reached its apex.

The romance of steamboats could not be taken from men like Andy Alcott. He was first mate on a sailing clipper now, "another breed, but the same kind of animal," he would explain. His love of boats had been conceived on the Mississippi, in this kind of vessel. He knew the day was coming soon when the sternwheelers would be gone forever, and he would miss them.

He was no longer the wide-eyed youth he had been at age 12, plunging from port to aft so that he could see everything there was to see. His father had laughed and given up trying to calm his usually placid son.

His father. Andy squinted into the sparkles that trembled off the water and thought of him. He wondered if his father regretted that trip they had taken together. It had given Andy a passion for the water that he had never gotten over. When he was 17, he had asked his mother and father if he could leave home—his future was not with the soil, but with rivers and oceans and seas. His mother had cried, and his father had nodded his head soberly. Andy was the firstborn son, heir to his father's land, his life's work. His father had made an investment in the soil that Andy did not want.

Now, eight years later, he never thought of that leaving-home time without a stab of guilt at the sadness he had caused his parents. Though they said they wanted him to be happy, to pursue his own dreams, he knew they were pained to see him go. One concession, he told himself, was that his younger brothers, Matthew and Daniel, loved the land, the orchard, and the horses. They had all the fervor for it that Andy lacked and eagerly took up the dreams of their father.

When Andy was 12, his father had taken him down the River, clear to the Gulf. It had been a wonderful, special time between them. The steamboat was already in its twilight, but Andy knew the vastness that stretched out from the Gulf was for him. En route they had visited with Patrick Cash, the man he called uncle, when in reality he was Andy's second cousin. Andy had been greatly impressed with the Cash plantation of Tanglewood. The climate, the mammoth cypress trees, the magnolias and their heady perfume, the big redbrick mansion, all had been so different to Andy from his native Illinois. His father told him he had felt the same way when he had first come south years earlier.

Andy had been equally impressed with his subdued and gentle "Uncle" Pat. Andy had always enjoyed drawing and sketching. His favorite subjects were boats and buildings. That his uncle was a talented artist only drew the two even closer. Cash lived alone in a huge house, and young Andy could not help but feel a depth of compassion and kinship for him.

As Andy had lain with his broken foot in the French quarter, he had thought of the lonely master of Tanglewood. Greenville was only a two-day journey from New Orleans. It had been some years since the family had had any contact with Cash. Andy decided he would go to visit. Two bachelors could have a fine time together, he reasoned. A telegram had been dispatched, and an enthusiastic welcome returned.

Now as he hobbled about the great sternwheeler, feelings of depression began to lift as the river fog had. Hawk had neither crippled him nor rearranged his plans permanently. The time at Tanglewood would surely be a wonderful and peaceful thing.

Mississippi

Rural America, and especially the South, had hardly been touched by the "gay nineties." Folks still burned kerosene lamps and went to bed with the chickens. Though American life was becoming increasingly urbanized and industrialized, on scattered farms and villages to the west and south of the Mason-Dixon line life still moved sedately, still demanded a precious physical toll, still kept a strong tie to the soil. The telephone, electric lights, elevated railroads, and even bicycles were part of city life back East. Magazines like *Ladies Home Journal, Colliers, The Saturday Evening Post,* along with the local newspaper, described Victorian society to lonely farm and ranch wives and their ambitious sons and starry-eyed daughters. Traveling vaudeville shows and minstrel troupes did their part to connect city and farm. The land was filled with new ideas, new inventions—and thousands of immigrants. From every European country, men, women, and children poured across the map, shaping their own destinies and their adopted home with their distinct influences.

The South had passed through tumultuous changes in the 30-odd years since Lee and Grant had amiably met at Appomattox Courthouse. The peaceable, healing reconstruction of Lincoln and then Johnson had been set aside. Radical reconstruction that followed had failed miserably. Gains that had been made for equality among all Americans quickly eroded. Heart attitudes—changing those were more difficult than pulling stubborn rocks from the Southern soil.

The power struggle between Northerners and the aristocratic Southerners had done nothing to heal the animosities and misunderstandings now heading into the new century. The black American's plight had not changed much since Mr. Lincoln's proclamation. He could vote now, but it was a vote often too costly to keep. White-robed figures in the night could terrorize him away from the ballot box. For those who braved the trip to the poll on election day, there was a stiff poll tax to pay before voting. With a heritage of slavery behind them, this was often impossible. The South was muzzling the black vote quite efficiently. Supreme Court decisions declared segregation legal. Separate, but so often unequal. Racial tensions remained—like a wound still festering.

The day was sultry as Andy rode toward Tanglewood. He watched the miles jog past with renewed surprise at such verdant and lush countryside. They passed few carriages on the gravel road, and Andy felt the quiet peacefulness he had instantly experienced as a boy. It reminded him of the night watches he sometimes took on board *Ivanhoe's Dream*, when the seas were smooth, shimmering panes of glass and the moon a golden disk slipping between veils of wispy clouds. Andy was grateful that the driver was a taciturn man who did not feel required to give the visitor a running monologue on local events and personalities.

Huge willows lined the road as they drew closer to Tanglewood. At an intersection, the driver slowed and Andy leaned forward. A horse and rider were in the center of the road, a Southerner in full regalia. He wore tight riding breeches tucked into tall black boots. He was in his shirt-sleeves, a silk scarf knotted lavishly at his throat. A broad panama hat shaded his face, a long Havana cigar projected from his mouth. It gave off a pungent smell that Andy detected when his carriage was still a length away. A large wolfhound stood tensely by the rider.

Drawing closer Andy could see the man was angry. Andy smiled. There was something about this man that made him think of his sister Meg. Seeing such a flamboyant character always made him think of her—and he saw a great many characters in his travels. He and Meg shared a mutual amusement and interest in the study of human characters.

The apparent objects of the rider's anger were a black man and woman and a mule. It seemed to Andy only the mule was unagitated as he reached for weeds along the roadside. Andy directed his driver to stop.

"Good morning!" Andy called out cheerfully.

The rider had been so intent on the couple in front of him that he did not hear the carriage till it was nearly beside him. He didn't like the interruption and eyed Andy with irritation. He managed a curt nod.

The black couple looked up at the young white man in the carriage, and Andy saw a quick flash of appeal in the eyes of the woman. He smiled gently at her.

"You're a Yankee," the rider finally said, without warmth or welcome.

Andy gave the man a slow, measured look. Andy was easygoing, hardly ever ruffled to anger. He shrugged.

"Guilty. Been one all my life."

The rider shifted in his saddle, tapping a nervous staccato on his boot with his riding crop. "Where ya bound for, Yank?"

Again Andy ignored the rudeness. "Tanglewood. My name's Andy Alcott."

"I go by Jeb Jackson French." He pulled out his cigar and examined it. The black man turned to Andy and spoke up eagerly.

"We've just been up to Tanglewood, yes, sir!"

"And the last time!" French snapped.

"Now, Mr. French, sir, I thought—"

"Better you didn't think, Seth Jefferson."

French had no qualms about showing a Northerner the ugly face of bigotry.

"It's my day off, Mr. French. Ain't much work at the warehouse now anyways. And—"

"There is work! Always work!" French flared. "Cash can afford to get picture frames from Vicksburg. He's trying to hire you out from under me!"

"Just to work for him on Seth's off days. Like today, Mr. French. 'Sides my man's better'n any Vicksburg carpenter," Viney Jefferson interrupted with spirit.

She stood with her hands on her hips, and Andy could see French's intimidation would not go far with this woman.

French's face turned very red, as red as a turkey's waddle, Andy thought.

"Did you say your name was Alcott, sir?" the woman asked cautiously.

"Yes, ma'am."

French inclined his head to get a better look at this oddity who called black women "ma'am."

"You're from the North—from Illinois?" she asked stepping forward.

"Why, yes."

She grew bolder. "Your daddy. He is called Ethan Alcott?"

"Yes, ma'am!"

The clear morning air was filled with the woman's delighted laugh.

"How did you know my father, ma'am?"

"I didn't know him, sir—"

"Please call me Andy."

She gave her husband a quick glance.

"Just like his daddy." She turned back to Andy. "My grandfather was a slave up at the Cash mansion. Your father came there years ago, before the war even."

"Yes, that's right. Your grandfather, his name was unusual . . . Goodnight!"

The black man laughed now. "Yep, that's him!"

"My father told me about him," Andy continued.

"Well, my grandfather told us kids when we was little about the spring a young man came from Illinois to see his kin in the big house. Never forgot that name—Ethan Alcott. Pappy told us again and again how nice the young man was. Wanted us to remember there was kind white folks in the world."

Then, as if by common agreement, Andy and the black couple swung around to French, who had largely been ignored throughout the conversation. French had sat listening with amusement; now his face flushed with embarrassment at the woman's words.

The tall black man stepped forward, reaching up a calloused hand to Andy. "I'm Seth Jefferson, and this is my wife, Viney. Welcome to Mississippi, Mr. Alcott."

"Thank you, Seth. It's Andy though."

"If my grandfather was still livin', he'd be glad to see ya too. He surely liked your daddy," Viney said happily.

"If I might be so bold as to interrupt this little reunion . . ." French blew a huge circle of smoke into the air.

Andy had to laugh out loud at the performance, it so reminded him of a child showing off. French looked at him sharply; he had said nothing funny. Apparently there were some Yankee half-wits in the Cash family tree.

Seth patted his wife's arm. "I'll go back to Greenville with Mr. French. You go on home."

"But it's your off day," she began to protest.

"Seth," Andy spoke up, "why don't you ride the mule. Your wife can ride up here with me." Andy glanced at the woman's rounded middle and smiled. "Doesn't look like you need to be riding a mule, ma'am."

French snorted.

"Then the driver will take your wife home after he drops me off," Andy continued.

With nearly any other white man, Seth Jefferson would have been suspicious. But he trusted Andy Alcott immediately.

"Thank you kindly, Mr. Alcott," Seth beamed.

"Welcome to Mississippi, Yank!" French yelled as he applied the crop to both his horse and Seth's mule. The Yankee still did not find much warmth in the welcome.

When Andy rounded the final curve to Tanglewood, he knew there was a different look, a different feel to the property. Thirteen years before, the place had looked occupied and not much more. It had given him the impression of loneliness.

Tanglewood mansion had kept the antebellum design and character that had given it grace and sophistication for years. It would take flood or fire to change that. Cashes of past generations had built the redbrick dwelling as a salute, a tribute to a singularly unique and refined way of life as permanent, as noble, as the magnolias and huge cypresses that shaded the house.

Four fine white columns fronted the house. Black shutters stood sentry at each window, which sparkled in the sun like gems. The lawn was perfectly manicured; a vivid flower bed bordered the gravel drive. Tanglewood, Andy decided as the carriage pulled to a stop, was looking impressively prosperous again.

A butler greeted him formally at the broad front door and led him down the hall.

"Mr. Cash is in his studio."

The changes were inside the house too, Andy mentally noted. Polished mirrors and wood, new carpets, huge vases of cut flowers everywhere. The parquet floors were gleaming. The dullness of Tanglewood was gone. Andy was intrigued. How would he find his uncle?

The studio door was opened, and Andy was greeted by the strong smell of paints and thinner. He found his uncle just where he expected, seated behind a canvas. Yet he did not expect that the artist would lean forward from a wheelchair.

Cash looked up, prepared to frown and fuss at the butler for the interruption. Instead his smile grew broad in his thin, pale face. He was very glad to see Ethan's son.

"Well, Andy..."

"Hello, Uncle Pat." They shook hands warmly.

"It's been a long time, son. Too long."

"Yes, sir, about 13 years, I think."

Cash nodded. "You were about two feet shorter then. You've grown up, Andy Alcott."

"Yes, sir."

Cash peered around Andy's shoulder. "Fenwick!"

The butler's appearance was instantaneous. "Sir?"

"Some sherry. A celebration for my cousin's son!"

The butler bowed and disappeared.

"He's a real English butler!" Andy exclaimed.

Cash chuckled. "Yes, straight from Manchester." He indicated a chair that sat before the large picture window. "You don't mind the smell, do you, Andy?" He swept his hand toward the bottles and jars.

"No, sir, it's fine."

"Good. This has always been my favorite room. Now though..."

He rolled his chair next to Andy's. They both gazed out upon the garden for a minute in silence.

"It's always beautiful here, Uncle Pat. The garden reminds me of my Aunt Wyeth back home."

"Thank you. It's even more beautiful at Tanglewood now."

Andy turned and looked closely at the older man. Patrick Cash looked frailer to Andy, his face lined, and totally confined to the chair. The same wistful look was in his eyes. But there was something else there now, and Andy did not know what it was.

"An English butler, flowers everywhere. Yes, sir, I can see that there are changes to Tanglewood, certainly more beautiful."

Cash laced his fingers in his lap, his eyes sparkling.

"But the most important change here, Andy, is one you haven't seen yet."

"Sir?"

Cash laughed again. "Forgive me, Andy. I'm relishing the surprise. I'm a married man now."

Andy's mind went blank with shock. "Married?"

"Yes. Last week was our first anniversary. I married a fine woman. Her name is Amy."

Andy reached out to shake his uncle's hand.

"Congratulations, Uncle Pat."

"Thank you."

"This would explain the changes I've seen."

Cash's eyes sought the garden again. His voice, always soft, grew even more so. "Amy's brought life to Tanglewood, Andy. Like...like a clean, fresh wind blowing through an old tomb!"

He turned back to Andy and smiled.

"You'll meet her day after tomorrow. She's been in Baton Rouge for three weeks, visiting a cousin there. Wasn't here when your telegram came. It will be a surprise for her, too."

His hand reached out and patted Andy's arm.

"I'm glad you're here, Andy. Hope you can stay a long time while you heal. Now, let's hear all about this business that's made you almost as lame as me!"

Andy's foot was throbbing when he stretched out in the huge four-poster that night. He wanted desperately to take some laudanum, but more than that he wanted a clear mind to sort through the impressions of the day. Moonlight and the scent of magnolias wafted through the lace curtains as he relaxed.

Patrick Cash. He was a survivor of a generation that had marched off to war for pride and glory. He had come back alive, but changed, even as Andy's own father had changed. Andy admired him, saw a courage and kindness that bullets and saber and privation and horrors could not steal or erase. He had seen that as a boy years ago. He had felt a kinship to the man even then.

He looked into the darkness and thought of his uncle's face lighting up when he had spoken of his new wife. He had not elaborated on her, however. They had talked of Andy and life on the oceans and family back home. It seemed easy, almost natural, for them to take up their relationship as if only a few months had passed and not 13 years.

Andy tried to picture what the woman must look like to capture his uncle's fancy at 58 years of age! He could not imagine his mild uncle being cowered by some ambitious Southern spinster or brainless, immature woman! It was silly, these thoughts, wanderings of his imagination that were groundless. He sighed, glad that his uncle seemed so happy—and hoping his stay at Tanglewood would be something close to his expectations . . .

It was a good thing Andy was bent over his drink, or his sudden, sharp intake of breath would have been too audible. When he straightened up, he cast his uncle a quick glance to see if this was some sort of joke.

Amy Cash had entered the library, a basket of beautiful cut roses in one hand and pulling off her hat with the other. Her hairpins had gotten caught, and now the hat was pulling down the tumble of gold-colored hair. The more she pulled, the worse it became. Patrick rolled his chair forward with a chuckle to help her. They were laughing together now, sharing a private moment as if Andy wasn't there. Andy could see Cash's hand linger a moment in the curls, tenderness filling his eyes. Then he pushed aside and let his wife see they were not alone.

Andy was too surprised to speak or even smile, and for just a fraction of a second he thought he saw the same reaction in the woman's eyes.

"Amy, dear, this is Andy Alcott. Ethan's oldest son."

She gave her husband a blank look.

"Ethan, my Illinois cousin," Cash added further.

Then recognition came, and Mrs. Cash gave Andy a dazzling smile. "Of course! What a wonderful surprise! Welcome to Tanglewood." She extended her hand, and Andy remembered to take it.

"Thank you, Mrs. Cash," Andy stuttered.

Like a sudden squall on the high seas, Andy's thoughts were thrown off-balance. This was Amy Cash. She was tall. She did not have classic beauty. Even in one swift glance, Andy decided that no feature taken alone was beautiful. The mouth was a trifle too wide perhaps, the nose slightly upturned at the end. The eyes were hazel, deep set, and not remarkable. The face was tanned, in complete rebellion to the creamy white fairness judged as the real beauty of the day.

What stunned him was her age. He glanced down at his boots, mentally calculating. Amy Cash had to be in her mid-twenties—at least 30 years younger than her husband.

Chapter 3

Tanglewood

◆◆ ◆◆ ◆◆

Creamy white candles in tall silver holders and waxy white magnolia blossoms floating in a crystal bowl formed the centerpiece on the glossy mahogany dining table of Tanglewood. Andy glanced down at the spotless linen and the pair of shiny silver forks and wondered whether anyone would notice if he picked up the wrong one. Spending the last eight years on a ship had given him little chance to learn the finer points of etiquette.

Amy was telling them about her time in Baton Rouge with her cousin. Andy felt vaguely excluded. He could see his uncle listening carefully, his eyes sparkling, his words to his wife affectionate and teasing. *He loves her. Well, of course*, Andy reprimanded himself. *What did you expect?* Andy sipped his wine and tried to sort through his thoughts.

What did I expect? A gray-haired matron! Heavyset, my mother's age, not my little sister's! She's so young. Why would Uncle Pat marry her? Why would she marry him? He swallowed with difficulty. *Surely not for money, for the possession of Tanglewood!* It was a shocking and disturbing thought. He felt eyes upon him and looked up. Amy was looking at him directly, almost as if she was amused about something concerning him. He felt angry. Innocent Uncle Pat! Taken in by this!

Andy had met many kinds of women in his travels, but this woman... designing and scheming. He recoiled from the thoughts he was having. But they had persisted since he had first seen Amy Cash. He had never thought of himself as the suspicious type, yet...

He glanced at the mistress of Tanglewood and frowned. There would be no bachelor atmosphere between him and his uncle now. No eating when and wherever they liked, no feet propped up on the furniture. The elegance of this meal alone testified to the dramatic changes that had come to the Cash mansion. If Amy had accomplished so much in one short year, surely she must be quite a strong-willed woman, a progressive Gibson girl like sister Meg always wrote about.

"Ever had such excellent lime pie before, Andy?" Cash was asking.

Too absorbed in his troubling thoughts, Andy had hardly tasted the pie. "Sir?" he returned absently.

"The pie," Cash said mildly.

"Oh, yes, the pie, it's fine."

"Amy made it," Cash continued.

"Oh, Cash, now—" Amy began.

"Amy, I cannot help but brag on your culinary skills. I'm confident Andy has never tasted better lime pie."

"I've never tasted any lime pie before." Andy colored with embarrassment. "I mean, I, we, usually have apple pie."

Cash tossed aside his napkin. "Ah, the Alcott apple!"

Still Andy remained silent, unresponsive and remote to his uncle's attempt to draw him into conversation. Cash's look was thoroughly puzzled as he shrugged at his wife.

Amy sensed her husband's confusion and spoke up.

"Cash has told me that your family grows apples. Only one kind?"

Andy barely looked up to answer. "No, there are several."

Silence again.

"It was your brother who bred the Alcott apple, correct?" Cash ventured again.

Andy nodded. "My younger brother Matthew. He and my brother Daniel and my father have a sort of lab on the property now."

"A scientist and a sailor. A diverse family you're from, Andy." Cash was smiling.

"How did your father take your leaving the family business for the high seas?" Amy asked, trying to sound relaxed and unannoyed, a very difficult thing to do since she was very annoyed with this interloper at Tanglewood.

Andy spoke tersely. "Fine. They wanted me to be happy."

He felt his face grow red. This rudeness! So out of character! What was the matter with him?

Cash leaned back in his chair. "Fathers often make plans for their children, but history doesn't always oblige them."

He fingered the rim of his glass. "I know that personally," he said softly.

Fenwick came to remove the plates in the stillness of the grand dining room. Andy sat staring into space, racking his mind for some topic to become even-keeled about, something to push aside the emotional turmoil he was feeling.

"Seeing your library this afternoon reminds me of the story my father has told about his encounter there with one of your neighbors. Bowers, I think his name was," Andy said.

Pat Cash chuckled. "Young Luke Bowers. I remember it well. Quite the drama in the Cash library."

Amy coughed nervously, but Cash did not seem to notice.

"Have I told you this before, my dear?" Cash asked.

Amy shook her head reluctantly that he hadn't.

"Well, Ethan and I, along with my father and about eight other planters, were in the library after dinner. The conversation turned to slavery as it was bound to in those days. Soon cousin Ethan was on his feet asking which one of us would trade places with a slave."

"Cash, perhaps it's best not to talk about those times," Amy suggested.

Andy ignored her. "My father was using an idea from President Lincoln."

"It caused quite a little stir that night. Sort of a prelude, I suppose." The older man's voice had dropped, and Andy did not see the look of warning Amy flashed him.

"Whatever happened to Luke Bowers?" Andy asked.

Cash pressed his fingertips together. "His family didn't . . . survive the war. They couldn't regain . . . like so many others. So long ago . . ."

He was gone from them, pulled into the past, 30 years before, when his sensitive young manhood had received its severest test.

Amy gave Andy a scorching look, angry that he had drawn her husband into painful memories. She leaned toward him, her tone restrained and formal. "I don't think talking about the past, the war years, is healthy."

Andy was never one to become defensive, but he bristled.

"Oh?"

They were both thoroughly annoyed with each other now and did not bother to conceal it.

"Sometimes antagonisms are still with us, still pulling North and South apart," Amy ventured carefully.

"I wasn't even born when the war was being fought." Andy refrained from adding, "and neither were you."

"I have no quarrel with the South. I've lived nearly nine years in and out of ports down here. But I defer to your wishes, Mrs. Cash."

He covered his acute embarrassment by carefully cutting his pie into two sections.

Amy's face was flaming. This was the rudest, most arrogant Northerner she had ever met. Her first quick impression, that of a kind, sensitive young man, had been quickly dispelled. She had thought him somewhat handsome at first look, but that too had changed.

"I am glad of your generosity, Mr. Alcott. The war years were not kind to Cash. I only meant to spare him."

Haughtiness was not in Amy Cash's personal makeup, but she had borrowed the voice of haughtiness with classic effectiveness.

Cash returned to them with a bland smile, hardly aware of the hot words that had passed between his young wife and Andy.

"Shall we take our coffee into the library, my dear?"

Amy Cash was careful to not intrude on the time between Cash and Andy in the following few days. It was obvious this Andy Alcott was suspicious of her, mistrusted her. He did not like her. Well, fine, she did not care for him.

Yet she could sense in her quiet husband some need, however indefinable, being met by Andy Alcott. For all his rudeness at their first dinner together, she knew his presence in the big mansion was good, perhaps even healing, for the melancholy man she had married. Yet she also resented Andy, for he seemed to stir up the past, the war years that had left Patrick Cash so troubled in body and mind.

She brought them a tray of drinks as the two men sat on the open veranda one afternoon. Cash's laughter greeted her as she placed the tray between them. It was good to hear Cash laugh. She wanted to withdraw, but a light touch from Cash's hand stopped her.

"Please stay." His voice was gentle.

Not looking at Andy, she sat down reluctantly. Cash returned to the tale he had been telling.

"We were camped by the Rappahannock in Virginia, late in August, '63. I can remember it so well because we'd marched by an apple orchard the day before. Some of the boys couldn't resist the green apples. Gorged themselves like pigs."

"Green apples can mess you up all right," Andy said with a laugh.

Cash nodded. "And being so hungry like we were—beans and hardtack every day—anyway, I remember I had a terrible headache. So a few of us wandered down to the river, thinking it might be some cooler." He closed his eyes. "I can still see it, a slow, brown river, well shaded. We were stretched out on the riverbank when we heard someone shout, 'Hey there, Johnny Rebs! Hey you butternuts!' We looked across the water, and there were about a dozen Yankees having come down to the water like us. Not one of us had a gun, and we saw that they didn't either. In their shirtsleeves, just . . . like us."

Amy and Andy exchanged a guarded look.

"So much like us, only their trousers were dirty blue and ours were dirty gray. Then one of us called, 'Good morning, Billy Yanks!' and there was laughter, all very friendly, like a fraternity or something. Then they saw we had tobacco on our side, and they called over to see if we would trade."

Amy was incredulous. "You were opposing armies! Wasn't there some hostility?"

Cash shook his head. "Not even a hint. They wanted our tobacco, and they had newspapers that our side didn't have. Hadn't had any news for weeks, in fact. So they huddled together and we huddled together and figured out who was the strongest swimmer." Cash laughed, "If our commander had found out! A fellow named Jess was elected to swim the tobacco over. A young boy, about 18. The reddest hair I'd ever seen . . ."

He drifted off, back on the Rappahannock again. He sat there silently, tears filling his gray eyes. Andy clenched his hands, regretting that he had provoked this conversation. Apparently his uncle's bride, no matter how young, understood her husband.

Cash cleared his throat. "Jess swam over, the bundle on his head. We watched as they welcomed him and gave him a drink of water. Then they gave him a little wooden boat made from bark to push back across. When he got back to us we found they had given us candy and an orange for each of us, besides the papers. They . . . gave more."

"Did you ever have time to paint during the war, Uncle Pat?" Andy asked, hoping to draw his uncle to a less tormenting subject.

But the grip of the past was a miser, unwilling to turn loose of Cash without payment. He shook his head.

"I had a paint box at the beginning . . . Do you know what happened the next day after that swim at the river? Do you know? Were you there?"

He closed his eyes again, his chin dropping forward, a hand resting lightly across his heart. Amy leaned forward in fear.

It was too vivid, even after 30 years. Dust and sunshine, horses screaming as they caught the errant bullets meant for their riders. Yells and curses. *Where was the glory in this?* young Patrick Cash was wondering as he swiveled his horse around, desperate for a moment of safety, a brief respite from the fury of violence all around him. Yet a Federal bullet found a target in the stallion's neck. Valiant . . . that was his name. Then Cash was trapped under the fallen horse, his own leg cracked in two places by the great weight of the beast.

He could see himself closing his eyes, desperately thirsty, agonizing along with the horse's dying spasms. He couldn't feel his own pain, and he couldn't stand the impotence he felt at being unable to help the wounded creature. It was too much. He worked his arm free and found his knife—a long, sharp, and expensive blade, a gift from his father. Tears were in his eyes as he quickly ended the animal's life. The knife was still gripped in his hand. It could be so easy, so quick . . . and no more battles, no more sickness, no more blood. . . . Then someone was saying his name over and over, pulling the dead horse off him, helping him to his feet. Bullets still screaming around him. A thud sounded beside him and the support was gone, crumpled at his side. Cash bent down in shock. The one who had helped him was gone. It was Jess.

Later when the fighting had stopped, when the men who had survived lay in exhausted heaps, someone spoke to him. He could not form words or complete a thought. Like a fragile twig, a pliant stem, something had snapped in Patrick Cash that day. It had changed him, stolen something and filled the vacuum with a frailty from which he had never completely recovered.

Cash's eyes were riveted on the horizon, seeing things that Amy and Andy could not see, would never see. Amy was shocked. Andy made no effort to conceal the tears that slid down his cheeks. He leaned forward in his chair, gently shaking his uncle.

"Uncle Pat, I'm so sorry. Sir?"

Cash turned his head slowly, his face still a mask of confusion.

"Ethan?...No, no, of course not. Ha, I'm getting old...Andy."

"Cash, let's not talk about the war anymore. Please," Amy pleaded.

"Yes, sir, it was my fault. The past—"

Cash gave them a trembling smile, as he waved a thin hand. "No, no, it's all right. I'm fine. The past, with all its haunts, has to be faced... sometimes."

It was a warm morning and Andy, Amy, and Cash were at the large white-fenced pasture watching the thoroughbreds that were being exercised. It was a wonderful morning, full of the richness of spring—trees in bud, flowers in bloom, the sky a cloudless turquoise-colored canopy.

Amy Cash had decided as she dressed that morning that their Northern guest was not going to ruin this lovely morning. He could say, or not say, anything. She would be civil, but not encourage him.

Cash had done most of the talking from where they sat in the buggy. He had told Andy the merits and lineage of every horse in front of them.

"I always thought my father kept fine stock," Andy said smiling. "But they're nags compared to these!"

"When your foot is healed and you're feeling up to it, you can try them out. They all have good dispositions. Amy doesn't have anyone to ride with. She could show you Tanglewood from our mountain border down to the river."

Andy merely nodded. Amy acted as if she had not heard.

Cash was confused. Why had Andy become so...so unfriendly, Amy so defensive?

"The old Natchez trace is a few hours' ride from here. It is a beautiful ride. Pioneers by the thousands came down it in the early part of this century. Connected Nashville and Natchez," Cash continued amiably.

Amy finally spoke up. "I'm not that good of a horsewoman, Cash, to act as a guide."

Andy did not want to be alone with his suspicions and Mrs. Cash, but he did not want to appear rude again. "Perhaps we could all go in the buggy sometime," Andy pursued.

Cash said nothing more on the subject—merely thinking, simply wondering.

"Do you like him, Amy?"

Cash and Amy sat alone together in the garden. She smiled. "Now Cash, why do you ask that?"

"You grow so quiet when he's around. Your words don't have their usual warmth," he said gently.

Amy felt her face flush with guilt.

"Andy was here for two days before you got home. He was animated, eager to talk. Now he seems like he closes up around you, downright Yankee-acting at times."

"Maybe..." Amy hesitated.

"Maybe what?" Cash pressed.

"Maybe he didn't like finding a bride at Tanglewood."

Amy Cash sat in front of the beveled mirror of her dressing table, slowly brushing her hair. She stopped a moment, looking down at the smooth, mother-of-pearl hairbrush in her hand. It was a brush that Cash had given her on her last birthday, one gift among many. She glanced around her beautiful bedroom at a big four-poster bed, satin coverlet, lace curtains, polished cherrywood furniture, and a thick, oriental carpet. This was part of everything he had given her—all of Tanglewood in fact.

They'd been married a year, yet the dramatic changes in her life still amazed her, still gave her feelings of uncertainty in the dark of night. "It's like going to bed a pauper and waking up a princess," she had whispered to herself.

But now she felt edgy, nervous. Besides the few servants, it had been her and Cash alone for the past year. The neighbors did not call. Patrick Cash had always been an oddity, cut from cloth other than traditional Southern weave. And then to go and marry a woman young enough to be his daughter, well, it was preposterous!

Now a relative of Cash's had suddenly come to Tanglewood. He had invaded their tranquil, private world, and Amy felt exposed. Surely the routine of their lives would be altered. Somehow his youth was even more disturbing. He must be her own age. She laughed out loud at the absurdity of her feelings.

But how could she explain her feelings to Cash, who was so obviously delighted to have Andy here?

She would just have to change, drop the cool formality she'd assumed when she was around Andy. Be herself, natural, realizing that his coming could not threaten their security or happiness.

The door to Cash's bedroom was closed, yet she knew he was an early riser and already downstairs in the library, waiting until they breakfasted together. She supposed he wouldn't read to her from the *Vicksburg Review* like he always did, little snippets of news that they laughed over.

She leaned over, breathing the rich scent of roses that stood in a crystal vase on the table. How grateful she was that Cash loved flowers

like she did, encouraging her in her gardening. Could she still push his
chair along the paths in the garden like they had always done, or would
that change too? One final brush stroke and a sigh.

Their guest at Tanglewood must feel welcome for as long as he cared
to stay. In spite of her annoyance with Andy, could she be the gracious
hostess of Southern tradition for Cash?

It seemed every time Andy attempted to be alone, he found himself
alone with Mrs. Cash. If he went to the garden, she was there clipping
roses. If he went to the stables, she was there helping the servants
groom the horses. She wore tan-colored trousers tucked into mucky
boots and one of Cash's old shirts, her hair piled lazily underneath an
ancient-looking straw hat. She certainly did not look like the mistress of
one of Mississippi's most impressive estates.

One night he'd slipped down to the darkened kitchen for a snack. She
heard his step before he could back away. He saw in one quick glance
that she was wearing something made of silk, that her hair was loosened
around her shoulders. She was munching on leftovers, a book in front of
her. He had noticed she had a book in front of her a lot. Seeing her there
annoyed him.

Their eyes locked in a challenge.

Finally, "Did you want something?" she asked coolly.

His reply was appropriately stiff. "No, thank you."

He turned and returned to his room feeling very awkward, very
foolish. In Tanglewood's kitchen, Mrs. Cash was smiling.

The next evening he found her in the library, curled up on the sofa.
Her feet were tucked underneath her. Andy decided she looked about
15, but he could not turn away so rudely again.

He hesitated, trying to think of something neutral and casual to say.

Amy's heart softened for just a moment when she saw his reluctance.
"I can share this room, Andy."

He took a step in. "Thank you, but I just wanted to return this book to
the shelf. What are you reading, Mrs. Cash?"

She held up the leather volume for him to see.

"*Further Adventures of Sherlock Holmes* by Conan Doyle. It's new."

"I've heard of it. Captain Treadle has read it. He blasts it for being
English, but says it's very good. Holmes is a detective?"

She nodded. "Yes, a very capable and creative sleuth."

Andy could have left then. But he suddenly felt a little creative
himself. "That would make it a story about . . . deceptions, wouldn't it?"

He tried to keep his voice very bland.

Amy had the strongest desire to laugh in his face. Such arrogance!

"Deceptions, disguises, plots, theft." She tapped the book with her finger. "It's all in here, and I find it very, very interesting. Would you care to read it when I'm finished?"

His reply was a mumble as he left the room.

They were on the sun-splashed terrace, dining on crabmeat salad, when a servant from the stable interrupted them.

"Excuse me, Mr. Cash, sir, but Miss Majestic is a foalin' and havin' a hard time of it."

Cash laid down his napkin. "She wasn't due to foal for nearly...How much longer, Amy?"

"At least three weeks. I'll go look at her," Amy said, rising.

"I'm thinkin' sir, that it will take some pullin', and I need help."

"I've helped my father with this a few times," Andy spoke up.

"Your foot, Andy. I don't think it will stand the strain. We certainly don't want you to injure it further or impede the healing," Cash pointed out.

"It will be all right," Andy returned, neglecting to mention the foot had been unusually tender all morning. "She...I mean, Mrs. Cash, cannot help...with that kind of thing."

"Mr. Alcott, I have helped with other foalings. I am capable of this. As Cash pointed out, you must be sensitive to your foot. I'll go change and be out in a moment, Sam."

Andy did not like to be reminded of his infirmity. He could not meet Cash's eyes and missed the look of amusement on the older man's face.

Andy laid down his fork. "Just the same, I think I'll go lend a hand."

Miss Majestic seemed entirely unconcerned with the events around her. She was receiving an unusual amount of personal attention, never mind a little discomfort. Amy was stroking the horse's muzzle, her voice low as she encouraged the animal. She had looked up with irritation when Andy entered the barn.

Sam had done the brunt of the work. Andy had braced himself against a wooden partition and pulled.

Then the mare had grown tired of her undignified position on the littered floor and gave one final, maternal effort. The new foal came out with such enthusiasm that Andy was sent sprawling on his back. He had lost his balance as he tried to spare his foot. The very healthy foal rested comfortably on his chest.

There was only the sound of Andy gasping, then Amy's very clear, very delighted voice. "Is that the way it happens when you help your father?"

It was nearly an hour later before Amy and Andy were ready to return to the house.

"You're a mess!" She could not help but laugh, but there was no animosity now.

He was filthy, his shirt plastered in dried blood and straw. When Amy saw the glob of manure on the back of his head, she leaned against the fence, doubling over in laughter.

"What are you laughing at?" Andy asked easily.

"Your...head...in the back..."

He felt the place and grimaced. "I guess I should go jump in the horse trough before I go in the house, huh?"

He was laughing with her. They had worked together. The last barriers were falling...

When they stepped into the sunshine, she could see he was limping.

"Your foot is hurting you, isn't it? Cash will be put out with you."

"It's all right. I'll just prop it up for a little while."

She smiled again. The Yankee could be nice...for a change.

A thin, slashing rain was falling the next morning when Andy eased himself out of bed and hobbled down to the library. The house was still robed in quiet darkness. He had hoped reading something from Cash's vast library would distract him from the pain.

Sometime later, a feather touch on his forehead brought him awake.

"Andy? Are you all right?"

His eyes fluttered open, and he couldn't help but groan. The pain was intense.

"Oh, Mrs. Cash. I'm sorry. I guess I fell asleep a minute. I—"

"Andy, for goodness sake, this is ridiculous. You can't be calling me Mrs. Cash! You're family here!"

He closed his eyes, surprised at the kindness of her words. How could his preconception of Patrick Cash's wife have been so wrong?

"I—"

"You're in pain, aren't you?" she asked gently.

"Well, a little. I thought by now... It's been six weeks."

"You're feverish. I'm sending for Dr. Browning."

"No, please. I'm fine. I don't want to be any trouble."

The doctor came and pronounced a severe infection in Andy's foot.

"Two weeks flat on your back. Sorry."

Andy groaned. "No, Doc. This...I feel so foolish! I didn't come here to be bedridden!"

The doctor shrugged. "I understand, but unless you want to lose that foot, that's the way it is."

It turned out to be a perfect arrangement for Patrick Cash. He hated to see Andy in pain, but it brought them closer together. He would wheel his chair into Andy's room where they could talk and laugh. Neither had any political interests, so their conversations were usually confined to books and travel, family and the past. Cash had spoken very little to anyone about those years he had tramped along with the Confederate army. He had told Amy bits and pieces, but now he found a man who was both a sensitive and understanding listener.

He spoke to Amy about the strangeness of it.

"Andy's father came here over 30 years ago from the North. We felt a kinship despite the obvious differences. Now his son is here, and I feel so close to him. Like he's partly... my own son."

Amy reached out and touched the thin gray hair.

"I'm glad he's here for you, Cash. You're both helping each other I think."

Cash looked up into her face, wistful a moment. "Are you happy here, Amy?"

"You don't have to ask that, Cash. You know I am."

Cash leaned back in his chair with a sigh. "Sometimes I think I'm a very selfish man to have you. The world out there, for you..."

He searched her with his eyes. "You knew when we married—"

"You're not a bit selfish, Patrick Cash, only very silly," she said softly.

Amy brought Andy's tray of dinner to him one evening.

A thawing had happened, ever since the afternoon in the stable when they had finally laughed together. Yet Andy still felt a slight discomfort when the young woman was near. She further unnerved him when she pulled up a chair to his bedside.

"Dr. Browning just called. He said he would be by in the morning."

"Thought I heard a phone ringing," Andy said as he took a bite.

"Cash had one put in last year. I think there are only half a dozen in the whole county."

"I certainly hope the doc gives me the okay to get up."

Amy laughed. "You men just hate to be confined, don't you?"

They both thought of Patrick Cash in his metal chair, and Amy sobered. "That was a thoughtless thing for me to say."

She looked down at her hands. "I'd do anything to make Cash well enough to be able to walk again."

"He only used a cane when I was here as a boy some years ago. How long has he been in the wheelchair?" Andy asked quietly.

"About a year or so—before we married."

Andy looked down at his food, thinking. Patrick Cash had married when he was in a wheelchair. There was an obvious, awkward silence.

"What does Dr. Browning say about his condition?" Andy finally asked.

Amy seemed reluctant to speak. "He took him to Vicksburg about six months ago, to a specialist. The doctors can't do anything about his spine. But it's his heart they're worried about now."

Amy smoothed her dress nervously. "It's been very good for Cash having you here. I hope you won't leave too soon if Dr. Browning lets you up."

"Uncle Pat was considerably cheered up before I came," Andy said, somewhat coolly and pointedly.

Amy inclined her head. "You think so?" Her voice was curious.

"I think you've done more for him than any tonic the doc could give."

She looked out the window, and Andy studied her profile. He glanced back down at his tray. There was no doubt—Amy Cash was beautiful. Seeing her in the soft light of the bedroom, Andy could see her as a young girl, with no illusions, no deceptions.

She turned back to him, their eyes meeting in the silence.

She had never trusted any man besides Patrick Cash, yet suddenly she wanted to understand, and to trust, this one. She drew a deep breath. "You're uncomfortable around me, aren't you?" she asked.

"I suppose I am, just a little," he admitted slowly.

"May I ask why?"

Andy was not prepared for her directness.

"I was very surprised when Uncle Pat told me he had married. Then I expected...I expected someone...different."

"Someone closer to his age?" she prodded gently.

Andy nodded. He watched her hands as they twisted her wedding band around her finger. "I think even Dr. Watson would know that you are as uncomfortable around me as I am around you."

She could not help but smile. It was time for honesty between them, if for Cash's sake only. "Yes, that's true. I'm sure you've noticed we don't have many callers here at Tanglewood. Cash and I are alone mostly and your coming...surprised me. I don't feel like the grand mistress of an estate. I feel full of flaws."

She had never even told Cash this. Suddenly she was telling her story to a young man who had been almost an adversary in the house.

"I felt like you could see every one of my...flaws," she added.

Andy's future was sealed with those words, though he didn't know that then. All he knew was that he had behaved shamefully toward this woman. He thought of Lilly. Why had he treated her so gallantly and Amy Cash so differently?

"Amy." It was the first time he had used her given name. She noticed that immediately. "I'm sorry...for my rudeness."

"Cash is very fond of you, Andy. You are all the family he really has here besides me. I'd like for us to be friends."

"Of course."

"Tell me about being a sailor on the high seas. I've never been on a boat in my life. I'm a confirmed landlubber!"

This was all it took for Andy.

"Never been on a boat!" He leaned forward, almost upsetting his tray. "This is absolute scandal at Tanglewood!"

Amy laughed delightedly. Their friendship now had a true beginning.

Chapter 4

Tanglewood

♦♦ ♦♦ ♦♦

*I*n the broad, stark, sunshine you could see the land for what it was, with all its flaws, with all its beauty—regenerating, changing by seasons, constant. A tireless firmament, a patch of earth for men and women to establish their homes, their personal dynasties.

Tanglewood lay in a fertile valley, 13 miles southeast of Greenville, Mississippi. It had seen the migration of buffalo, the silent trampings of the Indian, the seeking travels of the pioneer.

It had been claimed and fenced, planted, watered, harvested, and built upon. It had become a final resting place for the weary. It had been respected; it had been ravaged. In the mansion and in the cluster of well-built slave cabins, the plantation had witnessed the passages of life and death. In the generations it had been lived upon, it had seen five different masters, some kind, some harsh and arrogant, all tied and bound to the acreage that had been passed to them. If they themselves had not the thirst for being a Southern landowner, someone, male or female, of their bloodline did. For over a hundred years a Cash or Cash descendant had ruled this little kingdom now called Tanglewood. Some years in the future, a new master would come to Tanglewood, and the ancients, the ones who slumbered, would have been shocked beyond words to have seen him.

It had taken blood and toil to wrestle the wilderness out of the South. The early 1700s had been its infancy, and it had been an unruly infant at that. As the years passed it changed from a clawed-out existence to a place of civility, of harmony between land and man.

Then came cotton. A tiny seed changed the fate of millions and soul of the South.

Cotton and slavery brought prosperity to Tanglewood. The Cash fortune swelled with each harvest. Wealth afforded other interests besides the building of a classic redbrick mansion. It brought horses, blooded thoroughbreds, to Tanglewood. First it had been a hobby, purely a thing of sport and pleasure and status. Then it became a profit, and finally, a reputation.

Tanglewood thoroughbreds were known as far north as Belmont in New York. Patrick Cash kept a small but greatly demanded stable of strong, swift, and beautiful rich red horses. He had loved horses as a boy when the stables were at their apex. It was not for riding he loved them, but for their speed, their superb beauty. Muscles rippling, manes flying, slender legs stretched like perfectly poised arrows—motion and grace in one creature.

Andy was finally recovering. Except for a limp, which fatigue exaggerated, he was able to be about with the aid of a cane. Now, the whole of Tanglewood was to be explored. Driving Cash and Amy in a buggy became the focus of his spring days. They drove to the lumber and cotton mills of which Cash was part-owner, or sat in the shade of a mammoth cypress and watched the horses in the pastures. In sunshine—balmy, fragrant, warm—or in gray rain-scented breezes, they drove out with a picnic lunch, laughing and relaxed.

Amy was glowing with happiness. Cash had never looked so well, so animated. Often she would see his eyes rest upon his guest in affection. She knew the father role he had never occupied was being fulfilled in Andy. Seeing this, her gratitude for Andy grew. Now they were free to talk, debate, laugh, and tease.

When the weather was inclement or when Cash suffered from a bout of weakness, they remained in Cash's studio as he painted. One afternoon they were cloistered in the studio, Andy stretched out on a couch, Amy buried in a novel, and Cash wheeling himself from canvas to easel to the huge window, humming and bantering with Andy. A good-natured debate had risen between the two men.

"Are you saying that you can paint something you've never seen before? Like a street in New York?"

"Or Paris?" Cash countered easily.

"Like Paris, or Venice, or an apple orchard in Illinois . . ." Andy waved his hand to finish.

Cash did not immediately answer. It was not his nature or ambition to put himself forward.

"I could render a reasonable likeness, I think. Provided of course I had access to details that I needed about Paris, or the Swiss Alps, or—"

Andy sat up. "How about a clipper at sea, full sail?"

"Hmm."

Ivanhoe's Dream, somewhere on the Gulf."

"Time of day?"

"Sunrise."

"Hmm. Fetch me that sketchpad over there, will you? Yes, that one." Excitement was visibly growing in the older man. He reached for a leaded pencil, chewing the end in concentration.

"You'll have to answer all my questions to my satisfaction. Dimensions. Color. Everything I want," the artist demanded firmly.

"Think you can do it, huh?" Andy teased.

"Certainly."

"Men are so competitive," Amy said with a straight face as she looked up from her book.

"Is there a prize, a reward to me if I paint your *Ivanhoe* to your satisfaction, young Andy?"

Amy laughed. "Cash! He could say it was unsatisfactory even if it was a replica!"

Andy joined her laughter. "You sound just like my little sis."

Neither Amy nor Andy saw the odd smile Cash gave his sketchpad.

"I trust First Mate Alcott...with everything," Cash replied mildly.

"If you can't do it, I'll take my pick from any of these fine paintings I see around the walls here," Andy returned, knowing the full measure of his uncle's talent and the absurdity of the bet.

"All right. Still, what is my payment if I succeed?" Cash assessed the pad, then Andy, with a speculative eye.

"Name your price."

"That I will, when the work is done."

"That sounds very mysterious, Cash," Amy said smiling.

"Humor me."

"Sounds like you might get the short end of the stick to me. You know silver doesn't line my pockets. How can I agree to something I don't know the price of?" Andy was smiling, joking, the presence of laughter in his eyes.

Amy, looking up from her book, was struck in that instant with what a wonderful smile he had. She quickly returned to her volume.

"I am confident of my success and equally confident you won't mind the price," Cash said slowly, again with that mysterious smile.

"All right then, it's a deal! Paint away!"

Fenwick stepped into the studio with a judicious cough. His manner was so dignified, so emotionless. His disapproving, colorless eyes made you feel you should straighten your collar and smooth your hair.

"Ahem. Mr. Cash, sir, you have a caller."

"A caller?" Cash asked absently.

"Who is it?" Amy asked, rising.

"A Mr. French."

Amy turned to her husband in an unguarded moment, and Andy could see she was stricken. She was struggling with composure, and Andy was intrigued. Cash tapped his pencil thoughtfully as he debated with himself.

"I'll see him in the library, Fenwick."

The butler withdrew, and Amy and Cash regarded each other in silence. They seemed to have momentarily forgotten Andy's presence.

"Cash, I don't want you to see him alone."

"My dear, I am not afraid of this man."

"I know you're not afraid, Cash. It's just that..."

He rolled his chair across to her, pulling her down. Andy could see the tenderness. "He can't hurt us, Amy. He can't hurt you."

Then Cash remembered Andy. He turned around, his old levity and casualness restored. "Come meet a neighbor of ours, Andy."

Amy went to the window after the two men had left, her heart pounding, anger and fear battling inside her.

Jeb Jackson French was never without three things: his expensive Cuban cigars, his leather riding crop, and his huge Irish wolfhound. The dog now lay obediently outside the Cash mansion door. Some folks murmured behind French's back that those three things could tell you a lot about the man. Depending on the occasion, he also carried a small silver pistol. It had belonged to a locally famous Confederate officer, and French prized it highly. He had come by it honorably in a late-night game of cards.

French was a tall man, broad-shouldered, a commanding presence when he entered a room. His voice was fully Southern, his teeth very white, his lips, thin. Despite his imposing posture and manner, in profile he could almost look feminine. He was clean shaven but wore his nearly black hair long, in waves that fell just below his collar. It was an extravagant touch that mothers hoped their daughters did not admire too much.

He was shrewd, capable of great charm, loyal. All of which did endear him to women. He had a reputation that respectable women found interesting, and sometimes attractive. Other women found him captivating. He was not the kind of man you left your daughter or wife alone with. But he was generous and loyal to his friends, and that alone kept Jeb Jackson French tolerable to the community. He was a part of them, for better or worse, like Patrick Cash was in his odd fashion.

Now French stood in the Cash library, posed before the cold fireplace, gazing up at the huge oil that hung there. In the moments before Cash's entry, he had run his covetous eye over the room, missing few details. Before presenting himself at the house, he had ridden down to the famous Cash stable. He looked everything over; every horse was scrutinized. He was like that: confident, brash, dismissing Southern courtesy when it pleased his purposes.

He heard the wheelchair as it creaked across the threshold. He smiled to himself, and did not bother to turn but kept critiquing the painting.

"Good afternoon, Jeb," Cash called from behind. There was a note of forced ease in his tone.

French turned finally, smiling. "Afternoon, Cash."

"Jeb, this is my cousin, Andy Alcott," Cash said as Andy came to stand beside him.

"We've met," French replied curtly.

"Oh?"

"The day I arrived. We met on the road here," Andy supplied.

French gave Andy a long, perusing look.

"Still visitin'," French added.

Andy nodded. He had no quarrel with this Jeb French, yet instinct told him this was not a friend of Tanglewood. He could sense that French was waiting for something, or someone.

Cash was ever the diplomat. "Andy, will you pour us all drinks?"

The tumblers were poured, and French evaluated his with appreciation.

"What brings you out to Tanglewood, Jeb?" Cash asked, leaving his drink untouched.

Andy noted that Cash betrayed no nervousness or tension beneath his calm posture.

French tapped his crop against the chair leg. "I think you know what, Cash."

Cash shrugged lazily. "One of my horses?"

French leaned forward, his tone one degree less friendly.

"Not the four-legged kind." He smiled broadly.

Cash sighed. Andy rightly perceived his uncle had suddenly been drained of something and was tired now.

"I've never known you to be less than direct, Jeb."

The Southerner gave a curt laugh, a laugh with no real mirth in it. "You're using my Seth Jefferson. You're using him up. I consider that just a bit unneighborly."

Cash stiffened and was silent, sickened at heart. He'd had little contact with Jeb Jackson French over the years. He could see that this man had not moderated his bigotry, and it made him sad.

French became impatient. "How's your little wife?"

This was the impetus Cash needed. It broke and dispelled his melancholy. "You said you came here about Seth. What is it, then?" Cash asked tersely.

"He's working for you."

"True. I've engaged him to work carpentry on his days off."

"He's supposed to work for me."

"Has he failed to show up at work?"

"No, he's there."

"Then what's the trouble?" Cash's voice had risen with impatience.

Andy's curiosity was completely piqued now. There was more to this palatable tension than just a controversy about a shared worker.

"He's tired from his off day and doesn't work hard enough for me," French blustered.

Cash studied his chair, a slender finger tapping the frame.

"Then your quarrel is with Seth, Jeb. Not me."

Andy was amazed at his uncle's words of retreat. French's shocked look testified that he was also.

"Well, that's right. Exactly. Rode out here to tell ya, Cash, Seth doesn't have any more off days. He's busy at my warehouse. Just have to find ya another carpenter."

"So it seems, Jeb, so it seems." Cash's voice was bland again.

French was irritated; he was a gamy cock with no one to fight.

His eyes swept the room, finally resting on Andy, and narrowed.

"Aren't you a seafarin' man?"

"Yes, I am."

"Missed your ship?"

"No, an injury."

A long silence then; French inwardly cursing. He had accomplished none of his purposes in coming to Tanglewood.

"Neighbors don't see you much since your marriage, Cash."

Cash smiled benignly. "Yes, marriage sometimes makes a recluse of folks."

French laughed a short, hollow bark.

"Well, I'm off. Glad we're settled about Seth." He carefully arranged his hat and leaned forward almost confidentially.

"Didn't think you'd be wantin' to take what belongs to another."

Their eyes locked.

"Afternoon, French," Cash replied.

When the man was gone, Cash remained staring vacantly into space. French had stirred up memories and reminded him of an ugliness that war and time had not diminished. Patrick Cash had never been a fighter, never even as a young man. Now...now there was French...another little battle. He sighed with the weariness of it all.

"Uncle Pat?"

Andy had stood silently regarding Cash, slightly annoyed and disappointed at his words of concession to the belligerent and arrogant Jeb French. Seth Jefferson was a good man, and it seemed to Andy he had been treated as merchandise.

"Andy? Oh..."

"I'm sorry this man French upset you."

"French? Well, he is a man hopelessly frustrated. Can't seem to accept the end to slavery. Now, Andy, will you go and bring the buggy around? I think you and I shall go for a little drive."

Chisolm Crossing

If Seth Jefferson had known Jeb French had visited Mr. Cash up at the big house, he would have gone outside his cabin and split a cord of firewood—in about an hour. When Seth Jefferson was frustrated or angry, he worked it off, an intense kind of therapy that seemed to help him. Work helped him keep from smashing something or someone, or saying something he would later regret or pay for in some way. This solution had worked so successfully for so long he was known as a gentle, God-fearing man. And he was. His wife, Viney, had been his helpmate for 15 years. She could count on one hand the times she'd seen her big husband really angry.

One of Seth Jefferson's first memories was watching the Confederate soldiers marching through Greenville on their way north. He was seven years old at the time and very concerned by the scene. It was all his family and kinfolk, in hushed voices, talked about—the war and a man called Abe Lincoln and freedom.

From what he could figure out, wars were supposed to be "your side" fighting "my side." But "his side" was fighting to keep him in slavery, keep him and his family and his future bent over in a cotton field in the blazing Mississippi sun. So it was "their side," the blue ones, with generals named McClellan, Meade, and Grant, fighting to free his people. Yet there was the story old Harris liked to tell of a Yankee soldier slapping him as the Northerners ravaged the South. How could a seven-year-old mind unravel such a tangled problem?

Two years later he had gone hunting with his pappy to the mountains. From the summit they watched smoke rising southward. They did not understand it. It wasn't until a few days later that they learned the blue ones had burned Vicksburg.

And there was his own ancient granny who rocked on the porch and acted like a prophetess. She frightened him with her bulging eyes, toothless mouth, and words of gloom. She'd point her fleshless finger at him and say niggers would be better off being slaves. At least they'd have food and a roof over their heads. A black man freed was better off dead, she cackled. What fearful things Granny would say!

Seth Jefferson remembered her words. She might have been right in some ways. He was growing up and watching the government's policy of reconstruction unfold, one miserable failure at a time. He was still working under a broiling sun, but it was rice now, not cotton. His family rented from the son whose father had been their master just four short years earlier. Now they had a small salary to show for their long hours.

As Seth grew taller and bigger, his thoughts stretched—no different from any young man of any color who could dream. He had the right to vote, but he couldn't read. He could buy land, but he had little money. But he could pray, like the Jews in Egypt, he thought. He could pray!

With all his longings and all his disappointments, he had not grown bitter or violent. Not like Jonas Brown, who tried to kill any white man he saw and hid in the hills like an animal, out of reach from the law. But

Seth had neither given up nor grown complacent or uncaring. He was watching, thinking, and mostly praying. His watching had paid off.

When an opportunity came to work in Greenville, to make a bit more money and be out of the punishing sun, he carefully weighed the decision. He would trade one taskmaster for another—hopefully better—one. He would be working in one of the many warehouses along the waterfront of the city, shifting and loading cargo that passed to and from the boats that plied the Mississippi.

He took the job trusting that someday it would improve his future. There were days, years even, when he began to doubt the decision. Had he heard the Lord wrong? Or would that choice one day prove bigger than the best dreams of his youth?

His wife, Viney, was a part of his best dreams. Viney and now Micah, and the new little one, still bundled safe inside its mother. Viney, who made him laugh with her spunkiness, and smile with her love. Viney, who grew indignant when they watched the men of Greenville file into the building to vote while they stayed outside.

"You should be in there," she had muttered.

He smiled and patted her arm. But that attitude had changed when he had gone to work for the powerful Jeb French. A lot of things had changed. Viney had looked at Seth's employer with suspicion. But she had trusted her husband's wisdom and willfully kept her opinions to herself. She would have sputtered and perhaps become a bit fearful if she knew what he had done at work that morning.

Everyone had heard of the Klan, which fiery old Confederate officer, Nathan Forest, had started in Nashville after the war. He had taken the hatred and war wounds and stirred up a potent brew. More and more Southerners were sipping from the ugly cup. Beatings, burnings, sometimes even murder. It was whispered about, just as the war had been when Seth had been a barefoot boy.

He heard two men talking of it one morning as he swept the dimly lit building. He wondered what their business was so early in the day. He watched between the crates as one man pried the lid off a box marked "Nails, 10 lbs." But he pulled out a leaflet instead of nails. Thinking they were alone, one of the two began to read the paper aloud.

ATTENTION LOYAL MEN OF MISSISSIPPI!!!
THE IMPERIAL ARMY OF THE LORD
IS MARCHING TO MISSISSIPPI
AND WILL NOT BE STOPPED!!

WE ARE THE KLAN. WE ARE THE SELECT!
A meeting, Friday, at midnight,
Frazer farm

"See that this crate stays here for Greenville and around. This other one needs to go down to Vicksburg," one of the men ordered the other softly.

Then they had left the warehouse. Seth waited, tense and torn with indecision. He did not know where Frazer farm was, but he did know the significance of these papers. It could only mean more trouble, more hurting and bloodshed.

He stepped forward silently and quickly. The two crates looked like all the others piled around them. Seth pulled them away and placed two others in their spot. He hefted the two crates up and hurried to the darkened end of the warehouse where he tossed them into a pile of damaged crates that French had ordered hauled off and burned. French had given the task of piling the crates to Seth.

Before Seth had completed his sabotage, he had taken one of the leaflets and stuffed it into the pocket of his jumper. He couldn't read, but he could memorize the letters and look for more of these evil invitations.

He went back to his sweeping. It had taken only minutes to do the deed, but even big Seth Jefferson felt a little shaky.

Ford's Creek was one of the many legitimate cousins of the spectacular Mississippi River. It was a mild-mannered, even-tempered tributary. Because the Mississippi was a generous relative, the calm waters of the creek were home to prolific generations of trout and bass. That credential alone drew anglers, devoted and casual, from all over Mississippi and beyond to Ford's Creek. The creek itself had a role in paternity. It had given birth to a little, nondescript village called Chisolm Crossing.

Chisolm Crossing was a hybrid village really, looked upon with amusement, tolerance, and condescension by the more sophisticated cities like Greenville. It was a village that served the scattered community of blacks and poor whites within the valley. It sat at a junction of dirt roads to Vicksburg and Greenville, the creek at its doorstep, the piney woods its back porch.

One store, one small, vacant building, one church for the whites, one for the blacks, one wide, fly-populated mudhole between the two. One blink of the eye and the village was gone. Half a dozen gray, weathered fishing cabins were strung along the shoreline of Ford's Creek like discarded fishing bobs. Decrepit and rat infested, they commanded affection and high rent from the zealous fishing crowd.

It was late afternoon and warm when Andy and Cash rode through Chisolm Crossing. Only the storekeeper, who lazily swept his porch, and his wife, who was hanging laundry, noted their passing. It caused some speculation between them. What was the rich folk of Tanglewood doin' 'round the Crossin'?

Cash directed Andy to the cabin with little difficulty despite the fact he'd never personally been there before. Set among the fragrant and verdant pines, it was a simple log cabin, the true pioneer home that Victorian America had not yet encroached upon. A dogwood shaded the front steps, fading in its final performance of spring. A flat dirt yard kept tidy by a handful of fat hens was brightened by pennyroyal growing against the eastern wall and honeysuckle on the west. A carpet of wild primroses now drawing closed with penitent petals fenced the property from the pines. There were splashes of vivid red at the two front windows where geraniums were potted.

It was a mosaic of clean, honorable poverty and simple beauty. A visitor there could discern in a very short time that the real wealth of this place was in the family that resided there. Andy was thinking hard. There was a beauty here that Tanglewood with its precise gardens, wine-red brick, and white-columned mansion could never have. It was peaceful here, a tiny plot of Eden set down in rural Mississippi.

Before Andy had brought the buggy to a stop, a young boy had dropped from a mammoth, long-limbed cottonwood and was jogging alongside them. Andy thought he had never seen such a broad and beaming smile before in such a small face. They stopped.

The boy waved a friendly hand. "I say howdy to ya!"

Andy and Cash exchanged amused glances.

"Good afternoon, young master Jefferson," Cash returned cordially.

"You're Mr. Cash, I know," he piped.

"That's correct, I am. You're Micah."

"Yes, sir, that's the truth."

"Your father home yet, Micah?"

The boy nodded vigorously. "Just now. Givin' a howdy kiss to Ma. And those are fine horses you have there."

"Thank you, Micah. You like horses?"

Again that vigorous nodding. "'Bout think they're my favorite creatures. When I'm grown a man, I'm gonna have a whole herd of 'em."

A man came from the cabin, stepping into the sunshine, a thumb casually looped in the strap of his overalls. He was smiling broadly, calling over his shoulder, "Viney! Look who's come!"

He came up to the buggy.

"Afternoon, Seth," Cash said.

"Well now, this is a surprise, Mr. Cash, sir. Sure is."

"Hello, Seth," Andy spoke up.

"Afternoon, Mr. Alcott."

The two shook hands. Andy again assessed the tall black man before him. He moved with a sort of masculine grace. Yet there was no weakness in that. Andy sensed he was a strong man, imbued with carefully contained power. His smile was quick, his laugh deep and throaty. He measured his words before he spoke.

His wife came from the cabin now, hesitating a moment till she could see clearly who their visitors were.

"Why, Mr. Cash! Ya come here to the Crossin'."

"Yes, Viney, it has been a long time since I've been out this way."

"And how's your missus?" Viney asked, as if she were on the closest of terms with the mistress of Tanglewood.

"She's just fine, Viney, thank you. Was up to her elbows in flour when we left."

"Always said a woman in flour makes a mighty pretty picture, sure does," Seth said with a booming laugh. "Kind of makes 'em helpless-like too!"

Viney prodded him sharply in the ribs. "I reckon I can swat a big black boy as easy with floured hands as not!"

They all laughed at this exchange. But Micah was not to be forgotten.

"Say, why don't ya come throw a pole in sometimes, Mr. Cash? I can show you the best spots."

"I'm sure you can, Micah, and I appreciate that. Maybe I will. I'm sure Andy here would like that too."

Andy nodded. "It's been hard on me being away from the water so long. Will you be my guide, Micah?"

Micah swelled. He had liked the looks of the young man immediately. "Sure can. How 'bout tomorrow?"

"It's a deal. I'll tell Amy there will be fish for dinner."

"Ah, ever the confident fisherman," Cash said chuckling. Then his face became serious as he smoothed the linen of his trouser leg. Even young Micah could see in the thinness, the pallor, the occasional trembling, that Patrick Cash was not well.

"I'd like that this was purely a social call, Seth, but I'm afraid it isn't."

"I was suspectin' as much, Mr. Cash. Is there a problem with the frame plans?"

"No, no, not at all, Seth. The plans are fine." He hesitated, and Andy knew his uncle was reluctant to sober the pleasant visit. "I had a caller this morning, Seth. It was Jeb French."

Viney Jefferson's smile dropped, and her hand went lightly to her husband's arm—a feather touch, but eloquent. The tall man's face was riveted on Cash, no muscle or feature betraying agitation. Perfectly controlled, thought Andy with no small admiration. He was as outwardly calm as Cash had been at the library interview with French.

"French was complaining about your working for me. Says your work suffers at his place."

"Why that man!" Viney exploded. "Just ain't none of his affair! Sayin' your work suffers!"

Seth turned and smiled at her. A look passed between them and Andy knew Viney Jefferson was quietly seething.

"I'm sorry 'bout him botherin' ya, Mr. Cash," Seth replied slowly.

Cash shrugged, "No real bother, Seth. However, it did stir up some questions in my mind. You've worked for French a long time, haven't you?"

"Since I was 18. So that's 'bout, oh—"

"Fourteen years exactly. And worked hard," Viney sputtered like a fermenting can that would not stay closed.

"Yes, 14 years is a long time," Cash agreed slowly. "I'm wondering though if you'd consider a change."

"A change, sir?" Seth asked.

Cash laced his fingers together, leaning back.

"You are a man of great skill, Seth. You do marvelous things with wood. I want to offer you your own shop. A building I'd furnish and all the proper tools you'd want. I—"

"A shop of my own?" Seth's words came in a gasp.

Cash nodded. "Your own shop. We'd be partners."

It was completely silent. Even six-year-old Micah knew something very important was developing. Viney needed no restraint; she was too much in awe. Seth seemed to study the spokes of the buggy wheel. Cash continued, "I thought we'd convert one of Tanglewood's buildings into a shop. Plenty of good lumber about. Also, Andy's here and feeling much better. He could help implement our plans."

"Of course I'll help," Andy spoke up eagerly. "I think it's a great plan!" Andy smiled inwardly. Wasn't just a fraction of his enthusiasm rooted in the mental picture of a frustrated, arrogant Jeb French?

Finally Seth spoke, very deliberately, as if he were controlling his emotion with great effort. "I'm grateful to you, Mr. Cash, more'n I can tell you. It's just I've worked for Mr. French so long..."

"Well, I'd expect you to give him two weeks' notice. That seems reasonable," Cash admitted.

"I know, I know. It's just that..."

Andy hated seeing this kind man flounder.

Viney spoke, tears pooled in her deep brown eyes. There was no trace of bitterness in her words or tone.

"I'm right sorry for how I flared up earlier. Don't mean to bad-mouth anyone. Just, well, Mr. French has always been...about."

"About?" Cash leaned forward.

Viney looked embarrassed. "He's paid Seth a good wage most times. But he's over us, see? Pays the tax, then tells Seth how to vote."

Seth Jefferson's restraint snapped. "Viney!" He did not like to be reminded of French's power, which so compromised his integrity. He would have preferred not to vote again at all.

"He tells you how to vote?" Andy exploded. Cash could hear the echo of Andy's father in the son's voice. Without turning, he placed a quieting hand on the young man's arm.

"Go on, Viney," Cash said softly.

She glanced up cautiously at her tall husband.

"I'm sorry. I talk too much. Just Mr. French, he's..."

There was a lengthy silence. It was clear to everyone except little Micah. Too clear...

In many ways the new black codes in the South were stronger, more stoically enforced than those of slave days. And while many good and honest men and women of the South had changed, matured, or died and been replaced by compassionate generations, old ways, dark ways persisted in many hearts, played out a thousand times a day in segregated schools, markets, hospitals, hotels. From sidewalks to cemeteries, the Negro's position was clearly defined.

Andy was horrified as a transplanted Northerner; Cash grieved as a love-for-his-home Southerner. Cash glanced up at Seth, then to the dark, purple-shadowed pines, a tight muscle working in his slender jaw. Here was a man, honest and hardworking, legally protected, and defenseless. It was all too common.

He turned abruptly. He hated fights, struggles, tension—conflict by any name or description. Yet weak as he was, peace-loving as he was, a steel fiber ran through Patrick Cash. He had given his youth and health to the South three decades ago in a cause he had not believed in. Now he would take up a cause with the full flame of his convictions.

"I wouldn't want this offer to put you in a problem with anyone," Cash said firmly.

"I know that, Mr. Cash," Seth returned.

"You must choose. Make your decision on what you want, Seth. You and your family. Jeb French must not make this decision for you."

Andy suspected the black man was estimating, figuring, doing all to strike a balance with his future and Jeb French.

Seth turned to his wife. She was rigid with expectation. Finally she spoke. "Do as you're a mind to, Seth. Where you go, I'll go."

Cash spoke up again. "We can work together concerning any difficulties that might come about over this. I'll stand with you, Seth." He smiled. "Stand in my own way."

"And you can count on me as well while I'm here," said Andy enthusiastically.

"You can give me your answer another time, Seth. I don't want to press you," Cash said easily.

"No, no, sir. I'm... honored and proud to be your partner." His voice was tremulous. Then he grinned, his hand extended.

"When do we start?"

Cash was alone in his studio. Alone, but not lonely. A brilliant splash of ivory moonlight through the big picture window indicated it was approaching midnight. A soft wind was languidly tossing the magnolias and willows outside the studio. The artist had pulled on his frayed-at-the-cuffs, paint-splattered gray sweater. Despite his usual neat and careful appearance, he wore this old sweater. It was his uniform. His nimble fingers moved among the paint pots, mixing and daubing for just the perfect shade of blue. He must create the exact shade of cold, dark, ocean blue. Looking at the canvas must make one feel as though he were gripping the deck rail with both hands, feeling the salt-laden wind in his face. Cash was very happy and humming to himself.

He rolled back from the easel, tilting his head, evaluating. The mighty ship was crested on a wave, perched in foam and spray, proud. Sunlight, shy and nearly ineffectual, penetrated saffron and rose-hued clouds. Cash was satisfied; a few more hours work and the painting would be finished. He smiled to himself. Would the sailor concede he had captured *Ivanhoe's Dream?*

He was glad he was almost finished with the project. He had another painting, one more important to himself. And deep inside, Cash felt an urgency about it. Time was a luxury now.

He was tired suddenly. He laid down his brush and rolled away from the easel. He could feel his heart thudding erratically as it did so often lately. Not a predictable, healthy beat, but a swoosh, then a race, then a pause. He hadn't told Amy about these little cardiac dramas. Amy... she'd be upset with him if she knew he was down here working so late.

He picked the sketchpad with his new project. He had drawn it in rough lines of charcoal. He tilted his head and thought, then carefully sketched in the title. It would be his best work. It would be his last work. It was "Magnolia Remembrance," his final masterpiece.

He closed his eyes to rest. Perhaps that ride out to the Crossing had fatigued him more than he realized. Yet he was calm and confident he had done the right thing for Seth Jefferson. He only wished he had thought of it sooner. Seth certainly had as much skill with a plane and saw as he did with a brush, only Seth's skin was black and he hadn't been born into money like Cash had. Cash rubbed his forehead. Seth should have the opportunities that he'd had. Maybe . . . in this twilight of his life, Cash could effect changes in the lives of those around him.

Jeb French's face trespassed into his peaceful thoughts. Of course, the man would think Cash had done for the Jeffersons to spite him. French was the sort of man who measured men and their motives by a stunted yardstick. Cash knew he would be very angry. Another storm on the horizon, then. He would face it, but Amy must be protected from it at all costs.

He opened his eyes. He was no coward, but Patrick Cash could not help but be grateful that Andy Alcott was here with them. His youth and his strength gave security to Cash. Surely together they could face the battle.

Chapter 5

Peppercreek, Illinois

♦♦ ♦♦ ♦♦

*T*he man and woman were huddled together, chilled, but not by a frigid temperature. The doctor had snapped his black bag closed with a meaningful finality. He scarcely gave the couple a backward glance as he softly closed the door.

The woman, clutching her husband's calloused hand, was remembering her only daughter's birth some 20 years earlier. She would never forget the delight after two sons to have a beautiful, petite baby girl. She closed her eyes, recalling with amazing detail those baby days.

The man's eyes were not closed. His eyes were latched on the slight figure in the bed whose ragged, struggling breath so tortured him. His collar was damp from perspiring, and there was an arthritic throbbing in the stump of his left arm that always intensified under stress. He was thinking, debating whether he should assemble his family together as his daughter fought to stay alive.

She was so young. She looked 12, not 20, as he looked at her. So vulnerable. The pneumonia had thinned her, honed her down, pared away any excess, any beauty, any strength. He glanced out the window. A branch, fully budded, scratched against the pane. It was warm enough for shirtsleeves, yet his daughter lay bundled under a small mountain of quilts.

Every year it had been this way, this suffering from the long, hard winter. This time the spring warmth had been impotent to revive and to heal. Meg Alcott had remained tightly caught in the grip of a terrible taskmaster.

He swore suddenly, this imperfect father, profane as he had never been before. His wife's eyes flew open.

She gasped. "Ethan!"

He bounded up, his anger boiling over. "I'm sorry! I—God help us, Sara, we're losing her!"

She reached out to calm him. "Ethan...Ethan."

He paced the little sunshine-flooded bedroom, his arm gesturing frantically. "Sara, she's so young, and she's dying! You know it. She can't..."

He stopped before the window, barely seeing the orchard that stretched out for miles below him. His life-work, his dreams. He could hardly see them now.

"Every winter since she was a babe," he groaned. "Why didn't we move? Move south or west like Dr. Joe told us she needed. Stubborn—"

"Ethan, we couldn't just move all—"

"For our gal we couldn't? Of course we could! We should have sold every square inch of this land. If she lives, she'll never spend another winter here. I..."

He moaned and dropped to his knees. "God forgive me, a sinner."

He was sobbing, begging for the life of his only daughter.

"Take me, take me," he moaned. Sara was beside him, her arms around him.

The door opened silently, and Henri Mullins entered. He shuffled to the bed, ignoring the parents, focused only on the girl. His frail hand clutched the near lifeless one. His eyes were closed, lips moving in mute appeal.

Somewhere...far...warm, safe, lovely...She couldn't feel that awful pressure on her chest, that burning as she tried to draw a breath. She couldn't feel...anything. And those voices...Pulling her...She looked and couldn't see...But it was real, gently tugging at her. Not painfully, or forcefully, just persistently.

"Uncle Henri?" No one heard her thin, weak voice.

Then she saw her father, prostrate on the floor, her mother beside him, her head bowed. Meg had felt nothing but happiness, but the sight of her stricken father alarmed and grieved her.

She thought about those cords that had been pulling her. Were they prayer? Had it only been a dream?

"Papa?"

Ethan looked up and found her smiling at him. Such a radiant smile, it almost frightened him.

"Say that again," he murmured.

"Papa," she laughed.

Now there was laughter where there had been tears, sunshine where there had been shadow, praise where there had been petition.

Tanglewood

"Let's go to the library for some post-exam sherry before you go, Barrett."

Browning silently followed his host to the book-lined room where Cash poured two tumblers.

Cash took a drink, then peered over the rim of his glass at the doctor. Browning seemed lost in thought, his eyes fastened on the huge mauve roses on the carpet.

Cash made a wry smile. "That bad?"

Barrett looked startled. "Excuse me?"

"The diagnosis. That bad?"

Barrett looked back at the carpet, then to the frail man in the wheelchair.

"Part of the prescription of being a doctor is knowing the best time to speak and the best time to simply be silent. To know and to weigh what your patient wants to know...needs to know. Take Mrs. Charles Cassidy. One of the richest women in Greenville. My only Greenville patient. I'm speaking confidentially, Cash. What she needs is to give up, well..."

"Eating so many pastries?" Cash said, chuckling.

"Quite a few less. A few brisk walks around her estate wouldn't hurt either. That's definitely not what she wants to hear."

"Do you tell her anyway?"

"As diplomatically as I can."

"For Sophie Cassidy, I can imagine that's not easy."

"No, it's not. But you see how some want truth, some don't?"

"Truth is more palatable to me, Barrett, than professional evasion. I'm a big boy."

Barrett smiled. "I'm not a heart specialist, Cash, I told you that."

"You are my doctor, and I trust your judgment. You know a healthy ticker when you hear one."

Barrett stood up abruptly and stalked to one of the leaded windows. "Where did you say Amy was?"

"Went to Vicksburg. I insisted she go shopping, et cetera. Andy took her."

Barrett swung around, a small thought forming in his mind, a suspicion. He shook his head.

"Look, Barrett, don't feel bad. But I do need to know. It's important to me," Cash persisted.

"Your heart is very weak, Cash. I'm sorry."

Cash took a long drink. "Don't be sorry, Barrett." His voice gentled. "Thanks for telling me."

"Why, Cash? For Amy's sake?"

Patrick Cash sighed and looked at the huge oil painting that hung over the fireplace. "Confidential, Barrett?"

"Confidential."

"Amy will press you when she finds out you examined me."

"If you want, I'll be professionally evasive."

Cash tapped his lips in thought. "Well, there are three reasons for secrecy. First I want to finish something I'm working on."

"A painting?"

Cash nodded. "Call it artist's vanity; still, it's important to me to finish."

"What else?"

"I want everything to be in order for Amy. Tanglewood will be hers. I don't want any problems for her. Goodness knows she's had enough in her young life. Did you think us fools to marry, Barrett, like everyone else did?"

Barrett shrugged. "Not my place to judge, Cash. Ya'll look happy to me; that's what matters."

"Well, she's certainly been good for me. I want her happiness to continue even after I'm not here. She's too precious to spend her days entombed here at Tanglewood! I did that for years."

"Now, Cash, don't put more into my diagnosis than I meant."

Cash waved his words aside. "I hope that Amy will remarry. You were a candidate."

It took a minute for Barrett to understand Cash's words.

"Cash!"

"I decided that, fine man though you are, you're married to your work, Doctor."

Barrett was not easily shocked, but this! A man looking for a new husband for his wife.

"Cash, this is—"

"Don't be too disapproving, Barrett. Try to see it from my perspective. I love Amy, love her deeply. I've wanted to give her all I can to make up for the pain she suffered before she came to Tanglewood."

"And you have," Barrett interrupted.

"I hope so. I don't want her happiness to stop when I'm gone. I haven't been able . . . well, our marriage . . ." Cash stopped and studied his chair, his eyes troubled.

Barrett could suddenly see behind the veil of their relationship—a trembling and uncertain Patrick Cash had pulled it aside.

"Crippled as I am . . . not a young man . . ." Cash was speaking almost to himself now. "We're friends, husband and wife, not . . . lovers."

Barrett moved uncomfortably. In his profession he was privy to deathbed confessions, to intimate details of his patients' lives—vivid, human, touching, and often disturbing and tragic.

"Ah, but my love for her has been very real, Barrett!"

Barrett winced to see the tears that had filled Cash's eyes.

"I know it has," he replied softly.

Cash cleared his throat. "A good man for Amy, that's what I want. Someone strong and faithful, who will love her, protect her, and give her children."

Barrett attempted levity with a shaky voice.

"Since I've failed the test for suitors, any—" He stopped, the earlier suspicion crystallizing in his mind. "Cash, this sounds so cold-blooded! You're not throwing Amy and Alcott together, are you?"

Cash managed a guilty smile and spread his hands out in apology.

"He's family, and I'm very fond of him. He's a good man."

"He's also a seafaring man. Married to his work, like you say I am to mine."

"I know, I know. That is a problem I haven't yet overcome," Cash admitted.

Barrett laughed nervously. "I can't begin to imagine how outraged your wife would be if she heard this conversation. Let's change the subject. You said there were three reasons."

Cash nodded and tapped the side of his chair, his eyes becoming wistful. "This, Barrett. I've only been in it two years, but I'm weary of it. I want to walk again, feel steady and strong on my own two feet again. But I know that's one hope that won't be realized until my time here is over."

After the doctor had left, Cash remained in the library thinking over their conversation—the diagnosis and his confession. He thought of Andy and Amy in Vicksburg. He thought of his words to Barrett. *He's family, I'm very fond of him. He's a good man.*

"And he's young and strong," the master of Tanglewood whispered to the quiet room.

Cash was resting. Amy was working in the kitchen. Andy had taken his mail and wandered down to the stables. He climbed up into the huge loft filled with sun-warmed, sweet-smelling hay. He would stretch out here, read his letters, drift off into an afternoon nap. Just like a boy again, reading *Treasure Island* up in the Alcott barn.

He pulled out an apple from his pocket and laughed to himself. Amy had brought them from town, proudly presenting him one.

"I bought them to make you feel more at home," she explained.

He was in a teasing mood. He smelled it, rolled it in his palm, flicked the peel with his thumb, eyed it critically. He shrugged.

"I reckon you can call this an apple."

Amy had reached for something to throw at him as he backed out of the kitchen.

In the loft he again judged the fruit. He had the family bias well ingrained though he lived at sea—no apple was as good as the ones grown in the Alcott orchard.

He laid the two letters on his lap. Which to read first... He wished there was a third letter; he wished he had a letter from Lilly. But one missive was from his shipmate Ben, the other from his mother.

A bite of the fruit, then a quick slash of his pocketknife on Ben's envelope. He would read this one quickly, find out how his "family" at sea was faring.

He scanned the page. It seemed a normal enough voyage with typical trials, problems, and routines. The final lines held him.

"A week ago a very fierce storm came up. Treadle had been watching it all afternoon, trying to judge if we could outrun it and lay off in a bay till it was over. But it came suddenly, like a blast out of a cannon at us.

Young Greer Nelson was sent up with O'Murray to trim the topsails. It was his first time up. He'd been bragging he could do it with his eyes closed. You know how wet and wild it gets up there. He lost his footing. There was nothing we could do. I thought you'd want to know. And he left a wife."

Andy closed the letter soberly. "You know how wet and wild it gets up there," Ben had written. Yes, he knew. He hated to make "the climb." Few sailors he knew relished the task—unless they were part monkey and full of daredevil courage. He'd never forget his first trip up the sails. It had been around the Horn—a terrible indoctrination. If Treadle could have spared him, he would have. But every hand was needed. Andy would never forget the way the captain's pale and worried face hung over him when it was all over. The big man's rough hand had rested on his forehead when he thought Andy slept. It was the first glimpse Andy had of Treadle's softer side.

His first trip around the Horn, his first time up the sails—and very nearly his last. Every experienced crewman had told him to expect the worst when the ship passed around the southernmost tip of South America. They did not exaggerate.

The wind had been a heavy gale for two days. No sunshine, no break in the boiling black clouds. Everything on deck was lashed down. The sea churned, pitched, and heaved as if it were determined to toss out the manmade craft like a piece of cork. Andy had stood by the sputtering coal stove for precious little heat and wondered if he had really heard God's calling to come to the water. He wondered too if it could get much worse.

It got much worse. The mighty waves crested with a thousand feet between them. The wind became laden with sleet and snow. Men were posted to watch for mammoth ice floes that could slice the keel of a clipper like paper. The ship rolled badly, the lamps swung on their gimbals, and meals at the table were impossible. Who had a stomach for eating anyway?

Then the order had been given to go up and tighten the sails that were flapping wildly. *Up the rigging.* Each man dreaded those words. No one made eye contact. No one made feeble jokes. Andy felt like it was a death sentence. Who could climb, much less stand, in a fury such as this?

He pulled on the oilskin suit someone thrust into his arms. He grabbed the icy rigging and prepared to climb. But a hand on his shoulder stopped him. It was Treadle. He was cynical in those early days, still testing Andy's faith—and temper.

"All prayed up, lad?"

Andy turned away from him and climbed. He made it to the huge yardarm with the others. He gritted his teeth and went to work. They worked against the stinging wind and ice that blinded them and turned their faces raw and tore at their hands as if to pry them loose. A vicious wind. Then the cry was shouted to go down; it was finished. The *Ivanhoe* plunged sideways, entirely opposite to the direction it had been leaning, as if a giant hand had playfully slapped it. But it was a deadly slap.

Two of the veteran crew slipped and spun off into wind, then the ocean, their cries voiceless. Andy fell also. The rigging, like a net, caught him 20 feet above the slanting deck. With such weather and such danger, he hung upside down for ten minutes until the men could lower him. It was the longest ten minutes of his young life.

It took him three days to get his balance back and his color—a little longer to get over his fears. Treadle had been solicitous over him ever since.

Andy closed Ben's letter. Yes, he would pray for the sailor's widow.

The letter from his mother would be more cheerful. He knew what to expect in a letter from his mother. He enjoyed her letters, but they were predictable. She followed a formula—inquiries into his health, family news, closing cautions and advice, and a Scripture. He smiled, yep, Ma's letters were a slice of Peppercreek tucked in an envelope and sent through the mail.

She'd tell him how the trees were doing as though they were members of the family—their condition, their fruit, what they were going for at market. She'd give him a weather report of the day she wrote. He could see her at the oilcloth-covered kitchen table, chewing the end of a pencil and staring out the window. He'd seen her like that a hundred times. She'd tell him how his father was working too hard and what new mischief his brother Daniel was into. Though she wouldn't commit it to paper, Andy knew his mother thought her youngest the least responsible of them all.

She would tell him how big his sister-in-law, Millie, was getting with their first grandchild. Somehow in the lines she'd express that children really were a blessing. A wife and home were very nice too, in the proper order, of course. There she was again, on the campaign for him to settle down and start a family. She'd finish up with news about neighbors and folks he knew in town.

It had taken a few years for Andy Alcott to finally figure out that his mother took the time to write these long epistles because she was advertising—home. She missed him and wanted him closer.

And so she'd write about Meg and any of her new beaus, and any of the students at Peppercreek who were giving her trouble in the classroom. Meg needed a husband, his mother would write bluntly. Andy would smile. Mothers...always on the lookout for mates for their unmarried children.

But this time as he sat in the Tanglewood loft, the letter from his mother was not predictable. She had fooled him.

Dear son,

We almost lost Meg. I'm writing you now because I knew you'd want to be rejoicing with us, and thanking Him. She was a very sick girl. Her lungs were full of fluid, and she had a very high fever. Doc Smith had tried everything he knew and told us to prepare for her passing by morning. It was so hard to see my little girl so sick. I've never seen your father so grieved and tortured. If he could have laid down his life for her, I know he would have. We all prayed, and Uncle Henri came and laid hands on her. Meg is healed; she is well. She can breathe again. She's still with us!

The letter had slipped into the hay, forgotten. He could not remember a time when he and Meg had not been close. They had always played together. She followed him everywhere. His friends would complain and called her "Shadow." They would try to shame and scold and threaten her to make her go play with girls. Andy would listen, then sigh, then tell them to be quiet and leave her alone. After a while, they came to understand that where Andy went, Shadow was sure to go.

Andy and Meg became teens, and many nights they would sit on the front porch and talk and laugh and tease. Whenever she got into trouble, he was the first to defend her. He'd go and tell his folks they were being unfair to her. He'd take her to town to shop and tell her what color looked best against her hair. He wasn't too proud to tell her she was the prettiest girl in Illinois, even if she was his sister.

He looked out the loft window where Tanglewood was warming in the early summer sunshine. Meg almost died? *He* would have given his life for hers.

"You're so quiet this evenin', Andy. Are you all right? Is your foot bothering you?" Cash asked gently.

They sat in the library with the chessboard between them.

Andy sighed. "No, sir, my foot's fine. Just the...mail I got today. It was...Well, sir, I'm just glad I'm here with you...both. You see, a friend on the *Ivanhoe* wrote and told me about an accident—a crewman died. Then my mother's letter. My sister Meg was very ill. She almost died. I can't imagine life without Meg."

Amy had been sitting quietly across the room. She looked up from her embroidery. She watched Andy's face as he spoke. To be loved like that!

Greenville

Drunkenness was the weakness of fools, Jeb French had reasoned in his youth. The case was simple: Drinking to excess put you in something else's power. That was madness. Still, French was hardly a Puritan teetotaler. He had the amazing capacity to drink large amounts of liquor without intoxication. He gloated inwardly; he had triumphed over the bottle where others had hopelessly sunk. It was yet another measure of his latent strength.

Greenville, Mississippi, had colorful memories. Old-timers sat in the dusty and mellow sunshine of the courthouse square talking endlessly and with varying degrees of license about the delta town. Its existence had always been dominated by the aggressive Mississippi that flowed past its gate. Cotton flourished in the rich soil around Greenville, another gift from the river.

During the war between the states, Greenville had been burned to the ground by Union troops marching to Vicksburg, which lay south. The storytellers relished that drama among their repertoire of tales. Resurrected, the town had withstood near annihilation from yellow fever some 12 years later. Yes, Greenville was famous in its own unique way.

Saloons and grog shops were a part of Greenville, yet the city observed decorum and temperance by closing its Main Street doors every Saturday evening at six o'clock. Therefore Greenville was not a popular port for the riverboat crews. The city ministers felt they had done their evangelizing very well, and were just a little smug about it. The denominations felt they had defeated the devil at the dice, the card, the glass. Citizens felt their streets were very respectable, and very safe.

But a handful of "city fathers" of another sort met together in a jealous fraternity each Saturday night in the well-furnished back room of a Greenville bookstore. It was not unusual for thousands of dollars to pass hands at this little enclave of vice. Jeb French was always a predictable presence at these gatherings.

This Saturday night he was absent. He was in a very sour, very belligerent mood that several tumblers of brandy had not improved. He was in no mood for cards or dice or the company of his cronies. One wrong word from them might ignite his temper, and the little pearl-handled pistol would appear from its slumbering place. The wolfhound at his feet received the dark scowls and curses in his canine ears.

French had risen above his plebeian beginnings with a great deal of shrewdness and hard work. In that respect he was very admired. His varied investments and interests were far-reaching. He liked to have a hand in every pie that he possibly could. His bachelor home on Cable Street was impressive. He could, and did, boast he had installed Greenville's first telephone and electric lights. He was a well-informed man who knew the pulse of America beyond Greenville, Mississippi.

Yet for all of his financial gains, Jeb French's spirit was dwarfed. His character was narrow and corrupt. He hated everything about Southern-born wealth and position. There was something in these things that he could not work for, trade for, or steal. Marriage, a convenient ladder, was a thing he totally deplored.

French was seething. Patrick Cash in his weak yet superior way had bested him again. He poured himself another drink, his eyes narrowing. He would strike, but this time with very careful planning. A man could be patient when he needed to be.

New York City

Lilly O'Hara knew she should write Andy and assure him she had reached the big city safely. But it seemed to her when she had stepped off the train in New York, she had stepped onto another planet! So many people, so many accents and skin colors. A city of tall buildings and few trees, and a skyline that was an abbreviation—everything crowded right up to the edge of the Atlantic. It was certainly more than enough to make a country girl gawk. She needed to get settled, get some balance, before she wrote Andy.

Caleb Mullins had been there to meet her at the huge terminal. She had been very grateful of that, grateful to have someone say her name and reassure her everything was going to be all right. He had asked about Andy and about her trip, then had the courtesy to be silent as she leaned out the carriage and looked, and looked.

She was exhausted from the ten-day trip that had carried her across prairies, plains, and rivers, through mountains and sleepy little hamlets that had forgettable names. She felt she'd seen half the country from a grimy train window. She was tired of the noise, the jerky stops and starts, the hurried meals, and press of people sitting too close.

The mission was clean and homelike. The couple that served as the directors were old enough to be her grandparents, and treated her very kindly. They gave her a small, plain, but private room. It was the first time she'd ever had her own bed, her own space. She could sing softly without anyone telling her to hush up or to turn the light off if she chose to stay up late reading. It gave her a heady feeling of independence.

The first night in her room, she had sat on the edge of her bed, with the light off, staring out the window. She could finally see a decent patch of skyline. It was gray. But the night was alive with a horizon of lights. She stared until her eyes grew too heavy to stay open and she couldn't think anymore. Then she simply stretched out with her clothes and shoes still on, and slept. Oh, it was going to be fun to be on her own!

Her work at the mission was minimal, cleaning and helping with meals. It was her choice to stay and listen to the teachings from the Word. She stayed—it was food that her simple soul so desperately needed. But in her free time, she was on her own. Lilly could take the electric streetcars into the pulse of the city. She saw the big libraries, the art museums. She walked up and down Broadway and looked over the famous theaters and lesser-known playhouses. She stood in the alleys in the afternoons and watched the cast and crew pass in, and imagined that one day she would be joining them.

One afternoon she found a voice studio. She had asked around.

"Well, you sure need one, sister," a burly grocery man had tactlessly told her.

"Excuse me?"

"Your lingo, lady, your accent. I've lived in New York all my life, and I've never heard yours before. The way you say *a*...man, oh, man."

Lilly drew herself up impressively.

"I am from Mississippi, sir."

She marched out with her head held high, the first doubts growing in her mind. Did she really have such a dreadful accent that lessons might do nothing to improve it? She found the studio that was held in such high regard by the theater crowd. From the open window she could hear the practices—first the voice of the student, then the firm words of the coach. It would take months before she would be able to afford lessons; for now she'd just listen from the sidewalk for free.

Yet even as time passed and she had more money, she never took a single formal voice lesson. On days that were warm enough, she'd just listen from her spot by the street, then go back to the mission to practice what she'd heard. Years later she would enjoy telling this story to her wide circle of friends. She had been coached by a voice master and never paid a penny! She had become a true New Yorker, she'd laugh.

There was one sight in the vast city she saw in that first week that remained forever close to her heart, a personal symbol to Lilly O'Hara. She saw it one morning from the deck of a ferry when the fog was lazily rising off the Hudson River. Its proper name was "Liberty Enlightening the World." Some called it "Miss Liberty," or "the Statue." Some casually referred to it as "the Lady." No matter how many times she would see it over the progression of years, it would never be casual to her.

She didn't know it inspired others like it did her, those thousands who came to New York via the Atlantic and Grand Central. They were more friendless, penniless, and frightened than she was. Wave upon wave of those who landed on a patch of earth called Ellis Island looked up at that bronze woman as big as their ambitions. When Lilly struggled and was lonely, when she faced rejection and disappointments, she could glimpse the statue in the harbor and feel a surge of hope. Maybe . . . maybe her dreams weren't too big. She thought of Andy when she saw "Miss Liberty." She wished she could show it to him. He had become a part of her dreams too.

In those early days, when her faith was growing, when she was learning to live alone and make decisions, she thought of Andy often. It was a thing she probably shouldn't do, she told herself. A senseless thing; it had no future in it. He thought of her as a friend, a sister—and so it would stay. They were separated by thousands of miles. She had cast her future with this big city; he belonged to the world of explorers.

He had given her a priceless treasure, introducing her to the Lord. How could she ask for more? But she was flesh as well as spirit, and starved for the pure love she had never known. They would write each other, a relationship through letters. He would touch her that way.

Tanglewood

Andy sat in the shade of one of Tanglewood's many live oaks, waiting for Amy. They were going riding. He seemed to be dozing in the stillness of the warm afternoon but he jerked upright when he heard her step. She was smiling as she pulled on her broad hat. She wore crisp white linen riding clothes, a trademark of Southern women.

"Did I really take that long?" she teased.

He stood up, dusting off his pants. "Excuse me?"

"You fell asleep waiting for me," she said.

"Oh, I wasn't asleep. I—" he stopped. "I probably need to go shave after waiting for you." His voice contained forced lightness.

Amy had stopped smiling as she realized he had been praying. Somehow that made her want to look more closely at him. She felt uncertain. He was like no other man she had ever known.

They started toward the stables. "I wanted to make certain Cash was comfortable. I wish he was able to go with us."

Andy nodded. "I'm just grateful he has the use of his arms and can paint. It means so much to him."

Amy smiled. "Well, I can tell you *Ivanhoe's Dream* is coming along quite nicely."

Andy stopped walking. "You weren't supposed to look!"

"Cash said I could. Something about wifely privileges."

"You sound like you're certain I'm going to lose this wager, and glad of it!"

She burst out laughing. "Of course I am!"

"Any ideas about what my payment is to be?"

She was coy now, a skill she had not had much occasion to use in her young life. "Not a clue."

They were saddling their mounts in the sweet-smelling barn a moment later.

"Ever ridden a bicycle, Amy? They're quite the rage now, I guess," he offered.

She shook her head. "I've just taken up this kind of riding since I came to Tanglewood. Have you ever ridden one?"

"Nope."

"We're not very progressive, Andy. The world is spinning fast around us."

"That sounds like my sister. She always keeps me well informed on how fast the world is changing, and how she and I are missing it." He was laughing as he thought of Meg.

Amy noticed that reference to his sister again. He did not speak of anyone else so often from his home in Illinois as he did this little sister. *This must be what having a loving brother is like,* she thought. For a moment, she envied Meg Alcott.

"You're close to your sister," she said finally.

He smiled. "Meg makes me laugh like no one else does. We see things kind of alike, I guess. My brothers were always outgoing, easy-to-talk-to folks. Meg and I were—"

"Shy?" Amy offered.

He nodded. "You'd like her."

Amy had not spoken to Andy of her life before becoming Cash's bride. Cash had been silent on the subject as well. They had talked of his family back in Peppercreek, of his travels and the ports he had seen, and of current events.

"Have you any sisters, Amy?" he asked.

She turned away from him. "No," she answered softly.

The door to the past remained firmly closed.

Andy sensed that Amy was reluctant to pass through Greenville on their ride. However, Cash had asked Andy to go there on an errand for him. Andy would place the order for the tools that would make Tangle-wood's carpentry shop a fine one.

Their ride down the country roads that bisected large plantations had been a quiet and uneventful one. They had spoken very little and seen no one. Now as they entered the port city's streets, he could see a tenseness in Amy's posture. Her eyes were riveted to the space just above and between her horse's ears. For someone generally cloistered at home, Amy did not display any of the usual feminine curiosity about the fashions and theatrics of city life. Andy was intrigued.

"There's a tea shop, Amy. Let's stop in. I'm pretty dry."

Now in the subdued light of the little shop, Andy could see just how nervous Amy Cash really was. He regretted his decision, feeling a sudden wave of protection for her.

"Amy, are you all right?"

Her eyes met his over the table. "Yes, Andy, I'm fine."

Amy cared nothing for gossip, yet she knew the tongues would be wagging. Amy Cash was out riding with a very handsome young man. And not her husband.

It was at the city docks where Andy conducted Cash's business. It took only a few minutes, and Andy was grateful. He wanted back out on the sun-warmed, spring-fragrant road where quiet and alone, Amy could smile and be relaxed. It was crowded and noisy here on Greenville's busy front porch. Local plantation owners were sentimental about the shipping of their precious freight. The railroad was loud and crass; only the mighty waterway would suffice.

They had just stepped from the merchant's shop and remounted when an animal bolted from between two buildings. It was a large wolfhound. It nipped at the legs of Amy's skittish horse. Andy was shouting, trying to bring his own horse between Amy's and the dog. He knew Amy was a novice rider and very frightened.

His eyes glanced toward the boardwalk where a small group had gathered. He saw Jeb French above them all. He was placidly smoking and smiling.

"Call him off, French!"

French lazily pushed forward, emitting a low whistle. The dog came instantly to its master's side.

French looked neither at his dog nor Andy, who was red-faced and fuming. His eyes were only for Amy Cash. He smiled at her confidentially as he swept off his white panama hat.

"Afternoon, Mrs. Cash."

Amy did not speak, but she did not look away.

French turned to Andy, an arrogant, measuring look.

"Your dog, French, needs to learn better manners," Andy said stiffly.

French shrugged. "Oh, he has manners fine."

"Mrs. Cash could have been injured. If that had happened, I'd—"

"Andy, let's go," Amy interrupted hastily.

"You'd what?" French was still smiling.

When Andy did not speak, he turned back to Amy.

"So, why isn't your husband out with you, Mrs. Cash? Oh, yes... I forgot. You're awfully quiet, Mrs. Cash. Has your rise in fortunes made you snobbish?"

Amy and Andy turned their horses with mutual, silent agreement. Only later did Amy stop. She gathered a bunch of black-eyed Susans that grew by the roadside, finally relaxing. She could see that Andy was concerned for her. She smiled. "I'm all right, Andy, really."

He was startled at how accurately she had read his thoughts.

"I'm sorry about what happened back there," he said. "I'm sure Jeb French is just a little sore about losing Seth."

He hoped that was all it was.

Amy leaned forward. "Please don't tell Cash. It would only upset him."

Returning to Tanglewood, they passed under the archway of cypresses that lined the drive to the mansion. The Spanish moss swayed gently like a woman shaking out her fine Sabbath shawl. It was incredibly quiet, a tranquillity that was almost palpable.

"Do you feel it, Amy?" Andy asked with something of wonder in his voice. He didn't wait for her to answer. "It's so peaceful. No other living thing in sight." He did not mean to say anything intimate, yet it was out before he could stop. "It's like we're the only two people on earth."

Chisolm Crossing

Young Micah Jefferson left the general store at Chisolm Crossing later than he intended. It was really Mr. Chester's fault, the young boy reasoned. Chester always got to telling him stories and showing him the new merchandise he had. It must be fine to have a store like Mr. Chester did. Imagine getting up any time at night when you woke up hungry and just goin' in to help yourself to anything you had a fancy for. Maybe crackers and cheese or a can of those little fishes or Micah's favorite, a banana! Of course Mr. Chester probably didn't get to make many of those midnight raids. Nope, not with a woman like Mrs. Chester around.

So he left the store when the sun was easing below the fringe of pines. Just a slip of a disk and soon it would be dark. It would be a full moon tonight. Micah knew such things. But it didn't matter. He didn't need the light to help him home. He knew the woods like he knew every inch of the cabin he shared with his ma and pa and soon-to-be little brother. It had to be a brother since he'd been praying so hard.

He knew the woods because he tramped them daily in play or hunting coons or going down to Ford's Creek to fish. His ma sent him to the store for things like she'd done this afternoon. He knew them because he'd wait on the path for his father to come home from Tanglewood. He would always hide behind a rock or tree, then jump out to pull a fright on his pa. It never worked. His pa would shake his head and say, "Sure is a shame that a tired old man been a workin' all day come home to be jumped at by his own little boy."

Micah would say, "You ain't old, Daddy!"

And they would both laugh. It was the same every evening.

So he went down the path between the pines and old gnarled oaks and cypresses that were hung with moss. Noah's lace, Micah called it. It looked so old and gloomy. He hopped over rotted limbs, rocks and roots, whistling as he went and thinking about all the things he'd seen at Mr. Chester's. He had no reason to be concerned.

Only when he was halfway to his cabin did he come fully aware, like one coming from a deep dream back to reality. The woods had become dark and purple and shadowy. He hadn't noticed the sky when he left the Crossing. He didn't see that a storm was lying to the west like a promise.

He stopped in the middle of the path. With the wind and shadows, these woods could give a boy of almost seven a fright. Sure did look different in daylight or even early morning. They looked friendly then. Now...

He heard it. A laugh. A low laugh somewhere back over his left shoulder. He felt his skin crawl. Could Pa make a laugh like that? Pa should be home by now. Had he come out to the path to pull a fright on *him?* Must be.

He hooked his thumbs in his jumper and called out in a loud voice. "Pa!...You're too old to play games!"

He waited. Nothing. The wind had stopped as suddenly as it had begun. There was nothing now, not even the brush of the wind on a leaf.

"Think it's a shame for a poor ol' little boy to be comin' home and have a daddy try to pull a fright on him!...Pa?"

He turned back around. He could run fast if he needed to. But a hand grabbed him. Another hand clamped his mouth closed.

"Ever heard of the KKK, nigger boy?" the voice hissed in his ear. "Tell your daddy... Tell him to watch his step."

Micah thought his heart was going to burst through the front of his jumper. He could smell something. Something he had never smelled before. Not a bad odor, just, different.

"Micah?...Micah! You there, boy?"

It was his pa! He had come down the path to meet him.

The hands shoved him roughly forward. He did not turn around. He ran to his father.

Chapter 6

Tanglewood, July

♦♦ ♦♦ ♦♦

*T*he gentle Mississippi spring faded in the harsh strength of sum-mer's heat. Mornings were warm and balmy now; afternoons, hot and still. Evenings were spent on screened porches to find some relief from the humidity. The redbud trees, the camellias, and the azaleas still provided vivid splashes of color along country roads and gardens.

Dr. Browning pronounced Andy's foot completely healed. It was only a matter of waiting for *Ivanhoe's Dream* to return in early September. But now Andy had a new and absorbing addition to his days at Tangle-wood. He was working alongside Seth Jefferson as they converted an old overseer's cabin into the carpentry shop. Their hammers and saws beat a tempo as they reworked the building. They traded stories and some-times sang. Andy was enjoying himself greatly, relieved at last to be of some real benefit to Cash. Andy Alcott was of working stock, and idleness had not been comfortable to him.

Cash did not venture out very often, the heat seeming to tax his already frail reserve of strength. Nearly all his energy was directed to painting. *Ivanhoe* was finished, awaiting the artist's time to unveil it. He had begun a new work now.

At noon each day Seth and Andy came to the mansion for dinner. If Seth felt intimidated by the wealth of the place, he did not betray it in any way. He moved easily and appeared relaxed. He had made Cash throw back his head in laughter at the first meal. Now he leaned over and spoke confidentially to his new business partner.

"You know, that Fenwick is an intrestin' fella, sure is. Every time I see him he looks like he's smellin' a polecat!"

"I think he probably looked at the doctor that delivered him just like that. Told him to comb his hair too," Andy added.

They all laughed. Cash took a drink from his glass, his eyes sweeping the table. Amy looked so beautiful in her pale yellow dress, her hair piled high as a defense against the heat. He looked at Andy and Seth, who were laughing, and decided life had never been so good at Tangle-wood.

He was not surprised at the ease with which Andy turned the conver-sation to slavery. It reminded Cash of Andy's father. Nothing really alike in looks, still the boy reminded him in ways of his father. Seth accepted Andy's questions with equal ease. He had lots of stories to tell about the old days.

"What them slaves had was mostly hope, and hard times." He took a bite and meditated a bit. "'Course maybe those times were really better times," Seth reflected slowly.

"How so, Seth?" Andy asked in surprise.

"'Cause back then, with times so hard, folks had to look to Jesus more. He was all they really had. Now times is better, and folks forget some. Lazy like, they don't depend on Him as much."

Andy was amazed at the man's faith. Life was hardly a banquet for black Americans, even if some social strides forward had been made. Later that evening, Andy went out walking alone. He was thinking of his own heart, his own commitment. How strong was it, really?

Seth Jefferson went to bed each night tired from his construction work at Tanglewood. Yet there was a feeling of satisfaction even in his fatigue. And every night he lay there amazed at how his life had changed so suddenly from the drudgery and verbal abuse at French's waterfront warehouse to building a wood-working shop of which he would be part-owner. He had shared his amazement with Viney.

"Think of it, gal, turnin' that big old overseer's cabin into a shop for a black man. That overseer was master over hundreds of slaves."

"Mr. Pat is a different kind of man than his daddy was, and the others before him."

Seth nodded in the darkness. "Seems I can hear the songs of the slaves in them ol' timbers and see their tears. Sure am a blessed man, I am, Viney."

Viney hated to mention the fear that treaded lightly in her mind, yet it nagged at her.

"Seth, honey, you don't think Jeb French is still upset at you for quittin', do ya? Seems to me he'd be the spiteful kind."

Seth knew Jeb French was indeed the spiteful kind. But he could not voice that concern to Viney. It would alarm her ... and with a new baby on the way.

"Oh, he may be riled up for a little piece. But he'll get over it. Plenty of other good hands around to take my place."

He had comforted young Micah on the path that evening before the two had continued home, warning his son to say nothing to his mother about what had happened just yet. Give things a little time. No need to worry her when she was so happy over the new job at Tanglewood.

Micah had kept the trust, holding the incident in his mind—but not staying afraid. He did not want to be afraid of his woods. He'd just keep his hunting dog with him all the time.

"And you like young Alcott, workin' with him?" Viney continued on to a safer topic.

"Yep, he's a fine man...hard working. Tells me about being at sea. Makes me plumb glad I've got solid ground under my feet. He can keep his seven seas and big ol' oceans. I like it just where I am," he chuckled as he pulled Viney closer into the circle of his arm.

He yawned. "Funny thing happened today while we was up on the roof."

"What?"

"Well, we was a hammerin' away and a singin' at the top of our lungs—"

"Now tell me, how can Mr. Pat rest with such a choir of donkeys?"

Seth laughed. "Anyway, Miss Amy came out like she does sometimes, with something cold for us to drink. We scoot on down the ladder, and I take my drink and Mr. Andy takes his, only..."

"What? *What?*"

"Well, then they just stared at each other, like they had never seen each other before...or like they ain't seen each other in a long, long time."

Viney's feminine mind meditated on this a moment.

"How long was they a starin' like that?" she finally asked.

"Well, I didn't have a watch on," Seth protested.

She swatted his chest. "How long?"

"Maybe half a minute. I'm don't know...just longer than usual. And, it was the way they looked. I promise, Miss Amy turned pale and just turned around and went back to the house without saying a word. Sometimes Mr. Andy makes a place for her and she stays and asks how things is going."

"And Mr. Andy, how did he look?"

Seth's voice was puzzled. "Didn't do much singin' after that."

It was a definite commentary on the state of things to have the mistress of Tanglewood, a plantation of size and reputation, asking the cook of the manor her opinion on fabrics and fashion. Yet Amy Cash hadn't any close friends. In family, only one cousin, who lived in Baton Rouge and rarely visited. Patrick Cash had not moved in the usual circles of society that his birth and wealth created, even before his marriage. He was the local recluse. Then he married a woman who could have passed for his daughter and was from the wrong side of Ford's Creek. It was really too much for most of the wealthy families to understand or accept.

Amy Cash would have liked a girlfriend or two, but there was none, so here she was with the cook comparing shades and designs.

"I don't know about that yellow, Miss Amy. It's pretty, but..."

"Go ahead, Mary. What's wrong with it?"

"Well, it makes you look kind of sickly, washed out."

"I certainly don't want the washed-out look," the young woman laughed. "So, it's out. All right, what about this blue? Too light?"

"Hmm..." It was a difficult proposition for the cook, who typically wore black and daily dealt in menus and shopping lists.

"The blue," came a voice behind them. "Without question, the blue."

Amy whirled around, startled and embarrassed. Andy stood in the doorway of the large kitchen. If it had been Patrick, she would have smiled and been perfectly at ease. But it wasn't her husband. This was the man who only a month and a half ago had been a trespasser at Tanglewood. Now Cash's cousin was part of their home—and she could not imagine the day without his presence or what life would be like when he was gone.

"I came for something to drink," Andy explained easily. "Is this a dressmaker's salon now?"

Amy was fumbling around with the bolts of cloth, trying to act calm and normal. The cook spoke up in the awkward silence.

"Miss Amy is trying to select the right colors for some new dresses."

"I see. Well, what do you think about the blue, Mary?" Andy asked gravely.

"I'll get you and Seth something to drink," Amy interrupted.

"I think the blue is very nice," Mary agreed, warming to Andy's involvement.

"There, you see, Mrs. Cash. It's unanimous. I'm an established authority on colors. Next decision, please."

"You do a lot of that on the *Ivanhoe?*" Amy asked in an attempt to appear casual.

"I have escorted my younger sister on many occasions to the fine shops of Springfield, where my masculine perspective was highly valued. I have the reputation of being a very fair critic."

He was leaning against the table laughing at her.

"Anything else that requires my expertise?"

"Well, no, thanks... Here are your drinks."

"Miss Amy, have you forgotten the mint silk and rose taffeta? We couldn't decide between those," Mary pointed out.

Amy frowned to herself. If only Mary would stop playing along with him.

"Ah, mint silk or rose taffeta. A difficult situation indeed. Silk and taffeta are... so uniquely different, you know. Hmm. You must judge the feel, the weight..." He fingered the cloth with a very serious face, pulling at his chin. "Very smooth, fine quality... hmm."

"Don't you think Seth is waiting for something to drink?" Amy asked with feigned annoyance.

"He's happy to have this interruption, I'm confident. When he hears the seriousness of this silk versus taffeta conflict, well, I know he'll understand why I lingered."

Amy controlled her laughter. She did not want to encourage him.

"You must hold the fabric up to your face. It's the final test."

"Oh, I agree," Mary joined in heartily.

"I think we really have spent too—"

Amy felt Andy was standing too close. She wished he would get over this playfulness.

"Now, Mrs. Cash, please humor me. I'm a frustrated dressmaker at heart. Hold them, yes, just like that. Hmm...the silk is nice, rather ...green however."

"Yes, mint is green. Now, Andy, I really think you should—"

"The rose, please. Yes...all right, come closer, please. Mary, look carefully at this rose. We must be in agreement."

It had begun as a lark for Andy, as if he were laughing and joking with Meg. Then Amy held the fabric up to her cheek. Then, there in the Tanglewood kitchen, Andy realized this was not Meg.

"Well?" Amy asked impatiently. Andy was lingering on her face too long.

"The rose. It's...it looks good against your skin. I mean, against your complexion. It's like a rose against...a rose..." He was flustered and feeling very foolish. He wished Seth had come in for the drinks. "What do you think, Mary?"

"The rose is perfect, Miss Amy, just as Mr. Alcott says."

But Amy hardly heard the cook's words. She was still watching Andy, amazed at the change that had come over him. Now *he* was looking uncomfortable.

"Are you deciding curtain colors for Seth's shop, Andy?" asked a chuckling voice behind them.

They turned. Patrick Cash had joined them.

"For the two dresses I'm going to have made," Amy explained hurriedly. "Remember, I told you?"

"Certainly I do. I wanted you to have a dozen and you wanted only two. Another example of your power over me, my dear." He wagged a finger at her.

"I was asking Mary to help me choose from these samples, and Andy came in for a drink," Amy continued.

"And have you chosen?" Cash asked.

"Well, there's this blue. Mary agreed on that. And then, this mint... or rose..."

"Well, thanks for the refreshment. I'm back to work," Andy said cheerfully. But he lingered a moment.

Cash had appraised the fabric with his color-appreciative eye.

"The mint is perfect. Goes just right with the shade of your hair."
A silence, then Amy raised her eyes fleetingly to Andy's.
"The mint then. Thank you for deciding, Cash."

Chisolm Crossing

The doctor was working over the farmer's hand. The patient had been talking nearly nonstop since the doctor had entered the cabin with his little black bag.

"Glad you could come so quick, Doc," Willet Keller greeted Dr. Browning with artificial heartiness. "Martha's goose grease just ain't up to a burn like this."

Browning shrugged. "Your boy caught me at home for a change. Just prunin' my fruit trees. Mornin', Mrs. Keller."

The woman nodded. "Coffee, Doc?"

The doctor shook his head. He remembered Mrs. Keller's coffee from a previous visit.

Willet sat down at the wooden table and laid his burned paw before the physician. He didn't want the doctor asking a lot of questions, so he covered his nervousness with meaningless chatter. The doctor worked over the hand silently, his face emotionless.

"Reckon this will keep me from chores for a while, huh, Martha?" Willet said with a little laugh.

The woman looked up from the dishes she was washing. The doctor could see she was nervous too. He began to gather up his instruments.

"That's a nasty burn, Willet. How'd ya do it?" Browning kept his voice mild, as if he were asking about the cotton crop. He did not meet the farmer's eyes.

"Aw, you know how it is. Just got too close to the stove one mornin'. Still half asleep."

The lameness of the excuse fell like a thud in the quiet cabin.

Willet Keller had been on a midnight ride two nights previous, the next county over. It had been his first cross burning. He'd been very impressed with the night's activities—and a little too zealous. When a smoldering spar of wood had dropped at his feet from the burning cross, he had snatched it up thoughtlessly. One of the men beside him had chuckled and elbowed him in the ribs, ignoring the obvious pain the farmer was in.

"Wantin' a souvenir of tonight?"

"I just wasn't thinkin'," Keller had mumbled. "Meant to kick it back with my boot."

He hoped the others hadn't noticed what he'd done and think him stupid. He hoped if they had seen, they'd simply see it as a gesture of his sincerity and devotion to this important cause. He had felt very flattered when he was approached to join the society. It was coming to Washington County the "recruiter" had promised, slowly and carefully, it was coming. The county would have its own chapter. He could be one of the first, one of the elect, and someday soon, one of the leaders.

In his undistinguished, impoverished existence, Willet Keller had grabbed at the chance to gain some status, some importance—something beyond the sweat of sharecropping and a two-room cabin that he didn't own. He hushed his wife, who protested. The Klan was powerful, and growing more so. He could share in that power.

So he'd come away from that night with an impressive souvenir—a very burned hand, and a passion that only the Ku Klux Klan could admire.

"Interestin' mark, the stove made... like a brand," the doctor said.

"Yeah, interestin'," Willet agreed smoothly.

"Now, you'll need to change the dressing twice a day. Put this salve on thick."

"Sure."

The doctor decided to run one last gauntlet. Why not?

"Heard there was a cross burnin' in Maycomb County two nights ago. Heard talk of it in Greenville yesterday."

"Work of that Klan probably," Keller offered carefully.

Browning nodded. "Yeah, probably."

"Think it will come here, Doc, to Washington County?"

Browning held a scalpel to the sunlight as he polished it.

"Seems to me we have enough foolishness in the county without importin' more."

Willet cast a furtive glance at his wife.

"Well, not everyone thinks like you, Doc."

"That's a fact, Willet, that's a fact. It's just that I prefer to sleep on my bed sheets rather than wear 'em. Seems kind of silly to me."

The farmer turned red. "Ain't silly to a lot of folks," Willet said tartly. "Niggers are gettin' too uppity round here. Tryin' to vote, and own land. Takin' jobs that white men could have. Look at ol' Seth Jefferson for instance. Left a good job with French to work over there with that ol' coot, Pat Cash. Jefferson's just tryin' to act superior-like."

The doctor rolled the gauze smoothly and nodded.

"Heard about that too. Still, as far as I know, Mississippi hasn't made a law against a man changing jobs."

"No, there ain't..."

"I know if I was a... oh, a carpenter or laborer, I'd welcome a chance to go into partnership with a man like Patrick Cash. He's a fine man, and I'm sure he'll make a fine partner."

"He's makin' enemies, is what he's probably makin'," Willet said in a low voice.

Finally, the two men locked eyes.

The farmer stood up abruptly. "What do I owe you?" His voice was little better than a growl. He did not like having a doctor that worked for niggers working on him. But it was all he could afford. Someday that would change though...

Browning named a minimal amount, his voice still easy and light.

"Just keep your hands away from heat, Willet, and I'll be back by in a few days to check on it. Mornin', folks."

Tanglewood

From under the library door, Amy could see a thin filament of light. Surely Cash wasn't still up reading. She hated to go in and scold him. A man of 59 hardly needed a wife to mother him! She opened the door. It was not Cash...when she had needed it to be him. Andy stood in the center of the room, his back to her, gazing up at the huge oil painting that hung over the fireplace. He had not heard her, and she hesitated. Andy had been on her mind all evening.

She had brought Andy and Seth drinks as they worked that afternoon. Andy's shirt had been plastered to his body in sweat, his face grimy and in need of a shave. He had never looked worse to her—and never appealed to her more. She had handed him his glass, nodding mechanically at something he said, but not hearing a word. She had turned abruptly, her face flaming.

She went directly to the cool of her bedroom like a moth seeking a flame. Her mind was in a turmoil. She must admit it. She found Andy Alcott very attractive. She liked the way he thought, the way he smiled, the way he did not seem to mind the silence between them. At first she had distrusted him. Then slowly she had begun to think of him in a brotherly way. That was refreshing. But now...

He invaded her dreams at night, her waking thoughts during the day. She dwelt on stories he told; from her open bedroom window she could hear him singing spirituals as he worked with Seth. She would never forget how peaceful his face had looked when she had come upon him as he prayed.

She sank down on the bed, guilt washing over her. How could she be such a traitor to Cash? Cash, who had been nothing but good for her. Of course such thoughts about Andy were thoughts only. She was a married woman after all.

She sighed and stepped into the library. She stood beside Andy. He knew she was there, but did not turn.

"This is my favorite painting that Cash has ever done," she said softly.

"I wish my father could see it," he answered, still not turning.

It was a huge canvas, commanding immediate attention as one entered the room. It was a country road like any country road, dusty, tree lined, curving. Two men with their backs to the artist were walking beside each other, casual and friendly. One man wore a tattered blue uniform, the other, dusty gray. Yet somehow Cash had managed to capture dignity in the way they wore their uniforms. One walked with a cane; the other's sleeve dangled loosely at his side.

Amy felt a need to break the silence. "The original hangs in the gallery of the state senate in Jackson."

Andy nodded. "As you said, it may be Cash's best work."

Then he turned, reluctantly. He could smell the heliotrope she wore. He smiled wanly but did not speak. Amy felt very nervous.

"I ... actually, I thought Cash was still up ... in here."

It was so quiet she was sure he could hear her heart pounding.

She noticed the letter he still held in his hand.

"A letter from home?" she asked.

"Hmm? Oh, no. It's from a friend in New York."

It was the strangest thing, Amy reflected later. Wordlessly they had both sat in two leather chairs, facing each other, as if settling in for some long chat.

"It's from a friend," he repeated. "Her name is Lilly."

For over an hour Andy talked. He told her about meeting Lilly, about their friendship, the fight with Hawk, his injury.

"Her father beat her, so she ran away. Ended up in New Orleans and didn't know anyone, hadn't any skills really. She was pretty enough that she soon came to the notice of Max Hawk. She's so young. You may think this odd, but in some ways she reminded me of Meg. I could see the terror in her eyes. It was like she was in a steel trap, and Hawk wouldn't turn loose of her. Goodness knows, he had a hundred just like her."

He ran his fingers through his hair, lost in silence.

"I guess I just went a little crazy that last time Hawk came for her. He called her all kinds of things. I hurt for her, you know, just hearing it."

Amy sat with her hands demurely folded in her lap, her eyes riveted on him, scarcely breathing. It was amazing that from her past she had come into the presence of two such caring and gentle men.

"You're like Cash, in a way," she said suddenly.

He looked up then, seeing her again as if for the first time.

"Like Cash?"

"You rescued Lilly, just as Cash rescued me."

He smiled a genuine and gentle smile.

"Really, it was Lilly who saved me with a well-placed bash with the bottle. But you're paying me a very high compliment to compare me to Cash."

She was silent a moment, her eyes downcast.

"You've never asked about Cash and me—about our marriage," she said, almost shyly.

He gave a short laugh. "Certainly you have a low opinion of Yankees to think I'd just ask out like that. It's none of my business."

"But you've wondered?" she persisted easily.

Andy felt himself blush just a fraction. "Well, yes."

She looked to her lap. Oh, to be able to talk, to open up. Even with these feelings she was having, Andy seemed just right.

"Amy, you don't have to say anything."

"But I want to. You see, I've known Cash for a long time, since I was a girl in braids. I'm from Chisolm Crossing, Andy. Cash didn't marry into a blooded family. He married down. He—"

"Excuse me, Amy, but *down* is a perspective only, not a class of people. Please continue."

This eased the tension, and she laughed. "How like Cash you sounded then! Anyway, when Cash came back from the war, he let all of the old servants go. He wanted to start new after his father died. My mother was hired to help in the kitchen. Cash was a very generous employer and didn't mind Mother bringing me to work with her sometimes. Otherwise, she'd have had to leave me."

"Alone?"

"No, no. There was my stepfather and . . . brother." She shook her head, hurrying past what was obviously a painful chapter of her personal narrative. "So in a way, I grew up here at Tanglewood. When Cash learned that I loved to read, he loaned me books from these very shelves. He didn't seem to notice that he was Patrick Cash of Tanglewood and I was Amy Crawford from the Crossing. Those were better years for Mother and me."

Andy could see the cloud pass over her face, the knuckles whiten in her clutched hands. He leaned forward.

"Amy, don't talk about this. It's upsetting you too much."

"No, Andy, I need to. Please."

He leaned back, and she continued. "Then Mother stopped working here. My stepfather said he could make all the money our family needed."

"How old were you then?"

"I was 16. I didn't see Cash or Tanglewood for nearly nine years. My mother became ill. My stepfather refused any help Cash tried to give us. Tanglewood became like a memory for me, a very good memory."

She stopped and glanced up at Andy. He seemed so genuinely interested, so concerned. Now her words came slower and softer. Andy instinctively knew he was about to hear something as tragic as Lilly O'Hara's story.

"Jeb French is my stepbrother, Andy. He, he . . . was unkind to me. He—"

Andy stood up abruptly. "Don't say any more, Amy. You don't have to say any more." He stared at the flaming logs on the hearth.

Man's ugliness toward man never failed to shock and sicken him. Perhaps he should feel a violent rage toward Jeb French, something akin to what his more volatile father would feel. Yet he was unlike his father in many ways. He felt only a heartbreaking sadness. It had always been this way as long as he could remember. His sensitivity sometimes amounted to pain. He would always remember his father pulling him into a close embrace when he was a lad of nine. He was terribly upset and crying. His father had soothed him and told him he was like his namesake.

"The Andy you were named for was, next to your mother, the best friend I ever had. He was a soldier like me. He fought at Shiloh."

"Did he die in the war, Papa?"

He could still see the tears form in his father's eyes. "No, son, he died . . . of the war. He died in a Washington hospital."

"Where you met Ma?"

"Where I met your ma."

"How am I like him, Papa?"

"He was sensitive above all else. He felt other folks' pain."

He turned back to Amy. "I'm sorry," he said simply.

Amy was calmer now. She took a deep breath and plunged in again.

"My mother and stepfather died in the yellow fever plague. The property and the meager savings were left to Jeb. He made me a simple proposition. He said he was going to be very rich someday; said he'd have a fine house. He'd buy me anything if I'd become his mistress."

The word hung suspended between them.

"That night I took a small bag and a few of my mother's things and walked to Greenville. I wanted to go farther, but I had only a few dollars. I got a job in a hotel, doing laundry and whatever else needed to be done. Jeb found me, of course, threatened me. Two weeks later I ran into Cash when he was in town. He took me for a buggy ride and wanted to hear all about . . . the years."

She gave Andy a weary smile. "He made me tell him about French. Then the next day he took me for another ride and insisted I should marry him. He said we could help each other."

She stopped again, waiting and watching for anything that might reveal Andy's thoughts.

A temptress, a schemer, he had labeled her those first few days at Tanglewood! He could have laughed out loud at the absurdity of it.

"Cash was persistent. He kept asking me for over a year."

"A year!"

She relaxed and smiled. "Honestly, Andy, I couldn't keep sending him away. He looked so sad. He said, 'Let me do some good, Amy.' So, I came to Tanglewood."

Andy sat down again, facing her. "Like I told you when I came, you *have* been good for him. You've made him happy."

The soft lamplight brought out the golden highlights in his beard. The sun had chapped and blushed his cheeks. His eyes of steel blue were magnified as he looked at her.

Her voice was blunt, almost defiant. "I do love Cash."

He nodded. "It's...late."

He was a gentleman; she knew that implicitly. But if he made one move, gave one inch...She jumped up, freshly horrified at the direction of her thoughts. She had come full circle, talking of her past and about Cash—now she was back to Andy.

He stood up also, startled, his heart racing.

"Thank you for listening, Andy."

She turned and left. There was no more room for confessions this night.

Andy had been invited to the Jeffersons' for dinner. He accepted the invitation eagerly. He needed an evening away from Tanglewood. Perhaps the Cashes needed an evening alone as well...

So he sat in the humble dwelling at Chisolm Crossing, enjoying the food and enjoying the simplicity and warmth that the little family had welcomed him with. The cabin's furnishings reflected that Patrick Cash's confidence in Seth's talents was not misplaced. A fine carpenter was coming to Tanglewood. Viney had laid a simple meal of home-cured ham, fried potatoes, greens, and biscuits, testifying that Seth Jefferson was a fortunate man. After they had eaten, they sat in the cool shade of the front steps while Micah demonstrated his prowess with a harmonica.

"How come you ain't married, Mr. Andy?" Micah asked impulsively.

"Micah, mind your manners," Seth warned.

Viney tensed. Had her son overheard the conversation she and Seth had had concerning Mr. Andy and Miss Amy? Viney Jefferson would be mortified.

"Just askin'," Micah replied contritely.

"Well Micah, life at sea...would be hard on a wife. Most sailors I know are bachelors."

"Do they have to be?" the little boy persisted.

"Well, no. You could leave a wife on shore, while you went on a voyage. But it would be hard on her and the children."

Micah cocked his head at Andy. "How could there be kids, Mr. Andy, if he was on a boat far off and she was on land?"

Seth winked at his wife in the darkness, and wondered how the sailor was going to answer his son.

"You're absolutely right, Micah. It would be...difficult."

"See, you ain't got a wife, Mr. Andy, so you can't have little ones. That seems sort of sad to me."

"My mother would agree with you, Micah," Andy said laughing.

"Look at my ma. She's gonna have another one of us any day. Your kind, well, we need more of 'em."

"Now, Micah Jefferson, that's enought of such talk," Viney admonished. But she could not conceal her amusement.

"What is my kind, Micah?" Andy asked.

"I mean nice whites. We need more of 'em."

Andy looked out on the starlit night. A wife... All of the sudden his future looked empty, very empty. Where could he find a wife?... Young Micah had turned his thoughts in a direction he had tried to escape from...

Tanglewood

Andy was trying desperately to concentrate on the chessboard in front of him, but tonight it had been very difficult. He knew she was just a few feet away, even if she hadn't spoken a word since dinner.

Then Fenwick was at the doorway.

"Excuse me, Mr. Cash, sir, but Mr. Drummond is here."

"At this hour?" Amy exclaimed.

"Oh, it's all right, my dear. John is a businessman to the marrow. I'll go humor him for just a moment. Take him to my study, Fenwick." Cash pulled the shawl around his shoulders as he rolled his chair to the doorway.

"Not too long, Cash, please," Amy pleaded gently.

"No, not too long. Watch the board for me, Amy—I have Andy in an untenable position," Cash chuckled.

Then the room was quiet—painfully, personally quiet.

Andy studied his king and queen. Yes, he smiled inwardly, an untenable position indeed. He forced himself to plan his next move, to try some strategy his opponent wouldn't expect. He was frowning, and willing himself not to look up at her.

But he couldn't resist. He raised his eyes and found Amy looking at him. She was not looking at him generally, she was looking at him specifically, into his eyes.

He let himself look at her—a long, unguarded look. A look over her face and hair, her neck and shoulders. Amy didn't draw her own eyes away until she heard the roll of the chair.

"Was that too long, my dear?" Cash asked, laying a hand on her arm.

"No...it was fine." She stood up. "You'll have to play without my support, Cash. I'm tired." Her voice was shaky.

"Are you all right?"

"Of course, just tired. Good night, Andy."

"Good night, Amy."

After six weeks of steady work, the carpentry shop of Tanglewood was finished. All it needed were the tools that had been ordered. Already a small but impressive list of orders for fine carpentry work had been assembled, thanks to Cash's extensive business connections. Seth surveyed their work, his new shop, with unconcealed awe and humility.

Andy sought Cash one afternoon in the cool of the studio. He found the older man dozing in his chair, a thick pad of paper across his lap, a charcoal pencil idle in his fingers. His were the slender hands of an artist, yet networked with age. Andy stood watching him, thinking how frail he looked, and yet how peaceful. Andy realized how deeply he loved his father's cousin, this man he called Uncle Pat.

He glanced down at the sketch curiously, but his eyes held the drawing. It was a garden, arbored in magnolia trees, their blossoms prolific. A woman was seated on a bench. Even in profile, Andy knew immediately it was Cash's wife. In the austere lines of the pencil, there was no mistaking the curve of the jaw, the loosely pinned hair. It was Amy.

Andy looked at the sketch a long time, until he felt eyes upon him. Cash was awake and watching him.

Andy felt himself color, as if he had trespassed.

"Your new work?"

Cash nodded slowly. "New only to my pencil. It's been in my heart for a long time."

An awkward silence.

"The shop is finished," Andy said finally.

"I'm grateful to you, Andy. Very grateful. All those long hours you've put in out in this heat."

"No, Uncle Pat, I'm the fortunate one. It has been a pleasure to work alongside Seth. He's a fine man. I'm sure he'll make the shop a success."

Cash inclined his head, thoughtful a moment.

"I think you're saying goodbye, Andy."

The shock registered on Andy's face. Were all his thoughts that transparent?

He sighed and took a seat across from Cash.

"I suppose I am. I was planning to leave day after tomorrow."

"May I ask why?"

"I was raised with definite rules of hospitality. Being here nearly five months has about—"

"Aren't those rules void with family?" Cash asked with a gentle and affectionate smile.

"Now I'm sounding ungrateful. You and Amy have been more than generous to me. I . . . I just thought I'd go up to Illinois and see my family for a few weeks. When I join the *Ivanhoe* in New Orleans, I'll be gone for eight months or more. So, this will be the last chance to see my family for a while."

"What about that gentleman who specializes in breaking feet? Isn't he still a threat in New Orleans?"

"I don't think so. Anyway, I can't run from him forever. I won't be there that long. I'll go to Peppercreek first."

Cash turned from Andy, toward the window, seeing things that Andy did not. A sadness, a parting . . .

"Will you always be a seaman, Andy? Will *Ivanhoe's Dream* always be your address?"

"Well, I can't see any other future right now."

Cash roused himself. "The sun will be down in another hour. Throw the cover off that easel, will you? It's time for the unveiling!"

"Won't Amy be offended that we didn't wait?"

"She is a generous woman," Cash said with a wide smile. "Besides, she's already seen it."

It was perfect, and Andy was speechless.

Finally he spoke. "So what do I owe you, Uncle Pat?"

Cash pressed his fingertips together, that evaluating gleam again in his eye. "Come back to Tanglewood. Don't wait 13 years again."

"I—"

"When you return, Seth will have it framed for you."

It started as a slow, melodic rain during the early hours of the morning. By sunrise, a full-scale production of a summer thunderstorm was in progress, complete with splitting thunder and lightning. From any window of Tanglewood mansion, the visible world was a swirling gray tempest. Andy had wakened instantly as the storm intensified, his years of listening to the moods and manners of the ocean alerting him to weather changes. He dressed quickly, wanting to be outside no matter how inclement the weather. There was suddenly something very confining about the walls of Tanglewood. A tempest was growing inside Andy Alcott that morning. It did not match the violence of the rain and wind around him perhaps, but it was no less real.

Andy had a simple nature, a nature governed by kindness, integrity, and loyalty. He had embraced the spiritual heritage that had been passed to him. He had learned at his father's side, and learned well. So it was a matter of near horror that he should face this turmoil inside himself. How was it possible? When had it begun?

He had never loved any woman beyond his family. His life's work did not afford him the opportunities to meet women who possessed those qualities he so valued in his mother, aunts, and sister. He was no saint, but no woman had ever really tempted him. When he lay awake at night, he knew in his heart that the woman who claimed his love would claim him completely.

How could it be then that in one swift, crystallized moment in the library, he had known the evolution of his feelings for Amy Cash had changed. He could not think of her as a little sister any longer. He could not see, or think of, or speak to his uncle without feeling the penetrating immersion of guilt. He had flayed himself with the truth. Ducking his head, he dashed through the drenching rain to the famous Cash stables.

Amy lingered in the doorway, and Andy was unaware she was there. He was carefully grooming the mare that had been his favorite since he had come. She knew it wasn't a good idea, but she liked watching him work. When he stood up and wiped the sweat from his face, he saw her and colored.

"Cash told me that you were leaving tomorrow morning," she said softly.

He bent back down, brushing the horse's forelegs.

"Yes, in the morning." His voice was even.

She was quiet for a long time, uncertain what to say, knowing she should go back to the house.

"You don't have to go, Andy."

It broke the silence like a knife. He stood up abruptly and threw the brush across the room. The mare skittered beside him. Amy was surprised. He walked close to her and stopped. He was terribly, uncharacteristically angry. "Where is he?" he demanded harshly.

"He's resting."

Andy pulled her roughly into the interior of the stables. All caution was gone. He would be leaving tomorrow, and it didn't matter.

"Why do you say I don't have to go?" he asked her angrily.

"Because you don't. You're welcome here." Her words drifted away as his eyes tried to penetrate her.

"You know, Amy. You know I have to go...and you know why!"

He searched her with his eyes. He wanted to kiss her, to pull her into his arms, to finally know if her cheek was as soft as it looked. Just to kiss her—one, long, kiss. Finally she turned and walked away from him. He followed her.

"You know why!" he exploded again.

She whirled around to face him. "Yes! I know!" She was equally angry. But it lasted only a moment. "I know," she whispered.

He shook his head and walked back to the horse, picking up the tools he had scattered. She watched him, holding back tears that she didn't dare let him see.

He stroked the horse, not looking at Amy. His anger was gone. His uncle's face rose in his mind. He could not accept the gift of *Ivanhoe's Dream*.

"I'll leave in the morning, Amy." His voice was tired and flat.

"I'll never come back to Tanglewood. Never." For four years he would keep his word.

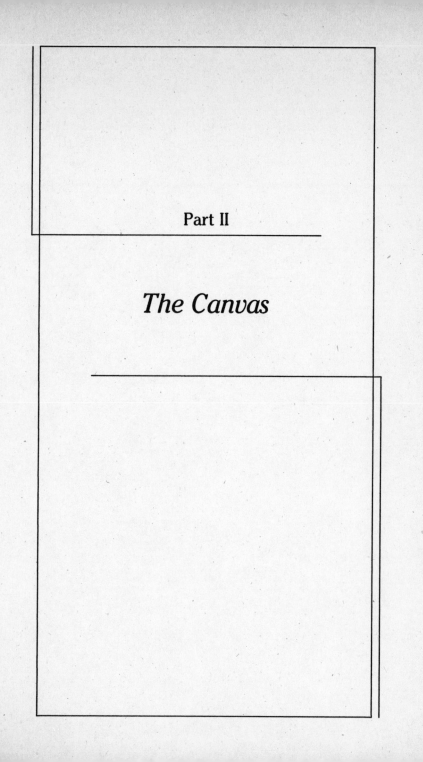

Part II

The Canvas

Peppercreek, Illinois
Summer, 1891

◆◆ ◆◆ ◆◆

*M*eg Alcott was thoroughly ashamed of her thoughts, but the visiting minister looked positively reptilian to her. She could hardly wait for him to use some gesture. It would surely be lizardlike. He was very tall and very thin, and his skin looked jaundiced. His gray eyes were swift and darting. *If he doesn't stick out a pale, pointed tongue, I'll be surprised,* Meg thought. It was his eyes, with those very full lids, slits most of the time. *Yes, definitely reptilian,* Meg smiled to herself. If Andy were here, he'd agree completely. She glanced at her father, who sat beside her. The minister had begun, and her father seemed wholly absorbed in the sermon.

Yet Meg could not seem to focus on the sermon. The windows of the little rock church were open, and a faint breeze was bringing her the scent of lilac bushes. It was a beautiful day, and her thoughts were far beyond the perimeters of the church property or Peppercreek or even Illinois. It had all begun yesterday when she'd gone riding with her father. She closed her eyes, hoping the minister thought she was in prayer, and remembered.

It had been more than just a leisurely outing with her father. His nervousness, his preoccupation, quickly dispelled that. He had planned this ride carefully. He had fumbled with his one arm as he saddled the horses, a task in which years of practice had made him swift and capable. They had left Peppercreek Orchard at a gallop.

Local farmers were praying that the rain would not come for another few weeks, until the harvest was in. The fields they passed gave off a rich, warm, earthy smell.

"Almost like bread baking in the oven," her father had said. He said nothing more until they rested their horses.

They rode nearly 15 miles west of their land, to where a rippling prairie in folds of brown and yellow stretched endlessly. The sky was vivid, piercing, cloudless.

Meg hopped down lithely and stroked the gelding while it grazed. To be a part of Peppercreek, you had to love horses. And apples. Even Andy with his passion for the sea spent hours riding when he was home.

"It's a beautiful day, Papa," she said at last.

He nodded absently. Then he turned abruptly and faced her. She was shocked again to see how he had aged so dramatically in the last few months. His thick hair was streaked with gray; the lines about his eyes and mouth had grown more pronounced. But he was still so handsome to her. There had been teasing in the schoolyard of her youth about her one-armed father. Yet she had always had two defenses against that: He couldn't spank very hard, and he was the very handsomest father around.

"It's warm today, as well as beautiful," he said carefully.

"Yes, deliciously warm. A perfect day."

He nodded again, still studying her without emotion. He pulled a letter from his pocket. "This came a few days ago."

"I noticed you've had something on your mind. Is it from Andy? He's all right, isn't he?"

"No, it's not from Andy, or about Andy. It...it came as a reply to a letter I sent." He handed it to her.

She read quickly, then reread slowly.

Ethan cleared his throat, shifting from foot to foot. "After last winter when we nearly lost you, I became determined that it would be the last winter you'd spend in Illinois."

"Papa—"

"Let me finish now. I know you're a young woman of 21—"

"Almost 22," she said smiling.

"And you have your own mind and plans. I thought of an old army friend I have who's in Texas now. He's a congressman down there."

"Sam Bass?" Meg knew the family stories by heart.

Ethan nodded. "He has a daughter in a seminary down on the Texas coast. Galveston. Meg, it's as far south as I could find without packing you off to the tropics of South America! Average temperature there in the summer is 85 degrees. It never drops below 65 in the winter. Think of that."

"Oh, Papa—"

"They need a teacher there. It's your position if you'll take it."

"But it's...it's so far!"

"Over a thousand miles. Believe me, I know...I know." He was terribly sad. Meg came to him, and he held her.

"What does Mama say about it?"

"It's hard to have you go, like Andy. But we both think it would be best. We want you to get your health back."

She didn't want to speak yet.

"I know you've always wanted to travel," he said, almost as an afterthought.

This is so hard for him, and he's trying to sell me on it, to be brave for me. She began to cry just for the love she felt for her father.

"How soon?" she asked softly.

"Two weeks. We'll all go. We'd come to see you in the winters, and you could come home in the summer."

Meg looked at the envelope, assailed by a thousand thoughts. "Galveston...Texas," she murmured.

Galveston, Texas

It was Meg's favorite time of the day, just at twilight. She'd take her tea (or a cup of chocolate, if she felt especially extravagant) and sit on her terrace. From her fourth-story balcony, she could see Galveston Bay. Thousands of colored lights bobbed and sparkled in the water, like some giant had scattered a handful of glass beads. It was a stunning sight. It made her feel almost cosmopolitan to live so close to this busy port, a traveler to the world by proxy. Strangely, out here on her balcony she did not feel lonely or sad. This was her refuge from the day. Alone and away from shrill voices and giggling, alone with her thoughts.

Meg had loved Galveston at first sight. In part perhaps because it was so different from her prairie home, an antithesis to the prairie with its towering palms, miles of white-sand beaches, and horizon of blue ocean. The streets were lighted at night by hundreds of gas lights. The buildings were very Victorian, yet proudly stamped with the Spanish influence of white stucco, red tile roofs, black iron grillwork. She loved the quaint touch of the knee-high curbs that lined the main streets. It had taken her a few moments to understand them—they protected pedestrians from mud slung by carriages. The climate was strictly tropical with salty, moist breezes. This was Galveston, sitting off the Texas mainland a mere two miles. It was the oldest deepwater port west of the Mississippi.

Bishop's Villa sat among a grove of palms on Broadway, only four blocks from the waterfront and the city's principal street, the Strand. A gleaming white Italian villa, with a red tile roof and black wrought-iron railings, it had impressed Meg greatly. It was considered one of the state's most exclusive schools for daughters of wealthy Texans.

Now, six weeks into her first term, Bishop's Villa was home. The entire fourth floor had been made into staff apartments. No dormitory life here. Meg had been hugely glad for that. It was furnished in French provincial, with a tiny kitchen and a panoramic view. Meg had never felt so rich and so independent.

But as much as she had taken the city to her heart and enjoyed the luxury of her new home, Meg was not especially happy in her new position. And because of that, she felt rather guilty. She knew the effort, the time, and the expense her family had taken to place her here so she could grow healthy and strong.

First, there was the adjustment of being so far from all that had been familiar to her. Then, there was the headmistress of the school. She felt the woman stiffen toward her from the first day. She would never know that the headmistress had planned to seat her own niece in the vacant teaching position. Then Senator Bass had landed on the Villa stoop, and, well, one couldn't say no to a senator. She had greeted midwestern Miss Alcott with polite and professional contempt. Meg's academic credentials were in good order, yet Miss Alcott was too young, too rustic. The three other teachers took their attitude from their superior.

Meg could tolerate the headmistress and her dragonlike personality. She could laugh about it alone in her apartment and write long letters to Andy about it. If that had been all, this time at Galveston might have been a grand adventure. It was more than that.

Teaching young, affluent women seemed to go beyond anything Meg had tackled before. These weren't squirming, eager-eyed children reciting their alphabet. Her scholars included 17 young ladies from age 15 to age 19 who, for the most part, felt learning archaic and boring. Meg was not much older than they were, and they let her know it. They had raised their eyebrows collectively and snickered behind their hands when they heard her accent for the first time. When they learned her only teaching experience was in a one-room schoolhouse, they felt insulted.

The first day of teaching at Bishop's Villa was a memorable one for Meg. The classroom she was given was impeccable and well supplied. Her students sat demurely with their hands folded on their desks. The room was frosty from rigid postures, unsmiling faces, guarded, suspicious eyes. All the young women wore dark serge skirts and crisp white blouses—all very practical and utilitarian. The wealth of their families would be reflected in other forms—the school dress code was intractable.

Meg mounted the platform and stood behind the expensive, carved desk. She had been introduced to the girls the evening before in the headmistress's spacious parlor. It had been meant to be an informal introduction between a new staff member and her pupils. It had turned into a stilted, awkward reception. Only a few girls gave her a shy smile and allowed warmth in their eyes. They were curious about this new teacher and willing to be a little friendly. But the majority of the class set the tone. This new teacher was a foreigner, and not to be trusted.

"Good morning," Meg greeted them.

No one stirred. No one flinched a facial muscle. A sea of frozen, staring eyes.

Meg smiled at them as if they had welcomed her enthusiastically.

"I've looked over the records and plans that your former teacher left. I've become familiar with what you've been studying, but I've also selected a new reading list for you. I think you'll enjoy the books. I've written the titles down. Would someone please volunteer to hand them out?"

They cut their eyes then, smothering little smiles. No hand was raised. Meg glanced down at her roll book, her heart thudding in her ears. What if she fainted right there in front of them? She could imagine the headmistress sweeping in with a triumphant smile to dispose of the pieces.

"All right, *I'll* volunteer Clarissa Barrows. Please raise your hand." The hand was raised very slowly.

"Thank you, Clarissa. Now kindly pass out these papers for me."

The young woman stood beside her desk, making no effort to conceal the smirk that she gave her classmates.

"Excuse me, Miss Alcott. What did you say? I wasn't sure what you just said."

An insolent reference to her accent. Meg took a deep breath and clenched her hands behind her. The tittering laughter increased.

"Please hand one of these papers to each of your classmates."

The girl raised her chin. "I do not pass papers around like a servant. Mrs. Ross always came to our desks."

There was a long strained silence. Meg felt herself redden as she passed out the papers.

No, the new teacher was not to be trusted. She was to be tested.

The "testing" went on for four weeks. Defiance, impertinence, haughtiness, pranks—Meg faced them like personal assaults and wondered how long it would be before she crumbled. Where had the strength she thought she had fled to?

The girls handed in their assignments as late as possible, and with an obvious lack of effort. Class discussions became embarrassing monologues. Only 3 girls from the 17 made any advances in friendliness and courtesy to Meg: Judith, Miranda, and Grace. Meg was grateful to them for their willingness to stand against their peers in this collective offense against the new teacher. But their overtures went only so far. She still went to bed at night and stared at the ceiling while tears slid down her cheeks. She had never felt so alone, so afraid. It gave her a sense of panic; this place seemed to be clutching at her.

Yet in the morning she faced them dry-eyed, pale, and firm. Warmth, smiles, and friendliness had not thawed them. So she became properly reserved like the other teachers. And it was not just the students she must contend with. The headmistress hovered like a spiraling hawk above her, waiting for an error, a reproach, a failure. She did not have long to wait.

"They are failing because they are not trying, Mrs. McCallas," Meg said evenly.

The headmistress pursed her lips as if she had just tasted something very sour. Another time Meg would have felt like laughing.

"Your entire class is failing, and you say it is because they are not trying? I find that difficult to believe."

"Three of the girls are not failing. They are trying," Meg said as firmly as she dared with such reproachful eyes boring into her.

"And why are the others not trying?" The headmistress's voice was snippy.

To answer truthfully, Meg must hand the woman a trump card. She took a deep breath. "They are doing it . . . because they don't like me. Call it spite."

"Miss Alcott, I must remind you these girls are from very fine families."

As if that explained anything. Meg felt very drained. She sat silently. If only her father knew what she was going through. But her letters home were newsy, cheerful—and false from salutation to closing. Meg could not tell her family the truth. This place was a horrible failure.

"I suggest you reconsider your teaching methods, Miss Alcott. What worked in a very small, 'primitive,' country school could hardly be expected to work here."

"I thought respect worked anywhere," Meg answered carefully.

The headmistress's eyes narrowed.

"I have spoken to a few of the girls. They have come to me with complaints. They say you are too strict. They say you play favorites with three girls."

"Too strict!" The Alcott temper finally found itself. "Too strict? I have allowed them all sorts of liberties I would never have tolerated from a class of eight-year-olds in my . . . my 'primitive' school back home! I've done everything I could think of to be friendly and helpful. I've done everything for them but wipe their noses!"

Mrs. McCallas was pleased. The new teacher was displaying distasteful temper. "Miss Alcott—"

"And as for the three that I supposedly favor, they are the only ones who have not shown me contempt. They've allowed me to be their teacher and treated me civilly."

The woman across the desk regarded her in frigid silence.

"Am I allowed to teach or not?" Meg asked with spirit.

The headmistress smiled a wintry smile and spread her palms up.

Monday morning at Bishop's Villa, English and Literature class— Meg gave the assignments in a weary monotone. It was the first of a new week, and already she felt exhausted.

"Miss Alcott, I have a question."

Meg tensed. "Yes, Julia?"

"*Caesar's Gallic Wars* is not on the reading list you gave us. The *Gallic Wars* have always been required reading for Bishop's Villa graduates. Mrs. Ross told us so."

"Mrs. Ross is not your teacher, Julia. We are not reading the *Gallic Wars* this term."

"Have you ever heard of *Caesar's Gallic Wars*, Miss Alcott? Did your little...scholars...at Pepper River read it?"

Meg was torn between the impulse to laugh or rush forward to choke the young girl. Instead she smoothed the essays on her desk with an unsteady hand. Oh, the arrogance of these gentleborn heiresses!

"Miss Alcott, I'm glad the *Gallic Wars* aren't on your list," Miranda Bass volunteered. "I think your list is much more interesting."

"*You* would," someone hissed from the back of the room.

"That's enough, girls!" Meg commanded sternly. "Go back to your work."

An hour elapsed without interruption or disturbance.

Meg watched her class, in their perfect uniforms, in their perfect rows, as they bent their heads to read. Gradually their faces and postures relaxed. They were good girls underneath, she was sure. Only girls. Spoiled girls...drifting from the safe harbor of childhood to the uncertain open seas of young womanhood. They suddenly looked so vulnerable. Meg's heart softened.

"I'm not going to leave," she said suddenly.

They cut their eyes at each other.

"I'm not going to leave unless I choose to go. You are not going to run me off. You can continue to hate me if you choose to. But I am not going to hate you...any of you. I have no reason to. I..."

She was going to cry. No, she could not do that!

She stood up. "Class is dismissed early."

They were subdued the next day. Still as expressionless, but without visible contempt. They listened attentively. They worked without complaint. Meg watched—and waited. Had her impulsive speech pushed them to sympathy, or further isolation? Aside from their haughtiness, Meg had found their manners genteel and proper; their Latin and French passable; their essays stiff, perfect, and dull.

In the end there was one last, one final, stand of defiance by the young girl who had been the leader in the campaign.

"Miss Alcott, you've marked my paper a *C*. Yet there is not a red mark anywhere on it. My paper was perfect! You made a mistake," the wealthy daughter said haughtily.

Rather than giggle as an encouragement, the class was silent.

Meg perched on the edge of her desk and appraised the young woman for a full minute. The class collectively held their breath.

"You're correct, Maria. Your paper was perfect."

"Well?"

"Your paper was perfect, stiff, and very boring. I think you're capable of much more creative work. That is why you received a *C*. The comments I've heard whispered about me indicate this entire class is far more creative than their papers."

The young ladies glanced nervously at each other. Meg burst out laughing.

"You've all been acting so superior! Ridiculing me because I'm from the Midwest! You ridiculous geese! Don't you know most people haven't even heard of your Galveston Island down here nearly in South America!"

Her laughter was young and fresh and good-natured.

"And you think I have an accent!" She mimicked them perfectly.

The entire class joined in her laughter, the perversity of youth breaking down the wall of disrespect. From then on, she was called 'Midwestern Meg' behind her back—and became the favorite teacher of Bishop's Villa.

Peppercreek

"When do you have to join your ship?" the older man asked.

"I need to be in New Orleans in about ten days," Andy replied without emotion.

His uncle quietly studied him a moment.

"Have you enjoyed being home, Andy? Or is the pull of the seas just too strong?" Henri asked with a smile.

"It's different without Meg here, but I'm enjoying it. I always do. I wonder why I leave sometimes. I love Peppercreek as much as Matt or Daniel does."

"But in a different way," Henri offered.

Andy nodded. "A different way."

He stood up and walked over to the bookcases, running his hands over the fine leather, reading titles of books he had cherished as a boy. Uncle Henri's personal library had always been a special place for him. The whole house was. This little white frame house was filled with memories for Andy Alcott. Perhaps if he had not been as close to his cousin Caleb as he was, it might have been different. As it was, no two boys could have been closer. They had been inseparable growing up. He knew this house as well as he knew his father's farmhouse at Peppercreek Orchard.

Andy had been quiet a long time, yet Henri knew it was wise to wait. He knew, even if everyone hadn't told him, that Andy was troubled, preoccupied this visit home. Henri suspected it was something beyond the longing to be out on another adventure. Finally Andy sat down in the leather chair across from his uncle, sinking his head into his hands with a moan.

"What is it, Andy?" Henri asked gently.

"I can't tell anyone. I can't tell my father. He'd be too disappointed. I can't tell Meg. I ..." he broke off.

"Go ahead, Andy. You can tell me."

Andy stood up and crossed to the window that looked out on his aunt's garden. This little house was modest and simple, but Andy knew the garden was surely a showplace in the spring, one of the passions of his aunt's heart. He turned back to his uncle.

"You've always understood me, Uncle Henri ... more than anyone else, I think. I wonder if you can understand this."

"Try me."

"I've met a woman—a fine, intelligent, beautiful woman. I ... I've fallen in love with her."

"Go ahead," Henri prodded.

"I love her, Uncle Henri! I love her like ... like a hunger inside me. Like I could never love anyone else as I love her."

Henri nodded, and Andy became agitated at his uncle's calmness.

"No, no, you don't see. You don't know!" Andy exclaimed in frustration.

"Don't know what love is, Andy? Is that it? A man of 65 is too old to understand?" Henri was chuckling.

"No, of course not, I just meant ..."

Henri crossed slowly and unsteadily to the window, and Andy winced again at how feeble his uncle had become since his last visit home.

"Ever notice that when I designed this house 20 years ago, Andy, that I put this big window where I did?"

Andy came up beside him. "I figured you put it here so you'd have such good light to work in at your desk."

Henri shook his head.

"Well, then it must have been to see the beauty of the flowers and herbs in bloom," Andy offered again.

Henri shook his head again. "No, not even the beauty of the flowers." His voice took on a dreamy, absent quality. "I hardly see the flowers if Wyeth is out there working. I put the window there so I could watch her ... so I could just sit and look."

Andy smiled. As a lad growing up he had quickly seen the love and tenderness between his aunt and uncle. He knew that the years had not changed those feelings.

"I faced my desk away from the window whenever I had a sermon to work on, or else I couldn't concentrate. There were times when Caleb

and Jenny were little, we'd take a blanket out there in the moonlight."
He smiled. "She'd protest and say I was acting scandalous for a preacher."

They returned to their chairs. "What about this girl you've fallen in
love with, Andy? Where is she?"

"She's in Mississippi."

"Ah, a Southern girl! You met her on a trip?"

"No, sir. She's at the home of Uncle Cash."

"Why does this sound so, so doomed, Andy?" Henri leaned forward
in his chair.

"Doomed is the right word, Uncle Henri. Hopeless."

"Now, Andy, it's not like you to be melodramatic. That's Meg's way.
Tell me, son, what's the problem?"

"She belongs to someone else."

"Ah." Henri sat back to study the young man's face.

Andy looked out the window again. It was so hard to say the words.
So hard to say them to a man who had such a pure and faithful love with
his wife.

"She's married, Uncle Henri. She's married." He stood up and began
pacing. "She's married to Patrick Cash."

Henri said nothing.

"You see, I feel so guilty," Andy said despairingly.

"Why?"

"Why! Because I'm . . . I'm coveting another man's wife, Uncle Henri."

The older man laced his fingers together and closed his eyes. There
was nothing pious or artificial in his gesture. He must know exactly the
words to say to this young man.

"I thought going to Tanglewood was the right thing to do. And I didn't
even trust her at first. I enjoyed being with Uncle Pat, and thought I was
cheering him up—"

"And I'm sure you did, Andy," Henri interrupted.

"Yes, while I was falling in love with his wife!"

He sat back down in dejection. "I never imagined the first woman I'd
ever love . . . that it would be like this. I can't understand God's way in
this, Uncle Henri. I feel like I'm trying to—"

"Navigate through a very thick fog? Pun intended."

Andy smiled at this. "You've always had advice for me in the past,
Uncle Henri. Is this problem too big?"

"I can recall quite vividly when you came to this very room and were
afraid to tell your parents that you wanted to leave home for the sea."

"And I felt guilty about that too," Andy admitted.

"Don't allow guilt to dominate your life, Andy. It's not from God, and
you know that. I preached it enough to you over the years."

"I never slept through a single one of your sermons, Uncle Henri."

The old man's eyes rested affectionately on his nephew.

"A high compliment. But your present trouble ... I have no easy or profound answer for you. Except that He who led you to the sea will lead you in His time out of this fog to something that is very good and perfect."

Andy smiled ruefully. "In my work, we call that sailing into a safe harbor, Uncle Henri."

Galveston

Meg was grading papers, hurrying through them because she was hungry. Tonight was her special time. It was a little tradition she had started in desperation for some variety in her predictable life. She would take the trolley down to an outdoor cafe on the Strand for dinner. She would listen to the music that wafted out from the restaurants like the fragrance of their specialties and watch the couples stroll by arm in arm.

"Excuse—" A head had popped in at the doorway to her classroom.

"Oh! Well!" A young man stepped into the room. He was smiling broadly. "Surely you're not one," he jerked his thumb toward the hallway, "one of *them.*"

Meg smiled in spite of herself. "One of them?"

"The straight-laced hags who try to broaden my little sister's mind."

"I am Meg Alcott. I teach English Literature here at Bishop's Villa."

His eyes went over her quickly and appreciatively.

"You're kiddin' me."

"No, I'm very serious."

He had perched on her desk. "Now, don't get too serious, Miss Alcott, or you'll end up like," he leaned forward conspiratorially and they whispered together, *"them."*

Meg was laughing. She had met Jerry Bass.

Jerry Bass, son of the congressman, brother of Miranda, heir to a fortune impressive by rural Illinois standards but a pittance by the mammoth scale that all things Texan were measured by. Jerry was 26 years old. A wiry frame, blond-haired, ruddy-skinned. He couldn't really be called good-looking on his features alone. But his friendly personality made him seem handsome. He was easygoing and fun-loving, which made it difficult to take seriously the empire his father was building. Somehow he could not be the ambitious heir. He preferred riding wild Indian ponies and working cattle with his father's paid hands to learning the business side of becoming a beef baron. His father would frown and wonder if he had been too lenient with his only son. He chewed his cigars when he watched the boy and wished he would settle down.

Meg liked Jerry immediately. He was a smile in a week of frowns, a Gulf breeze in a day that had been dry and tedious. He brought her laughter. Already he could parody the headmistress perfectly. She made him laugh too. He made no demands on her. He was her first friend in Texas.

He began to come nearly every Friday night to take her to dinner, to walk the boardwalk along the beach, or to a concert in the city park. Sometimes they took Miranda along; sometimes they went alone.

"Jerry, you can't come down here every Friday," Meg objected. "It's a long ride for you."

"What else have I got to do?" he asked innocently.

"Well, thanks a lot. I'm flattered," Meg returned dryly. "What about work?"

"Who works on a Friday night? Who would want to when they have such a pretty girl to come see?"

"Oh, Jerry."

"It's true, I do get tired of looking at horse faces all week."

She punched him in the chest.

Jerry made her week more tolerable. Their relationship also opened up a new avenue for teasing from her students. Now, however, their jabs carried no sharp points.

"Miss Alcott, is Jerry Bass your beau?"

"He is very cute."

"Maybe you won't be going back to Illinois after all."

Jerry pressed her to come to his home for the trimester recess.

"I don't know, Jerry..."

"You want to stay here? You want to spend your free time with *her*? You want to sit around in your cubicle and be lonely and weepy?"

"Now quit...I...well, your family..."

"Family? Meg, there are more bovines in my family than people, and they don't mind at all."

"Jerry, be serious!"

"I am. You've already met two-thirds of my family, and we all think you're great. That leaves Pa. He's already eager to meet you. Daughter of an ol' army pal. He wants to see the gal who's having such an influence on his daughter."

"Miranda is a good girl. That had nothing to do with me."

"And me. He wants to see who—"

"Who makes you leave your harem of mustangs?" she smiled.

"Come on. Austin is only a few hours from our spread. There's so much I can show you."

"The headmistress won't like me leaving."

"She doesn't like anything. Come on, Midwestern Meg..."

Meg saw Texas from a fringed surrey. Jerry talked the entire way, as he pointed out the sights with the end of his whip. He was like a boy about to share a treasured collection, wide-eyed and eager.

"Once you see how big and open Texas is, you'll forget about your Illinois prairie," he boasted.

"I don't think so," Meg laughed. "So, tell me, why is your farm called Nashville?"

"Ranch, Meg, ranch! They're ranches in Texas."

"All right, ranches. Why is yours called Nashville?"

"My father loves Texas. He'd never leave. But he remembers his boyhood home."

Suddenly Jerry's wealth became very real—and overwhelming.

"I think I'm feeling nervous."

Jerry laughed. "Don't. It's just a big old house with a widower, a few fussy servants, and a few shaggy cows roamin' around."

Within a mile of the Bass mansion, Jerry pulled the surrey to the side of the curving dirt road.

"What's wrong?" Meg asked.

"Nothing...well..."

"What?"

He slid across the seat and put his arms around her.

"Just that we're almost home, and it's about time I kissed you."

Meg was staring straight ahead, thinking. Jerry was fun, kind, generous. She could feel *some* attraction for him too. She needed to be wanted. Perhaps it would take the sting away from the past, when she'd given her heart and had it returned. She shook her head at the memory of that cold night in Peppercreek.

"You're shaking your head. Is that a no?" he asked with surprising gentleness.

She looked back at him. "No. It means, what's taken you so long?"

Sam Bass had come home to Tennessee from the war between the states just long enough to say goodbye to his family and head for the territory called Texas. He wanted to start a new life where men were not so bitter from four years of fighting. He worked hard and carved out a life in the Texas hills that was the envy of many. His wife died from scarlet fever when their two children were still young. He now applied the same energy to being a father that he did to ranching. He took the children everywhere, and they loved him dearly. When ranching became too tame, he entered the colorful, often volatile world of Texas politics. He was a success at that too.

Sam Bass loved a challenge, and in his own way, he loved Meg Alcott on sight. He was prepared to like her because his daughter liked her. He was prepared to be very grateful because she seemed to have steadied his flighty son in a few short weeks. But when she walked in the living room of Nashville, he was surprised. Very surprised. Of course, he knew the school lady had to be halfway pretty or Jerry wouldn't be going down to Galveston every Friday to see her. But he wasn't prepared for her beauty. He wasn't prepared for the charge that coursed through him. He smiled inwardly; this was better than the sight of a new heifer calf or a good fight on the floor of Congress!

This was Ethan's daughter...young enough to be *his* daughter.

He crossed the room in quick, graceful strides and took her hand. "Hello, Miss Alcott, welcome to Texas," he said gravely.

"Thank you, sir."

"From a pretty woman like you, I'd far rather be called Sam."

He bent over her hand and kissed it.

"Don't pull too much charm on her, Pa," Jerry said at his father's elbow. "I've just now kissed her outside Nashville's gates."

"Jerry!" Meg was shocked.

He shrugged sheepishly. "Well, it's true."

When Meg climbed into bed that night she felt a nagging, vague fear that coming to Jerry's home had been a mistake. Yet she had felt an unexplainable, instant attraction—for the lean Sam Bass. He was the man her father had talked about—the embodiment of a legend now standing before her with piercing dark eyes and a smile that was almost secretive. In a brief two hours, she could see the father was not like the son. Maybe in the morning he would look different.

Chapter 8

The Gulf

♦♦ ♦♦ ♦♦

They that go down to the sea in ships,
that do business in great waters;
These see the works of the Lord;
and his wonders in the deep.

*A*ndy closed the little leather Bible, quietly thrilled to the strength and beauty of the words he had just read. He tucked the volume back into the large pocket of his jacket and strolled to the railing of the forecastle. A breeze was blowing across the Gulf, ruffling the waves, waves of inky blue crested with a foam of pure white.

Sleek and swift, *Ivanhoe* carried three towering masts and yards of tight, white sails—the trademarks of the most beautiful and romantic sailing vessel, the proud clipper ship. These vessels knifed the oceans with their slender hulls. They brought the Orient to Europe and America in their cargoes of exotic teas and luxurious silks. When someone yelled "Gold!" in California, the clipper had ferried thousands from the East Coast around the Horn to San Francisco in less than a hundred days. Then gold fever broke out on the huge island continent, and the clipper sped to Australia. Wherever there was water and a bit of wind, there was a clipper.

In its prime, the names of famous clippers were known around the world. Clippers like *Flying Cloud, Sea Witch, Stag Hound,* and the *Great Republic* were setting records for speed, shrinking distances on the map, and bringing cultures closer.

Angus Treadle had been a young seaman on the famous *Cutty Sark.* The experience had given him a wealth of stories and respect from his own crew. To have sailed on the *Cutty Sark!* The crew of *Ivanhoe's Dream* were men who hadn't been lured away to ocean steamships that were replacing the clipper. They were a proud fraternity of men who believed the clipper was the greatest of all sailing vessels on the seven seas.

Andy had fallen under the clipper's spell the first time he had seen one. Every other ship in the harbor looked brazen and awkward compared to the graceful clipper. Meg had teased him.

"Yet another example of how old-fashioned you are, big brother. You were born too late!"

"I thought it was yet another example of what good taste I have!" he returned with mock offense. Andy thought of the memory and smiled. Thinking of Meg usually made him smile. Except . . . except lately her letters didn't sound quite the same. She didn't sound happy at her teaching position in Galveston. He frowned, wishing he could do something for her.

The ship's bell had rung the third watch of the night moments earlier. Instead of going below to his cabin for much-needed sleep, he had remained top deck, reluctant to break the hold the sea had on him. Granted he was tired, very tired in fact, for the months of leisure at Tanglewood had healed his injury but done nothing to maintain his discipline for the demands of life on the open seas. He should go below, but darkness and the still of the night brought things to his mind he hadn't the power to resist.

He was glad to have *Ivanhoe's Dream* under his feet again, to feel the surge and the rhythm of the ocean, to put as many miles between himself and Tanglewood, Mississippi, as possible. He didn't consider himself a coward, but the challenge presented at the home of Patrick Cash, he reasoned, could only be resolved through time and distance.

Captain Treadle was very grateful to have his first mate back. The substitute he'd hired in Andy's place had not worked out well. He was a skilled mariner. The trouble was that the man was youthfully arrogant, loud, full of new—and to Treadle's mind, worthless—ideas on navigation, and forever spouting the glories of the British Empire, the Royal Navy specifically. Treadle could not forgive him of that. In the end it was really very simple—the man wasn't Andy Alcott.

When *Ivanhoe's Dream* had eased into its berth at New Orleans, Treadle's calloused and irascible old heart had warmed instantly to the sight of Andy grinning broadly and running along the dock like an impetuous lad of nine! Then Andy had jumped the eight feet to the deck, aptly illustrating that his foot was healed and he was ready to set sail.

"When do we sail, Captain?" he asked immediately.

Treadle masked his smile effectively and snorted.

"It ain't dignified runnin' along the dock like that, not for the first mate of the *Dream.*"

Andy burst out laughing. The months had not lessened the crustiness of his captain.

"A compliment then, as I'd never want to be accused of dignity!"

Treadle stretched out his hand, and they shook warmly.

"We're going clear 'round the Horn this trip. To Chile. Taking cotton, bringing back coffee."

Since they had been sailing principally in the Caribbean the last several years, the chance to see the Pacific again appealed to Andy.

"Sounds fine to me," Andy replied. "Whose idea, though?"

Treadle shrugged. "Always the same, isn't it? Those tea drinkin' Englishmen! I'd just as soon have stayed where we felt homey this time of the year. Storms aplenty 'round the Horn."

Andy looked out across the busy harbor, so loud and chaotic, so opposite to the time he had spent at his uncle's home.

"Well I'm ready to go...wherever!"

The captain measured the younger man with his eyes as he would a length of rigging. "So, your months of loafin' seem to have suited ya."

An odd twist appeared at the corner of Andy's mouth, an inscrutable and fleeting smile. "I'm suited to sail, Captain Treadle...suited to sail."

An uneasy, sometimes volatile relationship existed on the *Dream* between an aggressive and thoroughly arrogant silver-colored cat and the crew. The animal sat regally upon a specially made cask on the bridge, its calm and proud green eyes observing the antics of the humans below with detached amusement. He permitted only the touch of the captain, and nearly every crew member had been scratched to prove its querulous nature. It delighted the crew in a perverse sort of way to encourage a stranger or new seaman to make friends with the animal. The results were always the same—a hiss, a flash of paw, a curse, then blood. Many of the crew would not have minded if some gale had tossed the surefooted feline to a watery grave. Yet it was a part of every voyage, a part of *Ivanhoe's Dream* itself.

The most vocal opponent to the cat's presence on ship was a sinewy man of 60 named Hannibal. He had served as Treadle's cook for 30 years. He believed animals were made for land, and land only. It boded nothing but evil to have them aboard.

"And what about the ark, Hannibal?" young Ben had asked the old man with a sidelong smile at Andy.

"Such believin' is foolishness, young Ben," he returned tersely.

"You think so?"

The old man nodded vigorously. "Arks, and men in whale bellies, and snakes temptin' women, and rocks fellin' giants, all foolishness!"

"You know a lot about the Bible, Hannibal," Andy remarked, not looking up from the rigging he was mending.

"'Course I do. Pappy made me read it when I was a boy child. Made me, till I was old enough to say no more. And think not you'll be proselytin' me, Andy Alcott!" He stalked away in a great huff.

"Sailors are a great lot for superstitions, aren't they, Andy?" Ben asked.

Andy nodded.

"Why do you think that is?" Ben persisted.

"I don't know exactly, Ben. Maybe it's the time they have to think when they're not working and confined to the ship. Maybe it's the variety of backgrounds they come from. The natural mind seems to gravitate to such gloomy things." He peered across the ship to where Hannibal was regaling a group with another story. "Either way, it's not healthy."

"You heard what he said when we shipped out," Ben reflected.

"I heard him. Everyone heard him."

Hannibal was a treasury of sailing lore. He knew the biographies of pirates, the statistics of famous clippers, and all the ancient and prevailing superstitions. He had been alarmed, appalled, and very verbal when Treadle had announced his intention to sail Friday from New Orleans.

"Captain Treadle! No! Not Friday!"

Typically autocratic, captains were known to dispose of disrespectful crew in very swift fashion. Yet Treadle had tolerated the scolding with patience. "Quit your blubberin', Hannibal. It's Friday."

"It's an ill-fated voyage that leaves on a Friday, I tell ya!"

Treadle's smile tightened. "We weigh anchor on Friday. Will you be a part of this ill-fated voyage or not?"

The crew that had formed a half circle around the old cook waited tensely. No one could imagine a voyage without him.

Angus Treadle sighed deeply, feeling all of his 60-plus years. He closed his eyes. His bunk was especially comfortable, the mattress filled with the down of a thousand English ducks. He was unwilling to get up, though he knew it was morning. Instinct told him it was morning, and rain was in the offing for the day. There was really no hurry for him to get up. He knew his ship was being navigated by capable hands. From his open window, above the lap of the waves, he could hear two voices, raised in obvious joy. The tenor belonged to Ben and was as good as any he had heard at St. Michael's in London. Andy's voice was softer, yet it blended well in the chant they always sang in the morning.

The earth is the Lord's, and all it contains
the world and those who dwell in it.
For He has founded it upon the seas,
And established it upon the rivers.

His crew worked well together, as efficiently as any he'd ever been a part of. He knew he was a fortunate man, and he knew a large measure of that was due to Andy Alcott. The man had a way of calming the petty squabbles that arose almost daily. Tempers were bound to flair among the collage of personalities confined to 200 feet of floating wood for months at a time. Complaints were not brought to Treadle, but instead to the fair-minded first mate. The men preferred Andy's calm firmness to the captain's uncertain moods.

The last note of their song died away, and he knew from habit they had moved to work at the stern. He laced his fingers together, well satisfied that everything was in order.

The morning sky was like an opal, variegated with shades of rose, shimmering close to the surface of the water where the first fingers of sun had reached. Andy Alcott believed sunrise could not be any more beautiful than it was on the Gulf. He thought fleetingly of Amy, thinking how with her love of beauty she would treasure this sunrise. He closed his eyes a moment to picture how she would look standing beside him, watching, then finally turning to him with a faint smile. He was grateful when a voice at his elbow interrupted him.

"Calm this mornin'," the man said gruffly. It was Jess Crow, newest member of the *Dream,* his first voyage in fact, and trying very hard to disguise his noviceness with brusqueness.

Andy nodded. "Should be like this pretty much for the rest of the week. We're in the 'variables of Cancer.' Breezes are always moderate here. We—"

A thin, shrill laugh just above where they stood stopped Andy's words. It was Hannibal, perched on a coil of rope like a monkey, gray eyes fastened to the west, peering as if his old eyes could see the coast of Mexico.

"First Mate calls this the 'variables of Cancer,' but there is another name for 'em, you know."

Andy sighed. Here was Hannibal doing what Hannibal did best, prophesying gloom and disaster, describing with relish anything morbid. The regular crew had been indoctrinated to the cook's ways when they first stepped aboard. His cooking rivaled any New Orleans chef, but his tongue was an implement of fear and superstition. Andy hated it and could never understand Treadle's tolerance of it.

On one of the early voyages, when his place was established, Andy had spoken of it with frustration.

"Why do you allow this, Captain? It stirs up the men. I've seen you dump men for less than this!"

"He's a windbag, Andy. I'm surprised that he bothers you that much. He's certainly failed the true test of a prophet by your own standard: He's never been right."

"He's more than a windbag!" He was risking the man's temper with his impertinence. "He's like...like a voice of darkness!"

Treadle calmly pondered the young first mate.

"I mean no disrespect to you, Andy, but you're our resident voice of light. Perhaps I have a perverse sense of humor, but I'm interested to see the outcome in the battle between darkness and light. Which will swallow the other?"

"That's why you leave him on? So he and I can spar?" Andy was incredulous.

Treadle chuckled. "Partly. Also, I'm very fond of eating well. I've never heard you complain about the man's cooking. Would you rather we had a cook who knew nothing but bully beef and hard biscuits?" He placed his arm around Andy's shoulder. "I'm a practical man, Andy. I live and work in practical terms. Seeing a philosophical or spiritual battle in progress is a change of menu for me."

"You're right, if I may say so, Captain."

"Right about what?"

"You do have a perverse sense of humor."

Treadle chuckled again. "If you're so sure of your religion—"

"My faith, Captain, my faith."

"Whatever, but if you're certain about your faith, and certain about the outcome as you've told me in the past, you've no real reason to be frustrated, now, do you?"

Hannibal's voice was raspy. "So do you want to know?"

Crow looked nervously from the first mate to the cook. The old man did tempt him with exotic stories. Hannibal did not wait for consent.

"These are the 'horse latitudes,' Mr. Crow."

"Horse latitudes?"

"You won't find them called that in Maury's charts," Andy countered.

"In colonial days, packets from New England to the West Indies becalmed here. Not a breath of wind for days and days. Horses started suffering from the water shortage. Finally pitched overboard. These waters were fine feeding grounds for sharks. Happened every year in the old days."

Crow laughed stiffly. "Not a very cheerful story, Hannibal."

"You've paid him a high compliment then," Andy muttered as he stood up.

The old man went into a spasm of laughter.

Andy stood on the port bow, the collar of his woolen peacoat turned up against the sudden chill. His eyes were searching, his ears straining. *Ivanhoe's Dream* was attempting to navigate the passage between the Falkland Islands and the coast of Argentina. Normally this 300-mile-wide stretch was easy. Yet for two days the ship had crept forward in a heavy fog, making bearings nearly impossible.

Fog was one of the many perils for a mariner. It muffled sound as well as vision. All that could be heard was the moaning of the ship's frame, the creaking of the rigging, and the thin flapping of the sail. Running into the reefs near either coast was a very real and ominous possibility.

All the crew was on deck, Andy noted, whether they were on duty or not. Every man knew that this passage was perhaps the most critical of the entire voyage. The sailors leaned forward, their faces white with tension. Tempers, Andy also noted, had grown remarkably shorter in the last few hours. A sailor coming up from the galley had tripped over the resident feline. His cup of hot coffee went flying. He gave the animal a curse and a well-placed kick. The entire crew swung around. The captain had seen it from the forecastle. The look he gave the man was icier than the wind. Everyone held their breath. What would be the penalty for abusing the captain's pet?

"You've spilled your coffee, man. See that it's taken care of," Treadle barked as he turned back to the watch. Everyone relaxed.

Jess Crow came up to Andy. "This blasted fog! How much longer do you think?"

Andy shrugged, thinking this new crewman might not be cut out for the rigors and dangers of life on the high seas.

"Hard to say, Jess."

"We could pile up on a reef!" he hissed in Andy's ear.

"We could. But I think more likely we're in the middle of the channel. The captain knows his stuff."

Crow cursed again. "Hannibal says it's because of that blasted cat! I think he may be right."

Andy gave him an easy smile. "Don't put your faith in his words, Jess. He makes a fine stew, but he's a terrible prophet."

Jess gave him a sharp look but was silent.

The fog lifted in a matter of hours, and the men cheered. The sky was a vivid turquoise. They had made the passage. Now, Andy knew, the real test of the voyage was soon to begin. Rounding the Cape was never easy, no matter the season or the vessel. Going around the Cape meant alertness and vigilance by every man on board. Erratic, unpredictable weather was part of traveling around this most southern tip of South America. These were the waters explorers like Magellan and Drake had navigated a few centuries earlier. They were a challenge then; they were a challenge still. Many men enjoyed the challenge, especially if the earlier part of the sailing had been smooth and uneventful, but many men dreaded it. Rounding the Cape could be treacherous.

Treadle had been barking and bellowing all morning—short, acid-toned commands. The crew moved quickly under orders, avoiding the man's penetrating, scorching eyes. His eyebrows were pulled down in a dark, threatening line, clearly indicating his mood like a vivid red flag. If the crew needed to communicate anything to him, they appealed to Andy to act as intercessor. The captain stayed top deck all day, never bothering to eat or rest—merely stalking the length of the clipper, glaring at the sea and horizon as if it was a truculent enemy.

Hannibal knew the captain's moods could get savage as well as anyone on board, but he preferred to think of himself as a privileged member of the *Ivanhoe*. Like the cat. But even the cat knew to stay wary in face of the big man's uncertain moods. Yet Hannibal continued his teasing or whining as it suited him. He ignored the red flag.

At noon, Hannibal brought up the bowl of potatoes he'd been peeling in the galley to sit in the sun. With the Horn a few days away, sunshine could be a premium. He was thinking hard on some tale he could tell his quiet, subdued audience. Something that they hadn't heard before. His croaking was a rude interruption in an interlude of peace.

Then in the cloudless sky, a bird suddenly appeared, flying over the ship effortlessly and without demand. The crew had been working, yet every man felt the shadow of the white seabird and looked up. With no visible land, where had it come from? Hannibal ignored the tension. He waved his knife at the gliding bird.

"Up there! Look at him, sailing smoother than we are! Heh, heh . . ."

He looked around. He could catch only Jess Crow's eye. For a veteran storyteller, two ears were more than enough. Everyone else seemed to be ignoring him.

"Know what it is?" he called to the novice seaman.

"A gull?" Jim Crow offered listlessly.

Hannibal's laugh was raspy. "An albatross. But you know what he *really* is, don't ya?"

Treadle turned from the spyglass he had been polishing to stare at the cook.

Crow did not speak, but merely watched the old man.

"An albatross is really the soul of a dead sailor, lost at sea! Yep." The little man was gleeful.

Everyone had heard this superstition except Jess Crow. Hannibal was irritated at the lack of response he was receiving.

"Hey, Jess, you reckon' it's ol' Greer Nelson up there over us? Heh, heh . . ." He went off into an irreverent spasm of laughter.

Treadle rushed forward and snatched the cook up by his greasy shirtfront. He shook the little man like a rag doll.

"If I hear one more word like that, I'll toss you over! Think of it, Hannibal, the cook will become the main course. Get my meaning?"

While Hannibal looked startled at the outburst, he did not look properly repentant to the angry captain.

Treadle's voice was still a snarl.

"Or maybe you'd rather be put off on a ship that works around the Chincha Islands. You know we won't be too far from them when we make port. How about that? Maybe you'd like to work on a bird dung boat!"

He shook Hannibal roughly again. But Andy had come to stand beside him. Seeing their captain in a rage could do as much damage to the crew as one of the old cook's stories.

"Captain, I have those charts ready. Can we look over them now?" Andy asked soothingly.

One final glare and Treadle stalked off. Yes, the captain's nerves were very strained...

Andy felt as if the *Dream* had slammed into a wall. It was if the vessel had stopped completely in the water, becoming abruptly motionless. Then silence. Everyone hurried above deck. The sky was purple, the wind screaming and full of ice. The ocean was suddenly churning, throwing the ship into troughs that seemed bottomless, then pitching it up onto the crest of mountainous waves. They were rounding the Cape, and Andy Alcott had never been in a worse storm.

A few men gathered in the galley were muttering that the old cook's words had finally come true. Another smaller group, including Andy and Ben, gathered to pray. Six hours later the storm slackened and the ocean was calm as glass. Only a sheet of rain fell softly, melodically.

Treadle and his first mate stood on the deck, ignoring the rain, amazed as men of the sea always are at the variable moods of the great waters.

"She can be a terrible mistress to be sure," Treadle said calmly. "Now look at her. A perfect mother, cradlin' her little one with nothin' but sweetness." He gave a tired laugh.

Andy noticed that the man looked older and wearier than he had ever seen him before. Indeed, the "terrible mistress" had taken a toll on them all.

Treadle noticed Andy's glance up at the yardarm, still frosted with ice. He knew his first mate was remembering his first time around the Horn.

"Glad I didn't have to send you up this time?" the older man asked easily.

Andy nodded. But he was thinking of the crewmen who had died so quickly and silently.

"My ma... When I told her about what happened, she cried and cried." He smiled. "She would have roped me to the front porch if she could have. She prays for me every day."

He hesitated, bracing for Treadle's caustic response.

"My mother's prayers protected me that day. The Lord didn't want to take me just then."

Treadle pulled out his pipe. He had no intention of lighting it; it was simply a habit to roll it in his calloused palms as he thought.

"Perhaps your proselytin' isn't finished yet on *Ivanhoe's Dream* with old sea dogs."

Andy gave him a wry smile, but took no offense.

"I would hardly call it proselyting. Perhaps the Lord is still working on *some* of the crew...through your nagging first mate."

The two locked eyes, then laughed.

"Well, your prayers were answered on this trip," Treadle said with unusual gentleness.

Andy turned to him, noting the usual humor and cynicism were gone. "Yes, you're right," Andy agreed with a faint smile.

The man continued gazing out at the waters he had called home for so many years after Andy had gone below. "Thank you," he whispered.

Treadle declared two days of rest for the crew in the aftermath of the storm. As violent as the storm had been, it had not been without benefit. It had pushed them forward to within three days of their destination on the coast of Chile. Every man looked forward to feeling land underfoot for a time.

Andy lay propped against a coil of rope, his hat pulled over his eyes. He could hear laughter in the distance. Undoubtedly Hannibal was not in the galley. The cook's audience of listeners had shrunk. It now consisted only of Jess Crow and two others. A perceptible feeling of thanksgiving hung over the ship. With the fog and with the storm, disaster had come close. Many of the crew who had been quietly skeptical of Andy's faith now began to examine it more closely.

Andy could hear only snatches of the tales Hannibal was embarked upon. "It was a clipper called *Eagle's Wing*...crossing the Atlantic ...ran into an iceberg the size of the clipper nearly! Sliced through the bow like it was a kiddie's boat...every man but one lost. Then there's the *Andrew Jackson,* fine and sleek she was. Stranded in a calm off the straights. Stuck there six weeks...ran out of water and food. When a ship finally sighted her, the crew were skeletons...fish food..."

His tales had been pure pessimism and fear. The cook was triumphant.

A muttered oath, then, "Can't you tell anything with a good endin'?" one of the lazing sailors complained.

Hannibal smiled benignly. "'Course I can. There's my personal favorite. 'Bout the Englishman who sails and is really a lord or something high and mighty."

"What's that one?" Crow asked.

"Seems there's this seaman who is really English nobility or something like. Rich as royalty but lives like us poor common folk. Don't want anyone to know who he really is."

Treadle approached from the bridge, the cat wrapped around his neck and shoulders like a cape. He observed the little knot of listeners with amusement. He was usually quite vocal on anything pertaining to the English. Despite the fact they were his very generous employers, he hated anything English. It was wise not to get him started on the subject. Andy had learned that from the moment he had signed on with the man. Treadle claimed to have been raised in Ireland. Andy supposed that explained the man's feelings for the Brits—it was almost genetic.

Treadle waited until Hannibal had finished the tale. Like a shifting wind, the cook had been restored to the captain's good graces.

"Of all your stories, my good cook, that one is the most outlandish. It couldn't possibly be true!"

Andy raised up on an elbow to hear better.

Hannibal bristled. "And why do you think it's so false, Captain?"

"Very simply, an Englishman would never play at being poor if he was really rich as royalty, as you say. He wouldn't give up his precious title. He's arrogant to the blood. That's one tale that is full of hot air."

Hannibal was visibly offended but kept silent. This time he would let the good captain have his opinions.

Jess Crow had made some complaint against the meal, and now the old cook, still smarting from the captain's humiliating treatment, loosened on the new sailor the very seasoned and choice language known to men of their profession. Jess grew red-faced.

"Look old man, it's the Chincha Islands for you, if the captain doesn't like your biscuits."

The crew laughed uproariously, the cook scolded even more virulently, and Jess felt vindicated. But it was Andy he sought out at the far end of the deck. It looked to him as if the first mate was very far away in thought.

"Thinkin' of a woman, huh?" Jess began lightly.

Andy shrugged and did not answer. He had in fact been thinking of Tanglewood...of the mistress there. He did not like the crewman intruding upon his thoughts.

"Been wonderin' about these Chincha Islands the captain threatened Hannibal with. Can you tell me where they are?"

Andy was irritated. He did not feel like jawing about anything to do with the cook.

"Three little islands about 12 miles off the coast of Peru."

His voice was clipped to discourage any further questions. But Jess was still interested in the subject.

"So, what's so awful about working off of them? They inhabited by cannibals or something?"

Andy frowned. "Look, Jess, Hannibal can tell you all about the islands. That kind of subject is right down his alley."

"He's in a huff at me just for mentioning the word to him. So I figured you could tell me."

"Three islands where seabirds and seals have lived and died for centuries. Solid dung. Someone figured out it makes great fertilizer, so ships from ports all over the world anchor for months just to get a shipment of it. It's pretty rank to transport, and an insult to have to work with. So you see, the captain was threatening Hannibal with a rather unpleasant situation."

"Well, I think the captain was being too hard on the old man. He wasn't hurting anybody with his tales."

Andy thought over his words carefully.

"Planting suspicions in men's minds can be dangerous, Jess. I have no objection to storytelling, but Hannibal trades in everything dark, gloomy, and fearful."

"He said this was an ill-fated voyage when we started out."

Andy nodded. "I remember."

"Well, look at the nasty weather, the dangers..."

"All a part of life on the oceans, Jess."

"Still, I think the old man...has a second sight or something. I think we should listen more to what he says."

Jess was pugnaciously holding to his opinion, Andy realized. *He is tangled up in the false prophet's power.*

He patted him on the back, and attempted some levity.

"I think it would be best if we just listened to him when he calls for dinner, Jess."

It was a moonless night, and seaman Crow sat in the shadows of the deck, his presence undetected by the watch. He had been observing the cat for several days. He knew its routines perfectly. After some vigilant spying, he discovered where the animal spent the dark hours of the night—and it was not obediently enthroned on the end of the captain's bunk.

Hannibal's ominous stories and prophecies found fertile soil in Jess Crow. The cook's words nagged at him while he worked and invaded his rest at night. Crow had become Hannibal's most avid listener, his appetite whetted for anything unwholesome. Crow dismissed Andy's countering words. The first mate seemed to have a mania for religion. Religion was for weak minds and cowards. Even the captain, who had such obvious affection for the first mate, seemed cynical about it.

More and more Jess Crow believed in Hannibal's pronouncement that this was an ill-fated voyage. He looked back at all that had gone wrong. They had narrowly escaped sinking in that terrible storm two days earlier. Some men were chuckling about it even now. Was he the only sane one on board? He and Hannibal. Yes, Hannibal had special insight. And he was always berating the cat.

Well, Crow would show some courage when the others would not. Never mind if the creature was the captain's personal pet. He wasn't going to the bottom of the Pacific because of a blasted cat!

It was nearly midnight. The animal came up from the companionway just as it did each night. It waited a moment as if testing the air, then dropped soundlessly into the cargo hatch. Crow smiled. A few more minutes. Everything was going just as he planned.

A clan of rats lived in the cargo hold of the *Dream,* kept comfortable by the sacks of grain stored there. But it was not a life without danger. The captain's pet was a capable mouser. Even now it was tensely perched on a grain sack, its eyes riveted to a stack of planking. It didn't hear the man as he descended into the blackness; the creaking of the ship and the ocean around him muffled all sounds.

Crow's plan was simple. Wait until the animal was feasting on its prize, then a quick fling of a tarp over its head, a rope around the neck to cut off any yowling, and then over the side.

He lit a match. The cat's eyes gleamed green. If the animal was disturbed by the man, it didn't show it. In his waiting, Crow had failed to notice that the tempo of the wind had increased. He rested comfortably against a stack of crates, watching the cat watch his own quarry—an odd drama in the hold of the *Dream.* He began to smoke while he waited.

Another seaman had given the cargo hold a casual glance after the storm around the Cape. All seemed fine, the seaman had yawned, nothing busted. What his quick look had not taken in were several highly stacked crates that had shifted precariously.

The cat pounced. Crow moved with surprising quickness as well. The canvas went over the cat in one swift motion. Crow had his prize, even as the cat had his. Just then the ship lurched ungracefully into a trough. The crates came crashing down on Jess Crow. He pitched forward, unconscious. His cigar came to rest in a small pile of cotton.

It was Hannibal who awoke first to the scent of smoke. Years of cooking had trained his epicurean nose to the smell of burning. Slowly, arthritically, he eased himself out of bed to investigate. Surely he hadn't left something on the galley stove.

Andy had wakened as the squall came up. Sleepily he decided it was too mild to get up for. He had dropped back to sleep instantly. Then he was awake again, this time sweaty and tense. He tossed the blanket aside. What had wakened him? A sound? A smell? He lay there uneasy and unable to go back to sleep. Something was wrong. He swung his feet to the floor and struck a match. Almost 3:00 A.M. He waited a moment. What was it? What was that muted creaking and snapping sound? A yell and a scream he recognized as Hannibal's reached him, and the sound of the dreaded fire bell. Fire...

Ivanhoe's Dream settled into its watery grave with an inglorious hiss. Andy closed his eyes as much from pain as from sadness at the sight. He clung to a huge spar, his feet already numbing from the cold Pacific, his right arm badly burned, his face blistered with falling cinders. It had all happened so fast. Could he survive until sunrise?

Chilean fishermen found all that remained of *Ivanhoe's Dream* the following day when the sun was a blazing half-circle on the horizon. Only four men from the crew of 12 had survived. Four men clinging to a piece of lumber—men burned, dehydrated, ravaged by a sea that had been a comfort and a provider. Four men and one cat, a silver-colored tom that sat on the wood, crying pitifully, a mere specter of its former defiant self. It now submitted eagerly to any caress, any attention.

The survivors were placed in the rickety little fishing boat and taken to the nearby village. Andy suffered from his badly burned arm. Ben and another sailor sustained only minor injuries. Andy was most concerned for Treadle. After two weeks of recovering, he still seemed so weak. None of the villagers, including the doctor with his meager supplies, could speak English. Still the medical attention had been sufficient. Andy had pulled the doctor aside, gesturing to make himself under-stood. The doctor looked thoughtful a moment, then rested one brown finger upon his own chest. Treadle's heart...

They shared a room in a small shack. One night, Treadle had grown talkative even in his weariness.

"Andy, if...I don't leave here—"

"What do you mean by that?" Andy asked quickly, ignoring the pain of his arm.

"Just listen carefully, will you?" Treadle's voice was almost pleading. "I want you to promise me something."

"I'll try," Andy agreed. His mind flashed quickly to another promise he had made without regard to consequence.

"When you leave here—"

"We'll leave together," Andy interrupted gently.

"I want you to go to London. I want you to go to a place called Havasham Court in London. Promise me you will."

"Why London? Why would you have me go to that city of despised Englishmen?" Andy gave a nervous laugh.

"I'd prefer to not answer that just now. I'd rather you just trust me."

"I always have in the past, Captain. But I'd prefer we face those tea drinkers together!"

Treadle smiled and looked up to the bamboo ceiling.

"We've had a few adventures together, Andy, we have. Faced many storms."

Andy's eyes filled. He knew the man was saying goodbye, and he didn't want to say goodbye.

"What do you think set off the fire, Andy?" Treadle asked slowly.

Andy winced, the tears spilling over.

"I don't know." He broke into a sob in the darkness.

"What is it, lad? What's the matter?"

"The fog, the storm, the fire, the sinking. Was it because of me? Eight men have died!"

Andy's sensitive soul had been more wounded than his arm.

"Because of you? What do you mean?" Treadle summoned gruffly.

"My sin! My loving something that wasn't mine to love."

Treadle was silent in the darkness as he tried to understand.

"You mean like Jonah? You think we went through that storm because of something you've done? No, no, lad, I won't believe that! You're sounding like ol' Hannibal."

"Hannibal," Andy moaned.

"Yes, the man is gone. He had time to choose, Andy... as I have. You're thinkin' only of judgment. What about God's mercy and forgiveness?"

Andy leaned forward slowly. "What did you say?"

Treadle managed a frail laugh. "Yes, there now. I know you've been frettin' over my soul. But you needn't any longer. I've prayed to become one of His crew. You've converted me at last, Andy Alcott! I thought it would quiet your talkin' about your religion so much."

"My faith, I've told you," Andy whispered huskily.

The old, rough, feverish hand sought the younger man.

"My faith... too."

Ten days later a passing freighter flying the Union Jack agreed to take the three men. Andy watched the coastline now growing thin, muted, almost swallowed up by the ocean. He gripped the rail tightly. He was leaving a very good friend behind.

Chapter 9

The Hill Country, Texas

♦♦ ♦♦ ♦♦

*I*n the first few days at Jerry's ranch, Meg seemed not to notice Sam Bass's age. His quiet charm veiled his years. He was simply another attentive, attractive man. She did notice he was quiet and unusually gentle for a man she had thought simply dusted off his jeans to work in the House of Representatives. He measured things in his mind before he spoke, carefully and deliberately. Not at all like his fun-loving son, who talked and teased from the time his feet hit the floor till he pulled his spurs off at night.

Sam smiled slowly with crinkles that spread out from his eyes. A kind smile, Meg decided, just like Jerry's. The only thing that seemed to fit the cowboy mold was his tall leanness, his tanned leathery skin. His hair was still a thick, sandy red, unthreaded by gray.

He noticed everything about her ... and forced himself not to stare. He could see she looked things over before she spoke, obviously thinking, taking the facts in. He figured she was bright in more than just academics. Dark, glossy hair, a firm red mouth ... When he thought of her mouth, a warning would toll somewhere in his mind, reminding him that she was little older than Miranda.

Sam had greeted her on the broad staircase that first morning when she came down for breakfast. He wore jeans and a white shirt open at the throat. His hair was uncombed, and he wore faded red carpet slippers. He held a steaming cup of coffee. He was headed for his office.

"Good morning, Meg." He bowed slightly.

"Sir ..." Then she laughed. "I ... Shall I really call you Sam?"

He thought of a provocative answer, but held it.

"Something wrong with Sam? My ma was always fond of it."

"Well, of course not. It's just ... well, I ... It only seems ..."

He leaned on the bannister toward her.

"You could call me Congressman Bass if that's easier."

His teeth seemed very white in his bronzed face. Meg smiled again; the son had inherited humor from his father.

"How'd ya sleep?"

"Just fine, thank you. Roosters woke me up."

His eyes went over her riding clothes. "I see Jerry got you up early for a ride."

"I think we're supposed to see all of your Nashville today."

He frowned. "He'd better not drag you all over the place. You'll get saddle sore and never want to come back to see us."

"I've done a little riding at home," she said modestly. "I think I'll survive."

"He's in there chowin' down; he didn't wait for you. Better hurry if you want anything."

They both laughed. But Meg did not move from the steps. And he did not want her to hurry away. Jerry would have her all day.

"Well..." Meg started to move. This man's masculinity waved from him like a fragrance. She shouldn't stand so close. She had come here with Jerry...

"Thank you for inviting me here. Getting away from the school for a while is like a holiday."

"I'm glad you could come. And I'm grateful to you for what you've done for Jerry."

"I—" she began to protest.

He held up his hand. "He's calmer, if you can believe that. Less like a shooting star..."

"Well, I'd better go eat," she said as she moved past him.

He nodded. He shouldn't stand so close to her. He followed her with his eyes. He went to his office wondering if he could concentrate on a bill that was coming up. The bill was what he needed to concentrate on, he chided himself—this was *Jerry's* girl...

Jerry was glad Meg knew how to ride. It would have been a disappointment if she hadn't—or worse, if she didn't like horses or was afraid of them. Jerry wasn't sure how easy it would have been to court a woman who squealed at the equines as if they were monsters. He was awfully glad he had gone to Bishop's Villa that day to pick Miranda up, and that he'd gotten lost in the hallways trying to hunt her down. His hunt had led to a real prize. Meg was the nicest girl he had ever met. She hadn't disappointed him in any way so far. Smart, witty, laughed at his jokes, good-looking, and liked horses. What else was there?

Meg was excited to be out riding the expanse of the Nashville ranch. It was so refreshing to be away from the school. Teaching had become more palatable since the girls had accepted her, but the "head" still was just as cutting and critical. It was a living, but deep down Meg was not happy with it. So coming to Jerry's home for a week had been a real treat. Out riding on the windswept hills or through endless fields reminded her of home. They couldn't possibly see all the place in a day, but Jerry had managed to show her a good portion of it—ranch house to bunkhouses to barns and corrals to stock tanks and wandering fence lines. They stayed out all day, spreading a picnic lunch that Miranda had packed for them under a live oak. Jerry fell asleep with his head in Meg's lap. She watched the clouds moving across the vivid blue sky like gigantic ice-white continents. He woke to find her smiling to herself. She pointed out a mammoth triangular-shaped cloud in the west.

"Penelope-asia," she laughed.

"What?"

"I just named that cloud over there. I used to do that when I was a little girl. Lie on my back and pretend the clouds were countries that only I could name." She laughed again. "See, I haven't really grown up."

He propped himself up on an elbow.

"Oh, I think you're pretty grown up, Midwestern Meg . . . Sure are nice to wake up to." He kissed her quickly.

Meg blushed. He had opened up the door to intimacy between them, and while she hesitated, she did not close it. He pulled her up to her feet.

"I think I could get pretty serious about you pretty quick," he said with untypical sobriety.

"I'm not so sure things that are serious should . . . happen quickly," she suggested.

He shrugged. "I figure you see something you want and you go after it."

He kissed her again, more possessively this time. It was only a matter of time, she told herself, and she would feel the same.

He was there before she knew. Reaching up to help her down. She really didn't need help, but it would be rude to refuse.

"The tank on that east section by the road is sure low. We need rain," Jerry was saying as he dismounted.

Meg leaned down into his father's strong arms.

"Yeah, we could use some rain," Bass agreed laconically.

But Meg could see he wasn't really listening to his son. Jerry was leading the horses away, still chattering, unmindful that his girl and his father were still standing in the courtyard.

His hands still lingered on her waist, hers still rested on his shoulders.

"Thank you," she murmured.

"My pleasure," he replied with an unconcealed twinkle in his gray eyes.

Meg had seen cattle branded before. She didn't like it. Burning cowhide was not an easy smell to forget. But Jerry had insisted she come along for a while. He'd be out all day with a dozen or so ranch hands as they branded the newest and youngest of the Bass herd.

"That's an unusual brand," Meg commented when she saw the long iron heating in the coals. "I'd expect a *B*, or *N* for Nashville."

"The Bass brand has always been the 21StILL. Don't you recognize it?"

"No...Wait, *ILL*. Does that stand for Illinois?"

"Yep."

"The 21st regiment from Illinois. The one our fathers fought with!"

"Yep. Pa calls them his bovine army."

Sam Bass had thought the 21st the best regiment in the entire Union army. Branding thousands of beef with that brand was yet another tribute to the adventures of his youth. Meg was beginning to see Jerry's father as both an unusual man, and a sentimental one.

It was dinnertime on the big veranda. Jerry had gobbled down his food, waved to Meg, then ridden back to the corrals. Sam watched him go in silence. Meg could only wonder at the thoughts that pulled his mouth down into a frown.

"You going back down there?" he asked abruptly.

"No, I told Jerry a morning of branding was enough for me. Don't be offended, sir, they are...cute cows."

His eyes crinkled up at this. "Cute cows! I tried to tell him brandin' was no place for a lady."

"Oh, I'm not squeamish. I just figured I could find something better to do."

He was smiling even more now. "Going to town with Miranda?"

She weighed her answer carefully. "Well, no, I hadn't really planned to."

"Good. Hitch up your skirts then, and we'll go for a ride."

They had ridden to a gently rising hill overlooking vast acres of grassland. When they reached the summit, Meg was surprised at the height. Hundreds, no thousands, of cattle were grazing below them.

"This is just about my favorite spot on the whole ranch," Sam said easily.

Meg sat down under the solitary oak to appreciate the panorama before her. Miles of green grass, a vault of blue—two oceans of perfect color washed in sunshine. It made Meg feel small and grand at the same time. Sam was leaning against the tree behind her. She squinted up at him and smiled.

"I think I know why this is your favorite spot. It makes you feel like a king surveying his kingdom!"

He laughed with her. She had never felt so comfortable with a man so quickly before. She couldn't quite understand it. Why this man? Why not...Jerry?

"I like this place because it's so quiet up here," he explained. "You can see the beasts down there, and you know they're chewin' and bawling but you can't hear a thing. I spent a lot of time up here when my wife, Anne, died. It was a real comfort."

He shrugged, a gesture she recognized as being thoroughly Sam Bass. It was the first time he had made reference to his wife.

"You never remarried," Meg ventured carefully. She could not explain to herself why she had asked such a personal question.

"Never found a woman . . . who wanted two kids," he said lamely.

"There are lots of women out there who would love your family!"

He cocked his head at her. "All right, then. I never found a woman who wanted to wear the Nashville brand."

Meg laughed. "If you think of women as heifers then I'm sure you won't find a wife."

"Guess I just never could find a woman to take Anne's place."

Meg picked at the grass. "A woman wants to make her own place, not fill another."

It was quiet up here. She imagined he could hear her heart beating. She could certainly feel the strength of his eyes.

"So we've come to the conclusion I know nothing about women—"

"I never said that!" Meg protested.

"All right. But let's make this real personal."

"I think we'd better be getting back to the house."

His laughter boomed out. "And you think I don't know women! So why aren't you married, Miss Alcott? From my perspective, you should have been snatched up long ago."

She took her time to answer. She must be flippant now. It was much safer. "I never found a man whose brand I liked."

As Meg had come to know, Sam Bass liked to think before he spoke, whether to his children, his opponents in the state senate, or his ranch hands. It made some folks think he was slow. It made others think he was wise. All he knew was that his ma had drilled it into his head when he was a boy, that is, bridling his tongue. In those quiet moments on that lonely hill, he thought of several remarks to make to the schoolteacher. He would have liked to say he hoped her coming to Nashville would solve her problem of finding a suitable brand. But he didn't say that. He wouldn't push Jerry's case. This young woman certainly had a mind of her own. And he wouldn't push his own case. Not yet anyway.

"I agree with you," he said simply.

"Oh? On what?"

"It's time to get back to the house."

When Meg went to bed that night, she talked very firmly to herself. This was infatuation, pure and simple. Well, simple anyway. It couldn't continue. It would only lead to embarrassment and hurt. She couldn't hurt Jerry.

Sam Bass was having a similar conversation with himself in the vast expanse of his four poster. This was Jerry's girl. But he really wanted to forget that. A woman hadn't made him feel this young since ... since he couldn't remember when. He wanted to forget her age—and his. He growled into his pillow.

"No fool like an old fool..."

Galveston

"Meg's girls" were having some difficulty concentrating on their studies. Miss Alcott had come back from the week recess looking tanned, healthy, and happy. One young student had ventured to whisper behind her hand, "Miss Alcott is glowing. She must be in love!"

Her classmates had tittered, then agreed, then pounced on Miranda for details. They knew Jerry Bass had come to Galveston for weeks, then taken Miss Alcott to his ranch. But they wanted to know more. There just *had* to be more.

Meg found them hard to control. She could only hope the headmistress would not suddenly decide to make one of her unannounced observations.

"Now girls, we must get back to these Latin roots. I want to finish before—"

A hand was waving with urgency. "Miss Alcott, we are all curious about something. And if ... well, if you could tell us we could go back to these very intriguing Latin roots."

The giggles around her increased like a ripple.

"Now, girls. If Mrs. McCallas were to walk in right now with you laughing this way, she'd have me for dinner!"

This sent the girls into full mirth. The girls loved it when Miss Alcott spoke so frankly.

"Girls, girls. Now, what was your question, Judith?"

"Well, it's just that we were wondering if you're going to marry Jerry Bass. You'd become the ... the, what was that word, Paula? What? Oh, you would become the matriarch of Nashville!"

Their laughter ended abruptly, and every eye focused on her.

"Judith, Latin roots are what we are to be discussing, not my personal life."

It was hard to be very firm with these girls that she had grown to like. She smiled, and that encouraged them.

Another hand shot up. "Miss Alcott, just think, if you married Jerry Bass and he's a wealthy Texan, you could have daughters just like us!"

Miranda waited by Meg's desk until her classmates had filed from the room. She hugged her books to her chest; her face was creased in concern.

"Oh, Miranda. Listen, I'm sorry about your classmates being so—"

"Blunt about you and Jerry?"

Meg smiled. She did like the entire Bass family.

"Yes, their bluntness. I'm sure it's embarrassing."

"Oh, that's all right. It kind of gives me status in the class. You know, my brother is the teacher's beau."

"I think you're very mature to take the teasing so well."

"I don't mind," she smiled. This was really a lovely young woman, Meg realized, with the best of her father, even in looks.

But her frown returned. "Miss Alcott, I wondered..." She grew agitated and drew invisible figures on the desk.

"Miranda? What is it?"

"About what they said, about you becoming the matriarch of Nashville."

"I know Miranda. It was very tactless."

The girl leaned forward. "But have you thought about it really?"

"Thought about what?"

"About marrying Jerry and living at our ranch."

Meg felt embarrassed now. But she couldn't be evasive with this generous girl. "I...Miranda, I'm not ready to get married."

Miranda was intent on explaining something to Miss Alcott. The teacher really did need to think about this.

"Nashville is very important to Jerry. It means a lot to him. Had you noticed that, Miss Alcott?"

Meg had noticed—and wondered if she should notice it even more.

"I know Jerry feels strongly about Nashville. It's his home."

"Well, sometimes I think he's just too tied up in it, Miss Alcott. Like that's all there is in the world. And a...a wife would be in second place with Jerry. I just thought you should know that about him."

Meg nodded.

"I hope, I mean, I didn't...I like you very much, Miss Alcott, and I wouldn't want to discourage you if you really like Jerry. If he chooses you, well..."

"I understand, Miranda. Thank you for your concern."

Lack of concentration was affecting the teacher as well as her students. As Meg sat in her apartment that evening, she could not seem to keep her interest in the papers in front of her. She brewed some tea, stirred it, then stared at it until it grew cold. She paced across the room a few times. She tried to read a novel. She started a letter to her parents, then crumpled it. A letter to Andy met a similar fate.

"Are you going to marry Jerry Bass?...Nashville is everything to him..." The words were playing over and over in her mind.

It was midnight when Meg Alcott finally sank to the floor beside her bed and prayed. She felt so tired.

"Help me to know if it's *him,* Lord. Please."

Nashville Ranch

Meg reasoned that there were few opportunities in life to make a grand and sweeping entrance. There hadn't been any in her years at Peppercreek, where socials were held in the church basement and dresses were ordered from the Sears and Roebuck catalog. So she should take advantage of this occasion. Would she ever go to a huge New Year's Eve party at a Texas ranch attended by cattle barons and their jeweled wives, politicians, and other luminaries again? Or would this be the first of many?

She was glad she had accepted Jerry's very insistent invitation to spend Christmas with him. She had been reluctant at first. But maybe, like the gorgeous night sky, things would become clear to her. So they took sleigh rides and played card games in front of the roaring fire. She and Miranda played war against him in the snow. She was having a very relaxing time, and trying not to notice that the congressman seemed to be spending a lot of time in his office.

So she brushed her hair until it reflected light. She wore a borrowed dress of Christmas cranberry and the little silver slippers Miranda had given her. Jerry's simple pearl necklace was her only jewelry.

Miranda went down the staircase first because she couldn't wait to see her father's reaction. She was gowned in ivory silk. She felt very grown up and was beaming at her father, who waited at the bottom of the stairs for them. She had told him to wait there so that she and Miss Alcott could make a dramatic descent.

"Jerry's bringin' the wagon around," he said gruffly as he looked Miranda over. He persisted in referring to the county's finest carriage as a hay wagon.

"So?" Miranda twirled in front of him.

He gazed at her critically. "Enough jewels for a jewelry store!"

"Daddy! They're everything you've given me."

"Don't see how you'll dance weighted down like that."

"Daddy!"

He took her hand and looked at her tenderly.

"Your dress is perfect, darlin'. You've never looked lovelier."

"All right, Miss Alcott, he's through with me. Come on down!"

It wasn't the most sophisticated way to be announced. But Meg came to the top of the stairs and slowly descended. The slower the better; it had more effect that way. Where was Jerry? She didn't want to watch the congressman's reaction, to boldly read his face. That would be too obvious. Yet it was difficult not to stare at him as she knew he must be staring at her.

"Well, Daddy, what do you think?" Miranda prodded.

But Sam Bass was saved from answering. Jerry burst through the front door. "We're ready. Golly it's cold out there—" He stopped when he saw Meg. She was smiling at him. "Well, you'll heat things up for sure!"

He hurried up to her and pulled the cape around her. He kissed her quickly and murmured in her ear. "One for the road. Ready, Pa?"

The congressman's face was a mask. Meg was disappointed. He had given her no more than a glance. She could have been wearing mucky overalls for the attention he had given her. He took Miranda's arm possessively.

"Yep."

There was no question she was the prettiest woman there. To Jerry's view, every other female looked dowdy in comparison. She had been introduced to the entire room of people, and promptly forgot most of their names. She'd struggled to understand everything that was said in their thick Texas accents, still heavy with German.

Jerry looked like he was going to bust.

"This is the limit, Meg! I've got the flashiest girl on my arm. Everyone is lookin' like—"

"Like you brought the prize calf?" Meg finished for him with a smile.

"Meg! You're turning Texan!" he beamed.

They danced throughout the evening. Jerry wasn't eager to turn her loose to any of the other young men in the room who could not conceal their open admiration of his date. Nor was Meg interested in leaving Jerry's arms. He was a remarkably good dancer considering he spent far more time outdoors than indoors. He had a natural grace, Meg decided— like his father.

The only cloud in an otherwise perfect evening to Meg was the congressman's conspicuous lack of attention. He had said no word to her all evening other than in making introductions. Meg did not know what to think of it. Had she offended him in some way? She was intoxicated by the gaiety of the evening, and she felt like being frivolous.

Jerry led her to stand by his father, who stood on the perimeter of the dance floor while he went for drinks for them.

"Watch her for me, will ya, Pa? Everyone is trying to pull her out on the floor."

Bass's tone was surprisingly testy. "Does that include me?"

Jerry was in too jovial a mood to be moved by his father's sourness. He simply squeezed Meg's hand, shrugged, and hurried through the crowd to the refreshment table.

Meg could feel Bass standing stiffly by her side. She was aware that he was trying to be unaware of her. It intrigued her feminine vanity. Tomorrow she would be sensible.

One minute, then two. Jerry would be back soon.

"You look very elegant in your tux this evening, Congressman," she spoke lightly.

He continued to stare straight ahead a full minute, as if he had not heard her. Then he turned, and his eyes did not travel. They were riveted on hers.

"And you, Miss Alcott, are a feast for the eyes."

She felt flustered by his unexpected intensity.

"I ... that's a compliment I'll always treasure."

He gave her the first smile of the evening then.

"I reckon I could come up with a few dozen more," he replied slowly.

Meg blushed and laughed—and looked for Jerry.

Jerry was parting the crowd with the energy of his conversations. A cup in each hand, he parried them effortlessly.

"Howdy ... howdy."

"Yes, sir, I agree, she's mighty pretty."

"I know I'm lucky ... So how's that new bull of yours?"

"Yeah, we need rain."

"From Illinois. I know, you'd think that pretty she'd have to be from Texas!"

"Miranda looks great, doesn't she!"

"I know, can you imagine havin' her for a teacher! How could you concentrate?"

Then he spotted them, 20 yards away. Meg and his father, facing each other. People crowding all around them, yet fastened on each other's faces as if they were in the room alone. He stopped in his tracks. He took a question at his side. He thought how funny it was you could talk on one subject while your mind raced away on another.

His father was looking at Meg. He hadn't seen his father ever look at a woman that way. With a jolt he recognized Bass had looked at Meg that way the first night he had brought her to Nashville. Only then, he had been too excited to give it consideration.

He didn't feel rage or jealousy or frustration. He didn't feel threatened. He knew Meg wasn't really his yet to lose.

"Well, you kept her corralled for me, thanks. Here's your drink, Meg."

"Jerry, if I care to leave the corral, will you object?" Meg asked playfully.

"Sweetheart, you can jump the fence if you like. Just come back at feedin' time."

"Oh, Jerry," she laughed as she punched him on the shoulder.

"Want to take her for a few turns, Pa?" Jerry peered down into his cup. "I give you permission."

The son and the father locked eyes for a fraction of a second. Bass's humor returned. "No, thanks, you do the dancin'. Big cattlemen like me don't dance. We just watch."

They moved away, and Bass did watch them. He would have liked to have watched them without interruption. But he knew it wasn't likely. All of 30 seconds elapsed before a friend stepped beside him.

"Thinkin' about the calf crop, Sam? Heh, heh. They do make an awfully handsome set, don't they? Have they set a date yet?"

"They aren't even engaged yet, Cole," Bass replied frostily.

The rancher moved away from the congressman's icy tone only to be replaced by another cattle cronie.

He stood beside the older Bass as they watched the younger one.

"She sure makes you wish you were young again, don't she?" the cronie asked as he jabbed Sam in the ribs.

Suddenly Sam Bass was wishing he had stayed home.

Meg could not be disappointed with the night. It was well after midnight before she dropped onto her bed. She was exhausted with the fun she'd had. Jerry had been wonderful. But it was not his words that lingered in her mind there in the darkness.

You are a feast for the eyes . . .

Peppercreek

Sara Alcott sat at her kitchen table with her daughter's recent letters spread out in front of her. A pale, wintry light streamed through the window behind her, a bare branch scratched the panes. Other than that there were no other sounds; the big house was quiet. She was glad Ethan had gone to town and Daniel was away at school. This time alone gave her opportunity to do something she had been wanting to do for a few weeks. But she didn't want to do it when her husband was around. He would tease her and say she was silly.

She did feel a bit like . . . oh, what was that fictional English sleuth's name who had become so popular? . . . Sherlock Holmes! Yes, a real Sherlock Holmes she was being! But Sara Alcott knew there was something in Meg's letters that nagged at her, planted vague questions and concerns in her mind. Now she must reread them and find a clue.

First, there were four neatly typed, thoroughly descriptive letters from her first months in Galveston. Newsy, detailed letters. Ethan was satisfied and pleased, but Sara wasn't so sure. She couldn't help but wonder. Meg's cheerfulness had almost an artificial taste to it. She said nothing to her husband; he would either scoff and tell her it was her motherly prerogative to worry over her children, or he would have become alarmed and ready to hop the next train south. So she waited. Each letter that came to Peppercreek she read out loud to the family, then privately to herself.

The fifth letter said things were much better. Sara had a triumphant look in her eye as Daniel read the letter over the dinner table. Things were better, much better, Meg had inadvertently written, fully implying things had not been good at all before. It was obvious, and she waited patiently for her men to scent out the truth. But Daniel had merely asked for more chicken please, and Ethan had said he was glad Meg liked to write long letters because the phone rates were ridiculous.

Sara Alcott pardoned them for their masculine dullness and continued her vigilance on Meg's letters. Then, the one had arrived saying she had met the congressman's son, Jerry. There were several paragraphs on him and what he was like, where they had gone together. Sara was pleased. He sounded like a nice boy. Then she had frowned. If Meg fell in love and married a Texan, wouldn't that mean she would have to live in... Texas! She was suddenly not so certain about this move to Galveston.

There were three more letters. Weather, progress with the girls. Less on Jerry. She had gone to his ranch. It was called Nashville. She had finally met the man who had secured her position at Bishop's Villa. Meg wrote a paragraph or two on the bigness of the ranch. Made the prairies of Illinois look miniature in comparison. Ethan had snorted at that and wondered if this move to Galveston was such a good thing after all.

Sara had paused on one paragraph in particular.

"Mr. Bass is nothing like I expected... He's very kind, attentive, and has a great sense of humor like Jerry."

After a few more lines like that, Meg had abruptly changed the topic. Still, there were more lines about the father than the son, detective Alcott discovered. She recognized an indefinable tone that signaled something was not quite right in these newfound relationships. Meg had met a wonderul young man, yet she didn't sound completely happy. That thread ran through the last few letters.

Sara folded the papers carefully. She would not say a word to Ethan— not yet. She closed her eyes and thought of Meg so far away. So lovely, this daughter she cherished. But the mother knew deep in her spirit, for reasons she couldn't put into words, the daughter was needing prayer.

Ethan came home 30 minutes later and found his wife still at the kitchen table—a smile on her lips, and at peace.

Jerry had been yawning since dinner. He could barely keep a conversation going. That meant Jerry was really tired.

"Son, you're about to fall into your soup. Why don't you hit the sack?" Bass asked.

"Aw, I'm fine." He yawned uncontrollably.

"Jerry, if you think you have to stay up for me, please don't. I'm just going to curl up in a corner and work on lesson plans," Meg said.

Miranda joined in. "You do need to go to bed, Jerry. You look awful."

Jerry frowned. "I think there's a conspiracy here."

After dinner he took to the couch and tried to stay awake. He yawned gapingly. "Say, Pa, why don't ya tell us one of your war stories? Like when you were at Shiloh with Meg's pa."

Bass had always enjoyed telling his kids about those days he had worn the blue and fought the gray. It made pretty good stuff for nighttime stories, especially when he spiced them up. They made him look like a hero, and they loved him even more for that. Bass didn't mind taking a few liberties with the truth. He figured that was one of the fringe benefits of going to war—like going fishing, you got to broaden and beautify. Like an artist.

But tonight he scowled at his son when he made the request.

"You've heard that story a thousand times, Jerry. And Meg's probably heard it from Ethan too."

His voice was rough enough to broach no argument. Jerry rolled his eyes at Meg and forgot about it. But Miranda, who had peeped around her book when she heard her father's gruff tone, guessed exactly what the problem was. She cast Miss Alcott a swift glance to read in her face if she had guessed also. Miss Alcott's face revealed nothing. But Miranda Bass had guessed correctly. Her father did not want to talk of the war years when Miss Alcott was around—it advertised his own age.

In a matter of minutes Jerry was stretched out and snoring. Sam regarded his only son with affection.

"I'll have to drag him upstairs. He always could fall asleep anytime, anywhere, at the drop of a Stetson."

Meg found her cozy corner across the room. She worked over her plans and perused the books she had brought. Miranda was curled in another chair writing a letter. Her father had pulled his chair up to the fire and propped up his socked feet on the fender. His head was leaning against his hand, eyes riveted on the flames. An hour passed, then another, while the fire crackled and Jerry snored.

Very homelike, Meg thought. Sam must have thought the same thing, for he turned suddenly and caught her staring. She lowered her eyes quickly and hoped Miranda had not seen.

But Miranda had seen. She hopped up.

"I'm off to bed. Good night, Daddy." She kissed the top of his head. "Good night, Miss Alcott."

"Good night, Miranda."

She paused. "Did you make the assignments terribly difficult?"

Meg smiled. "Terribly, terribly difficult."

"Well, maybe when you get tired of trying to educate the minds of young women..." the girl teased.

"Yes, Miranda?"

"You'll settle down and get married. Now doesn't that sound like a better challenge than giving young girls terribly, terribly difficult assignments?"

"A challenge, I'm sure," Meg laughed.

Miranda took a crumpled paper and tossed it at Jerry's nose. It bounced off without a stir from the young man. He needed to wake up. She had seen the look that had passed between her father and her teacher. She had little romantic experience herself, but that look was filled with significance! Miranda was easygoing and flexible, like her older brother. She would like Miss Alcott in the family no matter whom she went to.

"How 'bout some hot chocolate?" Sam asked Meg as he stood before her chair.

"That sounds good."

He snatched up her hand before she could protest and led her from the room, through the dimly lit halls, to the kitchen. Yes, now Sam Bass was moving with typical authority.

He fixed the drinks wordlessly in the subdued light of the kitchen. Meg watched him. Sloppy, slinging, slamming. The cook would not find her domain as tidy as she had left it.

"You make me think of something my mother always says," she said to break the silence.

He kept stirring and didn't turn. "Oh?"

"She says she'd rather have a bull in her kitchen than a man."

He brought her cup but did not lead her back to the library. They stayed there in the warm kitchen, standing a few feet apart, drinking their chocolate.

"This is very good, thank you...Congressman," she said lightly.

But he didn't return her lightness. Even in the dimness she could see he was frowning. He set his cup down. He took hers from her, though she had not finished. He stood very close, and Meg thought she was going to be dizzy.

"Are you going to marry my son," he asked bluntly. That was Sam Bass's way. Direct.

But she was not prepared for this directness, this personal question. "I...don't know. He hasn't asked me."

She felt very nervous.

"He will."

Meg could not take the power of his eyes. She looked down at her skirt, and down at his socks that needed mending.

"You could become the heiress of Nashville."

She was still silent. Her mind was racing.

"Will you take my son?" he asked again.

Her nerves snapped. "I said I don't know. I don't know. But I'm not...I'm not scheming for this ranch if that's what you think! I don't care about that."

He shrugged and finally smiled then. "Okay, okay. I didn't think you were. But I wouldn't mind if you were either."

Silence. She stepped back away from him.

His voice was softer. "I want very much to kiss you, Miss Alcott."

She looked up at him. "I...know you do."

She dare not speak her thoughts. She wanted very much for him to kiss her.

"I won't touch you if you tell me not to. I won't touch you if you tell me you belong to my son."

She thought fleetingly of Jerry asleep down the hall. She did not say a word.

He stepped close to her then, lifted her chin with his finger. He wanted to look at her as long as he liked. Make up for the night before. His finger traced the contours of her lips, and she closed her eyes. "I just want to see how soft they are," he whispered huskily.

He was going to kiss her, he really was. But something in her face stopped him. "You...you don't have the strength to tell me no, do you, Meg?" His voice was so kind, she could feel tears welling up in her eyes.

She shook her head.

"A Tennessee gentleman never forces a lady," he said with a sad smile. "I just can't bring myself to kiss you, Meg, if you're not going to let me have all of you... If you won't marry me."

She knew then what her spirit had been trying to whisper to her the night before. The thing that had awakened her in the middle of the night, the thing that had made her feel agitated and nervous all day. She wasn't in love with Jerry Bass. She wasn't truly in love with his father. A prayer had been answered, and she felt nothing but pain from it.

"No, Sam...I'm so sorry."
She turned and left the kitchen.

Meg dreaded the morning. She was leaving for Galveston, and she must thank Sam Bass for his hospitality. She must say goodbye. Jerry was stowing her luggage in the carriage.

"Jerry, I can't find your father. He's not in his office. I wanted to say goodbye."

"He's gone."

"Gone?"

"Left for Austin this morning. Told me to tell you goodbye."

"Oh." Jerry did not notice the flatness in Meg's voice. She knew the father wasn't like the son. A night could not heal disappointment. He had left early so he would not have to face her again.

Jerry came and took her hands. "Don't worry. You can thank him next time."

But Meg Alcott knew there wouldn't be a next time.

Peppercreek, 1892

◆ ◆ ◆ ◆ ◆ ◆

*E*than's face wore the look of a man weighed down by bad news, the wrenching look of a father who had lost a child. He had the telegram safely tucked away in his shirt pocket, yet he seemed to feel it searing through to his skin. He was already an hour late. Sara would be concerned. He dare not linger on the road much longer. It wouldn't help to pull the paper out and read the words again. Nothing would help right now. His throat felt constricted. There was a dullness in his limbs, a shortness of breath. The old pain in the stump of his arm began its predictable hammering, and he smiled bitterly. It had been gone over 30 years, and it still caused him pain.

Sara . . . Sara, still so beautiful to him. In his mind, still his bride. How could he possibly tell her? How could he say the words? He could burn the telegram . . . delay the pain . . . and be eaten up inside with the weight of it.

The horse turned mechanically at the lane that would take them home. He suddenly felt so old and feeble. Funny how bad news could drain you. He glanced up and saw there was another buggy in the yard. He squinted in the dimness. His son Matt was there. Matt and his wife, Millie. A birthday celebration for Matt. He had forgotten all about it. He groaned out loud as he brought the buggy to a stop.

Sara was out the door instantly. He felt dizzy as he climbed down.

"I was about to send the boys out looking for you. Did you forget the little party?"

She couldn't see his face clearly.

"Yes, I forgot."

Her arms went around him, pulling him close.

"We don't have to go in yet. I missed you," she said tenderly.

He forced a calmness in his voice. "I've only been gone a few hours."

"Too long." She was nibbling his ear, caressing his neck, kissing him.

"You're behaving . . . for a married woman of . . ."

She laughed and kissed him hard so he wouldn't say her age. After all these years, he did love to hear her infectious laugh. He tightened his arm around her.

Then 18-year-old Daniel was framed in the rectangle of light from the doorway. "Ma? Pa?"

They did not turn around.

"Oh." Daniel turned back to the room. They could hear his young voice clearly. "They're out there, just kissin'. Guess they'll be in after a little while." Laughter and piano playing greeted this.

Ethan spoke into her hair. "Sara?"

"Hmm?"

"Sara, I love you so much. Oh, how I love you!"

Now she could hear desperation in his voice. She was still in his embrace, the passion suddenly quenched as she waited.

"Sara, we trust, and we believe. We...hope. We trust!"

"Ethan, you're trembling. What is it?" She pulled away.

He glanced up at the lighted house, listened to the voices of his sons and daughter-in-law. He could take her in there, tell her with the others. But that would be cowardly. She deserved to have darkness cover her emotions for a time.

"Is it...Andy or Meg?" she asked quietly.

He pulled her to the porch, to the square of light, and took out the telegram. He read it, though the words were already imprinted in his mind.

"It's from Hawthorne Shipping in London."

He watched her face. Her hand went to her mouth.

"Andy..." she whispered.

"Ivanhoe's Dream missing. Last sighted off Cape Horn. Severe storms. No known survivors. More information as available. Deepest regrets. Hawthorne Shipping."

Galveston

The telephone line sputtered and crackled, an infant invention with growing pains.

"Meg? Are you still there?"

"Yes, Papa."

The flatness of her voice frightened him.

"Meg, if there had been any other way to be with you, we would have come. We couldn't write it."

"No, Papa, I know. It's all right."

"I love you, Meg."

"I love you, Papa. Tell Mama. Tell Dan and Matt."

Later, word spread to the headmistress.

"You have my sympathies, Miss Alcott," she offered in perfunctory tones.

Meg wanted to scream.

Alone in her apartment, Meg looked around as if she were seeing it for the first time. She felt detached, as though she were watching herself from some far and distant view, moving woodenly, scarcely breathing. *I feel as though someone has slapped me hard across the face,* she thought to herself. She was dry-eyed as she curled herself into a ball in the corner of her room, where she stayed cramped for hours as though she could hide from the terrible truth forever.

When the sun came up in a fiery orange ball over the Gulf, she got up. She stood at her terrace, stiff and dull-headed, weak with hunger and exhaustion. Another glorious sunrise. She could see that the same boats that had been at harbor the morning before were still there. The ice cart was rumbling down below her window like it did every morning. The bakery at the corner was rolling out its red-striped awning. The squeal of hot water pipes from another apartment and the drifting smell of coffee assaulted her.

She was stunned. A new morning, another day, and the world was still going on with its routine, predictable business. Yet a part of her world had vanished during the night. Andy was gone.

Tanglewood

It was a pale winter afternoon, winter in name only. Spring was the new tenant, soon to take up residence. Already tiny buds were erupting on bare branches. The breezes were softer, warmer, mellower.

Amy sat reading to her husband from the newspapers. The *Greenville Gazetteer* had been digested and now the *New Orleans Register,* with its global gossip, was being perused. Cash lay propped against his pillows, weak but alert. He was listening with divided attention. He heard her voice but was concentrating more on the lines, the curves, the shadows of her young face. Had he captured with his brush the beauty of his young wife? *Magnolia Remembrance* was finished and draped in the studio downstairs. He had not shown it to anyone. There would be time enough for that...

Amy looked up from the paper and smiled. "So, where do you think she is today, Cash?"

"Ah, let's see. Kibombo perhaps?"

"Kibombo! Where is that?"

He shrugged. "Somewhere in Africa, I think." They laughed together. "I read about it as a boy and liked the sound of it. So exotic, you know. Now, where *is* the intrepid young woman with the alligator bag?"

Miss Nellie Bly, reporter for New York's *World* newspaper, had captured the imagination of thousands around the world with her latest journalistic stunt and sent the circulation of Joseph Pulitzer's newspaper soaring. Her challenge was simple: She was attempting to break the record of circling the globe in less than 80 days set by Jules Verne's fictional character, Phineas Fogg. Newspapers across the country daily served their readers the latest dramatic account of the young woman's trip.

"Actually, she's in Hong Kong. Imagine…" her voice drifted off.

Cash looked steadily at her a moment. "Would you like to travel like that, my dear?"

Amy felt Cash needed a good tease. "With just one small grip for my luggage? No thanks!"

He joined her laughter. "I think that must be what fascinates women most about this round-the-world trip. Miss Bly is traveling with little more than a hairbrush!"

Then his smile faded. "I never intended for you to be a nurse to me, Amy, when I asked you to marry me."

Her throat tightened. "I know that. Do you think I mind? Cash, I'd rather be here right now than anywhere else in the whole world!"

His thin face brightened. "You are very beautiful, Amy Cash."

She blushed in spite of herself and looked down at her lap, twisting the diamond and gold ring around her slender finger. Cash had become even more tender lately, tender with his words, his eyes. It was unsettling to her somehow. Did it bring a new dimension to their relationship? Amy was uncertain.

She looked at him, their eyes probing into each other's with deliberate honesty. In an instant, Amy understood. Cash was telling her how much he treasured her, because he was going away. She need not feel threatened or guilty.

She reached out and took his hand, laying it against her cheek. She did love this man who had taken her as his wife. She loved him dearly as the older brother he had always been to her. They both knew this. But wasn't it forgivable if Cash grew wistful, if he dreamt of something deeper?

He reached up and stroked her hair. His voice was very faint.

"I was born too soon, or you were born too late, but God knows I have loved you."

Chisolm Crossing

Willet Keller had spent a sleepless night. In the morning, he spoke harshly to his wife and children. He didn't feel like working. He didn't feel like hunting or fishing. He definitely didn't feel like staying home where his wife's worried eyes followed him and stirred up more anger and a little guilt. So he rode off on the mule without an explanation to Mrs. Keller, who stood watching at the cabin door. She leaned her head against the doorframe. What was happening to Will? He had seemed

reasonably happy and content until this Klan business had started. It
was like an infection in the farmer.

Keller rode without plan or purpose, letting the mule settle in to a
comfortable lope while he fretted over the concern that weighed so
heavy in his mind. The mule followed a muddy track that curved,
sloped, and climbed three miles to the middle of Chisolm Crossing.

The farmer slid off the animal and stepped inside the mercantile.
Chester Chisolm was laughing at the far side of the room, slapping his
sides and wheezing. In his present sour mood, Keller was irritated by
the proprietor's joviality. He ambled across the store. Mrs. Chisolm was
rolling out fabric for one of his neighbors. She looked up and gave him a
curt nod. All you could expect from a woman who had ice water in her
veins instead of blood, Keller mused.

Chisolm was filling a box with groceries for the Jeffersons: mother,
son, new baby, proud and beaming father. They were all ignoring Willet
Keller entirely. And he did not feel like being ignored.

"You should hear him scream, Mr. Ches, louder than me!" the young
Jefferson was saying happily.

"Micah, I've told you, that is Gideon's cry. Not screaming," Viney
corrected with a smile.

"Why, Mr. Cash told me he done heard little Gideon night before last
all the way to Tanglewood. Our son's a little trumpet, Viney. Might as
well admit it," Seth added.

"Oh, Seth . . ."

Keller was leaning against the counter sneering.

"That your new partner, Seth? Mr. Pat Cash?"

They all turned, surprised at the sudden tenor of hostility in the
store. Seth nodded at Keller and turned back to his family.

"Gettin' high and mighty up at the estate, aren't you, Seth?" Keller
asked again.

Seth remained unmoving, as if he had not heard the taunt.

"That's about all on our list, Mr. Ches," Viney said softly.

"How 'bout a few bananas, Daddy?" Micah asked, hopping from one
foot to the other.

"I hear monkeys do like bananas," Keller said in a low, menacing
tone.

Low, but loud enough for everyone in the store to hear.

Seth Jefferson suddenly became very interested in the details of
Chisolm Mercantile. There were no crates to stack, no firewood to
cut . . .

Mrs. Chisolm looked up from her work, more concerned about her
little husband's slow, but definite fuse. Will Keller was in a testy mood,
acting as if he'd already been at a bottle this morning.

"Mr. Chisolm will be with you directly, Will. Keep your shirt on," she
called sternly.

He did not bother to turn to her. He called over his shoulder.

"I come in here to buy, not wait," Keller barked.

Chisolm laid a hand on Seth's arm, then stepped closer to Keller.

"I'm waitin' on the Jeffersons right now, Will. Almost finished. You'll be next." There was no mirth in the storekeeper's eyes.

"I came for tobacco," Keller reasserted with belligerence.

"And tobacco you'll get, when I'm finished with this trade."

Mrs. Chisolm had come to stand beside her husband. Willet Keller was being ridiculous.

"Now, Will," she soothed.

Keller was staring hard at Seth's back.

"Then you're servin' a nigger over me," he said acidly.

Seth spoke up quietly. "It's all right, Mr. Ches, we're in no hurry."

"I'm servin' the Jeffersons, Willet Keller, and if you can't wait, you can go to Greenville for your tobacco."

Mrs. Chisolm's eyebrows shot up. She had never heard her little man so firm before.

Keller smiled thinly. "Such ways could be bad for your business, Chester."

"I think there's another bad business going on around here," Chester replied pointedly.

Keller turned and left. He hopped up on the tired mule and spurred it home. He could work now. He smiled—his problem had just been solved.

He needed something with flair to prove his convictions to the cause. The recruiter from Maycomb had said so. The farmer must show his loyalty to the Klan with some specific act, something more than just words or an oath. A test, the recruiter had smiled benignly. Going into Chisolm's Mercantile had provided Willet Keller with the answer.

That night he rode to Tanglewood just after midnight. He was smart enough to know he should do a little reconnoitering before the actual deed. Was there any alarm, man or animal, on the place? Anything between him and his goal? Nothing. He rode home well pleased and fell instantly to sleep.

The following night he took another midnight ride. He tethered the mule and crept forward stealthily under a cover of moonless night. The great mansion was robed in darkness. Nothing stirred. He would pass the test with the dramatic flourish he had been looking for. It was pitifully easy.

He found neatly stacked piles of lumber. Little mounds of sawdust and wood shavings. Evidence of a prosperous, orderly operation. A stone foundation, a log structure recently remodeled. It would go up in flames before he was off of the Tanglewood property.

An English butler who rarely lifted anything heavier than a duster or tea tray, one young stable hand, one aging gardener, one middle-aged cook, a young woman, and a man in a wheelchair proved impotent against a building in flames. They could only watch.

When Patrick Cash heard Seth's cheerful whistle in the distance, his head sunk lower onto his chest, and he moaned aloud. Amy clutched his hand tighter. It felt so cold.

"Cash, I can stay out here for him. You shouldn't be out. You haven't slept. This is too hard…"

But even in his frailty he was determined. She could see that. He gave her a reassuring smile.

"I'm fine, my dear. Don't worry over me. Besides, you haven't slept either."

None of them had. They had stayed up even as the Tanglewood shop dwindled to a heap of blackened, smoldering embers—a skeleton in the raw light of morning. Mary had made tea. They had huddled in the kitchen, all six of them—exhausted, vacant-eyed, knit together by the shock that Tanglewood had been ravaged. It was clearly an act of human design, of hatred against something—or someone—on the estate.

Then the sun came up. The cook made breakfast without enthusiasm. Fenwick, the gardener, and the stable boy slipped away silently to their duties.

Cash had been staring into his cup on the porch.

"Can you get me another sweater, my dear? I want… to be here to meet Seth when he comes."

Seth was feeling especially good. Little Gideon had not "blown his trumpet" much that night, so his sleep had been undisturbed. He rode to Tanglewood with his mind full of praise for the clear, crisp morning— and plans for the day. Eight picture frames would be waiting in various stages of completion. He was thinking about tools, and types of wood, and how he loved the smell of newly cut lumber. To have his own shop… Was this really a dream he was bound to wake up from?

He saw Miss Amy first and was struck by how pale she was. He was surprised she was out this early. Then he saw the metal chair. And Mr. Pat up too? And outside? Only then did he smell the smoke. It had tainted the air for miles, but he'd been so caught up in his thoughts he hadn't noticed. As he moved further onto the property, he saw the open space where their shop was supposed to be. He stopped. He felt like he had walked into a wall of rock.

How could a building disappear? His breathing became labored. He stumbled past them, not meeting their eyes, not saying a word. When Amy saw his stricken face, she started to cry again.

He stood as close as he dared with the heat still so real. It was gone. All gone. The work he and Mr. Andy had done...the special tools Mr. Pat had ordered for him...the eight frames...the quilt box he was to deliver that very afternoon...the mahogany, cherry, pine and oak... the little wooden boat he'd been making for Micah on his noon hour ...the plans...

He sank down to his knees, just staring.

Finally, after minutes that seemed like hours, he stood up and slowly turned. He felt very tired. The Cashes were still there. He saw them as if for the first time. Mr. Cash looking so feeble and sad, Miss Amy holding his hand and looking afraid. He walked slowly toward them.

Patrick Cash roused himself. His heart was beating erratically, and he was feeling faint from shock and fatigue. But his eyes were clear and his voice very firm. He looked up at the big black man who stood in front of him humbly. It made his heart hurt to look at such sadness. He spoke only two words. Just two.

"We'll rebuild."

Amy walked with Seth down the drive of Tanglewood. It was good to get away from the house for a time, to get away from the strong smell of smoke. It had invisibly entered the mansion like a grim presence. Seth was going back home, though it was only midmorning. There was nothing for him to do, no work. He could not yet begin to clear away the charred embers and debris.

Amy stopped walking. "Seth, Cash and I want you to be assured of our intentions. You'll come back in a few days, and we'll begin the plans for the new shop. You heard what Cash said. He wants to build right on the old foundation."

Seth looked down at his feet. "Miss Amy, I do appreciate your kind words, more'n I can say. You and Mr. Pat have done so much for me."

"Now, Seth..."

"I keep thinkin' 'bout Mr. Pat's cousin—how much work he put in on the shop. He was sure excited about it." Seth shook his head.

Amy nodded. But she could not allow Andy Alcott's face to invade or linger in her mind.

"Mr. Pat...I'm afraid for him, Miss Amy. He looks so weak. Even before this. Now..."

Amy gripped her hands behind her. "I know, Seth, I know."

She faltered, the strain of the night and morning finally breaking her. She covered her face, sobbing. She was so worried for her husband. She had sent for the doctor. Pat Cash had taken to his bed—they could not know he would never rise from it.

Seth patted her arm. "Maybe we should put off rebuilding the shop for a while, Miss Amy. It's too much of a strain for him."

"I know, Seth, but we must. It means so much to him. He would despise himself if he couldn't do this. He . . . oh, Seth, he's too weak even to paint."

Seth groaned. The master of Tanglewood had done so much for him.

"It's my fault," he said brokenly. "I brought this trouble here."

Amy wiped her tears. "No, Seth, you mustn't think that," she said firmly.

"It's true, Miss Amy. I hate to bring it up now. But you and I, we got to have the truth between us."

"What are you saying, Seth?" Amy asked slowly.

"There's folks 'round here that don't like me being my own boss, partners with Mr. Pat. They're riled up about it."

Amy's heart thudded. The face of one man leered out in her mind. Would this evil forever be reaching out for her?

"What folks, Seth?"

He couldn't name names.

"Folks, Miss Amy, that just don't like me leavin' my old job and having such as I have here. That must be what happened. Them folks burned down our shop."

They were silent a moment as the grasp of hatred seemed to close around them.

"It doesn't change our plans. I know Cash has thought of these things even without knowing names. Seth, they'll have to burn down Tanglewood before they stop us!"

Brave and determined words—said with a bravery the mistress of Tanglewood did not feel.

Two weeks later the saws and hammers were ringing again at Tanglewood. It was music to Patrick Cash's ears as he listened from his first-floor bedroom. Amy sat beside the window and acted as his eyes.

"They have it framed . . . They're putting the roof on now . . . Seth says he'll have the doors fit this afternoon . . . Who would have thought Fenwick could swing a hammer like that!"

Cash smiled. It was good to see Amy excited, with the lines of worry and fatigue growing fainter. It was so good to lie there and just watch her, listen to the cadence of her voice. It was better than anything Dr. Browning could give him. It was like having a living painting from the brush of a master in front of you every day, looking at his young wife. And he knew he would not have much longer to look.

"Even Barrett looks like he's accustomed to using a hammer and not a scalpel!" Amy continued.

Cash nodded. "I'm most grateful to him. Between his practice and his own place, he's a fine man to do this."

A new building was rising out of the ashes. This time it was being built with more than just four hands. Along with Barrett, a handful of Seth's neighbors had come to Tanglewood, their tools slung over their shoulders and ready to work. But the real surprise had come the very morning the new frame was being raised. Amy still had trouble believing it—and Cash had smiled very broadly.

A beautiful carriage had pulled up on the circular drive in front of the mansion. A carriage as fine as any Cash owned, with horses just as blooded and sleek. Fenwick had greeted the owners with impeccable dignity and shown them into the library. Amy had been very nervous.

A father, mother, and two sons stood waiting for her. The father quickly extended a hand and a friendly smile.

"Mrs. Cash, I'm Walter Hudson. This is my wife, Irene, and our sons, Jeff and Jim."

"I'm pleased to meet you," Amy said cautiously.

"We're your neighbors about ten miles south," Mrs. Hudson explained.

"You own Three Oaks?" Amy was incredulous.

The ruddy-faced planter beamed. "Yes, ma'am. We heard about your fire, and we came to help."

Amy could only stare blankly.

"The boys and I are fair hands at carpentry. Put up a foal barn last spring that wasn't too bad. Just tell us what to do."

Amy looked from the kind face of the wife to the two smiling sons and back to the man.

"We can talk to your foreman and see if we need our own tools," Mr. Hudson expanded.

"My foreman is Seth Jefferson," Amy allowed carefully.

"Fine."

"He's black."

She saw the boys exchange smiles. Mrs. Hudson smiled.

"We hear he's a fine carpenter. We're eager to work with him," Hudson returned, smiling with the rest of the family.

Finally, Amy smiled. "Can I take you to meet my husband first?"

The shop was almost finished. All the materials and tools had been replaced. The new orders had been taken. Soon, Seth Jefferson would be planing and sawing and hammering again.

Cash had declared a barbecue must be held in the old style of the famous Tanglewood lawn parties.

He also hired a man he could trust to be Tanglewood's new grounds-keeper. It would be his duty to oversee the work around the estate. And to act as eyes in the night.

He surprised Amy with four Irish setter pups.

"But *four,* Cash!"

"Four pups with good strong voices." He smiled. "We'll hope they'll let us sleep at night, while they *don't,"* he said pointedly.

Watchdogs. Cash was worried about midnight visitors. Amy pressed his hand. "You are very thoughtful, Cash."

He had closed his eyes. Even talking exhausted him lately.

"I don't want any more fires at Tanglewood. I want this shop to stand...a monument, perhaps, that right prevails...that ugliness out there can't come to places like...Tanglewood...and Three Oaks, even if it surrounds us."

Amy fervently hoped this monument would stand as a tribute to a man who wanted only peace.

Amy was arranging mums in a vase when Fenwick approached. She could immediately detect something different in his usual cool manner.

He was hesitating.

"Ah, Mrs. Cash..." He looked at the ground. With the fire, with Mr. Cash confined to his bed, he did hate to bring the young woman more bad news.

She quickly laid down her scissors.

"Did Dr. Browning send for me? Is he still with my husband?"

"The doctor is still with Mr. Cash. He did not send for you."

"Fenwick, is something wrong?"

"Might I ask you a question, Mrs. Cash?"

"Of course."

"Do you recall the name of the vessel that Mr. Cash's young cousin sailed on?"

Amy tensed. "Mr. Alcott's ship?"

"Yes, ma'am."

"It's *Ivanhoe's Dream.*"

Fenwick regarded her a moment in silence.

"Registered in London?" His voice was probing

Amy nodded slowly. "I believe he said so."

He extended the paper to Amy. "I read this. I was concerned for Mr. Cash, that if he knew about the young man, he'd..."

Amy took the paper stiffly. "Thank you, Fenwick."

She waited until the butler retreated. She read the passage to herself. It was written plainly in black and white—there had been no survivors.

Amy stood at her bedroom window the next morning as a sliver of luminescent moon hung in a soft, azure sky. The sun was dimpling the eastern horizon, diffused in a hundred shades of gold, pearl, and scarlet. It would be a fine spring day. She pushed aside the lace curtains to see her quiet world a little better and hope that the peacefulness of it could somehow infect her.

She had gotten out of bed to forcibly push the reality—and pleasure—of her dreams away. To have lain there another moment would have kept the dream suspended in her desires. Better to put her feet on the floor, to see and touch the familiarity of her room and hug the flame of guilt that taunted her.

Andy had taken her in his arms and placed a kiss like a brand of hot flame on the nape of her neck. Why had she dreamed such a thing after spending a sleepless night chased by the stark and merciless banner, "Sinking—All Feared Lost"? Tears filled her eyes.

She glanced toward the door that led to Cash's room. He would be awake soon. He must not see that she had been crying. Fenwick had been right. It was better that the master of Tanglewood not know the tragic news. In a way, she wished that she had not known. No matter how indefinable her relationship with Andy Alcott had been, and how certain and definable it was with Cash, the young woman knew she was losing both of the men she loved.

London, England

These streets look straight from the pages of Oliver Twist or David Copperfield, Andy Alcott thought happily. And happy he was to be on English-speaking soil again. He only wished Treadle was with him. He smiled wryly to himself—if the old captain had been with him, he'd have been sending scathing curses down on the Englishmen he passed. Andy shook his head. Treadle and his merciless bigotry. Then his smiled deepened. Perhaps Treadle's newfound faith had wiped away his complaints against the people.

The London streets, with all their Victorian finery and sophistication, remained in some boroughs, alleys, and corners thoroughly Dickensish. Smoke belching from factory chimneys and gray fog rising from the Thames in blanket thickness were an eternal part of London, no matter what the century. Andy rode the trolley, nearly leaning out the windows, eager to see the crown city of the British Isles.

He had quickly dispatched a flurry of telegrams home to Pepper-creek, knowing what his family must have learned from the newspapers. One telegram would not do. In his eagerness and boyishness, he had dispatched three, all to confirm and reconfirm that he had not gone down on *Ivanhoe's Dream.* One had also been sent to Galveston.

Now he threaded his way to Havasham Court to fulfill Treadle's last cryptic request before he eagerly booked passage home.

He was shown into the spacious offices of Gladbury and Stirwell, a firm of lawyers. Gladbury was a thin, bespectacled barrister, and very professional.

"I was told by the late Captain Angus Treadle to come to Havasham Court, to see a Mr. Gladbury. He didn't explain why I was to come. He just insisted."

"Your name again?"

"Andy Alcott."

"Ah." Gladbury scanned a sheaf of papers before him. "The sinking of *Ivanhoe's Dream* has been verified. Lord Hawthorne's death certificate has been signed. The will has been read. No contests. All seems in order. I was Lord Hawthorne's attorney."

"Lord...Hawthorne?" Andy asked blankly.

"Of course." A thin smile flitted across the Englishman's face.

"I don't understand."

"Obviously. Your captain, Angus Treadle, and Lord Percy Angus Hawthorne are one and the same. Lord Hawthorne was an eccentric man. He lived a life quite uncommon to a man of title and substance. He—"

"Wait, wait," Andy said chuckling. "I think we have a mistake going here. I must be at the wrong Gladbury and...and Stirwell."

"There is no other Gladbury and Stirwell," the attorney said in comical arrogance.

"Well, we are talking about two different Angus Treadles then."

"There is, rather, was, only one Angus Treadle, alias Lord Percy Hawthorne," Gladbury returned with tired patience.

"Captain Treadle wasn't English! If you had known him, you'd know Treadle's being English was impossible...I mean laughable."

A rumor existed in legal circles that Charles Gladbury did not know how to laugh. "I did know him. I was his lawyer, for 30 years, as my father was before me."

"He wasn't wealthy!" Andy sputtered.

The lawyer peered across the desk at him with obvious amusement.

"Treadle was in his sixties. A big man, red hair," Andy said hurriedly.

"A thin scar across his chin? Received it while he was a young seaman on the *Cutty Sark?*"

Andy nodded mutely.

"Always professing to hate anything English, correct?"

"Yes...always."

"How many years did you serve him?"

"Nearly nine." Andy's voice was barely above a whisper.

"There, you see. He was a superb actor. He should have been on the stage and not the ocean. Lord Hawthorne carried out his charade for years, and only a handful knew it. Like myself. Don't feel bad that he had you duped as well."

Gladbury would not smile fully, but he could display a row of small, perfect teeth. "Lord Hawthorne owned a trio of ships. He preferred to live the life of a merchantman."

"A trio of ships?"

"I'm not at liberty to discuss the details of the estate, but there are three ships. The *Aunt Elizabeth,* the *Merry Widow,* and *Ivanhoe's Dream.* We know the fate of the *Ivanhoe. Elizabeth* is in dry dock, and that leaves the merchant vessel, the *Merry Widow.*" He leaned forward. "It has been left to you, Mr. Alcott, along with a small monetary gift."

"Left to me?" Andy was powerless to do anything but echo.

Were all Americans so slow? Gladbury shook his head mournfully. *How could they ever have beaten us?*

"The *Merry Widow* is here in London. You are the new owner. I should think Lord Hawthorne's last request is quite clear now."

"Quite."

"Shall we begin the paperwork, Captain Alcott?"

Two hours later Andy stood on the teeming docks of London. He had arrived the day before as a near-penniless survivor. He pushed his hat back and surveyed with wonder the proud masts of the clipper, *Merry Widow,* the legacy of the Englishman.

Tanglewood

Even the somber Fenwick did not look as disapproving as usual. His voice softened just a trace when he spoke to the mistress of Tanglewood. He made certain her meals were kept hot even when she neglected them. Once he had managed an awkward pat on her shoulder when he came upon her crying.

There was no mistaking it this time. Patrick Cash was dying. He would not see the fullness of another spring.

Barrett Browning came to the house each morning, soliciting a weak thrust at humor from his patient.

"You're coming around more these days...when there's nothing ...you can do...for me. Suppose I should feel...suspicious."

"I know I'm not earning my fee, Cash."

"I'm glad...you're not," Cash returned weakly.

Before Barrett had left the house one day, he took Amy aside.

"Amy, you've got to get some rest. Cash wouldn't want you wearing yourself out. There's nothing—" he stopped.

The young woman before him looked brittle with nerves and fatigue. Her gray eyes were flashing.

"Say it, Barrett! There's nothing I can do for him. Nothing I can do, when he's done so much for me."

The following evening they both sat beside Cash's bed. He had been incoherent most of the day. A distant crack of thunder had opened his eyes wide—he was 30 years old again and sweating another battle. They calmed and soothed him until he lay back.

"Amy?"

She took his hand. "I'm right here, Cash."

"Come...closer." His hand sought her hair. "Like...silk."

Barrett stepped back, feeling awkward to be witnessing this intimacy.

"Don't cry...Amy...don't cry for me..." His voice was a breathless whisper, his eyes closed.

"Oh, Cash. Do you know that I love you?"

A trembling smile. "Of course, I know...never a better wife..."

She was sobbing, wanting to be strong yet feeling so weak.

"I'm afraid, Cash. Afraid of not having you."

His fingers sought her face. "Don't be afraid, Amy. Please...be happy...live...and love again...love...again."

He turned. "Barrett, open the window. I...want to feel the storm. I want...to feel the wind..."

"Amy, I'm concerned about your being alone."

She wiped her tears. "Barrett, I'm not alone. Fenwick is here and the others. Seth will be here during the day."

"But tonight?"

"Tonight?" She glanced up at the oil painting over the mantel. "Tonight must be the first night of many nights alone." She gave him a smile. "I've got to start being a big girl sometime, Barrett."

The doctor admired her courage, and hurt for her in his own heart that was no stranger to loneliness.

"Anytime you need me, or need someone to talk to, or need help with decisions or anything..." he continued.

She looked up at him, seeing him as he was, a social outcast. Like her. She squeezed his hand. "Thank you, Barrett. I'll be all right."

Galveston

The delivery boy was pleased with the address on the telegram. Seventeen, Broadway Place. He could bicycle down the Strand and admire the swank shops and fancy cafes, then peddle up the hill to Bishop's Villa and all those girls behind the wrought-iron gates. Usually though, one of the sour-faced matrons took the messages. Still, he always hoped for a glimpse of the young ladies, cream of the Texas crop. Maybe his luck would be different this morning.

The headmistress was having a very difficult morning and was in a more menacing mood than usual. Classes were in session, her personal secretary was ill, and all the remaining staff was busy. She alone was left to deal with the good-natured young man who had finally come to fix the school's only phone. She had more pressing things to do—a little "conference" with one of the young ladies. *She's a born mischief maker,* the headmistress thought grimly. Heaven help her husband, if she ever landed one! She heard the muted chime of the front door to the school and hoped one of her staff would answer it.

Julia had been in high spirits all morning, and the music teacher could tolerate her no longer. She hoped the headmistress, with her severe looks and acid tone, could take some of the steam out of the young woman. When Julia heard the front bell as she passed through the hall, she was pleased and eager to open the thick, carved doors. It was like opening the door of freedom into this . . . convent!

"Good morning, Miss," the delivery boy beamed with obvious pleasure. She nodded with dignity.

"Have a telegram here, Miss," he said, producing the slim envelope. "You a student here?"

Julia took the envelope and scanned the address quickly. Miss Meg Alcott. Hmm. Who would be sending Miss Alcott a telegram?

"So, do you like it here, Miss?" he asked in attempt to draw her out.

She gave him a dazzling smile and spent the next 15 minutes in uninterrupted flirting. She tucked the telegram into her music composition book as she talked, fully intending to hand deliver it to Midwestern Meg. But it was completely forgotten when the headmistress swooped down on her. The telegram from London stayed unopened, undelivered, in the music book for two weeks, a message that could have brought such joy to her teacher had she known it. When Julia discovered the telegram, she was appropriately horrified, but too embarrassed to deliver it.

Tanglewood

The front door slammed open, impelled by a fury of slanting wind and rain. Amy, who was in the library, hurried forward as rain blew into the entryway. She stopped short. A figure had stepped into the threshold. It was a man.

The wind was wild and thrashing, heavy with rain, as Jeb French rode up to Tanglewood. The sky was ebony and churning, a spring tempest in the fullest sense. Jeb French had been in New Orleans on business and did not know Patrick Cash had died. The wind had tossed aside the black wreath from the front gate.

He sat in the shadows of the trees, watching the mansion, measuring it with his dark eyes. He hadn't any plan, any purpose. For once, the bourbon had blunted his typical caution.

Amy's heart thudded dully in her ears. Jeb swept off his hat in an exaggerated bow. The blowing, rain-slicked poncho made him look even more sinister.

"Evenin', little sis," he said finally, then laughed.

"Get out, Jeb! Get out!" Amy hurled at him with a vengeance that surprised them both. She clutched the stair railing for support, hoping her voice would carry to the servant wing where Fenwick was sleeping. Yet she also knew that with the late nights they had both been keeping of late, it was unlikely he would hear her.

"Not so quick, Miss Amy, not so quick," French continued blandly. "I was out ridin'. Thought I'd stop in and speak to your . . . *husband.*"

"What?"

"Sure. I want to see your old man. Already gone to bed without you?"

"Get out, Jeb, now!"

"Why, Amy! So unfriendly this evenin'. It's not like you. Cash may despise me, but at least he's courteous about it."

She waited. He would have his say and then leave. There was precious little she could do. She brushed past him into the dimly lit library, standing behind Cash's desk as a defense. *If only he doesn't see me shaking.* She knew that would be like the smell of blood to a man like Jeb French.

He followed her into the room. "I said, I want to speak to your husband!" he shouted at her.

Only then did Amy realize Jeb French had been drinking. Certainly this made him bolder, more foolish. Did it make him more dangerous as well?

"I'm telling you to get out." Her voice was calm now.

He leaned against a chair, his smile confident and brazen.

"Came here to tell your old and crippled man 'bout his wife. Tell him how cozy I seen her and that young cousin of his." He laughed and stepped nearer. "Tell him how cozy she was with me once."

The memory of a frightened nine-year-old girl came into Amy's mind suddenly and vividly. She could see Jeb's smile and feel his hands. Now these years later, Amy thought she was going to be sick. She flung open the desk drawer, finding the pistol she had expected to find. She grabbed it and aimed.

French's face paled just a fraction, and his laugh was forced and shaky. "Oh, little sis, what a way to act! Pullin' a gun on your—"

"Leave right now. I'll not tell you again."

"You won't? What will you do, Miss Amy? You don't look too steady to me."

"Steadier than you think."

How could this night be more horrible? With Cash gone from her barely 48 hours and a drunken madman threatening her, she laughed suddenly, hysterically. French's eyes grew wide.

"I'm going to shoot if you don't turn around this instant."

He stepped forward, confident, remembering the little girl he had bullied and abused so long ago. But Amy was not a little girl any longer. She pulled the trigger carefully.

Chapter 11

Galveston

◆◆ ◆◆ ◆◆

*M*eg could not wait for the privacy of her own apartment. Ever since her parents' phone call, she had felt like a tightly wound spring, just waiting to fly loose. Even at night she did not relax. Nights had been sleepless wastes of time. The darkness was like a gigantic window from which she watched all her horrible thoughts played out in vivid details: Andy smiling on the deck of the *Ivanhoe.* Andy's face etched in fear as he realized his ship was going down and he was going to drown. Andy asleep in his bunk, his face relaxed as the cold ocean waters prepared to swallow him. Every night produced the same graphic nightmares. Every night she wept and wished she could have told him one last time how much she loved him.

The girls of Bishop's Villa knew another broken romance had not turned their favorite teacher so pale and quiet, so rare to smile. They knew the truth. They could see that she had gotten thinner since she had first come. She gave assignments mechanically and without enthusiasm. Her face was emotionless, forbidding them to linger after class for a friendly chat. Midwestern Meg had gone and left only a shell.

She laid her head down on her desk and cried. It did not matter if the headmistress or one of her students swept in. Just now, nothing mattered. Nothing mattered because she was miserably unhappy here in Galveston, Texas, and miserably lonely. And Andy was gone.

Of course she had thought of Jerry Bass in her grief. Even Jerry in his own lighthearted way could have comforted her. She could imagine his arms around her and crying on the firmness of his shoulder. Jerry was kind; he wouldn't have scoffed or ridiculed her tears. But Jerry was gone. *Gone*—a four-letter word that carried so much heartache.

The visitor at her classroom doorway paused, pulled off his hat, and ran his hand through his hair. His face softened, and his eyes filled at the sight of the one he loved so dearly.

"You'll get your exams soggy like that, little sis."

Her head shot up as if she had been touched by a surge of electricity. Andy!

It felt like decades since she had last seen him. He was smiling the shy smile that was all Andy. He wasn't dead! He was standing there, just like old times.

She ran to him blindly through her tears.

She was sobbing. "You're alive!"

"Didn't you get my telegram?"

But she could only shake her head. Her voice was a whisper.

"Oh, Andy! You're real. You're not gone from me!"

"Don't cry, Meg. Don't cry," he crooned to her. He couldn't hold her tightly enough.

"Andy...I love you!"

Her head was against his chest, and she could feel him crying.

"I love you, Meg."

That first night they stayed up until after 3:00 in the morning, and Meg gave her students a holiday the next day. The headmistress was grim-faced and disapproving, but silent. Andy told Meg all about the sinking and about his arm, which was still healing. He told her about Treadle's death and his own rescue. But he did not tell her about his trip to London. He did not tell her his own vessel was now berthed in New Orleans. That would come later. She told him all about her students that night, and they laughed until their sides hurt.

She introduced him to her class. The young women were polite but unimpressed. The fashion of the day dictated that men did not wear beards, even if Andy Alcott's was neatly trimmed. A mustache was fine, especially a luxurious one with well-waxed, east-west, spearlike tips. And his hat! The black derby was the hat of the day, not that foolish cloth cap he had crumpled into his pocket.

"The girls told me, quite seriously of course, and out of genuine concern for you..." she said to him the next day with a laugh.

"Yes?"

"You're about two decades behind in your appearance."

"Oh?"

"My girls know about these things in great detail. It's very important to them."

"That will rule out romance with any of them then."

"I'm afraid so."

"I think I'm crushed," Andy replied gravely.

The next few days Meg showed Andy the sights of Galveston, as if he were not a seasoned traveler. Andy insisted they rent bicycles and learn this new craze in recreation.

"I don't have to be out of fashion with everything, do I?" he asked her. So Meg hitched up her skirts and Andy borrowed a bowler hat and they tried the bikes along the ocean boardwalk. It was the tonic that Meg had needed above anything else. She had never enjoyed anyone's company the way she did her brother's.

She held onto his arm possessively as they toured the city.

"I can tell by the smiles we're receiving that everyone thinks we're sweethearts."

He looked down at her and laughed. "My fortune and your misfortune then."

She jabbed him in the ribs. "Oh, don't play modest with me. You know you're handsome."

"To a Jamaican monkey perhaps."

"Ha!"

Yet it was not all laughter. They sat on Meg's terrace one night after she had made him one of his favorite dinners. The stars came out, shots of crystal through black velvet. The breeze brought them the smell of the Gulf. They sat in silence after the meal, listening to the sound of horse's hooves on the cobbled streets below, the thin whistle of a cable car on a distant avenue, muted laughter, a dove cooing in some nearby branch, the swaying of the stately palms.

"We've talked about me for two days," Andy said finally. "Now tell me why you are so unhappy."

Meg demurred. "What makes you think I'm unhappy?"

"Your letters for one thing; your eyes for another."

She sighed. "You're very perceptive."

"I'm your brother," he returned bluntly.

She smiled at him. "Matt and Daniel wouldn't understand. Even Papa wouldn't this time. Not after all he did to get me here. I'm not even sure I understand."

"What is it? Being so far from home? Your students? The head-mistress?"

She leaned on the rail, quiet for a full minute. She didn't want to talk about Jerry yet. She certainly couldn't talk about Sam.

"Mama and Papa want you to be happy, Meg. You know that. No matter what it took to get you down here," Andy said softly.

She nodded. "The girls like me all right now. They're less snobby than they were when I first came. But, Andy, these girls don't really care about learning. Most of them are just biding their time until the right man with the right bank account comes along. I feel useless here, Andy! I want to teach where I'm really needed! Where in this vast world is Meg Alcott really needed?"

He left her two days later with no answer for her question.

"You know what Papa and Mama would say about how you're feeling," he said as he took her hand.

"They'd say pray."

"That's what I say too. I'm going home first, then to New Orleans. You'll be hearing from me in a couple of months."

"That sounds very mysterious," she laughed.

He twirled his hat and grinned.

Peppercreek

Andy came home when the famous Peppercreek Orchard was in full bloom. From his open bedroom window, he slept wrapped in the intoxicating perfume of apple blossoms. Never had a homecoming been more poignant—one thought dead had come back from the dead.

Every light was on in his father's house the night he arrived. Every favorite food of his that his mother and aunt could think of had been prepared. His brothers, Uncle Henri, and Aunt Wyeth had all gathered to welcome him. His mother held him and sobbed until the room grew quiet. Then his father placed a trembling hand on his head and prayed a prayer of thanksgiving. It was well past midnight by the time he told them the whole adventure of the ship's sinking and his rescue. Their eyes grew wide as he told them the fantastic tale of the Englishman. He described every inch of the *Merry Widow* to them.

"So, I have this wonderful ship just waiting for me in New Orleans," he finished.

"Sounds like you're very eager to get started on a new trip," his father said with a smile.

"Well, with my own crew and cargo, and my own decisions to make, I guess I am pretty eager."

"You're not afraid then, to keep sailing after what happened?" his sister-in-law, Millie, asked.

"No more than Matt is when a horse tosses him. The oceans are usually very hospitable. Coming over from London gave me time to get my balance back." He met Uncle Henri's eye and smiled. "Over many things."

The next day he took his uncle aside in the cool, gray twilight of the front porch. The older man spoke first. "I can plainly see that things are calmer for you, despite what you've been through."

Andy nodded. Indeed the experience had been a crucible for his feelings, refining everything important to him down to the essentials. He would never be the same.

"I had a lot of time to think, even before the sinking, about my feelings for Amy." He drew a deep breath, and in the shadows Henri Mullins thought his nephew looked older. "I can't change the fact that I fell in love with her. I can't change what happened, but I prayed that I could go back to loving her like a sister."

"And you found that you couldn't do that," Henri offered gently.

"No, I couldn't. Before the storm came up, I was pretty angry."

"Angry with God," said Henri.

Andy was surprised. "Yes! I was angry that He had allowed this to happen. Then I saw my pride. Somehow I'd become proud about being, well, it's hard for me to say—it's so absurd. But I'd gotten proud about

being godly! It was like the Lord was saying, 'You're not above temptation, Andy Alcott.'"

He sat on the porch railing, suddenly feeling very weary.

"I prayed, Uncle Henri. I gave up loving Amy Cash like I knew was
wrong and found myself praying for her happiness. The anger seemed to
evaporate. I got calm inside again."

"The Lord could have someone else for you, Andy. The right sort of
love."

Andy shrugged, "Maybe." He patted his uncle's shoulder affectionately. "All I know is I never want to fall in love that quickly, or that hard,
ever again!"

When Henri Mullins lay down that night, he knew his prayer was very
different than his nephew would have expected. From his own experience he knew the painful truth: The hurting heart may have learned but
not yet healed.

Galveston

Meg sat very stiff and straight in her chair, waiting. There was really
no other way to sit when around Mrs. McCallas. Her rigid posture
seemed to influence your own. There was no slouching and definitely
no relaxing where Mrs. McCallas was concerned.

The headmistress was determined to ferret out the true motives of
this most remarkable defection in the ranks of Bishop's Villa.

"Miss Alcott, am I to understand you are resigning your position?"

"Yes, ma'am. I won't be returning next term."

"This is highly ... irregular!"

"Ma'am?"

"We have never had a staff member resign before. Never. Positively
never!"

The headmistress's face took on the coloring of a lobster.

"Well, you see, it's—" Meg began.

"Miss Alcott, are your parents aware of this plan?"

The headmistress's severe pinnacle of gray hair jabbed threateningly
at Meg.

"No, but—"

"There!" The headmistress was exultant. "I'm sure your father, who
went to such great effort to secure this most desirable position for you,
would be most alarmed at your intent."

"I—"

"I feel I have been most tolerant of some of your more unorthodox
teaching methods, Miss Alcott. The girls seem to have grown to like
you." The headmistress's face grew narrower and more pinched. Clearly
affection between teacher and student was not a credit.

Meg glanced down at her lap. "I'm very grateful. The school has been generous to me."

"Grateful," the headmistress chopped with distaste.

"You see, my brother called, and he wants me to come to him in New Orleans. I . . . I told him I would come."

"Miss Alcott! You are leaving your position on your brother's whim?" The headmistress was sputtering.

"I'm sure it isn't a whim to Andy. He's not like that at all. Whatever it is, I'm sure he's serious about it."

Now the headmistress used her final battle tactic. She was silent. Meg smiled inwardly. The headmistress was looking very owlish.

"Andy wants the best for me."

"You're determined about this . . . this foolishness, then?"

Meg hesitated only a moment as she wondered how someone's voice could be so contemptuous and cold.

She took a deep sigh and relaxed, smiling broadly.

"Yes, Mrs. McCallas, I am very determined!"

The old Midwestern Meg had returned. Her students were very glad, even if it was just until the end of the term. But the headmistress far preferred the subdued Miss Alcott. She was easier to intimidate.

An English lesson on the beach? Scandalous!

"It's an outing, Mrs. McCallas. A field trip," Meg explained patiently.

"It has never been done before," the matron faltered.

"All the more reason. We're studying poetry written about the ocean. It's the last outing I'll have with the girls."

"Yes . . . the last," the headmistress murmured.

So they trooped down to the Gulf beach, 18 young women full of Victorian modesty—their laughter preceding them like a banner. Sunshine, salty breezes, sand in their shoes, and verses by the water's edge. The young girls never forgot the delightful afternoon.

Meg was in the middle of a line of Tennyson when Miranda Bass interrupted her. "Excuse me, Miss Alcott."

"Yes, Miranda?"

"My father." She pointed to the boardwalk. "I . . . don't think he came to see me."

Sam Bass did look different, almost awkward, framed by the beach and ocean. He belonged to pastures and branding fires and corrals. Yet as Meg walked toward him, she could feel his commanding presence even in this new setting. He was frowning as he watched her.

"Well . . ." he drawled.

"Hello, Congressman Bass."

He smiled then and relaxed. His posture was true even if his environment wasn't—hands jammed in his pockets, head cocked to one side, leaning forward.

"Heard from Miranda you're leavin' in a week."

"Yes, I resigned."

"Leavin' Texas," he added with some distaste.

She nodded. "For New Orleans."

"Miranda says you're joining your brother."

"Yes, he wants me to meet him there."

The congressman looked out on the horizon, thinking, searching.

"You know, I never really thanked you for getting me this place at the school. I don't want to seem ungrateful," Meg said eagerly.

His smile was crooked and very brief.

"I reckon you thanked me fine." His piercing eyes held her until he finally looked away.

She could see he was groping, sorting thoughts, trying to weigh if the unspoken should be finally voiced.

"Then it's likely we won't see you again," he said gently.

She nodded, wishing she could make this easier for him, but knowing she couldn't.

He tipped her chin up with his tanned finger, made her look into his eyes. He wanted to remember this face for a long time.

"I hope you find nothing but happiness wherever you go, Miss Alcott. You'll make some fortunate man a very fine wife."

"Thank you . . . Sam," she whispered.

He tapped his heart. "I reckon you know . . . you take a little part of Texas with you."

The girls were giggly, and this time Meg did not mind. They were saying goodbye. They gave her gifts that reflected their personalities and passions, touches of affection from student to teacher.

Mrs. McCallas was formal, austere, and quietly triumphant. Her niece would begin teaching English Literature on Monday morning. Miranda Bass was the last to say goodbye. Meg invited her for dinner in her apartment her final night at Bishop's Villa.

"I'm sorry you're not going to be my sister-in-law," Miranda said bluntly.

Meg was momentarily embarrassed.

"I'm sorry things didn't work out between Jerry and me. Jerry's a wonderful man, and I know you'll have a sister-in-law one of these days soon."

Miranda nodded knowingly. "His last letter from Houston said he had met a girl named Renee. He spent an entire paragraph on her! She's another cattleman's daughter. Owns the Triple K ranch outside of Houston."

Meg meditated on this. She felt no pangs of jealousy, only gladness for Jerry. Still, she felt a twinge of emptiness suddenly.

Miranda saw the look that crossed her teacher's face. She pressed her hand.

"Oh, don't feel badly, Miss Alcott. I mean, about Jerry finding another girl so quickly. You really were very good for him."

Meg raised an eyebrow.

"Oh, yes, ma'am. I think you showed him women..." she cast around in her limited, Victorian experience for the proper phrase, "I think you showed him women can be more of a comfort than cows or horses!"

Meg laughed. She felt very flattered.

New Orleans

He came forward, smiling and eager. He had spotted her instantly in the crowded railroad terminal. Her broad hat, tied with a light-blue sash, bobbed along in a sea of derbies, bare heads, and hats like her own. Yet she stood out to him even in such a crowd. She stood clutching a little leather satchel, looking slightly bewildered and very young, and he admired her. She was his pretty little sister, and she had come when he summoned her.

"That was a merciless trip, Andy," she blurted out as he came up to her. Her smile was tired. "I endured a passionate, middle-aged shoe salesman who started out with the remedy for everything from broken arches to bunioned toes and finished with how my eyes are as blue as the Gulf!"

"A real romantic!" Andy laughed.

"Miles and miles of heat and dust, Andy. Enough heat even for me. I'm covered with dirt, internally, I'm sure. I hope this surprise is worth it."

He stopped walking and turned to her, his smile dropping a fraction, his eyebrows knitting together in concern.

"Maybe... maybe it isn't worth asking you to leave Galveston for."

She pinched his arm. "Are you serious? You rescued me from another term with the dragon lady and babysitting duties!"

"Still, you might be disappointed, Meg."

Only then did she see the lines and shadows of fatigue around his eyes.

"Silly, where's your sense of humor? I was just teasing. You look overworked, Andy. What have you been doing in the three months since I've seen you?"

"Well, I have been working pretty hard getting things ready."

"Getting what ready?"

His smile, his boyishness, returned instantly. "Tomorrow you'll see. First, to your hotel for a bath and rest."

She slipped her arm through his. "You're really enjoying this suspense, aren't you?"

"As one of your former pupils would say, 'I'm positively relishing it!'"

That night they dined at Napoleans, a restaurant in the French quarter known for its strolling violinist and spicy creole dishes. The view from the balcony was breathtaking.

"Don't you ever worry about running into that Maxwell Hawk fellow?" Meg asked just before she speared some shrimp.

"I have already," Andy answered with a mouthful.

"Oh, Andy! What happened?"

"He owns a tavern on the waterfront. I walked in, walked up to him, and told him I was back and Lilly was gone."

"What did he say?"

"At first, nothing I can repeat."

"Did he try to hurt you?"

"No, he'd thrashed me pretty soundly the first time and got it out of his system. He was quite calm about it. Besides, he was winning at poker and felt amiable toward everyone."

Disregarding Victorian propriety, Meg leaned forward to ask, "What would you do if you met up with one of his girls again?"

Andy swallowed but did not hesitate.

"I'd try to do for her what I did for Lil."

They ate for a few minutes in silence, and Meg thought her brother one of the bravest men she had ever known.

Finally Andy leaned back, appraising her.

"Now that you're cleaned up and reasonably rested—"

Meg dropped her voice to a conspirator's tone. "I know this isn't sophisticated dinner conversation, but the bathwater was mud, Andy! I brought half an acre of Texas soil with me!"

He laughed. "So, are you ready for a story?"

"Before you tell me, I want you to know how much this means to me, your sending for me."

A quick frown creased his face. "I don't think Mama and Papa will approve of it when they hear about it."

Meg's eyes brightened. "I'm growing more intrigued by the minute!"

"Tell me first. Is there anyone in Peppercreek or Galveston who will miss you, Meg? I find it hard to believe no man has won my sister."

Now it was Meg's turn to frown, a shadow of inner pain she could not share even with Andy. People were forever telling her she was pretty, yet she felt like a failure in matters of romance.

She sighed and toyed with her silverware. Seeing her grow so pensive, Andy regretted his question.

"Well, actually there was someone...in Galveston. His name was Jerry. He was very nice, very fun to be with. He..." She really didn't want to cry; it would make Andy feel bad. "I just couldn't seem to feel for him in...in my heart, you know? Oh, Andy, I really didn't mean to hurt him!"

"Meg, I'm sure you didn't."

"Then there was his...father."

"His father?"

She took a deep breath. "I felt things for him in a way I didn't feel for Jerry. I know it's hard to believe...or understand, but I didn't seem to notice his age."

"What happened?" Andy prodded gently.

"Well, it was the same thing—all of the sudden I could feel that he wasn't...he wasn't the one. I feel like such a failure!"

"Meg..."

She felt embarrassed in the silence that followed.

"It was like loving him just wasn't right," she added softly. She wanted to move from her own pain.

Impulsively she asked, "Did you ever feel like that, Andy? Like love for some reason was just not quite right with that person or at that time? And there was no real explaining it."

Andy thought he would choke on his shrimp. He was grateful when the waiter came and asked them their choice of desserts. This took Meg awhile, and Andy immediately put a new question to her on a safer subject.

"All right, let me ask you this. What would you do if you could do anything?"

She gave a nervous laugh. "That's an easier question? I don't know, Andy. That is the plague of my life. I don't belong in Peppercreek. I don't belong in Galveston. I don't know where I belong."

She looked out across the balcony at streets that were throbbing with laughter and music, and for a moment she felt utterly alone, separated from everyone, belonging to no one.

"I haven't any plans." Finally her smile returned. "My lesson plan is in your hands now, big brother."

"That's fine, then. Tonight I'll tell you about the Englishman. Tomorrow I'll fill in the plans."

It was a very warm morning on the busy harbor of New Orleans. If Meg listened closely enough, she could hear the languages of several dozen countries, a concentrated lesson in geography at arm's length. Hundreds of ships, thousands of men, tons of cargo. But Meg and Andy had eyes for only one ship berthed beside so many others.

Andy's ship was over 200 feet of classic clipper—three-masted with what seemed to Meg acres of crisp white canvas and miles of tight rigging. The flying jib was like a long, slender, wooden needle thrust from the bow of the ship, pointing the way, slicing through the ocean spray. The flags were bright yellow and snapping in the wind like a salute to her.

Andy was quoting something at her side, but she was only half listening.

"'To be a clipper of distinction, she must be sharp and sleek, with capacity for cargo over passengers, and very fast. She must be sharp as a cutter, symmetrical as a yacht, rakish as a pirate ship, and elegant in her cabins as a lady's boudoir.' From what you've seen, Meg, do you think she qualifies?"

Meg clasped her hands together. "Oh, Andy! It's a beautiful boat!"

"Vessel," Andy corrected happily.

"And it's all yours, Andy!" Meg whispered leaning forward.

Andy nodded. "Leaks and all. Yes, it's mine."

"Wait. What's the name on the side? The *Merry Widow?*"

"Uh huh."

"Hmm..."

"Something wrong?"

"Well, it's just an unusual name, not exactly what I'd pick for a vessel you'd own and sail. But—"

"Exactly, Meg. But you forget, I can change it to anything I like. *Andy's Black-Bottomed Barrel* if I want!"

She laughed with him. "Oh, no, Andy. Your ship must have a...romantic name. A name that will live up to its exciting and adventurous future!"

"Any romantic suggestions?"

"Well, that would take awhile."

Andy took his hat off, running his hand through his hair.

"Actually, Meg, I have changed the name already. A fellow comes tomorrow to repaint it. It's already in the registry under its new name."

"Oh, Andy, what is it?"

Andy smiled down into her eyes, greatly enjoying her enthusiasm. It made all the weeks of hard work worth it.

Meg could see the pride and happiness in her brother's eyes as he gazed out at the ship.

"You're looking at the *Magnolia Remembrance.*"

She was silent only a moment. "It's perfect."

"Romantic enough?"

"Completely romantic!"

"I knew you'd be the one to share this with, Meg."

She turned away from the rail to look closely at him. She studied the slender face, the brilliant blue eyes passed from their mother's side, the carefully combed short brown hair, the touches of sun upon his cheeks.

"Are you happy, Andy? I mean besides the ship."

He shifted. Suddenly Amy's face was clear and vivid in his mind. He evaded Meg's gaze. "Of course I'm happy."

"You should have a wife," she countered softly.

He threw back his head and laughed. "Meg! And you should have a couple of babies by now!"

She ignored his words. "You need a wife, Andy."

"If I had a wife, Meg, I wouldn't be here."

"A wife would keep you from this?"

His voice had become low, almost distant. "I wouldn't leave her, not even for this. Not if I loved her ... like I would."

Meg linked her arm through his. "Then the *Magnolia Remembrance* is your bride for now, big brother. Someday there will be someone—"

"For both of us," he interrupted with a smile.

He made her close her eyes as he led her down the narrow steps. When he'd flung open the door, the first thing she smelled was cut lumber and flowers. The first thing she saw in the oak-paneled cabin was a huge vase of pink roses.

Andy stepped up beside her, speaking hurriedly in his excitement.

"This will be your cabin, Meg. It was the captain's quarters, and I had that wall put up to divide it into two rooms. That door goes to my room. See the desk? It's bolted in, for you to write all your letters home and everything you see. See, here's the dresser for your clothes and the bed. It has the best mattress. I put it there so you'd feel the sun on your face from the window and smell the ocean. There's nothing like waking up to that. And these carpets, aren't they soft? They're from India. Your washbowl is bolted down, so no matter how rough it gets it won't spill. I think *Magnolia* will be gentle, though. It's all right, isn't it, Meg?"

She had gone forward to the little oak table to bury her face in the roses, and to cry.

"Meg?"

"Andy, it's all so beautiful ... and sweet of you. I—"

"We'll go to Europe, and I'll show you the Mediterranean in all its moods. You'll see so much, Meg!"

"How can I thank you, Andy?"

"That's easy. I'll be working hard with this new crew and everything. Just enjoy yourself, and make me laugh, Meg."

One week later, on a day of sunshine and blue-sky brilliance in which a breeze gently tossed the water in crystal ripples and waves, they stood together on the deck amid shouts and laughter, the smell of salt, the creaking of wood, and scolding gulls who spiraled overhead. Wind filled the sails like gigantic pocket handkerchiefs as she glided away from her berth. The maiden voyage of the *Magnolia Remembrance* had begun.

Part III

The Painting

Chapter 12

New York

♦♦ ♦♦ ♦♦

*L*illy O'Hara was enjoying herself greatly. Her new friends had given her a warm welcome. The "22nd Street Players" was an amateur drama group that met every Friday night in the basement of a shoe store. The members visited a few minutes, complained about the terrible winter weather, and forged friendships. Finally, they practiced their craft. The coach was a fat little man who'd had a bit part in an off-Broadway play once—or maybe he'd just been to see an off-Broadway play. The other members didn't question him too closely. All that mattered was that he was an organized leader, and knew more about acting than they did. And it was his shoe store upstairs. So he was their teacher, assigning them little parts, then judging their performances. He was both tyrannical and paternal, depending largely on how good business had been on Friday in the shop above.

Lilly O'Hara had approached him timidly about joining the group.

"I've heard you have a drama group that meets—"

"Don't be timid, woman!" he barked. "New York is no place to be timid! And you certainly can't be timid if you want to be a great actress!"

He expected her to shuffle out teary-eyed and chastised.

But he had just met Lilly O'Hara. Her spine straightened, and her chin went up. Her eyes were flashing; color had risen to her cheeks. The little man stopped in the middle of his dusting.

"Who are you, little man? A minion for the great George St. John? I demand an audience with the drama instructor for the 22nd Street Players, at once! Tell him Lilly O'Hara is waiting!"

She turned from him for a second, then spun around again. Her voice was sweet and wheedling.

"Say, handsome, do Lilly O'Hara a big favor. I need to see the drama coach right away. Hurry, sweetcakes!"

She dazzled him with her bright smile. She pinched him on his pudgy cheek.

George St. John laid his duster down and extended his hand.

"We meet at 7:00 each Friday night, Miss O'Hara. Welcome."

So Lilly had found some new friends and an outlet for her creative talent. A small, very informal, very amateur beginning, but a starting point. She looked forward to the Friday evenings. She could become a princess again, or an English maid, or a shrewish housewife. It was wonderful. She grew to respect the sometimes abrasive drama coach.

And he knew what the others in the group recognized as well—a real talent had joined them.

The Friday night session was over. Lilly felt exhilarated from the evening, yet tired. She had been up since 5:00 that morning, working at the mission house, then crossing the city with the director to visit a woman and her new baby. She had walked six blocks to the shoe shop to save money. One glance out the basement window told her she would have to take the electric streetcar home. The wind was howling down the concrete canyons of New York, threatening snow by morning.

St. John was scowling at the window.

"It'll snow tonight. Bad for business tomorrow."

Lilly pulled on her cheap wool coat and patted him on the shoulder. "Unless you have a good supply of snow boots in stock, Georgie."

St. John nodded. Lilly was the only one he allowed to call him Georgie. He didn't know why. Anyone else who tried it would certainly get an earful.

"Why do you bother to peddle shoes, St. John?" a young man asked who was pulling on his gloves. "Seems kind of..."

George did not like the slight. He did not like to be reminded of this mundane side of his life. He really belonged to the stage.

"Same reason you're not going to a classier theatrical group, Danny boy. We all like to eat," the coach snapped.

Danny Meyer bowed and turned to Lilly.

"How about going for coffee, Lilly? There's a place down the street still open."

Lilly hesitated. Dan Meyer had a reputation. Oh, he could act. But he was a smooth character, the other female players had warned Lilly. Still, a hot cup of tea before the cold ride home sounded appealing. She agreed. It was her first mistake since coming to the big city.

Meyer had talked and talked about plays and shows until Lilly was openly yawning. He finally leaned forward.

"You know, Lilly, you're the best one in our group. You make everyone else look like country hicks. That duchess you did tonight was great."

"A duchess with a Louisiana accent!" Lilly laughed.

Meyer shrugged. "Wouldn't it be nice to be part of a real theatrical group?"

Lilly frowned. "I consider the 22nd St. Players a real theatrical group, Danny."

He sneered. "They belong to... to country socials in the sticks!"

"I'm from the sticks," she returned archly. "But why are you there?"

"Purely entertainment for me. It's amusing. And..." he took a long drink of coffee for effect, "because I'm looking for real talent."

"Hmm..." Lilly was ready to go home.

"Ever heard of The Limelighters?" he asked.

Everyone who knew beans about theater in New York knew about the group. It hadn't taken Lilly long in the city to hear of them. They were an impressive off-Broadway club of aspiring actors and actresses, many of whom eventually went on to the famous stages.

"Yes, I've heard of them," Lilly admitted slowly.

"I know how you can become one of them," Meyer said with a big grin.

"Oh?"

He swelled with importance. "I know someone highly connected with the group."

"It would cost a fortune," Lilly said.

His eyes were riveted on her. "Not for you."

She felt herself tense. Something was coming.

"And why not for me?"

"This friend I have is a financial supporter of the group. Loves the theater. Has a box at the Roxy."

Lilly's eyes widened.

"You can have the open spot in The Limelighters, Lilly. No cost. No audition."

Lilly reddened. This sounded too familiar. She stood up and tossed some coins on the table. Her voice was icy and contemptuous.

"Good night, Danny."

"Wait, Lilly, wait." He followed her outside.

"You don't understand," he said eagerly.

"I'm new to New York, and I'm from the sticks, Danny, but I'm not thick. I understand just fine."

"Wait. Listen. Do you really understand what I'm telling you? This fella, well, I've already told him about you."

She stopped walking. She felt cold, and it wasn't from the weather. "You what?"

"You're a smart girl, Lilly. I saw that from the first night you came to the group."

Her vibrant red hair and good looks had distracted Danny from his lines. But only until he remembered his "friend." This friend was always looking for women with flashy looks like Lilly O'Hara.

"And..." Lilly prompted.

"And I told him how stylish you are."

She laughed in his face at this. "Stylish in a cheap tweed coat and woolen tam?"

He laughed too. "I can spot potential, Lilly. You have it. You belong to The Limelighters."

"Good night, Danny."

He said nothing to her again for several weeks. He acted as if the conversation between them had never taken place. Like a skilled hunter, he was letting her sniff the bait from every angle.

George St. John had taken her aside after one of the Friday night rehearsals. "So you're not concerned about my accent, Georgie?" Lilly asked.

He gave her one of his rare smiles. "Not a bit, Miss Lilly. It will be your signature!"

Then his face clouded. "I am concerned about something else, however. And far be it from me to meddle in my students' private lives."

"Yes?"

"You went for coffee with Danny boy a few weeks ago."

"Guilty."

"A word to the wise?"

"All right, I'm listening."

"Danny boy is a mediocre actor. I keep him around because he's useful. But I wouldn't trust him with my worst enemy. It's his eyes..."

She patted his shoulder. "Thank you, Georgie, for your concern."

But Meyer did approach her again.

"Thought it over? The spot is still open and still yours if you want it. But it won't last forever. My friend is still...interested in you."

"I wouldn't call the kind of man you're talking about a friend," Lilly replied sharply.

Meyer laughed. "See? I knew you had spirit! But you haven't even met my friend yet."

"Oh, yes, Danny boy. I have. Lots of times."

He decided to get a little tough.

"Then you know the score. You're a big girl. You know this is the chance of a lifetime. You're going to spend years stuck in two-bit groups like the 22nd. Maybe stuck there forever, and everything you dreamed about stays just that, a dream. Or you simply step into one of the most coveted theater groups in New York. How can you pass that up?"

"Easy."

But deep inside, Lilly O'Hara was tempted. She knew exactly what the deal with no cost and no audition really was. She knew exactly what Danny's friend would be like. Max Hawk with a New York accent. Yet it would bring her closer to her dreams. It would bypass years of work with little groups like the 22nd. To be a part of a group like The Limelighters!

"Lilly." There was a note of desperation in Danny Meyer's tone now. He had gotten an advance for "selling" Lilly O'Hara to his friend. And the friend was waiting.

"Lilly, listen. Lots of fine actresses do this kind of thing all the time.

How do you think they got to be where they are today? Not by being stuck with a dead-end bunch like the 22nd!"

He grabbed her shoulders. "Think hard about this, Lilly. It won't come again!"

She made the critical mistake of hesitating, of wavering.

"No promises, Danny Meyer. But I'll think about it."

She had done it before. Then she was desperate. She wasn't desperate now. Before she had been able to detach her mind from her "work." For a little while, for the chance of a lifetime, couldn't she do it again?

The Atlantic

Avoiding a severe storm had caused Andy Alcott to navigate the *Magnolia* into latitudes more northerly than he preferred to sail this time of year. The Atlantic at certain times and seasons could be treacherous with drifting ice floes—floating white caps, small peaks, frigid but innocent-looking with jagged, colossal craters of ice submerged under the cold, cold ocean waters. Icebergs were a mariner's nightmare. So silent, so hidden, so deadly—like gigantic knives ready to rip wide the hull of a wooden sailing vessel.

Andy pulled the woolen muffler around his chin and over his mouth. He was staring into the darkness and praying. A dozen other crew were stationed at points all along the ship, watching as well. A dark, cold night, yet no time for the comfort of a warm bunk. They must see the dull white glimmer before it was too late. By morning they should be through this dangerous passage. But tonight there would be little sleep. Down in the galley, Meg was helping the *Magnolia's* cook brew and serve hot chocolate for the crew waiting for their shift.

Andy should have nothing more on his mind this night than the serious business at hand. He should be thinking of precautions he might take, any other sentinels he should post. He should check the lines to the two lifeboats just in case...

But staring into the vastness, where the purple blackness melted ocean and night sky together, he could think of only one person: Lilly O'Hara. He hadn't had a letter from her in months. She had come into his mind suddenly the night before. It had stirred him from a sound sleep. Lilly. He had worked through the day, talked with Meg, ate meals. Yet there was Lilly in the back of his thoughts, never really leaving them.

Now he stood on the deck of his clipper, during the most dangerous time of the entire voyage—and all he could do was think of the red-headed young woman. Why?

He remembered something his Uncle Henri had told him. Something about persistent thought often being the call to persistent prayer. Uncle

Henri had said it eloquently at the time. Andy smiled. Yes, that had to be it. His prayers changed then, from the safety of his ship to the safety of the young woman alone in the big city.

Meg was writing in her journal. Last night's drama must be recorded. Some years in the future, she and Andy would read it and remember the tense night they had spent together in the Atlantic. But the passage had been made. It was morning, clear and sunny. The waters were free of the deadly ice floes.

Meg finished in the journal, then stretched out across her bed. She knew it wouldn't be long before *Magnolia Remembrance* would rock her to sleep. But she thought of Andy before she slept. She had taken him some hot chocolate during the early watch of the night and stood beside him, scanning the blackness, until her frozen feet sent her below deck. He had surprised her when he had asked her to pray. Pray for Lilly O'Hara in New York.

Now as she lay on her bunk, she thought again of that request. Could Andy secretly love this woman he had rescued in New Orleans? Had their friendship deepened? He wasn't giving up any clues to her. She could only speculate. She wished he'd have more success with romance than she did.

There in the Atlantic, a brother and sister were praying for the young woman who was facing her own dangers, as real and as deadly as icebergs in the ocean.

Lilly would have been very surprised to learn her case of the flu had been the answer to prayer. It effectively put her out of the grasp of temptation while she considered it. She was sick and recovering for nearly a month, confined to the mission home, seeing only the small staff and doctor. Outside her window, the world was a tumult of whirling snow.

"Is it still snowing?" Lilly asked the director, who had brought a bowl of beef tea to her bedside.

Mrs. Lewis shook her head. "Why, this is nothing compared to the blizzard we had a few years ago. Eighty-eight it was. Ask anyone who was in the city at the time and they'll tell you they'll never forget it! Four hundred people died. New York was so stranded that telegraphs had to go via London to get to the rest of the country. For 36 hours! No, this little snowstorm is nothing!"

To a Louisiana country girl it looked like another record-breaking blizzard.

"Is the tea all right?"

"Yes, ma'am, it's fine, thank you."

"Your color's better today. You know this snow hasn't stopped Mr. St. John from coming by to see about you."

Lilly smiled. "Underneath his flair and flamboyance he is really a very kind man."

"Hasn't stopped the young man either," the older woman said with sudden gravity.

Lilly paled a bit. "Young man?"

The mission director wasn't much impressed with theater types. This young man looked, well, Mrs. Lewis had lived in New York all her life and was used to seeing all kinds, shapes, colors, and sizes. He looked gaudy, almost like a gangster. She couldn't help but wonder about Miss O'Hara's choice in friends.

"Meyer was his name, yes, Danny Meyer. He's come by at least three times."

"Oh." It was all Lilly could say.

Lilly had had a lot of time to think while she lay in bed. When she'd gotten stronger, she read from the Bible Andy Alcott had given her. She loved to read about the woman at the well in the Gospel of John. It was one of her favorite stories. Jesus had been so compassionate and forgiving.

How could she have considered for even a moment returning to that life Andy had rescued her from? She blushed to the roots of her red hair when she imagined Andy's face if he had known of Danny Meyer's offer. If he had known she had entertained the possibility. She felt sickened at heart and filthy for what she had nearly done. All for a theatrical spot!

She prayed in those long, quiet hours for the Lord to strengthen her against the temptation and keep her with the 22nd St. Players forever if that was His will. She could not sell her body and soul for any price again.

Finally she was able to see George St. John.

"You're not coming back?" he had nearly shouted.

"I will come back, Georgie. Really I will. But I think I need some time."

"What's the problem, Lilly? You're better; you're well. So?"

She wasn't sure she could explain it to him. She wasn't sure he could understand. But she needed time away from something that had become too important to her.

"I'll be back in the spring, Georgie. Really I will."

Danny Meyer was very angry. The drama coach had told the little group Lilly O'Hara wouldn't be joining them for several months. She was still recovering, he said. Danny Meyer was convinced otherwise. She was hiding, and he knew why! He'd been paid $500 in advance to bring the redheaded woman to one of New York's many flesh peddlers. Five hundred dollars was a paltry sum to the peddler, but sudden wealth to the likes of Meyer. Now the goods had not been delivered, and Danny was seen about town looking like he'd run into a few waterfront thugs. A black eye, a lump on the cheek, a swollen lip. A real workover, but mild by tough street standards. Truth was, Danny Meyer was luckier than most.

He had found and delivered another acceptable girl in Lilly O'Hara's place. But it didn't make him any less furious or vindictive.

He sat in the corner of a little Italian restaurant, pretending to read the newspaper in front of him. He was actually hiding behind it and watching Lilly across the room. He had followed her to this place. He was ready to vent his anger. Lilly O'Hara needed some slapping around for the big trouble she had caused him.

She stepped out onto the twilight-brushed sidewalk, and he was instantly at her side. He twisted her arm behind her back until she cried out. "Be quiet!" he hissed. "This alley, here...Be still!"

"Danny Meyer, let me go! Please, you're hurting my arm."

"No promises, but you said you'd think about it!"

"I did!"

"You hid in that mission house for a month is what you did while I was looking like a chump!"

Lilly thought she was going to pass out. This was like the nightmare of Max Hawk.

"You lied to me!"

"No...no, I didn't! I did think about your offer. But I couldn't go through with it. Please let me go."

"Maybe just a little tighter, Miss. Maybe you'll remember not to play fast with—Awww!"

A large, hard, very cold ball of snow had hit Danny Meyer and fallen down the back collar of his shirt. He released Lilly and spun around. A barrel-chested man stood in the open doorway of the restaurant kitchen.

"Pardon me," he bowed with a mocking smile and a definite twinkle in his eye. "I heard a lady cry."

Danny brushed off his jacket, glaring at Lilly and the big Italian who could easily do much more harm than a mere baptism of snow.

"She isn't a lady!" Danny spit out. He turned and ran from the alley.

Lilly was weeping and cowering in the snowdrift. Look what her foolishness had almost cost her!

The Italian was nearly in tears as well. A beautiful woman in distress...was so distressing!

"Now, now, my dear young woman. There, there, don't weep." He was blotting her tears with his stained apron as if they were old friends.

"Don't worry. The stray has run off. You are safe."

"Thank you, Mr...."

He gave her a sweeping and extravagant bow. "I am Valentino!"

She smiled. "Thank you, Mr. Valentino."

"It was my pleasure. You know the scoundrel was in there watching you while you ate."

"He was? I didn't see him."

Valentino nodded vigorously. "Yes, he was very easy for me to notice. He picked at my pasta, and I was insulted! Now you will come in and get warm, then I will walk you to your trolley stop. I think my dear little wife has some boots you may borrow."

"You're an angel!" Lilly blurted impulsively.

A booming laugh from the Italian. "That I have never been called before! What is your name, my lovely?"

"Lilly O'Hara."

He motioned her inside his restaurant. "Lilly O'Hara, I think we are going to be good friends!"

Lilly returned to St. John and his players in the spring as she said she would. She never saw Danny Meyer again. And she never fell into temptation like she had. Lilly O'Hara was growing.

Chapter 13

Greenville, Mississippi, 1893

♦♦ ♦♦ ♦♦

*T*he young woman had sat through most of the trip leaning forward and looking out the grimy window, though mile after mile had grown predictably the same. A man across the aisle had raised and lowered his *New Orleans Gazetteer* just a fraction to watch her. He supposed he was being discreet.

She was all eyes. She looked like she was expecting something. It made him wonder. What was she expecting? Where was she headed? He ruffled his paper in irritation. He was old enough to be her father, yet something about the way she gazed out the window with such intentness made him watch her. Only twice had she relaxed, once to walk to the end of the car for a little paper cup of water, and once to blot her face with a dainty handkerchief.

He wondered if she was pretty. He wished his wife were with him; she could have told him immediately. She had a nice jaw, almost square, smooth, olive-tinted skin, and an abundance of thick, dark hair. As if feeling the intensity of his look, she had turned to him for a moment, smiling shyly before turning back to the window. He almost gasped aloud. Until then he had seen her only in profile. She wasn't pretty—she was beautiful!

It was his stop when Vicksburg came. He stood up quickly, glad to be home, glad to get out of the dust and heat. He leaned over the young woman's seat.

"Excuse me, Miss?"

She turned to him with a definite posture of reluctance. He smiled. *She's been fawned over because of her looks and grown tired of the fuss. She may fancy a good-looking young man's flattery, but not an old geezer like me.*

"This your stop, Miss?" He knew he was being unreasonably friendly.

"No, not till Greenville," she replied guardedly.

"Ah. First time in these parts?"

"Yes."

"Well, welcome to Mississippi!" he said expansively.

"Thank you."

"Just wanted to tell ya, not that it matters coming from me...and I'm a happily married man...for 30 years in fact..."

The woman's eyes were very green and very puzzled. Gorgeous eyes, he thought. Long lashes.

"Yes?" Her voice was low.

"Wanted to tell ya, though ya been told before, you are a lovely woman, yes, ma'am."

She smiled then, not a fixed or mechanical or perfunctory smile, but a genuine smile as if she was about to laugh.

"Thank you."

Well, I better go before I make a fool of myself, he thought. He doffed his hat, bowed, and hurried out of the car. She turned back to the window then, still smiling. It was her first welcome to Mississippi.

Meg closed her eyes as twilight approached. The view from the train was wrapped in shadows. A few more hours and she would be at her destination. *Destination.* She turned the word over in her mind. Another temporary stop in this journey to . . . to where? No, she wouldn't let any gloomy thoughts penetrate her optimism. All she needed to think about was the present. That was all she had, and her present was leading her to Tanglewood.

It was just as Andy had said. A train was an ungraceful thing compared to a clipper. She smiled. Andy and his prejudice. Yet after a year on the high seas, she had to agree. The *Magnolia* had been a cradle compared to this.

She closed her eyes in weariness, eager for the hotel bed she would get in Greenville. She was eager for a bath, and quiet, and no motion. She would spend this final hour on the train thinking over the past year. It would make the miles slide by faster. She was glad she had kept a journal. It swelled with the notes she had taken. "Meg's Memoirs," Andy teasingly called them.

They had seen so much together. It had been an experience to savor, to treasure for a lifetime, and all because her brother had thought to take her. Did a sister ever have a better brother than she had?

Magnolia Remembrance had introduced her to the Gulf, the Caribbean, the Atlantic, the English Channel, and the Mediterranean. While Andy was partial to the Caribbean, Meg had favored the warm Mediterranean with its beautiful coasts and exotic ports. For someone from a small, rural midwestern town, it was like stepping into the colorful pages of a geography book. She couldn't count the number of different accents and languages she had heard.

When fall came, Andy had settled her in Athens. He wouldn't risk her health. In a small, rented, white adobe house she became her own cook, maid, and mistress. She knew this lifestyle couldn't last forever, but while it did, she was loving it.

While Andy and his crew worked, she soaked up the sun and Greek history. Touring the countryside of bleached white houses, windmills, sleepy donkeys, vineyards, and women in dark robes had been a wonderful education for her, and she had loved every minute of it.

She had seen three European capitals besides Athens. Her memories of London were Big Ben, St. Paul's, Buckingham Palace, and a tea shop overlooking the Thames. She had even managed to drag Andy to a Shakespearian theater. Rome held the Colosseum, the Vatican, and lots of friendly, cheerful Italians. The letters home to Peppercreek carried no subtlety, no veiled unhappiness or worries for her mother. Meg Alcott was having the time of her life.

Paris was the last capital Andy had taken her to. It was like trying to capture the city in a picture postcard. But Paris was more than a flurry of sights and her portrait by a sidewalk artist. She would never think of Paris without thinking of the Frenchman she had met there.

She had met Paul at an outdoor cafe when Andy had been running errands for the ship. With only one table left, the waiter had seated them together as they entered the little restaurant. She had smiled—such presumption in this notorious city of romance!

"You would share the table, mademoiselle?" the waiter asked eagerly.

"Well...I..."

"I understand perfectly," Paul said in stilted English as he bowed. "I will wait for a table. Do not press this young woman."

Meg hesitated. Was this just another flirting Frenchman, which the country seemed to produce as prolifically as wine?

"I suppose it would be all right."

"You are American?" he asked.

She nodded and smiled.

"It would be a pleasure for me to dine with you," Paul said as he pulled out her chair. "I think cultural exchange is important; don't you?"

An innocent beginning. Meg was cautious and reserved. Paul was a serious-minded medical student.

Andy had protested immediately.

"Of course he's nice and friendly! I don't like it. I mean, I want you to have a good time, and goodness knows you're pretty enough for a rock to notice!"

"Thank you!"

"You know the reputation Frenchmen have, Meg."

"You're being silly, Andy. Stop worrying. I'm a big girl. He's showing me the sights of Paris. You've been along half the time. You said he seemed like a gentleman."

"'Seemed like.' You're making me feel like a doddering father, Meg! Watching over a headstrong daughter! Trying to keep the wolves away!"

He hadn't a clue how prophetic his words were.

They would be sailing for America soon and Andy was very busy with last-minute preparations. Paul invited her to dinner at a restaurant he boasted offered the city's finest French cuisine and breathtaking views. Meg had privately decided her mother's solid and simple home cooking was far preferable to the French food she had sampled. But she would go, one last night on the Continent with a Frenchman. What could it hurt?

But Paul had decided on a conquest. There must be a passionate heart beating underneath that very proper and cool reserve of the lovely American. While he had displayed the manner of a courteous guide and escort, she had responded as an interested, detached observer. When he had been friendly and almost filial, she had been friendly and almost filial. So if he became as ardent as his true nature, wouldn't the results be natural?

The food was as excellent as he had promised, Meg was forced to admit. The view from the restaurant terrace was as stunning as he had claimed. But she could not help but notice between the meal and the view, Paul the Frenchman was quieter than he had been before. And smiling more. Like he knew a satisfying secret.

"I think we should go back in. Our dessert is probably ready," Meg said as they sat in the cool shadows of the restaurant balcony.

"Do you? I think there is quite a dessert out here."

"Well..."

"Do you know I find you very lovely, Miss Meg Alcott? Very attractive, yes."

"I..."

"And how do you find me? Can you confess?"

"You...you are very nice. I've enjoyed what you've shown me of Paris."

"Ah...is that all? Nice? It is a word for a puppy, an old man in the park!"

She laughed nervously. "You are attractive, Paul."

He smiled and moved closer, an arm encircling her waist.

"Your hair is beautiful...so thick." He fingered it, moving closer. "The softness of your cheek, so smooth, like cream...I think a woman's neck is certainly a very lovely part of her, yes. Yours..."

He gave her a slow, soft kiss inside her wrist, and Meg closed her eyes. Back home this would have been a scandalous kiss, meriting a slap at the very least. But now...just for the moment...this was passion—French or American—and it was very real. When he kissed her lips, she trembled, a part of her mind warning her she should pull away quickly and rush inside the brightly lit restaurant. Something she thought buried had blazed inside her at his touch. She could feel his heart pounding, feel moisture on the back of her neck...

Her mind finally began to function properly. She stiffened. She made messes of men's hearts. Hers had been broken as well. She shouldn't be here, even if this was only one evening. Passion and pleasure belonged firmly in the past.

Paul had felt her response change. He had tightened his encircling arms.

"P-Paul...Paul...stop, please, stop."

"Ah...Miss Alcott, you do not really mean that. Your words say—"

"Stop it!"

A very American slap on a very frustrated French face. The cultural exchange was over.

Then the garçon had come to the terrace with a prudent, "Ahem... Your dessert is served."

She had regained her balance, regained her composure.

The *Magnolia* had sailed the very next afternoon. Hours later Andy had spoken to her, affectionately as always, but with a touch of scolding, adding, "So we leave France behind...and a broken heart?"

She squeezed his arm, shook her head, and smiled. She had learned her lesson.

Life on a ship had been as novel an experience to Meg as the exotic ports. It had taken some getting accustomed to. Not that the cabin that Andy had furnished wasn't perfect. Her little floating apartment had been ideal, a retreat, a place all her own. In the morning there was the sun in her face and the lull of the ship between the waves; at night, the million scattered stars and a moon that looked close enough for her to reach up and touch.

It had taken time for her to grow familiar with the ship. Her face reddened when she heard Andy's crew chuckling over her confusion between port and starboard, bow and stern, and the rest of the unique language of a ship. She still blushed at the thought of those first few days of the voyage when she walked on the deck like she had something more potent than coffee with her breakfast. A sudden plunge in the seas or a shift in the wind sent Meg grappling for something stationary, be it rail or mast or the arm of a passing crewman! Thank goodness her stomach had proved seaworthy. She had spent those first few days in a chair that Andy placed for her, with her parasol up, adjusting to the motion, giving a cautious smile to anyone who came near her.

"Not feeling queasy are you, Meg?" Andy shouted undiplomatically from the forecastle.

"Not a bit, thank you!"

Andy's deep laugh rang out over the stillness of the water.

Meg wasn't the only one who had some adjusting to do. Andy's handpicked crew were shocked when they learned a woman was to be aboard for the voyage—the captain's unmarried sister, no less! When she had toured the ship for the first time, they had been collectively horrified. Couldn't the woman have been, well, did she have to be such a "looker"? Those serious green eyes. Right off, every man knew there would have to be some personal discipline that other voyages had not required.

Andy had been uncharacteristically blunt in his speech to the crew. "You are all honorable men. (There were some sidelong glances at this. Was the young captain so naive or was he just foolish?) You have all met my sister. I want this to be a good experience for her and a good voyage for all of us. I want her to have complete freedom on this ship, to feel nothing but friendliness from you. I remind you she *is* my sister. Think of her as your sister too."

And the men of the *Magnolia* had done just that. After the initial awkwardness, they had become possessively proud of her. What other ship, clipper or otherwise, had such a tribute to feminine beauty sitting right in the bow? Ships had figureheads, graceful carvings in wood, but look what the *Magnolia* had!

In a matter of weeks they were able to tease and even flirt with the captain's sister. When she learned a handful of the crew were illiterate, the clipper became a floating classroom.

From her chair on deck, she could call to the man hauling in rigging on port bow.

"Jeffrey! Could you spell mizzenmast for me?"

"Now, Miss Alcott?"

"Please. And is it a verb or noun, Jeffrey?"

There had been squalls and storms in every ocean they traveled. Meg had grown very terrified, and very green. Huddled in her cabin, she wondered if she hadn't made a dreadful mistake in coming on this voyage and whether Andy must put her off at the first sight of land.

Mostly she cherished the time she had with Andy. He was generally very busy during the day, more so when the ship arrived at port to unload or receive cargo. But in the evenings, often with the lonesome melody of a harmonica in the background, they would sit on the deck and talk and laugh. Or be silent together as the sun would seemingly slip into the vast expanse of water, to be replaced by the moon.

The final night of the voyage, when the coast of Louisiana lay just beyond the horizon, the crew had thrown a little party on deck. There were contests, singing, and a little graduation ceremony for Meg's students. One of the devoted sailors came forward shyly to present her with a gift from the crew, a small jewelry box of inlaid pearl. Meg had been deeply touched by their affection.

Later she and Andy remained alone on deck.

"This has been a wonderful year for me, Andy, bigger and better than anything I could have expected. A treasure for me, really, to remember always."

He smiled at her as she held the rail, the Gulf winds blowing her hair and dress.

"*You* are a treasure, Meg. Someday a poor man will find you, and he'll become a very rich man."

There was a quality of sadness or loneliness in his voice. It was the sound of buried pain. But with his face turned toward the ocean, which was dark and crested in tiny waves, she knew instinctively he would not open his heart to her.

She let go of the rail. "You must admit I can walk on deck like a seasoned sailor now," she said lightly.

He laughed then, a sound of relief. "I will admit that the crew of *Magnolia Remembrance* will sorely miss your dramatic traveling from bow to stern!"

Mississippi

A woman stood in silhouette at an upper window of Tanglewood mansion. Her face was very sad. It would change in a few moments when she went down the hall to one of the freshly decorated rooms. But for now, in this unguarded moment, it was clearly etched in melancholy. She was looking out on a morning that was anything but somber. It was a bright, clear morning, freshly laundered and pungent with earthy smells from the rain the night before. She could see a thin tendril of smoke rising from the carpentry shop where Seth Jefferson was already hard at work.

Seth had brought "traffic" down Tanglewood's normally quiet drive. His reputation was growing. Granted, some thought his work excellent but were repelled by the idea that it had come from black hands. Others came, willing to ignore their bigotry for the sake of fine craftsmanship. Still others came who saw only the work and not the skin color of the carpenter.

Amy Cash knew Mary the cook was busy preparing the staff breakfasts downstairs. Fenwick was probably dusting. Amy smiled. The Englishman had a penchant for dusting. Or alphabetizing the library bookshelves when he had just done it the day before. Still, she liked the man and could not imagine Tanglewood without him. She knew if she had asked him to muck out the horse stalls, he would have bowed, changed into his second-best apron, and gone to work without complaint. The foreman would be snoozing in his cabin after his night watch. The stable hand would be grooming and feeding the horses. Like a well-oiled timepiece, Tanglewood was running efficiently.

Amy, even with so little experience, had kept the estate in good stead in the year since Cash had died. Had it already been over a year? It seemed like so much longer to her . . .

There had been no more threats, vandalism, or violence to Tanglewood. It had been a year of peace. Amy was busy, and her life had become even busier with a new arrival at the estate, which had brought her times of tremendous purpose and joy. But in quiet moments, sometimes, all she felt was loneliness. An emptiness and loneliness that Cash's death had created. She couldn't help but wonder if it wouldn't always be this way. It was a life of few dreams.

New Orleans

The *Magnolia* had returned to New Orleans; the year-long voyage was over. Now Meg sat in the darkened train bringing her closer to Greenville, Mississippi. Thirty more minutes exactly, the porter had announced. She looked out into the darkness.

What had prompted her to change her plans? Her intent had been to return home to Peppercreek. But return home to what? Even with the excitement and adventure of the voyage, there had always been that underlying thought, *What will I do when it's over? Where will I go? I'm 23 years old. No job waiting, no sweetheart. . .*

The night they reached New Orleans, they sifted through the mail that had never reached them. A tiny seed of a plan had taken form because of a letter from their mother.

Andy was reading one letter silently; Meg another. She happened to look up when a strong Gulf breeze rattled a shutter on her hotel room window. Andy had stopped reading. The letter hung limply in his hand. He was staring off into space with that look of sadness she had seen before.

"Andy?"

"Cash—Uncle Pat—died last spring. Heart failure. Mama had a letter from . . . his wife."

"I'm sorry. I never met him. You were very fond of him, weren't you?"

Andy stood and walked to the French doors. "He was a good friend." His fists clenched. "I hope I didn't hurt him." His voice was barely above a whisper.

"How could you have hurt him, Andy?"

Her brother remained silent, remote from her, grieving.

Over the next few days, Meg realized Andy could not shake off the sadness. It was like their final night on the *Remembrance,* only deeper.

"I think I've made my plans," Meg announced lightly one morning, hoping her mood would affect him.

Andy looked up from his plate. "I thought you were going home."

"Well, I am. But I'm going to Tanglewood first."

Andy stopped chewing. "Why?"

"Because I'd like to.

"You're talking with your mouth full," Meg added playfully.

"Why?"

"I don't know, I guess it's one of those habits Mama couldn't break you of."

He reddened and took a deep breath.

"All right, all right. Why are you going to Tanglewood?"

"Because I've never been. You've always told me how lovely it was, so different from home. Then too I've heard all Papa's memories of it. It's on the way home. And Cash's widow might like company, wouldn't she?"

Andy meditated on his next bite longer than necessary. Meg knew her brother's face plainly reflected his feeling. He was troubled about something.

"I don't know if she would or not."

"You've never told me much about her. You always talk about Uncle Pat. What's she like, so I'll know what to expect?"

"You shouldn't go anywhere with expectations, Meg," he answered brusquely. He saw her face cloud in confusion at his tone. "I don't know what she's like."

"You're repeating yourself," she replied, attempting to ease the tension.

His eyes were guarded, his whole body tense.

"I'm just saying I don't know that much about her."

"You spent over four months there!"

"Meg, that doesn't matter."

Meg leaned forward. "Andy, you are acting odd! Are you trying to keep me from going?"

"Of course not. Why would I?"

"I think we're about to have a fight. Why are you acting so strangely?"

"Now you're repeating yourself. Amy Cash is just Uncle Pat's wife."

"Was his wife," Meg added impulsively.

Andy paled, and Meg knew she had teased too much.

"Well, really, do you think she would like my company? I'd like to meet her."

"I'm sure she would, Meg. I'm sorry about acting odd. Guess I'm just tired."

"How about coming with me?"

"No," he replied firmly. "The *Magnolia* leaves in two weeks. I have a lot to do, you know." He took her hand. "Go to Tanglewood. You'll like it. It's as pretty as any place we've seen together."

They said goodbye a few days later. Meg sensed that despite Andy's attempt at levity and casualness, a wall had come up between them. Still his emotion was very real when he held her there in the train terminal.

"You know I can't tell you how much the trip has meant to me, and how much I love you for it," Meg said, crying on his shoulder.

"I know how much it has meant to me having you," he said, pulling away and looking deeply into her eyes. He smiled.

She could say nothing. It suddenly seemed wrong for her brother to go off alone, back to his ship and work with no one to care for him, to love him.

"Will you write to me, Andy?"

"From every port. I'll tell you how the fellows are doing in their grammar. And you write me, little sis. Tell me how you find Tanglewood."

Tanglewood

It was as beautiful as Andy had described—a classic Southern mansion and plantation now in the twilight of its days. Not a person was in sight as Meg stepped down from the buggy. Suddenly she wasn't so confident about coming here unannounced. How might Mrs. Cash receive her? She might be a formidable old lady, well versed in Southern custom and courtesies, and find a distant Yankee relative on her doorstep without invitation a rather unwelcome sight. She wished Andy hadn't been so strange about the whole thing. Meg was almost tempted to turn around and leave, but the mansion windows were like a hundred probing eyes. She drew a deep breath, fortified with a liberal dose of youthful curiosity, and approached the front door.

Fenwick was always mortified if Mrs. Cash had to answer the front door rather than himself. He had never forgiven himself for being asleep that dreadful night Jeb French had come to the mansion and Mrs. Cash had had to defend herself. The butler felt he had failed her miserably and had become only that much more devoted to her. Still, being in the garden fertilizing rosebushes, Fenwick did not hear the bell ring.

It was a young woman in a pale blue cotton dress who answered the door. She was not dressed like a servant, but neither did she wear a garment of wealth that one would expect from the mistress of a grand home. Her face was flushed from sunshine, her hair slightly disarrayed from the wind. The two women assessed each other in silence.

"Yes?" Amy's voice was low and cautious.

"Hello. I'm calling on Mrs. Cash, please."

A slight hesitation. "I'm Amy Cash."

"Oh, well, I mean Mrs. Patrick Cash. She was married to my uncle."

Amy gave her a long look. "Your...uncle?" Her eyes widened, her voice dropped almost to a whisper. "You're Meg."

Meg smiled. "Yes, I am. How did you know?"

Again Amy hesitated. "Your brother described you very well. You're as beautiful as he said."

"Thank you. I'm sorry I don't—"

"Please step inside," Amy urged.

They were both openly staring.

"I'm Cash's wife, Meg. Perhaps Andy told you..." Her words dropped off. She glanced away a moment, as if embarrassed. Meg's look was too intense.

You are my uncle's wife?" Meg blurted, inwardly furious at her brother. She could just imagine him laughing at her now. She laughed nervously. "I'm sorry for staring, I mean I ... I should be telling you how sorry I am about Uncle Pat."

"Thank you, Meg."

"We didn't get Mama's letter till last week. We didn't know, or we would have written sooner."

Amy Cash took a deep breath. "And you have my sympathies for your brother. I know you were close."

"Excuse me?"

"I learned of the sinking of *Ivanhoe's Dream* from a newspaper clipping. All the crew...lost."

Impulsively Meg grasped Amy's hands. "Oh, Mrs. Cash! Andy's not dead! He survived! We all thought he had perished. But I was with him this past year. I left him two days ago! Mrs. Cash?"

Amy had turned very pale as she slipped to the hallway bench.

"Are you all right? We've made a funny introduction, haven't we? If Andy were here he'd be laughing. I'm sorry I didn't let you know I was coming. This has been too much. I..."

Meg fell silent. The woman in front of her was trembling. In the hallway of the Cash mansion, there in the quiet, like reading the original manuscript of some play, Meg Alcott understood. One look at this woman and Meg could see Andy's face as it looked that final night on the ship, and as it had looked when he had read of Cash's death. A stricken look.

Her brother had fallen in love with a married woman. Knowing him as she did so well, she knew he had been burdened with guilt. Here then was the wall that had grown between them.

Finally Amy looked up, meeting Meg's eyes in one quick, unguarded moment. She smiled and stood up, attempting to recapture the composure that had fled so quickly.

"You're right, we have made quite an introduction, startling each other with our—"

"Expectations," Meg said brightly. "Andy warns me against having those." Now, she knew why.

After a short silence, Amy spoke. "You came to Tanglewood." There was gladness in her voice.

Meg nodded. "My father talked about it, and then of course, Andy. They both said how lovely it was here. I'm on my way home, and I suddenly found myself wanting to come here to—" Meg was suddenly shy, "to meet you." She shrugged and smiled.

Amy smiled deeply. "I'm so glad you've come, Meg. Welcome to Tanglewood."

Chapter 14

Tanglewood

♦♦ ♦♦ ♦♦

*I*t had taken Meg several hours and a basketful of crumpled paper before she was satisfied with the final letter. She was very tired and emotionally drained, a good enough excuse not to write, yet she had promised. And she had always kept her promises to her brother.

In the past, writing Andy had been so easy; it had been a natural flow of her thoughts and experiences onto paper. But this letter had been difficult to compose. She felt stiff writing it. Would Andy feel the stiffness when he read it?

She stared at the luxury of the elegant and spacious Tanglewood bedroom, so appointed in old Southern charm, without really seeing it. She should have felt nothing but excitement at finally being here, yet she felt only some degree of shock, outrage, and a thin whisper of disappointment like a softly played melody.

She closed her eyes in the darkness and replayed the events after she had stepped over the threshold of Tanglewood. There was the slender, lovely, and young Amy Cash. Andy hadn't elaborated about their uncle's wife, and to Meg's thinking now, for obvious reasons.

Amy had graciously led her to a sitting room for tea. Meg had given her the exciting narrative of the past year. She told her everything from the sinking of *Ivanhoe's Dream* to Andy's appearance in Galveston to the year-long voyage. Amy listened intently, silently, her face betraying no emotion. Only once had she interrupted.

"What did you call your brother's new ship?" she asked gently.

"Well, Captain Treadle had christened it the *Merry Widow.* But we both thought that was dull and unromantic. Andy renamed it *Magnolia Remembrance.* Perfect, isn't it?"

Amy nodded but said nothing. Watching her, Meg knew Amy Cash was a million miles away.

Suddenly Amy straightened in her chair, her head slightly tilted.

"The baby's crying. Will you come with me?"

That had been the harbinger of the shock to come.

"The baby?" Meg asked cautiously as she followed Amy up the broad, curving staircase.

Amy led her to a nursery of soft yellows and pinks. They leaned over a white crib. After nearly six decades, new life had come to Tanglewood.

"A baby!" was all Meg could manage.

Amy was wholly absorbed in the child she had taken into her arms, wholly oblivious to Meg's reaction.

Amy's smile deepened. "Isn't she beautiful?"

What Meg saw was a child with a crown of soft, golden-brown hair, slender face, and remarkably blue eyes...

As Amy fed the little girl, she introduced her to Meg.

"This is Melanie," she said proudly. "Her mother was a cousin of mine who lived in Baton Rouge. She never recovered from childbirth and died when Melanie was ten days old. Her father didn't want the responsibility of raising her, so he asked me to take her. I legally adopted her. Sleepy girl, here's another bite."

She was too involved with the child to notice the wall of reserve, an obliging cousin to suspicion and skepticism, that had risen in Meg's eyes.

Amy fingered the pink-blushed baby cheek. "Melanie's such a delight to me. She's given me such joy since I brought her to Tanglewood. With Cash gone, she's given me reason to live."

She shook her head at her melancholy tone. "My big girl! I call her baby when she'll be two in a few months."

Two years. Meg had always been quick at mental math...

Then Amy had looked at Meg directly, an appeal thinly veiled.

"Could you stay awhile at Tanglewood, Meg?" She dropped her eyes to her lap. "Your brother spoke often of you. In a way, I feel I know you."

Despite the tempest of thoughts in Meg's mind, she felt herself weaken at Amy's tone. She was drawn to this young woman. Was there any real hurry to leave Tanglewood? Wasn't there now more reason to stay?

"Yes, I'd like to stay awhile, Amy. I'd like that very much."

As she sat at her fine writing desk with the smooth, blank paper in front of her, she tried to sort through her rioting emotions. Unknowingly Andy had paved the way for a friendship between his sister and the mistress of Tanglewood. Yet Meg had not believed Amy's story of a cousin in Baton Rouge. It sounded like a fabrication through and through to her. She could still picture Andy's face of grief and guilt, and Amy's shocked face of relief when she learned that Andy had lived. And there was the child. Two years...

She had always thought of her brother as nearly perfect. He had never let her down. He had always been what she wanted and needed. In her immaturity she could not imagine him... *sinning.* There, she whispered the word to the bedroom. One word to contain all that she imagined. How could passion have swept away all the goodness and honor she had known in her brother? To have loved a married woman... How could she write him that a tiny daughter lived at Tanglewood?

Amy had rocked little Melanie asleep. She could get up and place the child in the baby bed without concern for her waking, but she continued to rock her. She did love to hold this little one who had come as a gift—and become as her very own. Didn't that alone prove the Lord's tenderness for her, giving her someone to love and be loved by? It made Amy Cash feel less destitute, though she was a very wealthy woman. Melanie gave her a measure of hope.

Now there was a guest in a bedroom down the hall. Another Alcott had come to Tanglewood, Amy smiled. She certainly didn't feel like she had when the first Alcott had come! She felt no intrusion, no threat over this woman. She felt an excitement she couldn't quite explain to herself. Here was a woman Andy Alcott had lovingly described in some detail. A woman only slightly younger than herself. It was pathetic in its desperation, yet Amy Cash was hoping she had found a new friend.

Amy slipped down quietly to Cash's studio after her guest had retired to her room. She felt silly—a bit like a thief in her own home! The studio looked very much like her husband had left it. She wanted to make sure one of the canvases was still draped in the corner of the room. Good . . . of course it was. No one in the house touched it—except her. Fenwick dusted only the paintings that were displayed. This canvas, however, stayed draped for now. She wasn't ready for it to be revealed. It displayed . . . so much. Like the pages of a diary.

Over the next few days Amy showed Meg all of Tanglewood, from the mansion to the gardens and pastures and from the stables to the carpentry shop. Seth Jefferson had greeted her warmly. "Mr. Andy's sister! Well, well, that's nice. A fine brother you have there, Miss Alcott."

"Thank you, Seth. Andy told me how much he enjoyed working alongside you."

Meg found the climate, the vegetation, and the land as impressive as Andy had. She felt vital in this warm, sunny, humid country where the afternoons were tranquil and heavily scented with magnolias. Meg enjoyed riding, and the Tanglewood stable offered her quality mounts to choose from. Amy had reduced the stable only slightly and encouraged Meg to ride.

One afternoon, gray and cool with low-hanging clouds, Meg went out riding from Tanglewood. She rode first to Greenville, where she posted her letter to Andy. She toured the town, drawing prompt attention to herself—a lovely young woman, carefully dressed, riding a well-blooded horse. Jeb French, who was supervising the loading of one of his ships, stopped in midsentence as she passed the waterfront district. By nightfall, he would know who she was and where she was staying.

A lonely-looking, spiraling road, well shaded with pines, drew Meg from Greenville. She smiled to herself. She was a girl again, without cares or concerns, exploring the cool, leafy trails around her girlhood home. The road wound and ribboned for several miles with Meg seeing only cottontails and red-tailed squirrels. She could hear the music of a river somewhere parallel to the road. The lane finally widened to a dry, dusty clearing. Meg had arrived at Chisolm Crossing. How could she know this place would forever alter the course of her life?

Seeing a mercantile made her realize how thirsty she was. Bright red paint declared that this squatty wooden building was called Chisolm's Mercantile. She entered and was instantly delighted. The old store reminded her of Bailey's General Store back home.

Although the rural mercantile was fast becoming a relic, the Chisolms had not surrendered. They still sold crackers from the barrel, not prepackaged like the current fad. They did no advertising in nearby papers, nor did they offer samples and promotions through the mail. The owner, Chester Chisolm, found such contemporary gimmicks foolish. His wife, Matilda, scorned his lack of business sense and progress.

Meg could see only the top of a man's very bald head as she approached the counter. He had heard her step but did not look up.

"You'll just have to wait. I'm with a patient here."

Meg leaned forward. The man was tying up a kitten's hind leg.

"Sprained it, I guess. I'm playin' surgeon. *She*," he jerked his head sideways, "says it's a waste of time, but I say what's the waste in helpin' a poor creature? What have I got better to do? Think it'll work?"

"I hope so," Meg replied.

When he heard her voice, he jerked upright, looking up into her eager face.

"Well, catfish in cowboy boots!" he sputtered. He laid the kitten down and quickly came around the counter. He was not much taller than the counter. "I declare, you'd make a picture for a man to wake up to!"

Meg blushed and laughed, not offended by the cheerful little man.

"There ain't a lot of meat on ya, but your bone structure is a credit to the Maker!" he continued.

Meg laughed again. "Thank you."

"So," he said as he continued to gaze on her. He was studying her hair. *What exact shade of brown is it?* he wondered.

"I wonder if I might purchase a cold drink. I've been out riding for a while."

"Certainly, certainly! It would be my pleasure to serve ya. How about a root beer?"

"That would be fine."

He handed her the drink. "You sound like you're from the North. Visitin'?"

Meg could not resist the jovial storekeeper. "Yes, I'm visiting."

"Well, now, that's just fine and dandy. I'm Chester Chisolm." He stuck out a meaty hand.

"I'm Meg Alcott."

"Alcott. Well, you surely are a looker!"

Meg attempted to draw him away from such embarrassing dialogue.

"How did your kitten hurt its leg, Mr. Chisolm?"

The man's jolly face sobered instantly.

"Met the unfriendly end of the broom, I'm afraid to say. *She* was scootin' him off the back porch 'cause he had messed just one too many times, and it's a bit of a drop off the back. Didn't say so, of course, but I knew she felt real bad about it. Didn't mean to hurt him. She says he'll be lame and my pretendin' to be a doc won't go far with him. Poor little guy."

"I hope your efforts do help him. I've seen my brothers do things like that and have them heal."

"Brothers, huh?" He was conspicuously lacking in subtlety.

"Yes, I have three." She smiled and finished her drink. "Could you give me directions to Tanglewood? I rode out this morning, and I'm not sure how to get back."

"Of course! So you're visitin' over at Tanglewood."

"Yes."

"Amy's a sweet young thing. Cash seemed a nice fella. Not that I knew him much, him being who he was and me the storekeeper at the Crossin'. You must be from his side."

"He was my second cousin. Do you know Amy?"

"Sure do. She's a Crossin' girl from way back. Been in my store when she was still in bloomers."

A flood of questions came to Meg's mind, but she kept silent. She was glad she had met this loquacious little merchant.

"I can see you're a woman of intelligence and wit. Delightful mix in a woman, given the proper proportions. And I do like a woman with the proper proportions!"

He went off into a wizened bout of hilarity, and Meg found herself joining him.

"Will ya come again, Miss Alcott? Bring Amy with ya. Ain't seen her in a coon's age."

"Yes, I will come again, Mr. Chisolm. I'd like to see more of this area."

When she rode away, the little man was waving his apron at her from the storefront.

A wounded shoulder had not deterred Jeb French from continuing to keep Tanglewood under a personal and secret scrutiny. The injury from Amy Cash's gun had not been a serious one—only enough to ache occasionally and remind French of his festering bitterness and hatred.

Patrick Cash was dead. The worthless old cripple had left the estate to his wife, his own stepsister. Smoking his cigars in the darkness of his study, he smiled at that . . . his own stepsister. She had shown surprising spunk to fire at him that night over a year ago, but spunk was really a laughable defense against a man like Jeb French.

For over a year he had carefully watched Tanglewood. He knew that young Amy was surrounded by a snobby English butler, a cook, a foreman, and a groom for the stables—an absurdly small staff for an elegant manor. Things would be very different if he were lord and master of Tanglewood. And a carpentry shop half-owned by a Negro! He sneered at the thought of that. Common to have such a thing . . . Seth Jefferson coming in the morning, leaving each evening. A pitiful entourage around Amy . . . like a sniveling bunch of spinster women!

He knew when Amy had gone to Baton Rouge and spent months there. He knew the very morning she had returned with an infant, bawling away at the quiet dignity of the Southern mansion. He knew . . . He remembered Cash's cousin . . . He laughed, then breathed heavily at the thought of his stepsister's buried passion racing through her while appearing so virtuous. It was French himself who had started the little whisperings of gossip—and secured Amy Cash in her isolation.

Greenville

The postal clerk felt as if he were being questioned by the local sheriff. The imposing Jeb French had strode into the little cubicle where the clerk was taking his midday meal. French leaned against the doorframe, pushed back his hat with his riding crop, and made the clerk feel rather small.

"There was a woman in here this morning," he said by way of greeting.

The clerk gulped a fortifying drink of buttermilk.

"Ah . . . there were customers in all morning, Mr. French. We were very busy."

The riding crop was jabbed nearly in his face.

"Yeah, yeah, you had customers. But this little customer you'd never seen before. And I wouldn't think you would forget her after you had. A classy lookin' lady, dark hair, young."

The clerk had known immediately whom the aggressive Jeb French was referring to. But it gave the timid clerk a bit of a thrill to know something the mighty French did not know. He would play him along as long as he dared.

"Classy looking . . . dark hair . . . hmm . . ." The clerk was searching the ceiling.

French grew impatient. "If you're half a man, or have two eyes in your skull, you'd notice her!" he snapped.

The clerk did not like this impatience and rudeness.

"A young woman...dark hair...classy looking...hmm..."

"Wore a dark riding skirt, white blouse, straw hat." Jeb French had missed few details when Meg Alcott had passed by. "Not from around here. Remember now?"

"I think I'm beginning to recall."

"Well, that's just fine," French said sarcastically. "Who is she?"

"I didn't ask, Mr. French."

The riding crop was snapping impatiently on French's boot.

"What did she do here?"

"Posted a letter, sir."

"Did you speak to her?"

"Not beyond, 'Good morning, ma'am'. She said, 'I'd like to mail this, please.' She had pretty teeth...My two eyes did notice that."

French's grin spread slowly across his face.

"Your memory is impressive now. So where was the letter to? What was the return address?"

The clerk looked like he would choke on his buttermilk.

"Mr. French! I am a postal officer of the United States government. I do not make it a practice—"

"I didn't ask you if you opened it. I asked you who sent it. Simple."

"Oh, I wouldn't know...I just took the letter."

He returned to his meal despite a feeling of agitation.

"The mail hasn't gone out yet," French stated flatly.

The clerk did not feel it would be wise, perhaps even healthy to offend one of the most powerful men in Greenville. If only his boss had come back from lunch, this wouldn't have happened to him. He mopped his suddenly sweating brow.

"I have to go back up front now. The outgoing mail is in that bin there."

Again that smile. It made the clerk think that was the way a snake would look if it could smile...

"There are three bins, and I don't have a lot of time," French pushed arrogantly.

The clerk laid his hand swiftly on one, then disappeared to the front of the office.

French found the letter quickly. Meg Alcott...to Andy Alcott...from Tanglewood. He tossed the letter back into the bin. The smile widened. Now a new beauty had come to Tanglewood, sister to Alcott. All very interesting and full of possibilities.

Meg had listened carefully to Chester's directions, but something had gone wrong. She had jogged down a long road without sight of human or habitation. The countryside grew more remote with each mile, and she knew she was lost.

Finally she rounded the curve to a small cabin. She must stop and ask for directions.

She called out hopefully, "Hello? Hello!"

She felt someone must be in the cabin from the gray filament of smoke that curled up from the chimney. Almost instantly, the rough cabin door swung open. A woman leaned heavily against the doorframe, one hand clutched at her throat, the other protectively over her rounded belly.

"You've come," she gasped. Even at the distance, Meg could see a measure of relief flood the woman's face.

"I'm lost," Meg said almost cheerfully. "I stopped for directions."

Meg's eyes widened in horror as the woman closed her eyes in a spasm of pain. She paled and stuttered, "I . . . are you . . . you see, I'm lost . . ."

"You've come," the black woman said again.

"Would you like me to go for your doctor? I can if you'll just tell me where to find him."

The woman turned, swallowed up by the dark cabin.

Oh, this is horrible! Meg's mind raced. Even in her naiveté she knew this woman was in the struggles of childbirth and in need. An ageless and great mystery was about to unfold for Meg Alcott, if she was brave enough to face it. She hopped down quickly, ground-tying the horse. She would go into the cabin, get directions, and ride for the doctor. It was the least she could do, yes, and it was the most she could do.

She was rigid with fear, dread, and reluctance as she stepped into the cabin, timidly calling, "Hello?"

It took a moment for her eyes to adjust. When they did she saw a rock fireplace giving little heat and even less light, and a table with a single kerosene lamp. Its faint yellow circle extended to a large, quilt-covered bed. Meg approached nervously. "Hello?" she called again.

A face blanched in pain and weariness looked at her, a mahogany face that could have been 20 or 50. The eyes were brown, bright, friendly. "I'm called Mim."

"I'm Meg."

"Meg? Not a name you would expect for—" Another contraction gripped the woman and silenced her.

Meg's hand flew to her forehead, a gesture reserved for times of intense stress. She breathed deeply, trying to calm the churning in her stomach. "How can I help you, Mim? Can I go for the doctor?"

"No, don't go, please. I done sent neighbor-boy Roddy for him. But—"

"Water! I can boil water! They always say there should be lots of hot water. I can do that!" She moved away quickly, not hearing the little voice from the bed that asked, "Could I have a drink?"

Meg was poking up the fire, hoping the woman in the bed could not see how badly she was shaking. *Palsied with fear, I am,* Meg scolded herself. Finding a wooden bucket, she dashed outside to the pump. She scanned the road, desperate for a glimpse of the tardy doctor.

She reentered the cabin as the woman moaned deeply. Meg felt a wave of nausea. The water set to heat, she hesitantly approached the bed. "Water's heating now. A rag! A rag for your head. My mother, she . . . she always . . . she was a nurse, you see, during the . . ."

Meg was definitely babbling now.

She went out to the horse and got her own clean white lace hand-kerchief from her bag, rinsing it in water. Her mind was in a whirl, and her own mother a nurse! How did she stand the smells . . . the wounds. *I never could stand the sight of blood! She'd laugh to see me now!*

Back in the cabin, she laid the cloth on the damp forehead.

"There, that should help."

The woman grasped for Meg's hand as her head went back in a voiceless scream. Meg clamped her eyes shut, trying desperately not to cry.

"I'm so sorry, Mim. I'll go look out for the doctor. He should be here by now, shouldn't he?"

"Could you just—"

"What, Mim?"

"Hold my hand. Just hold onto me."

"Hold your hand?"

The woman's eyes searched Meg's face with desperation.

"Angels, they aren't scared of black skin, are they? Thought you'd maybe be black anyway."

"What? Oh!" Meg gave a short, nervous laugh. Imagine being mistaken for an angel!

She reached out and took the clammy hand, feeling the thin roughness of it.

"There, there, that's what I needed. Won't be afraid now," Mim sighed.

How long Meg sat beside the bed she didn't know. It felt like hours and hours, though it was really only one. She felt awkward at first, then like her hardworking patient she relaxed a bit, resting between pains. The woman murmured incoherently at times, letting her eyes rest on Meg with a shy smile.

While resolved to not leave this woman alone, Meg felt mounting anger at the doctor. Didn't he care that he was desperately needed here? Meg, educated from the passions of farm-animal society, knew that birth was a progressive experience, and that this woman's travail would grow greater. What if the doctor still did not come?

The doctor enjoyed puttering around in his kitchen garden and among the trees of his small orchard. But he had very little time for it. If he wasn't on a case, he was studying from a medical text or reading a physician's periodical. His patients usually had the basic crop of complaints—fevers, lung congestion, sprains and breaks, birthings. Still he studied with a fervor to better serve them. This was a side of the doctor that his few friends and many patients did not suspect. With them he always seemed casual and a little preoccupied. But he was intensely dedicated to them. So he read about cancers and ulcers and a myriad of problems the big city physicians encountered so often.

He could remember the day as if it were yesterday, that he had told his father he wanted to be a doctor. He was a thin little boy of eight.

"Was out sittin' in the big oak, Pa, and I was thinkin'." He felt too shy to say "praying." But that's exactly what he had been doing. He had been listening carefully to the things he heard at the Sunday school his father sometimes took him to. When his father was able. "And it come to me, Pa, that I want to be a doctor when I grow up."

It was fitting that the elder Browning broke into a violent spasm of coughing. When it subsided, he tweaked his son's ear.

"Maybe you'll be able to patch up your old man, huh?"

"That's it, Pa!" the boy had eagerly agreed.

The man closed his eyes again. "Or maybe I'll be . . . gone by then," he whispered to himself.

The boy didn't like those dark, frightening words. He'd be all alone if his father died.

"Takes a lot of money to be a doc, son. To go off to school. Where could we get that kind of money?"

The boy shrugged. Suddenly his dream was crumbling. He felt like crying. But that would only upset his pa.

The father saw the sadness on his young son's face. It deepened the wound in his own breaking heart. There was so little he could do for this one he loved.

"Well, son, my ma was a prayin' woman, so . . . we'll try that. We'll pray for you to somehow become a doc . . . Yeah, we'll pray."

The father took his son's hand in his own, like a weak attempt at blessing—and fell asleep.

The doctor shook his head at the memory. He didn't like to think about the past. Good memories seemed to drift into unpleasant ones so often.

He dumped a bucket of water on a peach tree, then sauntered back to the house. He had two cases to check on before evening. He decided to fix himself something to eat first and maybe catch a few minutes' snooze in the sunshine. That's what he'd do.

His eyes fell on the medical journal he'd been reading earlier. Another article on birthing complications. He mulled this over in his mind as he headed for the kitchen. He didn't recognize the prompting in his spirit. His first love had grown dim, distant. So when there was a knocking in his heart, it was hard for him to hear.

Maternity. He had four maternity cases. Mim would be the soonest to deliver. And doin' fine. He frowned when he thought of Mim living alone. Maybe . . . no, he told himself firmly, he had just checked on her two days ago. She was fine. If he came again this soon it would just alarm her, make her think he suspected some trouble with the baby.

He lifted the knife, reached for the plate. He stopped and his frown deepened. He sighed and reached for his bag and hat.

The blunt nails dug into Meg's hand like razors.

"Mim, you're doing fine. It will be all right soon." Meg was crooning softly, not unlike a mother does for her feverish child.

Once in the long hour she had nearly laughed out loud when Mim had said, "I supposed you'd just quote me Scriptures and the like. You know, angel talk."

Meg did not feel it prudent to correct the illusion just now. What profit could this pain-racked woman gain in knowing her nurse was not a celestial visitor, but instead very mortal, tired, afraid, and remotely indignant at being thrust unwillingly into this drama. Perhaps years from now Meg would smile over this, maybe even chuckle at herself, but not now.

She glanced down at her gold filigree watch and frowned. Nearly four. Afternoon shadows were creeping across the plank floor. Amy would soon grow worried. Meg shook her head. *I should never have ridden out alone.*

Since there was no resident canine to herald a warning or greeting, Meg was not alerted to the truant doctor's appearance. She didn't hear his step even when he came to the bedside. Rather, she felt his presence, felt his shadow over the bed. She jerked upright, the muscles in her neck screaming.

Young Roddy had come panting up to the doctor's cabin just as Barrett was saddling his horse. As Barrett spurred the horse down the trail, he could not help but wonder at the . . . prompting that had prepared him for this. He was amazed when he entered the cabin. He expected his patient to be alone in her suffering, or exhausted with a newborn infant in her arms, or dead. Instead he found a white woman dressed in light-colored clothes seated by the bed, bent over it, one hand clasped in the black woman's hand, the other gently smoothing Mim's forehead. She was singing. Her words were rhythmic and unmistakably Northern-accented.

Meg's eyes flashed open, all the stress and fears of the last hour boiling over. "Doctor! This woman, Mim, needed you a long time ago. How unprofessional to keep a patient waiting this long! She could have died! Or the baby."

Meg instantly regretted her hot, impulsive words. She knew she had made a ridiculous accusation of a total stranger. The doctor slowly sat his black bag down, then straightened, grazing over Meg with cold, hostile eyes. She did not see the red that had colored the back of his neck at her angry speech. In his frigid look, she accurately realized she had made her first Mississippi adversary. He leaned over the bed.

"How goes it, Mim?" he asked gently.

"Dr. Browning," she breathed heavily.

"You're two weeks early, Mim. Why the hurry?"

Mim managed a smile, pathetic in its weakness. "Package just too heavy, Doc."

"Too heavy, hmm? Well, I reckon all mothers have been saying that since mothering got started. Little package must know the best time to arrive, right?"

He's trying to relax her, comfort her, Meg realized as she released the black hand.

"Let's have a look, see how things are coming along."

Meg stood up and crossed quickly to the neglected fire. The water had already cooled. She was irritated that the doctor would find her efforts lacking. Mim gave a high-pitched scream, and Meg backed out of the cabin. She leaned heavily against a tree, gulping in the cool, fresh air.

"You've got to come back. She's calling for you," the doctor said from the doorway.

Meg drew in a deep breath and walked back to him, regretting that he would see the tears in her eyes. "I can't. I'm not trained."

"The baby is turned wrong, or you would have delivered an hour ago. She and I'll do the work," here Meg noticed his tone grew more icy, "but she needs you to calm her. We can't stand here and gab."

Another scream. "Now!" he shouted.

Meg would never forget the next few minutes—nerve-racking, tense, fearful, then suddenly beautiful and poignant. In a tide of blood and water, a small brown body, a perfect baby, rushed from its mother's body, crying with the gladness of its new life.

Meg glanced up at the doctor. He was smiling at some private thought. She drew her breath in sharply. It brought such a change to his face. Granted she had little time to really look over the medical man, but the radiance was transforming. His eyes met hers for a second in a bond between two strangers over the miracle of life. Then he turned away sharply.

"You have a daughter, Mim." His voice was professionally calm.

"She all right?" Mim asked in a faint voice.

"Ten toes, ten fingers. Seems fine. Good pipes too."

Mim's eyes were closed, and she spoke slowly.

"My granny said that babies come into the world cryin' cause they just left the side of Jesus and they're just a mite sad."

"Interesting theory, Mim," the doctor replied as he examined the baby.

Mim gave a weak chuckle. "Ah, Dr. B., don't you know man can't live by theories alone?"

"Do you want this gal, Mim, or shall I take her home for my fee?"

He placed the infant in her mother's arms. Mim sighed that sigh of contentment as old as mothering itself. Meg felt the tears pool up in her eyes. "She's beautiful, Mim," she whispered.

"Do ya think so really? I'd think you seen all sorts of pretty little ones."

"She's lovely. Have you a name for her?"

"Susannah. She's called Susannah. After my ma."

Meg reached out a slender finger to stroke the downy softness of the baby's head. "A perfect name, Mim."

New life. Meg Alcott had never seen it so fresh, so new, so quietly peaceful. "She sure seems to have come straight from heaven, this little one."

"Like you," Mim said in awe.

Meg did not see the doctor's eyebrow arch, but she felt herself grow red. An angel! She wished the doctor would move away, not hearing this awkward explanation.

"Well, Mim..."

"You're going to have to introduce me to my assistant, Mim." There was a trace of sarcasm in the voice that Meg did not miss.

"Her name is Meg, Dr. B.! Seems like it was improper to ask though."

"Mim, you see, I'm—"

"You let a stranger in to help you, Mim? That's odd."

"Dr. Browning, be careful how you speak," Mim alerted.

"Why?"

Meg felt her embarrassment mounting. Her words were hurried. "Mim, I'm not what—"

"Dr. Browning, angels might have some power to strike you dead or something if you speak disrespect."

"Oh?" He turned his full, unfriendly gaze upon Meg. "So my assistant is an angel?"

Meg had a quick impulse to stick out her tongue at this man.

"I was praying hard for someone to come and help me, and then there she was, all in white, coming to help me so sweetly."

"I see." He crossed to the fireplace, and Meg could see he was making preparations for tea.

Meg sat back down and explained in a low voice her real identity.

Mim reached out and patted the soft white hand. "Well, seems like my prayers were still answered, weren't they?"

Meg smiled. "Thank you, Mim."

Then Barrett Browning returned to the bedside with the tea.

"Here's some tea, Mim," he said, extending a cup to the black woman with Southern courtesy.

He held out the other cup to Meg, his voice mocking, "Can you drink tea?"

"Yes, thank you so much, Dr. Browning," Meg replied starchly.

"Doctor, this is Meg Alcott, visitin' over at Tanglewood," Mim said happily. "A flesh-and-blood angel."

"Most practical kind, I reckon," Browning mumbled into his teacup.

When Meg offered to straighten the cabin and tidy up Mim and the baby, Browning spoke curtly. "No need, Miss Alcott. I can take care of that." His look spoke volumes. He was dismissing her.

She turned to Mim with the promise to return for a visit soon.

Mim was startled. "You'd come back here?"

"Of course," Meg smiled. "Is that all right?" She stroked the baby again.

"Don't get many visitors of any kind."

Meg suddenly felt awkward and unwanted. The "spell" so uniquely woven was broken.

Outside she made the horse ready. The doctor emerged from the cabin. He strode purposefully to the pump. She now had an opportunity for a careful scrutiny of the man.

Meg Alcott enjoyed playing a little game with herself, guessing a person's age. A face could be such a challenge to the writings of youth and age, with a multitude of emotions to line or lighten, to shadow or illumine, a window to the heart of its owner. Of course, guessing was just half the game. The concluding skill was getting the owner to unwittingly confess if she had come close, hit, or been wide of the mark. That, Meg knew, was the difficult part, often impossible.

His hair was sandy, already thinning and graying just a bit at the temples. His height and build were average. His face was tanned, as if he put in hours in the sunshine. She had noticed his hands. They bore slender fingers with red-blond hairs on the back. She had looked into his eyes only once; they were brown with little golden flecks. He possessed a straight nose, narrow face, and thin gold-rimmed glasses.

No, not a handsome man. His age? Early forties, she decided. Since she had no expectation of further contact with this unfriendly man, this was one guessing game she could not win.

He wore khaki trousers and a white shirt, worn, clean, and neat. His obvious care caused Meg to wonder if he was married. *Who cares,* she said to herself as she climbed into the buggy. *I was rude, but for some reason I suspect he would have been rude regardless. Doctors are often arrogant like that.*

She watched him rinse his face and run his hands through his hair. The action was somehow boyish, but the face was too tired, too troubled, too stern for youth. He gazed down the road a moment, hands on hips. Then he swung around abruptly and stalked to the horse.

"Are you married, Miss Alcott?"

Meg didn't know whether to laugh or be angry with his rudeness.

"No, Doctor, I am not married."

"I thought not. Well, then I'm sorry that you had to see this," he said, gesturing toward the cabin, "childbirth. Yet I needed your help."

"If you'll just give me directions to Tanglewood."

"I'll ride with you to the Crossing. You can find your way from there."

"No, thank you, directions will be fine." Her coldness matched his.

He studied her without embarrassment, and she stood firm, not flinching, and thankfully, not coloring.

He bowed, gave the directions quickly, and then reentered the cabin without a backward glance. One drama had ended; another had just begun.

Tanglewood

Jeb French's foreman wouldn't admit it to anyone, but he felt intimidated by the stately grandeur of Tanglewood mansion. Such meticulous care, such quiet dignity and prosperity. The foreman named Turner suddenly felt countrified and ignorant. But French had told him, no, *ordered* him, here. So here he was.

"I have business with the Tanglewood workshop," he told the worker he passed at the gate in his best French-like brusqueness.

He tied his horse at the rail in front of the shop. He wasn't afraid of the big carpenter—that was ridiculous—nor did he have any scruples about the spying that French had ordered. He had worked long enough for the waterfront lord to not have very many scruples left. He'd done all kinds of illegal, immoral, shady, and suggestive duties for French in the 18 years he had worked for him. It was just that this little chore seemed so transparent. Even Seth Jefferson should see through it.

Seth was sorting lumber beside the shop. Only when the foreman's shadow fell across him did he realize he had a customer.

"Why, Turner! This is sure a surprise! Ain't seen you in a long spell."

Turner managed a long and arrogant look that would have made his boss proud. "Not since you left French."

His tone was uncommitted to either friendliness or unfriendliness, but Jefferson didn't seem to notice.

"Looks like business is pretty fair for you," Turner remarked.

Seth nodded happily. "Yes, sir. I'm lookin' to hire another helper. Already have three. Just can't handle all the trade myself."

Turner could hear the saws and hammers ringing in the shop.

"Lookin' to apply?" Seth asked as a joke.

But Turner was not smiling, certainly not in the mood to swap jokes with a black man.

"Came for business, Jefferson," he said curtly.

Seth did not miss the tone this time. "All right, sir."

Seth moderated his cheerfulness. He had not forgotten the testy temper of Turner. *Like a shadow of his boss,* Seth thought regretfully.

"Wife's havin' a baby," the foreman said.

"Well, congrat—" Seth began. But Turner cut him off.

"Thinkin' on a cradle for it. Want to know what you can do and what you charge."

"Come on inside, sir."

Seth showed him samples of his work, displayed different woods for him to consider, estimated costs. But the foreman would commit to nothing. They had stepped back into the sunshine in front of the shop.

Turner glanced casually at the house. His tone was mild again.

"Heard Mrs. Cash has a guest."

"Miss Alcott from Illinois, yes, sir," Seth answered easily. "Brother was here a year or so back."

"What's she doing here?" Turner ventured with bold bluntness.

Seth shrugged. "Just visitin', I reckon. They're family, you know."

"How long she staying?"

Turner had childish skills as a spy. He wanted the information French wanted quickly. He wanted to leave, to ride away from this snobbish place and this uppity black.

Seth Jefferson had one of those rare moments of sudden, clear understanding. Knowledge that came unexplainably. He saw the hawkish looks the foreman was giving Tanglewood mansion. The man hadn't placed an order because he had no intention of ordering anything. This was his intention—to know about Miss Amy's guest.

He forced a chuckle into his tone. "Don't know how long she plans to stay. They wouldn't need to tell an ol' black carpenter now, would they, Turner?"

The man looked at Seth sharply. This was all the information he was going to get on the Yankee woman. Let French get whatever else he wanted, for whatever reason. Wordlessly he mounted his horse and rode away.

Seth was thinking hard now. He felt as if trouble was connected to this man, and trouble was coming to Tanglewood through him. He stood there in the sunshine and felt as if a chill wind had blown across him.

Chapter 15

Tanglewood

◆◆ ◆◆ ◆◆

*I*f Patrick Cash had been alive, his artist's passion would have found the subject irresistible: two young women, lovely in their pastel dresses, seated at a white iron table with delicate tea things between them and blazing colors of the garden in full bloom behind them. Smiling, talking, laughing, and sometimes silent, they were yet growing daily as close friends who had found each other.

At first Meg had tried to find a deceptive or seductive side to Amy Cash, something to explain how her normally steady brother had been lured. She found nothing. Or perhaps... perhaps Amy Cash was superb as an actress, a grieving young widow, generously raising her cousin's baby.

But what Meg was slowly finding in Amy Cash was the same gentleness that was in Andy. She was vaguely irritated by it. It didn't make her original determination to dislike and distrust the mistress of Tanglewood any easier.

Amy talked at length about Cash and running Tanglewood alone. Meg talked of her teaching experiences and the sights she had seen in Europe. Neither talked of Andy's time at Tanglewood. Meg was resolved to prompt no confession. Amy must speak freely on her own.

When Meg returned to Tanglewood from Mim's, she was exhausted from her "nearly a midwife" encounter. Her paleness and fatigue alarmed Amy, yet Meg had managed to breathlessly relate the event. Amy controlled a strong desire to smile with difficulty.

Meg took another deep drink of tea, her hands still trembling.

"It was dreadful, Amy." She glanced out over the lawn, now drawing on its bedclothes of gray. "Yet somehow it was beautiful." She shrugged, unable to say more.

"I know what you mean," Amy replied. "When Melanie was born—"

Meg was too weary to pursue that subject. She laughed shakily. "Just think if that doctor hadn't shown up! No, I don't want to think about it."

"That was Barrett."

"Mim called him Dr. Browning, I think."

"Yes, that was Barrett Browning."

"What an interesting name." Her voice was tinged with scorn.

Amy nodded.

"Well, he certainly wasn't..." Meg continued. "He seemed to me a very arrogant man."

She conveniently neglected to tell Amy her own ill-chosen words.

"Really? You thought Barrett arrogant? He's always been kind to me. He was Cash's doctor."

"He was my Uncle Pat's doctor? And a doctor to the . . . blacks? That's rather different."

Amy smiled. "That difference may be what you mistook as arrogance. He's from the Crossing. He went back East to medical school, yet came back here to be a doctor to the black community. Most whites have little to do with him. Cash and a few others were his only white patients."

Meg kept silent. There were mysteries around Tanglewood—mysteries for a Yankee schoolmarm to decipher?

It was a lonely-looking house, having somehow assumed the emotions of its tenants over the past years. It was a house well built, but without much glory in its history. The building materials had been pulled from the land itself, a kind of birthing of massive timbers and gray-bleached rocks. Its walls were stout pine logs, the foundation, rock. It lacked any grace, any charm. A well-built house, yes, but desolate.

Its east side commanded a panoramic view of the sweeping fields below it. But the view had never been used to advantage. The back of the house, the east side, was a broad porch. It could have been a peaceful, restful retreat, catching vagrant breezes. Yet it had been boarded over and was now the dusty domain of a fat gray mouser.

The property wasn't untidy exactly; it simply seemed to sit among the pines in dejection. On closer inspection, you could see it was an unfinished house, a house that had ambition years ago. But something a casual visitor couldn't know had stayed the hand of the builder.

It was the residence of Dr. Barrett Browning. He had ridden in from Mim's, slid off the mare, and tossed the reins aside. He pulled off the saddle in one quick gesture. He patted the horse's rump, knowing she'd find food and water on her own. Man and beast alike had to be self-reliant on the Browning place. A hound came wiggling up, and Barrett ruffed its ears absently. He had been up since 5:00 and was bone tired.

He could see only dimly through the front door, but he knew every inch, where to lay his hand or place his foot without stumbling. With one hand his hat went on the peg in one swift motion, while his other hand gently dropped the black medical bag on a stool by the door. Over to the basin he went, sleeves up, arms scrubbed, face washed until it was glowing. Still he didn't bother to light the lamps, though the sun was creasing the hills and leaving the valley in muted colors. He yawned deeply and set the coffee on to boil. He waited for it, staring fixedly into the flames.

A new life, a healthy new life, had come into the world, and the mother was doing fine.

He yawned again and searched among the stack of dirty dishes for a reasonably clean cup. He hacked off a thick slice of coarse bread, spread a veneer of butter, and topped it with a slash of molasses. That was the doctor's dinner. He pulled off his boots and threw his socks in a dark corner. Barrett eased himself into a creaking willow rocker, the cushion well-stained and cat-haired, and slowly ate his spartan meal.

The unmistakable imprint of a bachelor was inside this house. Rooms lived in by a very busy man whose creature comforts were very few and came by his own hand. No curtains hung at the dirty, mullioned windows. Nothing gentled or interrupted the barren walls—no trophies, no samplers, no photographs. No jelly jar of wildflowers. No plant taking root on a sunny windowsill. The furniture was serviceable, nothing more. No touch of a feminine hand could be seen.

Nothing in the house testified to there ever having been a feminine presence in the house or on the property. But there had been. All traces of the former mistress were gone, dispatched and buried long ago with no apparent sentiment. The house looked, with its scattered newspapers and medical journals, sturdy masculine furniture, assorted muddy boots and crumpled laundry, dirty dishes, pipe ashes, and fishing rods propped in the corners, to have been Barrett's forever.

Of course he did not mean to live slovenly, but the business of a growing medical practice took nearly all his time. For the young doctor was not much richer than his poorest patient. Getting paid in garden produce or knitted socks and fresh-baked bread did not pay for medical supplies. For that, he farmed the broad rice fields below the house. It was a meager living at best, but it was what he had known most of his 35 years.

When his bread and coffee were gone, he stared into the flames, his mind replaying the afternoon's events. His face softened, relaxing a fleeting instant when he thought of Mim's assumption of her angelic "nurse" and the nurse's obvious discomfort at the mistake. Then his eyes swung around to a closed door and lingered there.

It had been a bedroom originally; now Barrett used it for supplies and his laboratory. But his mind was not on supplies. He thought of the trunk that was pushed into one corner, covered over in moth-eaten quilts.

He stood up, hating his decision yet determined, almost gloating in the pain it stirred inside him. The door was quickly unlocked, a lamp finally lit. He angrily tossed aside the quilts, his breathing labored with emotion. The trunk was not locked, and he flipped it open. He stood there, silent, like stone, angered at the smell of herbs and roses that clung to the contents and drifted up to him. He hated that smell.

Impatiently he pushed aside the leather, the silk and lace, and the cotton quilt until his fingers touched cold metal. Clutching the object he stalked back to the fireplace. He quickly placed the lamp on the mantel, where it threw a homey glow around the room. If only the room could have infected the occupant.

Barrett squatted down before the flames, tense and rigid, morbidly fascinated with the object he so despised. He stared into the picture frame. It was a daguerreotype, flecked with age yet preserving the somber face of a young man and the laughing face of a beautiful young woman. He stared into the woman's face, so carefree and young. He was not surprised to feel warm tears slide down his cheeks; it happened every time he looked at this photograph. This time, however, he looked at the woman's face with a new and different perspective. It seemed to the very tired Dr. Barrett Browning that the face which looked back at him was the face of Mim's angel.

Jackson, Mississippi

The Klan leader was unimpressed with the membership in Washington County. In a word, it was feeble. He stood in his personal study and looked over the state map on his desk. With meticulous care, he had pinned paper crosses in each county of Mississippi to represent a Klan group. Beside each cross was a membership tally. Parts of the state were definitely growing in Klansmen; others were weak in the mighty race warriors. Weak, feeble, and casting aspersions on the entire state. It didn't look good to the higher-ups, these spots of weakness. Mississippi must be growing in the Klan in every county!

He perused the list of county leaders. He had placed a little question mark beside each name that led a small group in his county. Each name had been invited to Jackson. He settled into his deep leather chair. He was waiting for one of the county leaders now. The man was late. He pushed aside the Klan documents and scanned his Sunday sermon.

Willet Keller was shown into the study minutes later. He looked like an excited schoolboy who had come to the big city for some honor. He had carefully greased and slicked down his hair. His black suit was stiff and rusty looking. The reverend frowned; the farmer looked like he was on the way to a funeral!

Keller perched carefully on the edge of his chair while the two engaged in meaningless chitchat. Finally the leader opened the red leather volume in front of him again. His eyebrows drew together in a hard line. Keller became even more nervous now.

Another inch and he'd slip from the chair. He twisted his hat in his hands to keep his hands from shaking. He wished he'd taken a few swigs to steady himself. He felt cold, hot, and clammy all over. He would try to keep the tenor of his voice even. It was an honor to be invited to the home of the state leader. But even countrified Keller knew it wasn't for praise and accolades that he had been summoned. Quite the opposite. For Willet Keller was a better farmer than recruiter.

The reverend started with a brief overview of Klan philosophy. That took little time. He moved to the successes of the Klan in the Southern states and the growing interest in the North. A tide, he explained with passion, that would only swell. Nothing he said was confidential. That would be absurd to share with the farmer.

Keller listened intently, nodding eagerly. The reverend's lips drew together in a tight smile. He read figures showing the growth of membership of several counties in the state—imposing figures worthy of applause. He was building his case, coming to the point. In Keller's lingo, he was "about to tree the coon."

"Now, Mr. Keller, we come to Washington County." He let the words dangle for emphasis. "Being the organizer of that county you are aware of the membership total."

Keller wasn't sure what to say. Should he go on defense or offense?

"Well, yes, Reverend, I know the total, but you see—"

"Sixteen!" the leader exploded with unexpected ferocity.

"Yes, sir, 16."

"Pitiful! You can understand our concern, Mr. Keller. Washington County has come to the attention of those at regional level."

"It has?"

"Yes, it has. And not for the kind of recognition it needs! They are concerned about the choice of leadership."

"I...see..."

The reverend assumed the gentler expression he reserved for counseling wayward parishioners.

"I am willing to hear your explanation, Mr. Keller."

Keller was thinking of this flip side to power. He was thinking of the constant disapproval of his wife over Klan matters. He was starting to squirm.

"Well, I'm not certain, sir, exactly what the problem is."

The reverend's eyes narrowed. He waited.

"We don't doubt your conviction, Mr. Keller. But we do doubt your ability to recruit and lead. You understand, of course."

Keller did not want this little grab of power taken from him. He had proven his loyalty with the arson at Tanglewood. They had seen and been impressed with that. It had gotten him this far.

"I'm glad you see how serious I am about the Klan, Reverend. Niggers and Jews are just—"

The reverend waved Keller's words aside like an annoying gnat. He said these same words, heard these same words nearly every day. He did not need to hear them mouthed by some obscure little dirt farmer.

"I have discussed your problem at some length with the others," he conceded significantly.

Keller tensed. "You have?"

"Yes, and we all agree it is time for a new line of action for Washington County."

Keller swallowed a feeling of panic and nodded.

"A little incident to wake up, to arouse, to incite the good men of your county. They must see, graphically, the threat the nigger poses."

"An incident, sir?"

The reverend gave the farmer a condescending smile.

"Don't worry. We would not expect you to come up with a plan. We will decide where, when, and who. You will merely put the incident into effect. We will be in touch with you concerning it."

Keller wasn't sure he liked the idea. But what could he say?

The reverend stood up, terminating the interview.

"You have the list of men you should contact in your area?" he asked.

Keller nodded. "Still have it."

"I suggest you take it out, look it over, and make the contacts again. Use your eloquence to convince these men of standing of the political, the economic, and the spiritual good of joining our cause. It will benefit your record, Mr. Keller. Good day."

Viney Jefferson agreed with her oldest son. Miss Meg Alcott was the prettiest white woman she had ever seen. Miss Amy was pretty in her own quiet way. But she looked sad so often. Because Viney knew Patrick Cash had been an artist, she compared the two women this way: Miss Amy was pastels, Miss Meg was vivid colors. Viney was quite pleased with her analysis.

Viney sat outside the Tanglewood carpentry shop on a bench Seth had made for customers. Micah was in helping his father, young Gideon toddled around his mother's skirt. Meg had come from the mansion with glasses of lemonade for them all, and apple turnovers just from the oven.

"My, don't those look good!" Viney exclaimed. She was still a bit amazed at being served by a wealthy white woman! *Just like her brother, and their father before them.*

"I hope they are," Meg laughed. "I haven't made them in years."

Viney told Meg about her own grandfather, Goodnight, and Ethan Alcott. Meg had never heard the story before. But she was not listening with all her attention to Viney's words. She was thinking about Amy Cash... and her brother. She tried not to let her thoughts develop very far in that direction. But an innocent remark, a sudden look, had sent her mind that way.

She had been in the kitchen, working alongside Mary making the turnovers. Amy had entered with Melanie balanced on her hip.

"Those look wonderful!" Amy said.

Meg made a face. "Well, I don't know how they'll turn out. The apples weren't the best quality. But—"

Amy burst out laughing.

"What did I say?" Meg asked.

"You! You sounded just like..." Amy's laughter dwindled. "Your... brother. He teased me about some apples I bought once. They weren't as good as Alcott apples."

A look passed between them, an attempt to read each other's thoughts, to probe, to discover. But Amy had become nervous. She smiled and left the kitchen.

Now Meg sat with Viney. It was time for a little detective work.

"You met my brother when he was here two years ago?" Meg prompted.

"Oh, yes, ma'am. Met him as he was a comin' to Tanglewood, right on the road. We had just left talkin' with Mr. Pat, and there was Jeb French a bullyin' us. Mr. Andy and Seth worked on the first shop together, and Mr. Andy came for dinner at our place one night. He was real kind."

"The first shop?" Meg asked. She pointed behind them. "This isn't the first carpentry shop?"

Viney shook her head. This was not a pleasant memory to resurrect.

"The first shop burned to the ground one night... after all that work they did."

"Why did it burn?"

"Someone came and lit it up."

"But why?"

Viney had never understood that mystery herself. Seth had been subdued on the subject. She knew him well enough to know he was coming to his own quiet conclusions.

"Don't know who, don't know why, ma'am."

"Was Mr. Cash still alive when it happened?"

Viney nodded. "He died a few weeks after this new shop was finished. My Seth surely did think powerfully of Mr. Pat."

Meg swirled the lemonade in her glass and digested this news. Why would Tanglewood have such an enemy?

She glanced up at the house where Amy was tending to Melanie.

"I didn't have many letters from my brother while he was staying here. I wonder, was he really enjoying himself?"

Meg Alcott was shamelessly laying a trap for the voluble Viney Jefferson. But it didn't stop her.

"Well it seemed to me he was enjoying himself, Miss Meg," Viney said eagerly. "Workin' alongside Seth. Goin' ridin.'"

"My uncle could ride? I thought—"

"Oh, no. Mr. Andy and Miss Amy went, or the three of them drove the carriage," Viney explained. "Mr. Pat and your brother came out one afternoon to our place when Mr. Pat asked Seth to come to work here."

Viney would have liked to elaborate on this happy memory, but Meg was on a trail, with that Alcott tenacity.

"Miss Amy must have enjoyed those rides I'm sure," Meg said slowly, "since she couldn't get out with my uncle."

"Yes, ma'am. Seth said Miss Amy looked happier than he had ever seen her when she was with—" Viney froze. She remembered the night Seth had told about the long look that the mistress of Tanglewood and her guest had exchanged. Suddenly Viney had the revelation that perhaps she was talking too much.

But it didn't matter, the sleuth had heard enough.

Jeb French had spent considerable time thinking of how to effect a meeting with Meg Alcott. Boldly approaching the door of Tanglewood did not appeal to him—not because of fear, but because of his natural tendency to exercise shrewdness and cunning. When he finally came upon a plan, he was very pleased with himself.

Despite the fact she knew no one besides the Hudsons, Meg was enjoying herself. She felt a little like a newspaper reporter covering her first Southern lawn party. Because she knew no one, she carried an air of anonymity and detachment. She was void of preconceptions, a curious observer in a very colorful scene. But she drew immediate attention from Tanglewood's neighbors. Here was a Yankee woman staying with the reclusive widow, Amy Cash. And Mrs. Cash hadn't even come! Smiles, whispers, nods, questions, and flattery were directed her way. The afternoon was interesting, even amusing, until the end.

"How long are you planning on staying in our area, my dear?"

"A pity Mrs. Cash couldn't come."

"I'd sure like you to meet my son, Alex. My unmarried son, Alex..."

"And how is Mrs. Cash's baby? A girl, isn't it?"

"So sad about Patrick. He is missed."

"Wasn't your brother here a few years ago?"

"So, are you engaged to anyone back East?"

"My dear, you have a gorgeous complexion! How do you do it?"

"Charming accent..."

After two hours Meg felt pinched in her tight slippers, and tired from nodding and smiling and trying to remember names. And tired of the older gentleman who was determined she would come to some marital agreement concerning his son, Alex! She sat in one of the many wicker chairs scattered on the jade lawn that was as smooth as carpet. She drank something cool and tried to sort through impressions and remember the funny things to tell Amy.

She looked up and found herself being watched by one man in particular. She had felt his eyes; they lingered boldy on her bare shoulders. He smiled a careful, uncommitted smile. She instinctively knew he was waiting to meet her, waiting until the crowd around her thinned. She did not see the wink he had given the host of the party. Their plan had succeeded.

He stood before her, tall and imposing in his crisp white linen suit. He bowed over her hand, a modern day cavalier.

"Are you enjoying yourself, Miss Alcott?"

Jeb French smelled of cigars and bay rum aftershave, a virile smell that Meg did not mind. Since he was so tall, so powerfully built, she had to lean back to see him better. She had to admit he was handsome, yet it was a handsomeness that both attracted and repelled. She knew from his smile, from his eyes, he was making her a conquest.

"Thank you, I believe I am."

"I am Jeb French."

He said his name in such a confident fashion, as if he expected her to recognize it. And Meg did, but she could not remember where she had heard it. Jeb French...

"You're surprised to be enjoying yourself? If you weren't, it would be an insult to Mississippi!" he smiled.

"Oh, it's not from a lack of hospitality I say that. It's just that I came here today not knowing a soul."

"I hope I can change that," he bowed again and smiled broader. "It's a pity Mrs. Cash couldn't come."

She studied his face a moment to understand the amusement in his tone. "She doesn't feel comfortable leaving the baby," Meg replied.

"Ah. Mrs. Cash wasn't much of a socialite before her baby arrived, so I'm not really surprised." He took a long drink and turned momentarily away from her.

"I think the last time I saw her was nearly two years ago," he continued, "out riding with your brother. She looked very cheerful that day."

French was a practiced gambler, and he was gambling that the fearful Amy had not told her guest about the shooting.

"Of course, with Cash as he was, she didn't have much of a chance to get out," French said pointedly.

Meg did not feel inclined to speak. Somehow this man was holding her captive with his words, his manner. In the first few moments, she knew he was carefully calculating everything he said. She wondered why.

"So, who does the heiress to Tanglewood favor? Mother or father?"

Meg tensed. She didn't like discussing Amy with this bold man. She glanced around, hoping someone would come to interrupt this conversation. He obviously wanted to talk about Amy, and Amy's baby.

"I don't know. I'm not good at evaluating that sort of thing."

A safe answer. She drew a deep breath, steadying herself. Whatever his reasons, whatever his motives, she could not let this man trap her. She smoothed the silk dress that Amy had loaned her. A Yankee schoolmarm draped in Southern finery! Only her accent belied her.

"I knew Amy as a child. She was very pretty then. So, if this child—what is she called?"

"Melanie." Meg's voice was curt now.

"Melanie . . . Melanie Cash. A good Southern name. If she's as pretty as her mother then Amy will have young bucks around Tanglewood in a few years! Wonder if she and that English butler fella can handle it."

He laughed dryly.

Meg was shocked. Local opinion must think Melanie was Amy's own child, no matter who the father. Should she tell this arrogant man Amy's claim? She could imagine his eyes mocking her even before she spoke.

"Well, I certainly think it will be more than a few years, Mr. French."

"You Yankees sure speak proper."

"I'm a schoolteacher, Mr. French."

"I'm glad we're off the subject of babies and onto you."

"Oh?"

He leaned slightly toward her. "I arranged this party so you'd be invited. I wanted to meet you. You're a very lovely woman, and you caused quite a stir when you passed through Greenville some days ago."

"You arranged this party, counting on my coming?"

"Women like parties and a chance to dress pretty. I counted on you being all woman on the inside, as you are on the outside."

Suddenly she was sickened by his smell of cigars and bay rum aftershave. Did he suppose she'd be impressed with his power and his desire to meet her?

"It seems to me you put our host to a lot of trouble so we could be introduced. You could have come to Tanglewood if the need was that pressing."

French's smile dropped a fraction and froze. This was no brainless beauty like the women he was accustomed to keeping company with. This young woman had wits. This woman could be a challenge—and he liked that.

"You've proven you're a very capable horsewoman, Miss Alcott. I'd like to escort you some morning, to show you more of Mississippi."

He had arranged this meeting. He had purposely spoken of Amy and Melanie. He knew something of Amy's background. He might unlock more of the perceived mystery around Tanglewood. He was a man to be cautious around, but she could keep him at arm's length and use him.

"Perhaps some morning...that would be nice, Mr. French."

Plumes of clouds with purple undersides, hanging idly on far horizons, saved the sky from being a smooth vault of vivid blue. The fragrance of wildflowers and lilac and magnolias scented the air, so warm with the richness of earth. Meg rode out alone, wanting no company, especially that of Jeb French. She would ride with him another day. She wanted to return to Chisolm Crossing, to the jovial little storekeeper who gave her such an uncomplicated welcome. She couldn't exactly explain the pull of the Crossing, nor could she ignore it. There was a calm peacefulness there. She wondered when Andy had visited this place, and if he had felt it as she did.

As she rode, she thought over the lawn party she'd attended a few afternoons earlier. The invitation had come, and Amy had demurred without explanation. Still, she urged Meg to go.

"It's a chance for you to meet my neighbors."

Amy's motives had been genuine. She wanted Meg to enjoy herself. She worried that Meg might grow bored with the almost monastical quiet of Tanglewood.

She had smiled, and even laughed when Meg had related the details of the party. But her face had gone white when she heard about the attentive Jeb French.

"He said he had arranged the whole thing so we could meet. I wonder why?" Meg puzzled.

Amy was hesitant. "Well, you are a very attractive girl, Meg."

Meg shrugged. "I don't know. I felt like there was more to it than that. Anyway, I just can't remember where I've heard his name before..."

Meg told her he had invited her out riding. Amy chose to say nothing, but Meg could clearly see she was distressed. Meg waited, yet Amy remained mute. Meg was troubled. She had told Amy about her childhood, about her past. Amy had merely stated that all her family had died.

Meg was still a mile from the Crossing when she spotted a tumbledown fence, overgrown with wild roses. She reined her horse and rode over to get a closer look. The roses were beautiful; she would gather some on her return ride. Then she heard voices not far distant, somewhere just beyond the pines and brush. She strained to hear more clearly. Young voices, one leading in words she could not discern. And after that, singing. They were singing an old hymn she had sung often! She was intrigued. She slipped down, tied the horse, and went forward softly.

It was a cathedral, a forest cathedral drenched in mellow sunshine, made holy with the worship of five young children. Four were sitting on cottonwood stumps, the fifth and oldest stood before them. Meg's eyes widened. The two boys wore overalls; the girls were in calico dresses, well-faded and patched. One girl was weaving a wreath of wild roses as she listened.

The leader spoke again. "Now, we sung and prayed and I preached."

"Wish you could read from the Bible 'bout Noah or Jonah and the big fish. Ain't perfectly like church without Bible readin'," the boy listener said.

The preacher frowned. "Ain't got a Good Book like you know, Micah. Couldn't read it if'n I did." His face became proud and stern.

"Pa's taught me Scriptures though. 'Thy word have I hid in my heart so's I might not sin against thee.' See, if I got it in my head, what does it matter that I don't have a Bible?"

"You're the best preacher, Tick, that there ever was!" one little girl shyly allowed.

The boy called Tick swelled at this praise.

"How did your pa know them Bible words if he ain't never read nor had a Bible?" Micah asked.

Tick's smile was broad. "His pappy taught him when they was in the fields. Taught him when they was pickin' cotton and needed to think on something 'stead of how hot it was or how their backs was achin' so. Taught him and he's teaching me, and my grandpappy says I'm the richest boy he knows. Now in heaven there ain't no crying or achin', no, sir!"

"Amen!" the three worshipers chorused.

"We ain't shouted the glories and amens and hallelujah Jesuses yet," Micah protested.

"Got to do that."

"When Sister Taft shouts and raises her arms, the skin underneath shakes and shakes 'round," one of the little girls offered seriously.

"How we gonna do that?"

Meg stifled her laugh.

The leader took the question with commendable gravity.

"Don't have to do ever single thing, Missy."

Meg backed away quietly, not wanting to intrude or be discovered. She had heard enough to keep her smiling all the way to the front of Chisolm's Mercantile.

A young black man greeted her from behind the long counter.

"Mornin', ma'am."

"Good morning." She glanced around for the friendly merchant. The young man understood her look.

"Mr. and Mrs. Chisolm pulled in 'bout five minutes ago. Been to Vicksburg and back. I watch the store for them when they're gone."

"Oh, that's nice."

"You're 'bout the fourth customer in this morning. Guess what I've been doing when I ain't waitin' on folks."

"What?"

"Learned *r.*" A long, slender finger traced the letter on the polished counter. "Am up to *r* already. Oh, I forgot to ask ya, can I get you something, ma'am? These peaches are just as tasty as they are pretty." He indicated a basket of the dusky scarlet fruit.

"Yes, I'd love one."

"Grown over at an orchard 'bout two miles east of here. Best in the county." The youth leaned forward conspiratorially. "Mrs. Chisolm says I should say that, and Mr. Chester says I should just let 'em speak for themselves."

Meg bit into the fruit. "They're both right."

"*P.*" He was beaming.

"*P?*"

"Peach starts with *p.*" His smile dropped anxiously. "That is right, ain't it, ma'am?"

"Yes, exactly right. You're learning your letters?"

"Yes, ma'am. Up to *r* so far."

Meg reached for a bolt of ribbon on the counter.

"Ribbon starts with *r.* And *r*abbit and *r*iver."

"Yes, ma'am, and..." His brown eyes searched around the store. "And *r*ope?"

"Perfect! You're on your way to learning to read. And *r*eading starts with?"

"*R!*" His mind was opening; he was triumphant, and Meg was excited. It had been too long since she'd had an enthusiastic pupil.

"Yes, ma'am, I want to read a powerful lot. Maybe have a store like this of my own someday. Forgot to tell ya, my name's Sawyer."

"Sawyer, I'm Meg Alcott."

A door opened then, and a woman emerged. Her manner radiated briskness and efficiency as she tied a snow-white apron around her formidable midsection. Her husband was close behind her.

The Chisolms were an interesting couple. Chester Chisolm was a rotund little man, as broad as he was tall. His hair was, as he put it, "part of the vanishing West." A gray fringe around his head, just above his ears, saved him from complete baldness. When folks commented on his vastly receding, soon-to-be extinct hairline, he would reply philosophically, "Saves combin' time considerable."

His face, his whole head in fact, was one smooth, pink globe. He spoke with a perpetual wheeze and was known for his frequent bouts of mirth. He would rock back and forth wheezing and laughing, turning a brilliant shade of red, and Dr. Browning would privately fear the fat little man wasn't far from a stroke.

For all his friendly cheerfulness, Chester Chisolm was no buffoon. He was a careful businessman, scrupulously honest and unambitious. Behind the gay exterior was a sensitive man. Being the proprietor of a rural general store did not afford Chester much opportunity to exercise his deep thinking, except in matters of the human condition. And around the Crossing, there were plenty of human conditions to observe.

Only in her weight was Matilda comparable to her husband. She matched him ounce for ounce. Her hair had gone gray also, yet it covered her head in stiff, New England-proper thatches. She believed in what could be touched or counted. Anything else was poetical and foolish. She trusted that deep thinking and emotions were generally a complete waste of profitable time. Chester and Matilda were as mismatched as any couple ever, with Chester overrun in good humor and Matilda sadly deficient in it.

What saved Matilda from being a shrew to the marrow was a generosity in heart, a compassion that, while stunted, had never withered away completely. It woke from slumber from time to time, much to her irritation. Perhaps that is what kept the two together. Matilda thought her husband silly and impractical; he thought her unfeeling and rigid. Yet they had been devoted to each other for over 40 years.

"Well, britches flyin' in the wind! Look here, 'Tilda! She came back."

He winked roguishly at Meg and whispered, "Said ya would."

"Hello, Mr. Chisolm."

Matilda Chisolm stood in front of Meg, hands on ample hips, carefully studying the young woman as if she were a new shipment of dry goods. Her eyes were neither hostile nor friendly. Merely calculating.

"This here's my wife, Miss Alcott."

"Pleased to meet you, Mrs. Chisolm."

Matilda's head jerked forward. "Mr. Chisolm has raved about you ever since the first time you came, Miss Alcott. You've been the topic at every meal."

Meg shifted uncomfortably.

"She's as pretty as I boasted, ain't she, 'Tilda?"

"You're a real stimulant to my vanity, Mr. Chisolm," Meg said, laughing. "I can't come back here if you keep this up."

She wanted to divert the conversation from her looks. Chester's wife looked like she could speak frankly, and with needlepoint sharpness.

"I'll allow that you weren't exaggerating *this time,* Mr. Chisolm. Sawyer, you're loafing. I see Clive Taylor driving up. He'll be here for his feed."

"Yes, ma'am." The young man moved off reluctantly, giving Meg a shy smile.

"Keep at those letters, Sawyer. You're doing fine," Meg said warmly.

For the next hour the three talked—Meg, perched on a stool, Chester leaning forward, absorbed, Matilda dusting the shelves with Puritan vigor and not missing a syllable. Meg told them about her family and her teaching experience. Riding home later she could not explain why she had been so verbal. There was Chester with his friendliness, Matilda with her reserve and unhidden suspicions.

Meg stood up to leave. "I should be leaving now. I happened upon a group of children as I was riding over. They were singing in a field near here. One was named Tick."

Chester laughed. "That would be Tick, all right. Bet he was preachin' too!"

Meg joined him in laughing. "Yes, I think there was some evangelizing going on."

Matilda's frown plunged to greater disapproving depths. She snorted, a mannerism that Meg would come to know well. "Such pretending may be near irreverent and should hardly be encouraged."

Matilda whisked past the counter as the front doorbell rang and customers entered. Meg and Chester watched her, and then Chester leaned forward.

"It's a comfortable habit, Miss Alcott."

Meg smiled. She knew he referred to his marriage.

"I'll walk out with you, Miss Alcott."

"Mr. Chisolm—"

"Chester, Miss Alcott."

"Chester, I'm wondering something. Your helper, Sawyer, and the children I came upon—they couldn't read. Where do they attend school?"

They stopped on the store's front porch.

"Ain't no school for them, Miss Alcott." His voice was genuinely sad.

"No school for them anywhere?"

"Not for black children. Some years ago, ten or more, the Freedman's Bureau set up a school over near Greenville. For one reason or another, it closed. Too far for children around here anyway."

"That was ten years ago! Nothing since?"

His head wagged again. "Missionary came through once and started a Saturday school in the black church. But he was scared off by white folks who didn't cotton to blacks gettin' an education. Seems like I recall hearin' old lady Collier kept a primer class in her kitchen for a while. She'd been a slave when she was young—had a master who believed in teaching his slaves to read. She died though."

Meg was too shocked, too grieved, to speak. The beauty of the day, the delightful worship service she'd witnessed, the friendly chat with Chester Chisolm, paled. How could this happen?

Chester patted her arm. "Please don't be too upset, Miss Alcott." His round face was anxious. "Don't mean you won't come back to the Crossin', does it?"

She gave him a wan smile and shook her head. No. What she had seen, what she had heard, only strengthened her ties to this place.

Chapter 16

Chisolm Crossing

♦♦ ♦♦ ♦♦

*W*illet Keller had returned from Jackson with his ego trounced in the dirt and his ambition fired up. He would go to Jackson again someday under vastly different circumstances. He would go to receive commendation for the explosive growth and the rabid devotion of Washington County to the Imperial Ku Klux Klan. In his mind it was a simple equation—just like farming. You plant, you water, you harvest. The problem was clear to him now. He hadn't been as energetic physically to the cause as he had been philosophically. He had spent too much time farming, too little time converting and campaigning. Now it must become just the opposite. The burden of his new conviction fell on his two oldest sons. They would have to leave school for a time and take up the responsibility of earning the family living. And he would ignore altogether the protests and the nagging worries of his little wife.

Greenville

Approaching Jeb French was nearly as unnerving as approaching the state Klan leader. But French's name was prominent on the list the organization had given him. He could not ignore that. French was an influential man with many potential Klansmen in his employ.

French was leaning back in his chair, peeling an apple when Willet Keller was shown into the waterfront office. This time the farmer wore clean trousers and a new shirt. No Sunday duds, no dusty, patched overalls. And this time he had nursed from the dark brown bottle just a bit.

"Afternoon, Will," Jeb said lazily and without rising.

"Howdy, Jeb!" Keller returned heartily.

"What brings you to Greenville?"

"Business, Jeb, purely business."

"Sellin' turnips?" French asked mockingly.

Willet was not deterred or intimidated by this arrogance. He launched into an impassioned sell of the Klan. In his own way, he was eloquent. French listened without comment, without movement or obvious emotion.

"So, you see, Jeb, we all work together to keep the blacks in their proper place." He had a sudden inspiration of originality. "Keep 'em underneath our boot!"

He expected French to say something, but French said nothing. He almost looked like he was falling into an afternoon nap.

French yawned. "Don't see how it benefits me much, Will, runnin' around burning crosses," he finally said mildly. "And wearin' bed sheets..." He shook his head and laughed scornfully. "Seems kind of childish to me."

Keller turned very red. This talk with French was not going as he had hoped. And these remarks about bed sheets. He had heard them before.

"Think of it as a uniform, Jeb. It gives us a kind of mystery. Keeps us secret. 'Sides, it scares the daylights out of the nig—"

French held up his hand. "All very fine for some men, Keller, but not me."

Keller felt his nervousness fleeing, his temper rising.

"You sayin' you don't care about niggers gettin' jobs over white men or voting or owning land! What you said about the sheets is exactly what Dr. Browning said. Are you like him?"

French was fingering his riding crop silently.

"What about Seth Jefferson?" the farmer burst out hotly. "Look what—"

"What about Seth Jefferson, Keller?"

A tense silence filled the office. Keller jumped to his feet.

"Reckon I'm wastin' my time, French!"

"Reckon you are, Willet."

"I thought you were a man of...of..." He was searching for the word that the reverend had used so freely. "Vision! I thought you were a man of vision!"

French continued smiling.

Keller did not care if this was the mighty Jeb French. He closed the office door with a vicious slam.

French remained at his desk, though there was pressing business for him to do. The smile faded. His handsome face was set in a dark scowl. He didn't like Keller's reference to Seth Jefferson. He didn't like what must be local opinion—that Jefferson had in some way dumped his boss. He didn't care for that conclusion at all.

Joining the Klan was not for a man like Jeb French. It wasn't a doctrinal disagreement—he agreed with every evil word they spewed. But it would have put him in a structure, with authority over him. He wouldn't be in control of decisions. He preferred to stalk and strike as *he* planned. He had been ignorant of the Klan propaganda that had passed through his warehouse. No midnight rides in flapping bed sheets, no symbolic cross burnings. That was too obvious, too blatant and cheap. Those were the ways of a lion; his were the ways of a snake.

The president of Greenville's largest bank was a thin, bespectacled man who had spent more time counting other people's money than he had with his own family. The years of worshiping mammon and position had made him a stranger to his family. Therefore it was no surprise, and no secret, that his children were wayward. His only son had run away from home when he was 15. His only daughter had a very soiled reputation in parts of the city. And she suited the Klan's purposes quite well.

Martha Keller had a dozen or more chores she needed to be doing. Since her boys were farming, many additional things had fallen to her, like bringing in the stove wood, feeding the stock, and weeding the garden. Then there were the inside chores, the cooking, laundry, and mending. But on this cloudy spring morning, Mrs. Keller wasn't doing any of those things. They could wait. They would still be there in an hour, and they would come back the next day.

She sat on her front step and tried not to let herself slip into the chasm of depression. But it was so hard. She was so disappointed that Willet had taken the boys out of school. Taken them out so he could spend more time...She groaned out loud.

Her husband was being sucked into this madness! She had seen a tornado once. That was what was happening to Willet; he was being pulled into a whirlwind, a vortex, of hatred and violence.

Martha Keller had no political views. She didn't understand economics. She had no opinions on the social position of blacks. All she knew was they'd been happy until this Klan business started. She was a petite woman with very plain features. But she was mighty in prayer. All she could do was pray for Willet. And pray that this madness would stop.

Dr. Barrett Browning rode to his next appointment not thinking of the gouty-toed man he was going to treat, but of what the last patient had told him. Or more precisely, the husband of his last patient. He had finished examining the very pregnant Mrs. Evans. Her young husband walked out to Barrett's horse with him. He was looking concerned, even though the doctor had said the pregnancy was progressing just fine.

"Somethin' troubling you, Tom?" Barrett asked.

"Yeah, Barrett, there is. Didn't want to say anything in front of the wife. She gets upset when she hears anything about the...Klan."

"The Klan bothering you?"

"They're wantin' me to join them. Will—"

"It's all right, Tom. It's Willet Keller, right?"

The farmer nodded. "Yeah, he's going around talkin' and stirrin' folks up. Word is he took his two boys out of school so he could do Klan business full-time. Anyway, he wanted to use my place as a meeting place. Wanted to have this meeting where he'd explain what the Klan is all about and how it's an honor to join. Even said it was the American thing to do, and the best thing for our kids. He got real heated up about it."

"Why your place?"

"He said it was central to the other farms. Then he put on a little whitewash and said I was real respected around here."

The farmer looked down at his boots. "I told him no."

"Guess he was pretty mad at you," Barrett suggested.

"Mad enough to cuss me pretty good. But that ain't what bothers me."

Barrett pulled off his glasses and sighed. He was feeling tired all of the sudden. He let the young man take his time.

"What bothers me is that he found another farmer who said yes. Barrett, I'm hearin' more talk about the Klan every day. I hear it over at Chester's; I hear it over the fence. More and more men are talking about it. I hate to see it spread to this county." He shook his head. "It can't mean anything but trouble, maybe even bloodshed."

Barrett knew Tom Evans spoke the truth. He was hearing the same suggestions, the same muttered threats, the same propaganda. And he was hearing it from each house, each patient he visited. It was growing just like the farmer said.

"You're right, Tom. You'll pardon the obvious illustration, but it's like a virus."

"I don't want my kids growin' up with their white neighbors terrorizing their black neighbors! What can we do, Doc?"

Barrett didn't have an easy answer. Some viruses were easy to diagnose, and so difficult to cure.

"If you're a prayin' man, I'd say pray, Tom. And keep your eyes open."

Now Barrett rode along, the question blazing in his thoughts.

"What can we do, Barrett?"

It didn't make sense for him to be thinking on this problem, then have his mind suddenly switch to another track so dramatically. Yet it did—back to his boyhood days. He was ten years old and listening to the Sunday school teacher. He couldn't remember her features. He didn't remember her name. But he did recall that she always wore black and looked very hot. He also remembered some of the Bible stories she told: Noah, Goliath, David and Jonathan, Queen Esther.

Queen Esther. His next patient thought the doctor seemed more preoccupied, more remote than usual. He made the exam, gave the advice. He was gone.

Barrett couldn't stop thinking about the Jewish queen. Why? It was silly. It was...

Mordecai was pleading with the beautiful young woman.

"And who knows, but that you were raised up for such a time as this."

Barrett ate his dinner. He scanned the newspaper. He washed out a pair of dirty socks. He got ready for bed. But before he fell asleep, he suddenly realized why he had been thinking on the biblical story all day.

Now he knew what he could do. Now he had an answer for the farmer.

Seth Jefferson was behind his cabin plucking a pair of chickens for Sunday dinner. Micah was helping him, Gideon was scampering about with chicken feathers in his woolly crown. It should have been a peaceful morning for Seth to enjoy his family. But he didn't feel at peace.

He kept glancing at the woods, at the cabin, at the path that led to town. He didn't hear half of what Micah was chattering about. Finally his young son noticed his behavior.

"Somethin' wrong, Daddy? You're actin' fidgety like Mama says I get sometimes. What ya fidgety about, Daddy?"

"Feel a storm comin', Micah."

Micah scanned the sky. It was clear, cloudless, bright. He trotted quickly to the front of the cabin where he could get a view of the horizon. Nothing but a smooth arch of blue.

"Not a cloud anywhere, Daddy!"

Seth Jefferson shook his head at his son. He couldn't explain it; the boy wouldn't understand. It was so indefinable he had said nothing to Viney. Yet it was there. Trouble, like a storm, was coming. He could feel it.

Fittingly they met beside the manure pile behind the barn. It was the only place Willet Keller could think of for privacy at such short notice. The rider had come up to the cabin just as the family sat down to their evening meal. One look and Keller knew who had sent this stranger. He watered the man's horse and led the way to the back of the barn.

Keller had been excited to see this emissary from the reverend. It made him feel important to be entrusted with this responsibility. But as he listened, his excitement turned cold. He didn't like this plan for rousing Washington County at all. He chewed a straw stem and frantically tried to think of excuses, anything to slow this plan down. This "little incident" was too dangerous, too difficult, and maybe just a little cruel.

But the emissary had brought the plan. He was not prepared for questions, arguments, or refusals. He rode off into the darkness, leaving the farmer sickened at heart. Keller slumped to the ground and leaned against the old barn with a moan. He didn't want to do this deed.

Mrs. Keller had heard every word from the shadowy edge of the barn. She wanted to rush to her husband and comfort him. She wanted to tell him he must drop out of the Klan before it was too late. But she knew he'd be angry at her spying and disgusted with her suggestions. She slipped back to the cabin, as burdened as her man.

Greenville

He could hear the mocking words of the reverend in his mind.

We'll provide the who, the what, the when. You simply put the incident into effect. Keller gritted his teeth in frustration as he rode through the darkened streets of Greenville. He didn't like this test of his loyalty. He had already earned that with the burning at Tanglewood. He didn't get into the Klan for this kind of thing. Still, if it worked, it would accomplish a great deal. Klan membership would soar. Well, he'd better see that it did succeed.

He had trailed the banker's daughter for two evenings. He knew the pattern of her nightly outings. She merited her tarnished reputation, he decided grimly. He passed this information to the stranger who was registered at a Greenville hotel. The girl should leave the waterfront tavern around midnight. She would be alone.

He slipped to an abandoned shed where a group of blacks were huddled over a game of dice. He watched them, then signaled to one from the shadows. They had spoken before. The young black man approached this stranger from curiosity. Keller led him to a deserted street and offered him a bottle and some quiet conversation. How would he like to earn some money? It would be very simple. The young man listened to Keller's fabricated plan while he sipped from the fine whiskey. He was known on the docks for his strength and his fondness for drink. He knew Keller was setting him up for some shady deal, and he didn't mind. Before long he was well on his way to drunkenness. Keller could have ordered him to do anything, and he would have obeyed. But the farmer merely had him follow him. Keller began to think this was going to be childishly simple and that all his worries were foolishness.

He delivered the black man to the warehouse where the stranger was doing his part. Keller suddenly felt sick when he heard her screams. This was the part of the incident he didn't like. The only consolation was that they hadn't asked him to do it.

Just knock her around, a few bruises, a torn dress. That's all. No worse, and probably better than she'd gotten from men she had associated with on the waterfront. Still, Keller felt himself go weak and sweaty. *Remember, this is for the Klan, for the good of all. She's only a small part, a sacrifice.*

The stranger came to the door panting.

"Keller! Have you got him?"

Keller slid down from his horse. The black man was singing something, and hiccuping, and laughing. They hurled him into the darkened building.

"Now go for the sheriff," Keller screamed. "Hurry!"

The Klan could not have hoped for better timing. This could only help their case. Word was filtering down from the northern part of the county. A Democratic town mayor had been defeated by a Republican candidate, thanks to the large turnout of black voters. It would have stayed the most talked-about county event, except a young white woman, daughter of an influential citizen, had been brutally assaulted by a black man in Greenville. That was the news the county was buzzing with.

Many of the citizens of Greenville felt a shocking outrage. A seemingly tender, innocent, respectable young woman had been beaten by a black man. Their fury was spreading across the county and beyond. In a matter of days, all of Mississippi knew of the tragedy.

"Can you *imagine?*"

"The poor, poor girl . . . and her family!"

"I say string the nigger up! Forget a trial!"

"Folk, folks, a little rational thinking here! We don't know all the facts."

"You don't suppose she could be in the family way now, do you?"

"All our daughters are unsafe, I tell ya!"

"And look, they're voting too!"

"Folks, don't be so bloodthirsty! He hasn't been proven guilty."

But the ground was fertile for a sowing of hatred. What would the harvest bring?

Everyone was talking about it, gossiping about it, embellishing it, from town to the isolated country farms to Chisolm Crossing to the kitchen at Tanglewood. Most everyone around Greenville knew the banker—some knew the truth about his daughter. The waterfront crowd, black and white, knew of the young accused black man. He was known for his oxen strength. And he was known to be the favored worker of Jeb French.

Keller knew the appearance of over a dozen men at his farm could mean only one thing. The horrible plan had worked. He was elated, thrilled, beside himself with the resurgence of power and importance. Now watch the membership of Washington County grow!

They met inside the barn this time, sitting casually on boxes and barrels and listening to the fervor of Willet Keller with rapt attention.

What had happened up north in the vote and what had happened here...It was too much. They were eager to join. They would be as zealous as any Klansmen anywhere. Keller was delighted.

"I tell ya the truth, Mr. French, as well as I remember."

"Tell me again, Silas," French snapped. "And don't leave anything out!"

The young black man was huddled in the wet, cold, county jail cell in Jackson. Jeb French had been his only visitor.

"I's playin' dice, just like I do every Friday night. Was doing pretty good." He scratched his head. He had never felt so much like breaking down and sobbing. If only he could clear the fuzzy cobwebs out of his mind.

"The next thing I knowed was a gal screamin' somewheres near me and the sheriff is shoving me against the wall. Kicked me in the face, called me all sorts of names. Next morning I hear what it's all about. Sayin' I beat up that white gal."

French lit a cigar. "You think you did, Silas? You think you were drunk enough to attack a white woman?"

The young man still felt like weeping.

"I..."

"Tell me!"

"I was pretty far gone drunk, Mr. French, but I don't think I beat up no white woman!"

French considered this as he drew a long pull on his cigar.

"There's a big gap in your story, Silas," he said bluntly.

"Yes, sir."

"From playin' dice in that shed to a warehouse a block away. That's a pretty big gap. The sheriff ask you about that night?"

Silas shook his head. "Just threw me in here and won't let me say nothin' or see my family. Just cusses me."

"Tell me who you were playin' dice with that night."

He gave French the list as well as he could remember.

French studied the young man sitting abjectly in front of him. He felt no pity, no sudden evaporation of bigotry. He didn't want to lose his most valued worker. There was something about this that didn't smell right.

"You should have listened to me about your drinkin', Silas."

"Yes, sir."

"Didn't see anyone else that night but the dice crowd?"

"Not that I can remember. Been tryin' to think it all out."

French prepared to leave. "Ever play chess, Silas?"

"Chess? No, sir."

"I think this was a setup, Silas, and you were the pawn."

"Sir?"

"I'll look around, but your drunken foolishness has put your head on the block, boy. I don't know if even *I* can get it off!"

Chisolm Crossing

Seth and Viney Jefferson were sitting side by side in their cabin. Their sons were asleep. Neither one felt like they could sleep though it was late.

"I just feel so sad for Silas's ma. She just swears that her boy couldn't of done it."

Seth nodded. The storm had broken over them.

"Silas is known for being wayward," Seth admitted. "But I just don't think the boy did this."

He rubbed Viney's hand. "Seen his pa this mornin.'"

Viney waited; she could sense his reluctance.

"They're leavin' in the morning," Seth continued. "Going to his family over near Vicksburg till this thing blows over."

"Will it blow over, Seth?" she asked as she molded herself closer to him.

He might as well tell her the truth. She was bound to hear it sooner or later.

"They got their barn burned down and the cows run through their cornfield."

"Oh, Seth." Viney was crying now.

"That's the fourth fire in two weeks. Folks is in a rampage, Viney."

"Folks, Seth?" Viney sputtered with renewed spirit. "Devils, you mean! Runnin' round in sheets!"

"Viney, the Lord's gonna watch over us, gal. I just know it."

She squeezed his hand. God really was their only shelter in this storm.

While Keller was in the middle of his gloating, a worry nagged in the back of his mind. It was a small thing, he supposed. But he hadn't been happy to learn the victim of the plot was a prized worker of Jeb French. Surely the black was too drunk to remember Willet Keller. The papers were saying nothing of the accused or his defense. Keller should feel safe. There was really nothing to worry about.

Though the membership of the Klan had grown in Washington County, the whirlwind of violence surrounding the Greenville incident had subsided. Most of the members had little time to ride around the county blustering and bullying blacks. That was night work, and there was a living to be made in the reality of morning. Their fervor was real enough. They would commit to only one night a month, to meet at Willet Keller's farm. They must come to any urgent meetings Keller chose to call. He insisted. So now 45 men of Washington County had been enlisted, indoctrinated, and initiated into the fellowship of the Ku Klux Klan. Willet Keller was very pleased.

But the state leadership was still unimpressed. Their plan should have swelled the membership to hundreds. Perhaps the problem lay with Keller. He was, after all, nothing more than a poor, semiliterate sharecropper. Perhaps he needed to be replaced. Or perhaps the county itself was simply too rural and unconnected to big city ideas. It was a puzzling problem to solve.

Martha Keller was a meek woman who rarely confronted her husband. But the strain and tension of the last few months had taken their toll. The Klan had met the night before. The front yard was littered with horse manure and cigar stubs and a few bottles. Her tiny flower bed had been trampled. She was a simmering pot ready to boil over.

"Willet. Willet, please. This Klan business . . . I don't like it."

He observed her coolly. "Don't get worked up, Martha. It doesn't concern you."

That was the worst thing for the farmer to say.

"Don't get worked up? It doesn't concern me? What happens to *you* concerns me!"

"And what is happening to me?" he sneered.

"You're becoming *ugly*, Willet! Filled with hate!"

"Nothing is happening to me. You're acting like a crazy woman, Martha. I'm the head of the Klan in this county. Most Klansmen have wives that support them, not badger them!"

"Willet," she pleaded. "I don't mean to badger you. I'm just so worried about all of this."

"I told you. Stop worrying," he said cuttingly.

"Willet, what about that girl in Greenville who was beaten? What about her?"

His eyes were cold and suspicious. "What about the little tramp?"

"She . . ." Mrs. Keller felt helpless. Willet was as hard as stone. She was having no effect, not with anger, not with tears, and not with reason. "What about that poor boy who sits in jail for something . . . he didn't do? How can you sleep at night, Will—"

"What do you know about that? How do you know he didn't do it? Of course he did!" His temper was fully ignited. "He's where he belongs!"

"Oh, Willet." She broke down in sobs. How long would the truth choke her?

If Barrett Browning had been a drinking man, he would have taken a sustaining measure before going to see Willet Keller. But he wasn't. So he set aside his loathing and put the dangerous charade into effect. He found the farmer in his fields. Barrett was instantly grateful for the remoteness, the quiet. Anyone who observed them would think they were discussing a case. No one would overhear their conversation.

"Mornin', Will," Barrett began affably.

Will nodded and continued hoeing. He was not in a sociable mood, especially with the medical man.

"I have business with you," Barrett said easily.

Willet looked up and speculated on Barrett with unveiled hostility.

"I didn't send for you, Doc. Neither did the wife."

"I didn't come as a doctor."

"What do you want then?"

Barrett had rehearsed the words in his mind, but now that the time had come, he felt dry-mouthed and nervous. He had to be convincing!

"I've been thinking a lot about your . . . work lately."

Keller knew the doctor did not refer to farming.

"Oh, you have?" Keller returned coldly.

"I don't like what I see happening around here. It's one thing to free niggers from slavery, but it's another thing to let them have the liberties they've been taking. This business in Greenville, for example. Probably wouldn't have happened if we had a curfew at night for blacks in the city. They have it in other cities."

"I seem to remember a little joke about preferrin' to sleep on sheets rather'n wear them."

"Yes, I did say that at the time. But I've come to see the wisdom of it. For me, it would make perfect sense. I'd have to cloak myself from my patients."

The farmer eyed him suspiciously. "You sayin' you want to join the Klan? You sayin' you hate blacks?"

"No, I don't hate them, Willet." Barrett could not lie on this. And besides, he already felt like he was choking. "But as I said, I don't like the power and position they are assuming that rightly belong to men of our color. It's that simple."

"You doctor 'em!"

Barrett shrugged. "You farm. It's a livin'. Besides, I treat whites too. I'm too poor to move on to a new practice, Willet. Maybe someday I won't have to treat . . . darkies."

If Keller's superiors had heard the doctor they would have heard a Judas warning. For Barrett Browning was a very good doctor, but a mediocre actor. But Willet Keller was inwardly elated. He felt his power had won the doctor. Here was a real convert! A week ago, farmer Evans had joined, today the local doctor!

"We meet here at my place two weeks from tonight. Welcome to the Klan, Doc!"

Chisolm Crossing

When Barrett Browning stepped from the cabin one midmorning, he was surprised to see two riders on the road parallel to the house. He frowned when he recognized them. They both wore long riding skirts; one was light blue, the other was tan. They both wore white blouses. One wore a hat with a white scarf around the crown, the other was bareheaded. The breeze and the ride had loosened the rider's hair. It was long, full waves of auburn. From where he stood it looked silky to Barrett. One of the riders saw him and waved.

"There's Barrett," Amy said to Meg, who rode beside her. "Let's go say hello. I haven't seen him in a while."

She didn't wait for an answer but reined her horse to the right. Meg wanted very much to protest.

"Good morning, Barrett!" Amy called.

"Amy." He was polishing his glasses, trying to keep his hands occupied so he wouldn't openly stare at the two lovely ladies mounted before him. "Miss Alcott."

"Good morning, Dr. Browning," Meg replied with Yankee coolness.

"If you're delivering Mrs. Evans's baby, Barrett, I think we're right on time. Especially since Meg is such an old hand..."

The beauty of the morning and Meg's friendship had put Amy Cash in a joyous, teasing mood. This jest was more for Meg's sake than the doctor's.

Barrett acknowledged the joke with a thin smile. Meg blushed.

"Not this morning, another week maybe. How's Melanie?"

"A little cranky the last few days. Mary is watching her now, or actually spoiling her shamefully while we're gone."

"Perhaps Miss Melanie is experiencing growing pains," the doctor suggested with a slight smile.

"Perhaps. Well, we're off to the Jeffersons. Just wanted to say hello."

Barrett nodded. "It is a beautiful morning for a ride."

He looked directly at Meg then. He wanted to say something, anything. Meg met his eyes with a question in her own. She wanted to be cordial, to say something, anything.

Amy looked at them both. A person would have to be blind not to see the stiffness between them, as tangible as a wall. She impulsively decided on a direct approach.

"Meg has decided to lengthen her stay at Tanglewood. Isn't that wonderful?"

Barrett had known Amy Cash long before she had become Amy Cash, mistress of a large estate. They had been friends for years. He knew her enough to know she was challenging him.

He had not forgotten that somber evening when Patrick Cash had died and how frail, lonely, and hopeless she had looked. Or how frightened she had been when the fire had consumed the carpentry shop at an arson's touch. Now she was bright, teasing, animated. It was Melanie, and it was this Miss Alcott.

"Yes, Amy," he said finally, and with a genuine and affectionate smile. "It is wonderful." But that sounded a little too personal, a little too cordial. "For you," he amended quickly.

Meg smiled her first smile at him—inwardly laughing over his awkwardness and arrogance.

Viney was expecting her company. She had made coffee and a pound cake. She had made her husband put on a clean shirt and had scrubbed the faces of her little boys. She had swept the floors and dusted—and barely tolerated Seth's teasing.

"Wish we'd have company more often, sure do. This pound cake looks mighty good. Ain't seen one too often."

"You're worse than Micah! Now you keep away from it, no pinchin' a sample from the edges. I know your tricks, Seth Jefferson!"

Seth put on a pouting face. "Won't let me pinch the cake. Won't let me pinch...anything."

She couldn't help but laugh as she snapped him with a dish towel. Seth was pleased. Viney was smiling and laughing. For the last few weeks her smiles had been far too rare.

Meg and Amy arrived and they all sat down for coffee and cake. They talked and laughed and enjoyed the two little boys and the mellow sunshine that flooded in through the open cabin door. Micah brought them each a bouquet of wild daisies.

"Thank you, Micah, that was very sweet of you," Meg smiled.

"Yes, thank you, Micah. You are a gentleman already," Amy added.

"What would you like to be when you grow up, Micah?" Meg asked impulsively.

Seth and Viney exchanged a look. No telling what their energetic, precocious son would say.

"I'd like to be like you, Miss 'Cott."

The adults were puzzled by this.

"Like me?" Meg asked gently.

"Heard you're a teacher up North. I want to get some learnin' so I can be a teacher and find children ways out in the country that don't have a school or teacher or nothin'. I could teach 'em readin' and how to write and...and..." He suddenly became shy in front of the four adults.

"And what, son?" Seth asked.

"Maybe I can make...I can help 'em with making their dreams come true."

Meg Alcott typically kept her emotions under guard. But there were times, like this, when they rioted against restraint. Here in this little rustic cabin, a barefoot boy had opened his heart up to a near stranger. The tears came to her eyes and spilled over. She took his hand as she tried to steady herself.

"I...I want your dreams to come true, Micah. I really do."

Amy had seen the wall of reserve crumble in Meg, and it made her think of her tenderhearted brother. Seth and Viney saw the tears and felt an assurance that not every white in Washington County was against them and their race.

"Like to see the creek, Miss 'Cott? It's just a hop from the back door, and it's real pretty with moss and little flowers. I can show you where I got the daisies."

"Yes, I'd like that very much, Micah."

"A mighty nice young woman," Viney said after the two had left the cabin.

"Like her brother," Seth added.

"Yes..." Amy agreed. "There was a reason I wanted to visit today. It reminds me in a way of when Cash and Meg's brother came here."

Seth and Viney nodded. "Sure was a big day for us," Seth remembered happily. "Changed things..."

"I came here to ask you if you'd be interested in another big change."

Husband and wife leaned forward with expectation.

"I know you love living here by Ford's Creek. This is certainly one of the most beautiful spots around the Crossing. You've made a lovely home."

"Thank you, Miss Amy," Viney managed, though her heart was pounding. These Cashes did bring surprises!

"I wonder if you would consider moving to Tanglewood. I don't know why we didn't think of it sooner. It seems so natural. Meg thinks it's a great idea too. Seth wouldn't have the near hour ride to and from work. He'd have Micah to help him in the shop like we talked about. And..."

She reached across and took Viney's hand in hers.

"With all that's been going on lately...I think you'd be safer at Tanglewood."

They were silent.

"There's that rock building that used to be a big summer kitchen years ago. It could be fixed up for a fine house. But I don't want to pressure you," she added hurriedly.

Seth patted her hand, and his smile was wide.

"We think your offer is sure generous and kind, Miss Amy. And we're gonna pray on it real hard, yes, ma'am!"

Chapter 17

Tanglewood

♦♦ ♦♦ ♦♦

*S*culptured in drab, olive green, marbled with yellow-green and
higher up, shades of blue, then purple, a low range of mountains
quietly lay west of Tanglewood. Fields of yellow rose up on an undu-
lating valley floor, a shimmering mist at the foot of the range. Meg
had wandered alone to the edge of the Cash property. She stood
watching the sunrise, her mind full of competing thoughts. Andy loved
the sunrise. Was he in some foreign port or sailing the Caribbean?
Andy . . .

The land in front of her was so beautiful. Despite her turmoil at
finding a child at Tanglewood, the place had drawn her. She had found
peace here. She bowed her head to pray.

She knew her family in Illinois was waiting for her return, eager for
her to come home. Hopefully, she was strong against harsh prairie
winters now. Still, she hadn't written them to say when she was coming
home. She was waiting. Waiting for what?

In her mind she could see the face of the young black boy with the
odd name of Tick; the eager, proud face of Chester's helper, Sawyer; Seth
who carried written orders to Amy. None could read. And of Micah—she
would never forget the little boy's selfless ambition. It was perfectly
outrageous. Generations were passing into illiterate oblivion.

It was obvious what she must do. Yet her mind rebelled at first. The
challenge was too big, too radically different from anything she had
done before. Different from teaching in Illinois, absurdly different from
Bishop's Villa in Galveston.

She squinted into the sunshine that grew warmer on her face. A
Scripture she knew came to her there on the crest of land. "My soul
waits in silence on the Lord." She had been waiting. Now what? Children
needed an education. Did geographics, or economics, or skin color
matter? She breathed deeply and smiled.

Seth looked up as her shadow crossed the sawdust-covered shop
floor. He smiled; Miss Alcott did look healthy. Must have been up walkin'
early, he mused. Her cheeks were blushed pink.

Excitement made her unusually direct. "Seth, I need to ask you a few
questions."

"Surely, Miss Alcott."

"Would you or your neighbors allow a white woman to come and
teach your children?"

"Ma'am?"

"Seth, I want to open a school for the children around the Crossing," she said hurriedly. "I want to stay in Mississippi!"

Seth slowly laid down his tools.

"Miss Alcott, my Viney has been prayin' for over ten years that we'd learn to read and get some education one day. When Micah was born, she prayed even harder. I can't wait to get home this evenin' and tell her, her prayers been answered!"

Amy knew from the sparkle in Meg's eyes that something exciting had happened. Meg told her quickly.

"What do you think of my plan, Amy?"

Amy straightened up from the rosebushes, smiling happily.

"I think it's wonderful!" Amy's face softened. "I'm glad about the school, Meg, and glad for the children. Still, my motives aren't entirely pure. I'm being selfish. I didn't want you to leave too soon."

That shadowy feeling, kept at bay in Meg's heart, surfaced again, causing a fleeting frown. This was the woman who had led her brother ... If only Amy were easier to dislike. If only she wasn't becoming the best girlfriend she had ever had.

"Thank you, Amy. I do want to stay here. Do you think they'll let me? You know the last teacher was discouraged by the whites in the area."

"I think you can make it work. I don't think they can stop you. You can be a very determined young woman, Meg Alcott!"

Meg laughed. "I've heard that before, from my parents especially, and I've always had the feeling it wasn't quite a compliment!"

Chester Chisolm was beginning to feel possessive about Miss Alcott. Already he secretly pretended she was the daughter he never had. He supposed he would do anything she asked. If she had waltzed into the store and demanded his apron, he would have shrugged and handed it over. He liked her very much, and his heart warmed to think she liked him too. There was no explaining it, of course, but it surely had brightened his days. Chester knew it was prudent to edit and greatly condense his remarks to his wife—she would only snort and call him foolish.

When Meg rode up to Chisolm's, she wondered if she'd have a long wait before she could speak to the storekeeper. There were several wagons pulled up front. Apparently it was shopping day in the Crossing.

She opened the door, and was immediately greeted with Chester's syncopated laughter. She scanned the store. Matilda was working over a bolt of fabric with two women, Sawyer was filling a box with canned goods, Chester was leaning on the counter, talking with another man. Meg decided to mill about the shop until Chester wasn't busy. But he had spotted her.

"Howdy. Howdy there, pretty lady!"

Matilda looked up and frowned. Meg felt herself blush. Chester was waving her over. The tall man turned slightly, as if reluctant to allow a third person into the conversation.

"Here she is! Mornin', Meg."

"Hello, Chester."

Still the man kept his side to her, his eyes focused on the counter. It was Barrett Browning. Meg's blush deepened. Oh, if only Chester wouldn't keep on about her looks!

"Meg, this is Barrett Browning. Doctor to our local parts." He laughed at his own joke, not noticing that Meg and Barrett were stone silent. "Anyway, we're lucky to have such a man of medicine," Chester enthused.

"We've met," Meg said evenly, still looking only at Chester.

"Met already? Well, that's fine." Chester slapped Barrett lightly on the arm. "Miss Alcott proves Yankees can be mighty pretty, doesn't she?"

Barrett shifted and cleared his throat. "I need to be going, Chester. A pound of coffee will finish my list."

Meg felt as if she had been slapped. She turned then and faced the doctor squarely. "How are Mim and her new baby, Doctor?"

"Doing fine, thank you."

Chester scratched his head at the obvious tension.

The doctor paid his bill and left without another word. Chester felt embarrassed and awkward. For once, he didn't know what to say.

"Northerners don't have the corner on rudeness, Chester," Meg said shakily, trying to make the merchant comfortable.

"I know, I know. But don't take offense at Barrett. He's a very nice fella when you get to know him."

"You're the second person to try to convince me of that. What I came for was to talk over something very important with you, Chester."

"Let's go into the back room. I'm all ears, Miss Alcott."

Meg laid her plan before him, wanting his enthusiastic support. She genuinely valued the storekeeper's thoughts.

"Chester, will the blacks accept me?"

He patted her hand. "Reckon they'll take to you like buzzin' bees to a flower garden! They accept 'Tilda and me, don't they? And we're not near so nice to behold!"

"Chester, it's my competence as a teacher that matters, not my looks. You know these people."

"Yep, I do. They'll take to you."

"What about the white community?"

Chester rubbed his chin. "They might take some persuading, I'll admit."

"I'm not afraid of them! They can approve or disapprove, but I'll stay!"

Chester smiled.

"Are they all as rude as Dr. Browning?" Meg asked cautiously.

"Oh, now don't take a notion against Barrett. He's all right." Chester looked away a moment. If only he could explain his old friend to his new friend. "Barrett's a good man. He just..."

"Just what?"

"Has his own private devils, things he can't turn loose of. He'd pitch a fit to hear me say that."

"Private devils? That sounds frightening."

"Well, things of the past, hurts of the past. Yet I've seen him cradle a babe and bandage a knee and hold the hand of one that's dying. He knows these folks, and they trust him. Couldn't be a doc to 'em if they didn't trust him. He's white, and they let him birth their babies and bury their dead. You just got off on the wrong foot with him."

Meg chewed her lip thoughtfully. "Maybe. Chester, will you help me? Can I do this?"

"Do you want to, Meg? Do you really?"

"Chester, it humbles me to say so, but I think the children of the Crossing... need me!"

In the long, lazy days of summer the only news was cotton prices and farm foreclosures, a tornado in far-off Kansas, and some political debate in Washington, D.C. The story of the Greenville banker's daughter was history, as much as the accused who sat dejectedly in the stifling jail cell at Jackson. The anger, the indignation, the hot-tempered speeches would revive again once the black man came to trial in the fall. But for now it was filed away. And for Meg Alcott's plans, that was very beneficial. An inflamed citizenry would vehemently protest a school for blacks. So the timing of Meg's project was nearly perfect.

Meg made discreet inquiries in Greenville and Vicksburg for a week, finding the proper authorities to which to submit her proposal. It was a tedious, frustrating week, and the first test of her resolve.

Vicksburg was sweltering in the noonday heat, exhibiting all the glory of a very hot, very dry Mississippi summer. Shade and cool drinks were at a premium, covered porches and electric fans a prize. Women took baths after breakfast and sought the gray coolness of their bedrooms; men sought saloons that offered drinks with shaved ice; children, swimming holes.

Meg had waited for a full hour in the sultry outer office of the county's school superintendent. This was the man to whom she had been directed, who held the power to grant or deny her request.

The man who was sitting behind the desk barely acknowledged her presence when she was shown in. He continued reading her application, so she swung her eyes around the room.

The first thing she noticed was the thick, burgundy book that propped open the room's one window. She decided the superintendent must have little regard for *Mississippi Natural History* from its unfavored position. The spine was cracking, and Meg wondered if the window would come down in the middle of an interview such as this. The second thing she noticed was the brass cuspidor that sat beside the desk only a few feet from her own hard, wooden chair. It was very used. She tried hard not to look at it. She tried not to notice that one entire wall of the office was covered in fading photographs of stern-faced Confederate officers. Meg tensed. Would this man have any sympathy or understanding for a Yankee schoolteacher?

Yet the sober-faced Colonel Higgins turned out to be a very considerate listener. He listened patiently as Meg explained the need of Chisolm Crossing and her own plan for meeting that need. He asked no questions, made few notations. Finally he leaned back and regarded her as he had the documents spread before him, as if seeing her for the first time.

"All very interesting, Miss Alcott . . . very interesting. I think I can say for my superiors that your plan can be approved. All that remains—"

"Are you serious? Just like that I have my school?" Meg interrupted excitedly.

"Ahem. As I was saying, all that remains is finding a building to use and discussing your salary. Is there a school building at the Crossing?"

He knew there wasn't!

"No, there isn't a building, Colonel, but I'm sure that—"

"The state cannot possibly afford to erect a building or pay rent on an existing building." He spread his hands apart in mute appeal. "And without a building, there is little hope for a school."

Meg was furious. So this was one of the discouraging ways that Chester had hinted at. Meg took a deep breath.

"This situation reminds me of my mother, Colonel."

His bristly gray eyebrows lifted, yet he said nothing.

"My mother left her home when she was a young woman and went to the nation's capital—"

"Excuse me, Miss Alcott, which nation was that?"

"Washington, D.C. She wanted to be a nurse in the war effort. She—"

"Was that the war between the states, Miss Alcott?"

Meg's cotton shirtwaist clung to her back with perspiration. She could feel the dampness on her neck, imagine the Rebel officers breathing down her Yankee neck. Perhaps this illustration hadn't been a good idea.

"She faced a rather formidable amount of opposition to becoming a nurse. Still she was persistent."

"And I can see you are your mother's daughter. I can admire perseverance, Miss Alcott, but the fact remains you have no building to use as a school."

"I'll get one, Colonel Higgins, if I have to build it myself!"

They faced each other there in the heat, silent, determined. Was this a reenactment of Gettysburg or Cold Harbor? Meg focused on the man's beard; it reminded her of a Bible patriarch. Andy should see a beard like this...

"We'll just set this building matter aside for the moment. Your salary is another point to consider. Let's see," Higgins continued.

The man's slowness was maddening. Meg thought she might scream.

He peered critically over the rim of his glasses. "Salary for teachers is set at thirty-one dollars and sixty-four cents per month."

"Thirty-one sixty-four! I get double that back—"

She stopped, furious at her own impulsive words.

"Miss Alcott, the salary is thirty-one dollars and sixty-four cents, yes, ma'am. You're doing a sight better than a colored teacher. He gets nineteen thirty-nine."

"Nineteen thirty-nine! That's outrageous!"

The colonel leaned back in his leather chair. He was very amused.

"I'll take nineteen thirty-nine as my salary, Colonel Higgins."

"What's that?" His chair came down instantly. He was exhibiting more energy than he had for the entire interview.

"I'll accept the colored teacher's salary as mine. Dismissing unfairness can begin with me."

Meg had never looked more virtuous.

The superintendent smiled benignly. "The state is always glad to save a few dollars. Mississippi accepts your generosity, Miss Alcott. I'll be waiting to hear from you about a suitable schoolhouse. Good day!"

He watched her from his window, watched her cross the chalk-white road quivering in heat, her proud head held high.

"Yankees," he muttered. "Pretty little thing despite her highfalutin ways. Nice ankles too." He returned to his chair and settled into an afternoon nap, confident the Confederacy had prevailed.

Chisolm Crossing

Barrett Browning found the friendly storekeeper anything but friendly the next day. It went against his grain, but Chester managed to appear aloof and preoccupied. Living alone, Barrett had fallen into the habit of dropping into the mercantile each evening on his way home from rounds. Chester had a way of bolstering his confidence, or just making him laugh. A grim diagnosis, failing cures, various heartaches seemed to melt away for the time he spent with Chester. And the serious-minded doctor needed that very much.

Chester's voice was clipped as he greeted Barrett.

"What's the matter, Ches?"

"Matter? Matter! What's the matter with *me?*"

Barrett had to laugh. "Yes, you."

"There ain't a thing wrong with me, Dr. Browning! It's you who... who... Yesterday! Never seen ya act so rude and irregular! Just what's got ya all fussed up 'bout Miss Alcott?"

Barrett frowned and drummed the counter with his fingers.

"She's a Yankee!"

"Uh huh." Chisolm shook his head sadly and noisily sucked his peppermint.

The storekeeper made Barrett feel like a naughty schoolboy. Chisolm began to elaborately dust the shelves, disapproval radiating from his rotund little frame.

"All right, Ches. Say it. What's in your craw? You're about to bust your suspenders!"

Chisolm stopped his dusting and climbed back up onto the stool.

"We got enough bigots 'round here, Barry, my boy."

"Now, Ches, you hold on. Just because I'm not overly fond of Yankees is no reason to call me a bigot!"

Chisolm shrugged, then his eyes grew piercing. He leaned forward.

"Just remindin' ya, Barrett, North and South fought more than 30 years ago!"

Jeb French had business in Jackson anyway. He would drop in at the jail and put a question to his accused worker. While Silas had been frightened and pathetic on French's first visit, now his fright had turned to anger and panic. He nearly pounced on French when he stepped into the cell. French stepped back in undisguised disgust.

"Mr. French! I's so glad to see ya!"

"Get back, Silas! You smell."

"Mr. French, please, sir, I feel like they done dropped me in here and forgot me! Please, sir! You gotta help me!"

French was unmoved. "I don't have much time, Silas. I didn't come all this way to visit in a hot, stinkin' jail cell!"

"Sir, tell me, what's going on out there? What about my case?"

"Silas, the fact is, you'd better be grateful that you're in here and not out there. There's a Klan man around every corner and behind every tree just waitin' to get his hands on you. So simmer down."

"Is there gonna be a trial or somethin', Mr. French? Don't I get a lawyer or... anything?"

"How are you going to pay for a lawyer, Silas?"

The black man slumped to the ground. Mr. French hadn't brought any good news—no hope, nothing. He had just come to taunt him.

"Ain't got nothing then," he sighed.

"They told me your trial may come up next month, or the month after. You get a court-appointed lawyer, but as you can imagine, no one is overly eager to touch this case. Either way, you'll be swattin' flies here all summer."

Silas was silent. He was accused, condemned, forgotten. What did it really matter that he was also innocent?

"Listen up, Silas, cause I'm fixing to leave. I talked to your dice buddies."

Silas lifted his face.

"They have far better memories than you. They told me an interestin' fact that the sheriff never bothered to look into."

"Sir?"

"They told me you were playin' when you got up and went and talked to someone in the shadows. Of course they couldn't see who it was or hear what was said. They—"

"I . . . talked . . . with someone?"

"They said it looked like you left with the mystery man. Clear the fog away yet?"

"I . . ."

French rapped impatiently for the jailer.

"Think on it, Silas. It's all you have right now."

"Wait, sir. I . . ."

The alcohol had spread a blanket over his mind, a thick blanket that was so hard to pull aside.

"What is it, Silas? I need to leave."

"I . . . I did talk to . . . someone. I did."

"Who was it, Silas?" French snapped.

"I can't see his face or hear his voice in my mind. I . . ."

French moved to go. "Tell me next time I'm in town."

A tiny edge of the blanket fell back.

Silas grabbed frantically at French's arm.

"Mr. French! He . . . I can see . . . I remember looking down at his boots!"

"His boots?"

"Yes, sir!" Silas agreed eagerly. "They was ugly and had mud on 'em. They was thick-soled, like . . . farmers wear!"

Despite her husband's near adoration of the young schoolmarm from Illinois, Matilda Chisolm did not resent Meg. She knew a large part of her husband's feelings stemmed from the void of not having his own children. In a buried reserve of her heart, Matilda Chisolm, now past childbearing years, grieved at her barrenness, grieved that she'd not been able to give her man something he so longed for. She was an energetic, thrifty, capable businesswoman—as much as a rural mercantile could demand of such skills—but she had failed in the one area so tender to Chester's heart. She fussed and upbraided him about the time he spent with the young woman, but secretly she understood, and it comforted her to see him so pleased.

Matilda knew in Chester's and Meg's enthusiasm for the plan of a Chisolm Crossing school, they had all but forgotten the obvious lack of a building. They were like children really. But Matilda had not forgotten.

"Blacker'n the inside of a cow in here!" Chester exclaimed.

"Mr. Chisolm, light the lamp, will you?" Matilda demanded sharply.

"I'm tryin' to, 'Tilda, I'm tryin'. Calm yourself. There."

Chester, Matilda, and Meg stood in the fourth building of Chisolm Crossing, peering into the dusty darkness, trying to breathe, unable to see much from the small arc of light thrown from the sputtering kerosene torch.

"This place has been empty for nearly 20 years," Chester explained to Meg. He lowered his voice. "And for 20 years she's been tryin' to get me to burn it down."

"And aren't you glad you did not listen to me!" Matilda retorted. "I was the one that thought of this place, Mr. Chisolm, when you and Miss Alcott were so stumped!"

"Yes, thank you, Mrs. Chisolm," Meg said as she moved cautiously forward.

The building was stifling in the evening heat and the smell of mold and filth, rats, and a few generations of tomcats.

"Used as a cotton warehouse originally. That's why there ain't any windows," Chester elaborated.

"There would have to be windows, of course, if this were to become a school," Meg replied slowly.

"Easy to accommodate that. I'm a fair hand at carpentry," Chester boasted.

Matilda snorted, then screamed. Her foot had plunged through a rotting floorboard to midcalf.

"'Tilda! You all right?"

"Don't just stand there! Pull me up!"

That was no easy task, but between Meg and Chester, Matilda was hoisted up. She was breathing heavily, rather embarrassed for her ungraceful scream. "We should have waited till morning to look this place over. As you can see, Miss Alcott, it would require considerable effort to make this building habitable."

Meg could not help but think of her clean, well-supplied, airy little schoolhouse sitting so picturesquely on the windswept Illinois prairie.

"Yes, I can see that, Mrs. Chisolm."

Matilda rubbed her ankle, her voice querulous.

"Take all summer to get this place ready for the fall. Also, Mr. Chisolm has a store to manage."

"Now, 'Tilda, I think we all know who manages the store! A genteel woman like Meg will need some—"

"Oh, no, Chester. I can work on this place, really," Meg interrupted hurriedly.

They stood on the sagging front porch, twilight coming on, stirring the pines in a much-needed breeze. Meg looked around. It would require a terrific amount of work. Still, it was a building! She smiled roguishly at the thought of Colonel Higgins.

"I need to know, what would the rent be?" she asked the couple at her side.

"No need for rent, Miss Alcott. We've managed this long without it," Matilda answered in her most superior voice.

Chester was beaming. He repressed the impulse to squeeze both women.

"Really?" Meg asked incredulously.

"I'm not given to pretending or jokes, I remind you, Miss Alcott."

"Oh, I know that!" Meg blurted, then colored. Chester coughed discreetly. "I mean..." Meg impulsively hugged Matilda. "Thank you both so much! I have a school!"

The lean hound was whining and smiling up at her, clearly eager for her to climb down and shower him with affection.

Barrett had tossed the ax aside and was pulling on his shirt. She glanced away from him and back down to his dog. This man made her nervous, that was the truth. Perhaps it was because he seemed so calm, studying her just a bit like she was a specimen under glass. She felt he tried to penetrate her thoughts.

He walked up to her, wiping his forehead with a handkerchief.

"Good morning, Miss Alcott. This is a surprise." He was tempted to ask if she had lost her way, but refrained. She could read nothing in his passive voice, find no trace of pleasure in his seeing her.

"Good morning, Doctor. I need your help. I—"

"Lost?" he could not resist.

She reddened more quickly than even she thought possible. With anyone else she would have joined in the laughter at herself, but with him she was unwilling. She tilted her chin a bit higher, an unconscious habit she had developed when she was feeling intimidated or uncertain. The doctor did not miss it and smiled to himself.

"I need your assistance, Dr. Browning. Perhaps you have heard I'm trying to establish a school for the black children in the area."

"Yes, I had heard that, Miss Alcott."

"Well, I wondered if you could confirm or add to the list Mr. Chisolm gave me of families who have children."

"I'm sure Chester is thoroughly knowledgeable of the folks in the county," Barrett replied quietly.

Meg bit her lip, thought a moment, then smoothed the list on her lap. She read the list aloud and waited.

When he did not reply, Meg felt a bit of irritation rising, replacing the nervousness.

"Anyone else, Doctor?" Meg's tone was very formal.

"Had you planned to visit each family personally, Miss Alcott?" he finally asked.

"Why, yes. I planned to encourage them to come to the school."

Another long, uncomfortable silence. Finally he spoke again.

"May I ask why you want to begin a school, Miss Alcott?"

She had not expected this question, and he could see her visibly stiffen. "I am a certified teacher, Dr. Browning. There is in my estimation a desperate need for a school in this area. The children have nothing."

"You are aware that Minnie Collier kept a school of sorts in her cabin until last spring when she died," he stated.

"Yes, I'd heard that. Yet there is no formal schooling for the children now." Meg was clearly irritated. Why was this man refusing to help her? What were his real objections?

Barrett reached out and stroked the horse's muzzle a moment.

"I'm sure your motives are sincere, Miss Alcott," he said slowly, not meeting her eyes.

Meg instantly bristled. "I think I see your train of thought, Doctor. You think I'm just an empty-headed little do-gooder on a mission here! Is that correct?"

Barrett looked at her now, and she felt that same sensation of being scrutinized. "I think you're a *wealthy, white, Northern* woman." He had emphasized each adjective with a choppiness that infuriated Meg. "You propose to teach *poor, black, Southern* children. I think you fail to see the difficulties of the work before you. I think this work would be vastly different from teaching middle-class white children in Illinois."

Meg felt the despised blush rise to her cheeks.

"And I think you are the most arrogant man I have ever met, Dr. Browning!" she replied hotly.

"Now, Miss Alcott—"

"Your self-righteous attitude is—"

"I'm sorry. I didn't mean to offend you, really. I was merely giving you my personal evaluation."

"Thank you so much, Doctor."

The buggy lurched forward as she applied the whip to the startled mare, her original opinion of the doctor very well intact.

With a newborn baby to examine, there was nothing suspicious about the doctor's presence at the Evanses' farm. And too, they were now Klan brothers. It was the access he had as a physician that made Barrett Browning valuable to the cause—even Willet Keller could see that. But this passport was also valuable to the doctor for his own personal reasons. He heard the gossip, the opinions, the fears, the bragging, and the heartfelt convictions of his patients scattered around the area.

Now he met with the Evanses in the kerosene light of the cabin. The newborn was sleeping, but Mrs. Evans was included in this meeting. She sat wide-eyed as she listened to her husband and the doctor. She refilled Barrett's cup and sliced him another piece of raisin pie.

"I understand why you and Tom have done what you have," she said slowly, "but it still worries me."

Her big husband smiled. "So far, Nell, all we've had to do is listen to the rantin' of Willet and a few others. The other night, Barrett about toppled off the hay bale asleep!"

Barrett chuckled. "Yeah, it had been a long day."

"But it won't stay like that, Tom, and you both know it," Nell Evans pressed. "Sooner or later something will come up, and you'll have to ride . . . or worse. What will you do if they expect you to burn someone's property or bully some poor farmer?"

Her husband's smile dropped a fraction.

"I don't know. We'll have to see when that happens."

"It sounds so dangerous," she said softly.

Barrett sighed. "Believe me, Nell, if there had been some other way to slow this thing down, I'd have done it. This way we're on the inside. We know what their plans are. We can find out who they target, and hopefully warn them."

He pushed his cup and plate aside. His appetite was gone. He hadn't had much lately anyway.

"Actually, something has come up. Thought I should talk it over with Tom."

Tom and Nell Evans tensed and waited.

"There's a Yank—a woman from up North, a relative of Patrick Cash, who is going to try to start a school for the black children between the Crossing and Greenville. Her name is Meg Alcott. She's staying with Amy Cash at Tanglewood now. She's got Chester pretty excited about her plans."

He smiled a moment to himself. *Miss Alcott has the little shopkeeper wound around her pretty finger.*

"I have the distinct impression she'll get this school," he continued. "She's a determined woman, I've judged."

Tom Evans' voice was grim. "Willet and the others won't like that at all when they find out about it."

Barrett nodded. "Exactly. That's why I plan to ride over to Keller's after I leave here, and tell him."

"Why, Barrett?" Mrs. Evans asked anxiously.

"If it comes from me, mixed with a little—"

"Klan foam and froth," Evans interrupted with a dry smile.

"Right. Anyway, it will help my credibility. But mostly it will give me the chance to encourage patience on the Klan's part. Let Miss Alcott try to put the school together. Let's just observe her efforts for a time."

"What if Willet or anyone else finds out that you two are traitors?" Nell trembled.

Evans soothed his wife. Barrett prepared to leave.

"Silas is still sitting in Jackson. His accuser is still being pretty silent on the whole thing. While things stay this calm, we have to do our part. When it comes to trial, Keller will probably be pressured to become more visible and active. Fortunately there aren't many of us—"

"*Them,*" Evans corrected with a smile.

"Them. Maybe we have a chance to poison this thing from the inside out—and kill it."

Chapter 18

Gulf Coast

*S*he was a pathetically lonely-looking girl sitting hunched over on a sand dune on a Gulf Coast beach. Her mother was back at their rented cottage—probably thumbing through a stack of magazines. Her father was in Greenville behind his expansive, walnut desk, a fortress of figures, stocks, bonds, mortgages, loans, and stacks of other people's money. He was the very efficient, hardworking banker of Greenville. The girl's only brother hadn't been seen or heard from in three years. They had been close when they were very small, so she idly wondered what he would think of this scandal she'd brought on the family. He'd probably laugh.

Her father had sent her away from Greenville for the summer. He had told her it was to get relief from the heat. It was for her and her mother's health. They were both looking so fatigued and pale. But she knew her father's real reasons—they were as obvious as a neat column of black figures on white paper. She reminded him of the attention she'd brought to him. "Unpleasant" would be the word he would choose, or "distasteful."

He had been carried along with the outraged public sentiment following the beating. He had been the most vocal in his demands for harsh retribution for the treatment of his innocent daughter. But in the evenings, when they had to face each other, all he could see was her promiscuous, disappointing behavior, which had caused the trouble in the first place. Even in her tarnished heart, she knew he didn't really love her—not as a father who loves a child in the corrupted face of any sin. She felt despised.

She stared out at the ocean without seeing it or the gulls with gray-tipped wings that danced above her and hopped in the sea grass. They had kept her a prisoner at home and withheld any information about the black man. That was the only way she knew him—the accused, the nigger. He had no face, no name, no identity, no history. He was just the hands that had beaten her in the dark warehouse.

Until now. Now he had a name. Silas. She had learned it from the newspaper she had found in the seat beside her as they took the train from Greenville to the coast. Her mother had been asleep or she would never have permitted it. So this was the man who had beaten her. It was a very small article on the back page. Held without bail in Jackson . . . a short trial expected in September. Her stomach churned at the thought of a trial.

She had given the sheriff her statement only one time, on the night it had happened. He hadn't talked with her again. She was whisked away, closeted. She'd been hysterical that night and in pain from a dozen cuts and bruises. Now she wasn't hysterical. She was very calm and clear-headed. And things were looking a bit different.

It had been such a foggy night. It had happened so fast. Someone grabbing her, hitting her, pushing her around. Then the panting breath had stopped and there was the strong smell of alcohol. The accused was stumbling around. She was crying and wondering if he was going to hit her again. For all her grown-up ways, she was really only a little girl.

He had stopped and slumped over in a corner. She was afraid to move. The next thing she knew, the sheriff was helping her to her feet.

"Who did this to you, Miss?" he had asked.

Terror. The face of her condemning father rose in her mind. She pointed to the crouching black figure in the corner.

"He did."

"Didn't he?" she whispered to the ocean.

Tanglewood

It was well past midnight, and Meg was walking the hallways of Cash mansion. Amy had finally fallen asleep in a library chair. Fenwick lay sprawled on a sofa. Meg could not help but smile, the proper English-men looked anything but dignified. They were all exhausted from taking care of Melanie, who was suffering with a fever and earache.

She had rocked the little girl with no success, so now she walked with her, as much to keep herself awake as anything. She had put in a long day at the Crossing, firmly believing a century, rather than a few decades, of dust and debris had settled into the abandoned building. Except for a few floorboards, it was still a sound structure, but that was about all.

"This is one of my pessimistic days," she had greeted Amy when she returned to Tanglewood earlier that day.

"Why, Meg?"

Meg slumped down in a chair. "Oh, Amy, the place is dreadful. There's so much to do! I'm sorry, I'm already complaining."

Amy smiled. "You never thought when you knocked on my door you'd be staying here and cleaning out an old warehouse—"

"Full of mice," Meg interrupted sourly. "Hundreds of mice, thousands of mice, aeons of mice! All have lived in that one building. Every mouse in Mississippi! Came over on the ark, the first pair!"

Amy was laughing. "Maybe this will cheer you. Seth came to me today and asked if he could help you. He said other men, his neighbors, would like to help also."

"Really, Amy?" Meg asked as she roused herself up.

"Yes."

A loud cry from the nursery stopped their conversation.

"Is that Melanie? I didn't know little ones could cry that loud." Meg was tired, and in no mood for a screaming child threatening the peace of the evening.

Amy stood up quickly. "She has a fever. It's been like this all day. Dr. Browning was here earlier." Knowing Meg's feelings, she could not refrain from slyly adding, "You missed seeing him," as she hurried up the stairs.

Meg attempted a Matilda Chisolm-like snort. "Missed him, ha!"

Cradling Melanie in her arms, Meg wandered into Cash's old studio. She wished this uncle of hers had painted a self-portrait as some artists were known to do. She wished she had something besides what she knew about him from her father, and Andy, and his young wife. Amy had shown surprising openness when she talked about him and their brief time together. Still, Meg noted that she made no reference to the disparity between their ages or how the older man had courted, and won, such a bride.

One night they had stayed up very late, like two adolescents, laughing over fashions in the latest magazines. Then Amy had stopped laughing and grown quiet, her eyes filling with tears.

"I miss him," she had whispered.

Meg had held her breath—she was about to hear a confession.

"I do miss Cash so much..."

Amy had shown the studio to Meg during her first days at Tanglewood. It was not kept locked as though it were a shrine. Yet it no longer served a purpose. The tools lay still, the artist was gone forever. It did have the best view of the garden, however, so Meg went there, enjoying the view so bathed in pale moonlight. She could feel the child relaxing against her. Soon she would be sleeping soundly.

Meg turned from the window; she would look at the paintings along the walls and pick out her favorite.

Of course she had seen the famous oil that hung in the library. In a letter home, she had described it in detail. Amy had also shown her the oil that hung over Cash's bed.

"That's *Ivanhoe's Dream!*" Meg had exclaimed.

Amy nodded. "Did your brother tell you about the little wager he and Cash had over it?"

Meg turned to Amy. "No, he didn't tell me."

Amy was disturbed by the unguarded look of suspicion Meg Alcott gave her. Why had she suddenly become so aloof? Amy turned back to the canvas.

"Andy didn't think Cash could paint something without seeing it, so he challenged Cash to paint his ship. If Cash couldn't do it, he was to give Andy any painting he chose."

A long, contemplating silence followed.

"Obviously he captured it perfectly," Meg prompted. "What was Andy to pay Uncle Pat?"

"I don't know. Cash never told me. He never told your brother either."

Now Meg spotted an easel draped in the corner of the studio. She had noticed it the first day. Amy had mentioned it casually.

"That was Cash's last painting." She made no move to unveil it.

Meg went forward, and pulled off the cloth.

Chisolm Crossing

She looked immaculate in her cream-colored linen suit. It was a simple outfit, certainly by standards back home or at Tanglewood, but suddenly here, driving down dusty country lanes in rural Mississippi, Meg felt overdressed.

The first house on her list of prospective students was supposed to be just around the bend in the road. She lifted her chin hopefully and brought the buggy to a stop in the clearing in front of a crude cabin. Two young boys sat on the steps. They gave her no greeting, but stared apathetically. Here must be two of her future students. She gave them a bright smile and called out a cheery, "Hello!"

The tranquillity was instantly shattered. A vicious-looking, multi-colored dog bounded from the back of the cabin. He crouched near the buggy, his growl throaty and serious.

"Little boys! Is your mother or father home?"

The two little brown bodies did not bat an eye or move a muscle. "Hello!"

The hound was now nipping at the mare's legs, and normally placid Rosie was becoming skittish. Meg tightened her grip on the reins.

"Boys! Could you call your dog? Please!"

The buggy was lurching as the horse avoided the dog. Meg knew enough about horses to know that she could not keep control of the mare much longer. Rosie was about to bolt. She maneuvered the buggy around and headed back down the lane.

The hound chased behind them for a few minutes before retreating. Meg brought the buggy to a stop under some trees. She would let the horse graze while they both regained their composure. Run off from her first prospect by a mean hound! Ridiculous!

A large-boned black woman was stirring a steaming kettle when Meg rode into the littered yard that was next on her list. Chickens and pigs squealed their greetings, then scattered. She drew a deep breath, smoothed her skirt, and hoped for better results than her first visit had brought. She saw no dog in sight, much to her relief.

Half a dozen children stopped their play to stare at the white woman perched so primly in the buggy. Their eyes were round. They had never seen someone so white...so clean.

The woman did not stop her stirring or even look at Meg.

Meg smiled awkwardly. "Good morning!"

The woman shifted a baby to the other hip and poked at the fire underneath the big pot. Meg realized the woman was doing her washing.

"It's a warm morning to be doing laundry," Meg said nervously.

The woman finally gave her an impersonal glance.

Meg consulted her notebook. "You are Mrs. Mayhew? Abby Mayhew?"

The woman wordlessly handed the baby to another silent child and ambled over to Meg's buggy.

Meg was shocked. The woman's face was a network of tiny white scars, her eyes ringed with fatigue—and something else. *She reminds me of a caged animal,* Meg thought, *full of fear and... hatred.*

"What you wantin'?" she asked in a coarse, unfriendly voice.

Meg squirmed on the leather seat. "I...you are Abby Mayhew?"

"I'm Abby. What do you want?"

Meg took a deep breath. "I'm Meg Alcott, and I'm organizing—" She stopped. Perhaps organizing was too big a word. "I'm establishing—" She stopped again. *Good grief, the woman probably thinks I'm a half-wit.* "I'm making a school!" she blurted. "A school for the children in this area. I'm here to invite your children."

Meg paused and drew out a handkerchief to wipe the perspiration from her forehead. She waited for the woman to speak, but Abby Mayhew just continued to regard her with hostility. Meg noticed her eyes follow the dainty white handkerchief. Meg blushed. She knew the woman's thoughts. Something so clean and delicate did look absurd in these surroundings. She hastily stuffed it back into her bag.

"I'm turning the old Chisolm warehouse at the Crossing into a schoolhouse. I hope to begin classes in about four weeks."

"A school, huh?"

"Yes. To teach reading, penmanship, arithmetic, geography, and history. We will have Bible and music as well."

She waited for the big woman to speak, but Abby Mayhew was silent.

"I know my plans, I mean my academic plans, sound rather ambitious...I mean, well..."

Meg knew she was floundering in the face of open unfriendliness.

"What my chillins need book learning for?" Abby asked in a tight voice.

"Excuse me?"

"Book learning, why do my chillins need it?"

Meg felt suffocated in the bright sunshine. She wanted to fan herself, to ask for a cool drink of water, to step into the shade, anything to get out of the heat and away from the woman's penetrating stare.

It was deathly quiet in the dusty yard. The Mayhew children had crowded around their mother.

"How's readin' and numbers gonna help my younguns? Tell me. Is it gonna get 'em good jobs next to white folks? Is it gonna help 'em own land or vote?"

"It, it, should," Meg stuttered.

"*Should,* Miss white lady? Should? Ha! It won't! It won't change nothin'! No matter how much learnin', it won't change a thing! And why? Why, Miss white lady?"

She leaned against Meg's wagon and hissed. Meg bit her lip to keep from crying. "It won't change nothin' cause my chillins got black skin. Black, you see! You white folks tryin' to do your Christian duty, huh? Help the blacks read a primer. Your Freedman's Bureau helpin' us? Now go on and git. Git off my land!"

Well beyond the Mayhew place, Meg pulled her buggy over. Her body was shaking as she tried to control herself. What a horrible, horrible beginning!

Two hours later, with the sun at its peak, Meg found her third address. It had taken two hours of jogging down wrong roads and making wrong turns to finally find this cabin. She was completely exhausted, and without a single pupil enrolled!

The black woman at this cabin greeted her far more cordially, enthusiastically in fact. Mrs. Tidly gestured to her to step down and stay awhile. Meg was elated.

It was only after five minutes together that she realized the woman was a deaf-mute and could understand very little of what she had been saying. Three young children had smiled and shyly fingered Meg's hat and hair. They could no more speak than their mother could. Meg was shocked. She climbed back into the buggy, waving and smiling cheerfully as if she and the little family had communicated perfectly.

It was early afternoon, and Meg Alcott could not handle another rejection. She would return to Tanglewood. Tomorrow was another day, and maybe things would go better.

"How much worse could they get?" she muttered to herself. Only three contacts from a list of 16.

One final wrong turn and Meg was caught in a deeply rutted mudhole that Rosie failed to negotiate. Here was the perfect ending to a dreadful day—stuck in a quagmire with no one for miles to help. She bit her lip in frustration. Even if there was a cabin within walking distance, would anyone be willing to help?

Meg tossed aside the reins in exasperation.

"This is just fine! Just fine!" she said threateningly to Rosie's rump.

She carefully stepped down and daintily picked her way to the grassy edge of the road. She sat down, fanning herself and trying not to notice the beginning of a very promising headache.

She thought of Barrett Browning. How he would chuckle now if he saw her predicament. So superior and self-righteous! Her agitation grew as she thought of his words the last time she had seen him. She stood up abruptly, looking at her spotless attire with disgust. She took off her shoes and squashed her way to the back of the buggy.

Meg had seen her brothers lift the back of a buggy up before, perhaps she could as well. What other choice did she have? She braced her shoulder and pushed. She was encouraged by the slight movement and summoned all her young strength for one final shove.

"Go, Rosie; go, girl!" she called sternly.

The mare, somewhat shocked with the tenor of her mistress's voice, hopped forward obediently and enthusiastically.

The buggy lurched forward, and so did Meg Alcott. She lay flat in the middle of the stinking, thick mud, right in the middle of the road.

Thirty minutes later the Cash buggy passed briskly through the Crossing. Meg was horrified to see Chester, Matilda, and Dr. Browning in conversation in front of the store. She had planned to stop, to pour out her tale of woe, but now, with the arrogant doctor there? Never!

From the corner of her eye, she could see them stop and stare. They could not miss the brown uniform she wore. Nor could they fail to see the higher tilt her chin suddenly took.

She saw Browning turn away quickly, and she knew he was embarrassed for her. He was gentleman enough, she supposed, to wait until she was out of sight to give way to laughter.

Barrett shook his head. "Looks like Miss Alcott met the Carter Road mudhole personally."

Viney sat very primly with Gideon in her lap as the buggy traveled the dirt roads and cow tracks around the Crossing. She wore her best summer Sunday dress that was starched to within an inch of its life, and a broad straw hat with fake cherries on the brim that Seth had bought her a few years ago in Vicksburg. She hoped she didn't look too smug, though it was hard not to. She supposed some of her less generous neighbors would think Viney Jefferson was putting on airs riding in the Tanglewood buggy. If she was, she hoped she'd be forgiven. She didn't put on airs very often. This morning, already so warm, was still a beautiful morning. She felt so blessed and in love with life. There seemed to be nothing to threaten her happiness just then. She laughed out loud suddenly, for the sheer joy of life. Little Gideon clapped; Meg gave her a sideways glance, then joined her laughter.

In that one morning they had visited eight families, all with children, all quietly curious about this Yankee woman who was a reality and not a mere rumor. Viney was the ambassador, the diplomat. Her disarming friendliness put her neighbors at ease. They listened attentively to Meg's plans.

"I'd say we had a very successful morning, Viney," Meg said happily. "Certainly better than I could do alone."

"Oh, Miss Meg, you did fine by yourself. You're just a surprise to folks. It'll take 'em a piece to warm up, but they will."

"I think Abby Mayhew was a little too . . . warm. Steamed was closer to her temperature!"

Viney laughed. "Abby Mayhew is a tart one, all right. Don't know her real well, she lives so far out, like Mim."

"Well, I'm going to have to work my nerve up and go back and see Mrs. Mayhew and Mim," Meg said firmly.

Viney studied the white woman a moment.

"You feel like this is home, Miss Meg?" she asked.

Meg gave her a dazzling smile. "Haven't you noticed my attempt at a Southern accent?" They both laughed again, and Gideon clapped again. "Yes, this is home, Viney, for . . ."

A farm wagon was approaching them on the road from Chisolm Crossing. It held a man and a woman. Viney tensed and drew Gideon closer. Willet Keller's scowl was recognizable even from a distance.

Meg was prepared to nod a good afternoon and pass by. But the wagon stopped, and she knew that meant in wagon courtesy that she was to stop also.

"Hello," she said easily.

Already the woman beside the man was looking anxious. Apparently this was not a social stop along the road.

"You're the Yankee woman," Keller said by way of greeting.

Meg glanced at Viney. Viney was nervous too. Was this a local character that she hadn't heard about?

"Yankees are generally unwelcome down here. Yankee woman startin' a . . . nigger school is even more unwanted."

Meg saw the woman's hand rest lightly on the man's arm. *She's trying to restrain the rude ol' coot,* Meg decided. She was too startled to know what to say. She had not met such open antagonism before, excepting Abby Mayhew.

"Your school won't open," he boasted. "Or if it does, it won't stay open. Take this advice, Miss Alcon—"

"Alcott," she corrected crisply.

He gave her a contemptuous smile. "Alcott. Go back north, Miss Alcott. We don't want your school here. We won't have 'em."

Meg did not feel intimidated, nor did she feel like talking or defending her plans. Her eyes sought the eyes of the woman beside the man. They were fearful and pleading. Meg knew she was apologizing for him. Meg smiled at the woman. She suddenly thought of Andy and his humor. Her smile widened.

"Yes, it is a lovely afternoon. Well, good day!"

She snapped the reins and jogged past them. She waited till they were out of sight.

"Who was that, Viney?"

"Name's Willet Keller. Wife's Martha."

Willet Keller. Meg sighed and supposed it was a name she should remember.

"Thank you for coming with me, Amy."

The two rode along in the buggy toward the Crossing. Meg was paying a return call on Mim as she had promised. Amy adjusted her own hat and Melanie's bonnet. "Well, if I didn't, no telling what condition you might come back in. Or you might get lost again, or come upon another medical emergency!"

They were both laughing. "I could see you growing a bit white over the sight of blood," Amy teased.

"A bit white? I can see myself passed out in a dead faint!"

"Since your mother was a nurse, I'd imagine she finds you very amusing."

"A scandal to my poor mother, yes," Meg agreed.

Amy smiled. The roadside was beautiful, and she did enjoy being out. Yet she had not really wanted to come. Leaving the safety of Tanglewood was difficult. She might tease Meg for her weaknesses, but Amy knew well her own cowardice. She wasn't afraid of her neighbors, no, it was more a wariness, a caution. And the Crossing folk. She had grown up with them; they knew her. What did they think of her marriage? Now she owned one of the oldest plantations in Mississippi.

Greater than any of those concerns was the chance of encountering her stepbrother. She had not laid eyes on him since the night she had shot at him. He had vanished into the night, his blood staining the carpet as a grim reminder. Only Fenwick knew of the shooting. Who had French told? Even in this summer heat, the thought of Jeb French cast a chill over her.

Mim felt it her good fortune that she'd had the energy the day before to clean her cabin. Not that there was much cabin to clean. Yet she would not be ashamed of any filth. She tried to calm herself when the buggy with two white women drove up. Visitors!

Meg went forward quickly, wanting her to feel at ease.

"Hello, Mim! I brought Amy Cash with me. This is her little daughter, Melanie. How's Susannah?"

"She's fine. Come in and see her. She's a sleepin.'"

Meg leaned over the big bed. The little baby was a beautiful child. But now in the clarity of daylight Meg could see her skin. It was a soft tan. Meg was startled—that could only mean...She lifted her eyes and found Mim staring at her with the same look of sadness and pleading that she'd seen before.

"Isn't she as beautiful as I said, Amy?" Meg said.

"Yes, she is. You have a lovely daughter, Mim."

"Thank you both. You're so kind."

They sat at the crude wooden table as Mim served them cool water in tin cups. Meg tried not to notice that the woman's hands were shaking.

"Do you live here alone, Mim?" Meg asked gently.

"Yes, just Susannah and me. Few neighbors scattered about, that's all."

"Mim, I'm starting a school this fall for the black children around the Crossing."

"A school?"

"Yes, in the building by Chisolm's Mercantile. Would you tell your neighbors about it? My efforts so far—"

"I don't get out much. Don't see my neighbors."

Meg had grown very nervous. She had wanted this visit to go smoothly, to cheer up this woman who seemed so lonely and isolated, like Amy Cash.

"Well—"

A shadow blocked the sunlight from the open doorway. The three women turned. Jeb French stood before them.

His companion wolfhound brushed passed him, inspecting the place quickly, but not threatening them. It was evident to the two guests that the dog had been here before. Melanie began to scream.

The riding crop flicked against French's boot with a quick motion, and the dog was instantly at its master's side.

Amy had turned away from the doorway, her back to French. She crooned softly to her daughter. In one swift glance, Meg could see she was shaking and pale. Mim was rigid, her face fastened on the tall man.

"Little socializin' goin' on here? A missionary circle or quilting bee?" His laughter was mirthless.

Susannah had begun to cry, and Mim scooped her up.

Meg followed French's eyes. "And a nursery even! What are you servin' the ladies, Mim?" he peered over the table. "Just water!" His voice was mocking. "That the best you can do, Mim? These fine ladies are accustomed to better than that."

His eyes rested on Amy. "Greetings, little sis. So that's your girl, hmm? Heard you had a little one, sure did."

Amy still did not turn, her face buried in the child.

"You've turned so unfriendly, Amy girl." He looked directly at Meg. "Not like the old days."

Meg felt weak with shock and fear of this man. She did not want him to see her fear; he was the type of man with predatory instinct. She controlled her voice with great effort.

"Mr. French, you've interrupted our visit with Mim. If you wouldn't mind..."

His brilliant white teeth flashed in his dark face.

"Ah, Miss Alcott! You're looking very fine this morning." His eyes raked over her brazenly. "Very fine. I came by a couple of mornings ago for that ride you promised, but you were out. Least that's what Mr. Butler informed me."

His boot was possessively propped up on a cane chair. He leaned forward. The other two women were excluded; French had honed in on Meg exclusively.

"I've been very busy, Mr. French."

"Needn't be Mr. French to you. Been busy, have you?"

"Yes, now—"

"Been busy with that nigger school you're startin'?"

"Go on now, leave us!" Mim suddenly flared, the baby clutched tightly to her chest.

French pulled his eyes from Meg, his face changing from lust to anger in a flash. But his voice was controlled, tempered, biting.

"Mind your manners, Mim."

Meg was shaking and furious. Yet what could she do? Suddenly, unexplainably, she thought of Barrett Browning. Surely he was out on rounds, perhaps at a nearby cabin. If only he would come and check on little Susannah. She realized how strange it was to think of him now as help.

French swept the room with his eyes, resting on Amy, then Meg. A sudden snap of the riding crop, and he was gone from the cabin.

When they had passed through the black iron gates of Tanglewood, Meg pulled the buggy under a spreading live oak and stopped. Being back on the grounds of Tanglewood meant safety.

Neither woman had spoken since leaving Mim's. From the corner of her eye, Meg could see that Amy sat rigid, staring straight ahead, her eyes dry.

"Amy...Amy, are you all right?" Meg reached out and touched her arm.

Amy glanced down at Melanie sleeping in her arms, her smile very faint and trembling. The tears spilled over then; still, she did not look at Meg.

"You care," she whispered.

"I care? Oh, Amy, of course I care!"

"It's just that sometimes there comes a look in your eyes...like you don't trust me...or you're angry with me."

Meg felt a wave of shame and guilt. Yet she could not address those feelings now.

"Amy, I'm so sorry about what happened back there. I know why you don't like to leave Tanglewood."

"You understand?"

"I think so."

"He's an evil man, Meg."

Meg felt her heart breaking for the sadness she saw in the young woman's eyes. "I can see that he is, Amy."

Willet Keller had been rude and irritating, but French...She searched her mind a moment to find the right word to describe Jeb French... Ominous. That was the word. She would never forget the look of fear and pitiful defiance she had seen in Mim's eyes. It was evident that innocent little Susannah was the result of French's cruelest arrogance, and evident too, he held Amy in some kind of power.

"We don't have to talk about it, Amy. You don't have to tell me anything."

Amy took her hand, finally meeting her eyes.

"Meg, you said you care about me. I can trust you. I can tell you about Jeb French."

Barrett Browning was pleased to be riding to Tanglewood. He couldn't, or wouldn't, explain or admit the reason why. Maybe it was the relief of being away from the tension around the Crossing and the dangerous charade he was playing. Maybe it was the contrast of treating a patient in wealth and luxury to a patient in poverty. Perhaps it was because he enjoyed the friendly banter with Amy Cash or watching the antics of Melanie. Or maybe...maybe, it was the perverse pleasure he experienced in seeing this stranger who caused him this...irritation.

Fenwick dutifully led him to the sunny parlor where Amy Cash sat with her foot immersed in a pail of warm water.

"Running after Melanie or chasing a wayward pony, Mrs. Cash?" he asked as he pulled up a chair in front of her.

"Hello, Dr. Browning! You look awful!"

He laughed deeply. "Let's see the foot."

He examined the bruised, swollen ankle carefully. He tried not to notice that Miss Alcott was conspicuously absent. And he tried not to notice his disappointment.

"How'd you manage this? Hurt there?...There?"

"Ouch! Barrett, do you have to be so brutal?"

"I'm barely touching it."

"I was chasing Melanie. She has this new fascination for the fish pond. I tripped on the steps. Very ungrace—ouch! Do you have to do that?"

"Melanie's a better patient," he said in an attempted mumble. "Nothing broken; just a nasty sprain."

He cared for the foot, then sat back in his chair with a deep sigh.

"Will you stay for tea?" Amy asked.

He paused. "Are we alone? I mean—"

"You mean, is Miss Alcott here?"

Barrett hoped he wasn't blushing or admitting anything with his eyes. "Miss Alcott seems to find my company disagreeable."

"Well, Barrett, have you tried to be friendly, civil, sociable?"

He put on a very thoughtful face.

"I'm a doctor, Amy. I don't know how to be any of those things!"

They laughed together at this. Then Amy sobered. She leaned forward to touch his arm.

"Barrett, you do look awful."

"Thanks."

"I'm sorry, but it's true. You have bags under your eyes, you're pale, and you look like you've lost weight."

"Bad advertisement for the physician to look ill. I'll take a dose of tonic when I get home."

"Barrett, I'm serious. There's something in your face besides the other."

The doctor moved uncomfortably in his chair. Amy Cash knew him too well. "If you probe too deeply, Mrs. Cash, I can't stay for tea," he said lightly.

"Don't you trust me, Barrett? It's more than your patient load, isn't it?"

He leaned back in his chair and closed his eyes.

"I'm tired, Amy...very tired."

Tears came into her eyes at the sound of the sadness in his voice.

"The Klan is stirring around the Crossing," he said abruptly.

"Oh, Barrett, I wish there was a law against hateful groups like that!"

"It's like a weed, Amy. Not very strong, not growing, but not dead. Miss Alcott's school..."

"Barrett?"

He didn't know why he was telling her this. He shouldn't be. But it was so lonely never having anyone to talk to about it all...to have to keep the hurts and fears always inside.

"She's going to stick with it, isn't she?" he asked.

"She's working there now. She thinks she can open the doors by the first of September. Barrett, the Klan won't—"

"Amy, this conversation is just between you and me, all right?" His eyes were piercing.

"All right, Barrett."

Their jesting had turned to an earnestness Amy had not anticipated. "She's putting herself in the path of trouble with the Klan."

"But you said they're small and weak."

"They are going to have to bring the young black man to trial about the beating in Greenville sooner or later. When that happens, it will bring Klansmen from other counties in. They'll see the school as another threat. They may not tolerate it as the Klan here locally has. Or the Klan here will have to prove itself, and that school is pretty convenient. She could be in danger."

Amy Cash sensed she should not press this old friend. But how did he know all these things?

"Barrett, what can we do?"

He knew she would come to that question.

"Right now, nothing. I don't imagine she would quit if you urged her to."

"No, she wouldn't. That school is the right thing, Barrett. It's important, isn't it?"

He smiled wearily. "It's probably one of the best things to come to Chisolm Crossing in a long time ... barring, of course, that it comes from the hand of a ... Yankee."

Amy relaxed a bit. "Meg will be pleased to hear that."

"No, Amy." His voice was sharp. "This is between you and me, remember? It's safer this way."

She gave him a coy smile. "Are we talking about the Klan or about feelings, Barrett?"

He was mercifully saved from answering. Melanie entered, pulling Meg along behind her.

"Amy! Mel told me—" She stopped short when she saw that Amy was not alone. "Oh."

The doctor diagnosed the "oh" as decidedly a disappointment.

"I didn't know. Are you all right? What happened?"

Amy proudly displayed her bandaged foot.

"It would be funny if it didn't hurt so much," she said. "A bad sprain and nothing worse, the doctor has decreed. So how were things at the mouse den today?"

Meg felt very embarrassed. She was filthy, smelly, bedraggled, and being scrutinized very coolly by the doctor. Was he repulsed by her looks?

"Fine. Things went fine. I'd better go clean up."

"Barrett's staying for tea," Amy ventured roguishly.

"No, Amy, really, I'd better be going," Barrett said lamely.

"Of course you're staying. You said you would earlier. You'll want to hear about Meg's school. It's in your neighborhood after all."

Meg cleaned up faster than she thought she could. She told herself she was hurrying because she suspected they had, or were, talking about her! She felt as if she had intruded on some degree of intimacy...and she wondered why the doctor looked so ill himself.

She brushed out her hair and tied it back with a white silk ribbon. She slipped into a very simple, butter-yellow dress. There! Let the doctor scrutinize her now!

The Gulf Coast

Her mother had fallen asleep on the sofa, so the banker's daughter slipped from their cottage. She couldn't stay there any longer. She needed some fresh air. Maybe the crisp sea air would clear her mind and blow away the dark clouds in her thoughts. This time of rest her father had proposed had turned out differently. All she could think about was the scandal and the man who was condemned.

She wandered down the boardwalk in the late afternoon sunshine. Couples strolled and children scampered ahead of their parents. Their cottage was located not far from the fringe of town. She could see red, green, and yellow lights. She could hear music and laughter. These were familiar sounds, comforting sounds. But she walked past them. She walked out to a stretch of grassy beach where a colorful tent was pitched. She had the strangest feeling she was being pulled along. There was music at this place too.

"Yes, brother!"

"Amen!"

"Praise the Lord!"

"Hallelujah!"

She stopped. A tent meeting! Oh, no. But she stood there at the edge, where the horses and buggies were tethered, and listened to the singing. She liked it. She could see a sea of backs. And black faces. She should turn away. But she didn't.

Boldly she climbed to the seat of a vacant buggy and listened. She stayed when the preacher came to the pulpit. She heard every word he said. Every...healing...word. When it was over, she waited in the shadows, ignoring the curious glances that came her way. She waited until the crowd around the preacher had thinned. Then she went forward. She had to talk to him.

Frederick Dilling was a ramrod straight man of 40. He'd been preaching for nearly 25 years. He was educated and articulate and had traveled extensively. But he went to where the people were, rather than accept a pastorate. His younger brother Ambrose had done that. Frederick had felt this calling to carry the Good News when he was a young boy living in the slums of the nation's capital. He was ten when he had read the New Testament Captain Ethan Alcott had given his family.

When he saw the young white woman walking toward him, he knew now why the Lord had told him to hold one more meeting. He just *knew*.

She was tempted to turn away when she saw how weary he looked. But he had seen her and smiled as if it were not the least unusual to see a solitary white face in a meeting for blacks.

He mopped his face and took a sip of water.

"Rather warm tonight," he said.

She nodded.

"I'm Frederick Dilling."

She didn't want to give her name. Surely everyone had heard of her. "You have an accent; you're not from Mississippi."

"No, ma'am, I'm not. I lived most of my growing-up years in Washington, D.C."

Then he leaned forward. "How can I help you?"

She told him everything—except her name. He listened, he nodded. Of course he had heard of this sad case in Greenville.

He was the first black man she had ever talked to besides giving an order or summons. He looked so understanding.

"So you see, I've been thinking day and night about it. It haunts me at night... the thought that it... wasn't... him. I don't think he did it, Mr. Dilling! He was pushed into that warehouse. Someone else grabbed me off the street and beat me up."

Dilling was praying furiously, though his eyes were on the young woman. "They framed that young man," he finally said gently.

"But why? Who would do something like that?"

"That's the hard part, Miss, except that men's hearts are evil and sinful until they're washed in the blood of the Lamb. But that young man is innocent, and only the folks who set it up, and now you, know it. We can calculate that they aren't going to confess what they did, so..."

"That leaves me," she said slowly and with tears in her voice.

He dared to touch her then, to take her hand in his.

"Let's pray together, Miss."

Chapter 19

Chisolm Crossing

♦♦ ♦♦ ♦♦

*N*ell Evans had a lot of time to pray, now that she had a newborn to hold and rock. She had never been much of a praying woman, but Tom's involvement in the Klan had sent her looking for help and peace. She began to reexamine and think about those truths she had heard as a child. And she was praying...

Martha Keller was on her knees in her cabin a few miles south of the Evans farm. She knew folks thought she looked haggard and thin, but the truth was, Martha Keller had never felt more at peace. There had been no moving Willet. Now her appeals went to One so much higher than her husband. And she believed *He* was listening...

Very far north, in a quiet, sparsely furnished bedroom, a black preacher was on his knees. He had not forgotten the young white woman he had met a few weeks earlier. He had promised to pray for her. And the Lord always helped him keep his promises...

His prayers had started out so simple, so pleading and urgent.
"Lord, please, please help me."
Like Nell Evans, he had time to pray—lots of time. A jail cell with nothing but a hard bunk for a bed saw to that. He had no companions but the rats who looked as desperate and thin as he did, no visitors but the mean-tempered jailer. This foul hole had been his home for over eight weeks. His desire for drink had driven him nearly mad. But now at least that desire was gone. His smile was sad. Mama would be glad to hear that. But it looked like Mama would never know.
He had time to pray, lots of time—and every petition began the same. "Lord, sir, this is...Silas...."

Meg never thought she'd enjoy scrubbing floors, but with Seth and his neighbors hammering and singing up on the roof, she really didn't mind. Viney was at another end of the schoolroom; Fenwick was scrubbing walls. Amy and Matilda were preparing dinner for them at the Chisolms' kitchen. Chester was working in the store and popping out on the front porch at regular intervals to check on the progress. It was just like a big happy family, Meg had smiled to herself. With each thud of the hammer, her school was coming closer to reality. Children were going to come and fill the big empty room. They would become her children, just as her new friends in Mississippi had become her family.

They ate dinner in the shade of the schoolhouse. Meg could not help but nudge Amy. Fenwick was eating fried chicken with his elbows on the table, jawing with Chester as if they were old friends.

"More than a few miracles around here," Amy whispered teasingly.

Meg drifted off on the course of her own thoughts. She was so tired, but so pleased with the remodeling of the school. Now she was thinking about the mail she'd received the day before: a newsy letter from her mother, a letter from her sister-in-law, and a short letter from Andy in some port in the Caribbean. She hadn't written him much lately. But the fourth letter claimed her thoughts. It was a hastily scrawled note from Jerry Bass. She had written him. And now he had written her. A $100 bill was tucked into the envelope.

> ... Figured you'll huff about this little gift, but I wanted to contribute to your new school project. Sounds like a great plan and just like you. Name a hitchin' post or a swing set after me. By the way, I'm finally engaged ...

She smiled. She would always smile when she thought of Jerry Bass. Sometimes she thought of his kisses and how he had held her like a prize. Now, there was no one to tell her she was pretty, to want her ...

She had folded the note carefully.

"Just think, Amy, I could have been the matriarch of a ranch in Texas!"

"Oh?"

"But I'm in Mississippi starting a much-needed school for black children."

"Regrets?"

"None. I'm exactly where I want to be!"

The banker of Greenville was feeling smug and very pleased with himself. His wife and daughter had returned from the coast looking healthy and rested, just as he had planned. But his daughter was quieter, more subdued, somehow altered from her loud, defiant ways. The banker watched her with suspicion for the first few evenings. He expected her to leave the house for her old crowd of friends and return after midnight, singing and laughing. But she didn't go out. She stayed in her room. She was busy with several things.

First, she was trying to decide at nearly 21 years of age what to do with her life. She hadn't any prospects for marriage. She wanted to leave home; she could no longer stand the loveless atmosphere of her father's house. So she tried to determine what her skills, her talents, and her interests were.

But more importantly, she was trying to work up the courage to tell her parents the truth about that awful night in the spring. Every time she tried to talk about it, it stuck in her throat like a dry wad of food. They would be angry with her. They would be disappointed again. They would be horribly embarrassed.

As boisterous and bold, as rebellious and riotous as she had been in the past, now she trembled to think of confronting them. But it must be done! She could not listen to the terror. A black Yankee preacher was praying for her—and waiting for her to throw open the jail cell door.

Chester Chisolm loved a party. He loved any reason to celebrate, to pay tribute, to do little more than tell stories, laugh, and tease. And eat. He loved all the food that was testament of a party. So it seemed natural to him to host a party in celebration of the soon-to-be-finished Chisolm Crossing school. Everyone around the Crossing must be invited. He would make a proud little speech on the front steps and present the schoolmarm with a shiny new brass bell. He could hardly wait for the Saturday to come. He was like a child, too excited to sleep at night.

Matilda Chisolm was far more practical. A party would create added work—and added business for the store. She couldn't depend on her jovial little husband to make the arrangements or figure details. She would have to do it. She would shake her head and wonder how the store would prosper if she weren't there. Chester couldn't even find his own socks in the morning!

They were behind the long counter making preliminary plans when Barrett Browning entered. He had come for his mail. Chester looked up and was very glad to see him. He hadn't seen much of this friend lately.

"Just in time, Barrett. You can be the first to know, and spread the word."

"What are you cookin' up now, Ches?" Barrett asked good-naturedly.

"*I* am figuring it all up, Mr. Chisolm," Matilda reminded pointedly.

Chester winked at Barrett. "Barrett, they just threw away the mold when they made my gal, they sure did. She's just as efficient as ... a clock from Sears and Roebuck!"

"If I ever find a woman to court, I'll remember not to come to you for romantic illustrations, Ches."

"Now if you two are quite finished with your silliness ..." Matilda reproved.

"We're gonna have a little celebration, Barrett. Celebrate the opening of our new school. Gonna invite everyone, have lots of food and fun. Yep, it'll be a big day at the Crossing!"

"Two Saturdays from tomorrow," Matilda added.

"You'd better plan on filling up, Barrett. You're lookin' a little like one of the cows in Pharaoh's bad dream!"

"You're the second person who's told me that. I think I'll take some time off and go on a fishin' trip."

He had said it without seriousness, but it sounded pretty appealing. It would be good to get away for a while. *You can't run away now though, Barrett,* he whispered to himself.

"Well, take it after the spread, or you'll miss a mighty fine time," Chester enthused.

"What do you think of our plan, Doctor?" Matilda asked directly.

She and her husband had noticed the doctor had not been around for any of the Saturday workdays on the school. Had he simply been too busy with patients? Matilda knew Chester was annoyed by the doctor's absence, but silent on it.

"Well, it certainly is looking like a well-built school. You have done a fine job. I...I don't know...what I might be tied up with on that Saturday." He knew it sounded stilted.

"Well, like I said before, you could help spread the word about it," Chester said with sudden asperity.

Barrett took a deep breath. He was about to sacrifice a friend. He hoped it would only be for a short time. But this celebration was just the thing that Willet Keller would want to mix in.

"To tell you the truth, I don't know that it's such a good idea."

"What?" Chester snapped.

"Well you see, I—"

"It's a fine school and a great idea! What could be wrong with it? I just don't understand you, Barrett!"

"Let the doctor speak," Matilda said firmly.

"I'm just trying to say I think the more visible you get about the school, the more trouble you invite from those who are opposed to it."

"Those opposed! Those opposed! Who's opposed?" Chester sputtered indignantly.

Another time and Barrett would have smiled and told the shopkeeper to calm down and remember his heart. But he did not dare smile.

"Well, Ches—"

"Ya been noticeably absent while the school's been going up. Not that I don't allow you have plenty of work of your own. But it lays... disturbin' in my mind when I put this with how cold you are to Meg." Chester was red-faced and fuming.

"Ches—"

"I thought you were a big enough man to put this Yankee hatin' aside. Now it's lookin' like you've taking up hatin' people of color!"

Barrett was very grateful the store was empty of customers.

"Mr. Chisolm! Will you please? Your tongue is taking off like a team of runaway horses! The doctor is your friend, and you are ... are scalding him unfairly," Matilda inserted.

Chester pulled out his red handkerchief and mopped his face.

"You're right, you're right. I'm sorry to carry on so, Barry."

"It's all right, Chester. Look, all I'm saying is that I do hear things as I treat folks, and not everyone is happy about a school for blacks. It's the first in this area."

"Now don't get started again, Mr. Chisolm, but the doctor is right, whether we like it or not. We'd be foolish to think everyone is delighted about the education of poor, black children. Not everyone is as broad-minded as us."

"But ... but ..." Chester had lost his steam.

"Think of Willet Keller if you must," Matilda continued with authority. "It's no secret he's the Klan leader around here. And there are others with him."

"Willet Keller is a windbag! A toothless dog! A peacock!" Chester growled. "His poor wife comes in here looking like she ain't seen the inside of a smile in a year!"

"Windbag or not, Keller and his kind won't like the school. The point is, will he be brave enough to do something about it?" Matilda persisted.

Barrett was grateful for Matilda Chisolm just now. She had made his case effectively and eloquently. But now the couple turned their questioning eyes on him.

"All right, so you hear things, Barrett. Will Keller do anything? Are you sayin' we shouldn't celebrate at all?" Chester asked crisply.

"I think I'd reconsider inviting everyone. Just invite those who have worked on the school and the families with children who are planning to enroll. Don't advertise it here in the store."

"Will that keep Keller still?" Chester persisted.

"Keller may be satisfied; he may not. I don't know. Well, I'd better just get my mail and be on my way."

Chester Chisolm dusted his shelves and waited on customers for the rest of the morning with untypical sobriety. At times, he stopped working altogether and scowled. Barrett had dumped cold water on the flame of his exciting plans. But he didn't fault him that. Barrett had reminded them of the opposition to the school. But that troubled him the least at the moment. Chester Chisolm was agitated with the doctor himself. Why was he so distant lately? Why did he hold himself apart from the dealings with the new school? How could he oppose a school for the very people he tried to keep healthy? It was a puzzle Chester

Chisolm was determined to solve. And maybe Matilda would help him on it.

It was Evans who had the idea, though Barrett was eager to talk with Keller about the school celebration.

"I guess it will work," Barrett admitted slowly. "It won't hurt to try, and I'm too tired to think of anything better."

"Good. I'll drop in at 7:00, and you get there by 7:30. That'll give me 30 minutes to get worked up and let Willet get worked up. Then the two of us together should be able to push him over. He's not a very original thinker, Barrett, and I don't think he has much nerve. He's a puppet," Evans said eagerly.

The farmer had miscalculated on that point, however.

"It's a stall, Tom, and we both know it. I'm happy to try your plan, but I think we're prolonging the inevitable."

"What other plan do we have right now, Barrett?"

"A little miracle would be nice," the doctor said with a sigh.

Evans had never seen the doctor so low, so pessimistic before. He put his arm around Barrett's shoulders.

"Come on, Barrett, this is a fight, and we're on the winning side!"

So far, Evans's trap had worked smoothly. He lured Keller out to his barn, offered him a choice plug of tobacco, talked about how dry and hot it was. Then he skillfully mentioned the black school. As he expected, the Klan leader launched into an impassioned tirade. Evans waited awhile, then added a few of his own words of vehemence.

"It makes me sick to see it," Keller seethed. "Little Yankee woman didn't take ol' Will Keller serious. Well, she'll surely wish she had!"

"She has Chisolm all taken with her plan," Evans interrupted. "Even saw a few white fellas helpin' put the roof on the other day."

"It's a fine lookin' roof, Tom, but it'll burn as well as any other," Keller said with significance.

"Evenin', fellas." Barrett stood in the open barn doorway.

Keller had jumped and cursed. "What do you mean by sneakin' up on us like that, Doc?"

Barrett laughed easily. "I wasn't sneaking up, Will. The door wasn't closed. Could have heard you two over a church choir!"

Evans laughed, but Keller was not smiling.

"Came by your place, Tom, to check on your little one. Nell told me you had come out here. I thought maybe I had gotten my nights mixed up and this was a meeting night."

"No, it ain't," Willet snapped irritably. "And your woman shouldn't be knowin' I'm over here, Tom."

"What's the problem, Will? I told her you were coming over here to talk about mules," Tom replied with a straight face. He dare not look at Barrett. "Anyway, we were talking about the darky school, Doc."

"Oh."

"I think it's time we—" Evans began.

"It's time to do something about it," Keller blustered. He was jealous of his power. He did not want any plan to originate anywhere but in his own mind. He had been pushed once before against his will. This time he was in control.

"Well, Chester is planning a potluck picnic in a few Saturdays to celebrate the completion of the school," Barrett reported.

"That's a fine thing to hear," Keller gloated. "A real fine thing."

Evans and Barrett exchanged quick looks. Will Keller was responding with ugly predictability.

"I'll call an emergency meeting for tomorrow night," Keller said with a smile.

"What do you have in mind, Will?" Evans asked.

"Oh, a little added . . . entertainment at their party!"

All three men laughed.

"We'll just ride through and make it look like a tornado touched down!" Keller boasted.

Barrett closed his eyes. All he could see in his mind were things trampled and broken . . . children crying and screaming . . . Chester furious but helpless . . . Miss Alcott wide-eyed with terror.

"That'll wake 'em up to how serious the Klan is!" Evans said loudly. It was Barrett's cue. But Barrett was pale and silent.

"It's a plan that the devil himself would approve!" Keller was rocking on the hay bale with laughter.

"Barrett? Barrett!" Evans prodded.

"Hmm? That would be a dramatic move all right, but maybe not quite the best way just now."

"Why not?" Keller asked testily. He had a grudging respect for the doctor. But he wanted no arguments, no preaching of patience. This was all his plan, and it was perfect!

"Well, there're a couple of things. First, it's in broad daylight."

"That's true," Evans echoed.

"So what?" Keller countered.

"So it takes away from our valuable ally of surprise. Sheets or no sheets, a lot of folks know our horses. If I'm recognized I could lose patients, and I have to eat."

"Barrett has a good point," Evans said hurriedly before Keller could protest.

"In daylight they see who we are. We lose our mystery and the power of fear. Some of the men there may get confrontational. I don't think we're strong enough for that yet."

It was very reasonable, and Keller didn't like any of it. He was like a pouting child who had just had a favorite toy taken away.

"Well, we just can't let this thing go on! A nigger school ain't right!" Keller shouted.

"I agree, I agree, Will. I just think we should come up with something else. Your plan is a good one, but subtlety might be more effective right now," Barrett soothed.

Keller did not want to ask what subtlety meant.

"That sounds good," Evans jumped in. "We do a little here, a little there, like . . . like steps of fear. That'll shake the Yankee up."

"That's the idea!" Barrett enthused.

"Like what steps of fear?" Keller asked.

"Like some warnings every so often, some little reminders that the Klan has its eye on her and the school," Evans continued like one suddenly inspired.

"Maybe a few of those reminders for Chester Chisolm too," Barrett offered.

"And we would leave them at night for her to find in the morning. She might not be so bright-eyed and eager to teach!" Evans chuckled.

"Might just help her pack up her bags and head north!" Keller added. He had finally caught on to the spirit of the thing.

Evans knew he must stroke the leader's vanity one last time to ensure the plan. "So, what do you think, Will? It's up to you."

Keller knew these two men were smart. Smarter than any of the other Klansmen he knew. He did not want to offend them, but he was still in charge. He was not overly eager to have one of his plans fail. His had been dramatic, but open to things going wrong . . . people getting hurt.

"We'll try it for a while," he compromised.

Evans and Barrett dared not exchange a look. It had bought them a little more time.

Jackson

It was one of those days Silas knew he was dying by slow inches. He couldn't go on like this much longer. He didn't want to go on like this. He remembered the Bible story of Joseph, the young Jewish boy thrown into the pit. But this pit had swallowed him up.

"Hey you, boy!" the jailer called. "You have a visitor!"

A visitor! Had they finally allowed his family to come? Had French found the truth at last?

The visitor had paid the jailer $20 in order to see the boy from Greenville.

"I want a full hour for my money," the visitor said firmly. And oddly enough, the jailer did not argue.

The visitor stepped into the sweltering jail cell. He carried a wooden stool in one hand, a Bible in the other. It was the biggest Bible Silas had ever seen. The tall man was dressed in white trousers and a white shirt. A white jacket was slung casually over his arm. He was bareheaded—and the most handsome and impressive black man the accused had ever laid eyes on.

"Hello, Silas," he said in a deep, Yankee-tinted voice, "I'm Frederick Dilling, and the Lord told me to come see you. We have only an hour to get acquainted and for me to acquaint you to the Lord."

She was preparing to leave for Tanglewood when she found the note in her buggy. It was late afternoon, and she glanced around quickly. No one was in sight. The scrap of paper contained only two lines.

> I would sure like to help you with your school, Miss
> Alcott. I feel bad that I can't. Maybe I can help you in some
> other way.

It was unsigned. Someone wanted to help but couldn't. Someone was going to help in his own secretive way. She knew there was some controversy surrounding this school, but there had been no tangible threat so far. She studied the note a moment longer before she stuffed it into the pocket of her apron. She would show it to Amy—maybe she would recognize the handwriting.

She thought of Dr. Browning. It would be like him to leave an anonymous note rather than speak to her directly. She would trust he had his own reasons.

Amy Cash had never been busier. There was the work at the Crossing school. There was the renovation on the building that was to become Seth and Viney Jefferson's new home. She was so thankful they had decided to move to Tanglewood. Micah would help his father in the shop in the afternoons. In the mornings the Tanglewood buggy would carry him to the Chisolm Crossing school. She would enjoy having Viney close by and young Gideon for Melanie to play with. She smiled at the thought of some of her aristocratic neighbors seeing the black child and the white child playing together. But perhaps she was just carrying on the unconventional ways that her late husband had started. He would love to see the changes that had come to Tanglewood. She thought of him often, as the loving brother she had never had.

When Meg's mail came to Tanglewood, Amy thought of Andy. So distant, like something of her imagination. It was senseless to dwell on him.

Jeb French had a varied menu of things on his mind. His shipping interests were expanding and prospering. But they demanded time, travel, and effort. He didn't mind. The success pleased him and fed his ego, but did not satisfy him.

Amy Cash was on his mind. She was always lurking somewhere in his thoughts. She was the one prize he hadn't captured—yet. There was her Yankee visitor. Here was a beautiful woman capable of stirring a man's blood...

Seth Jefferson. French felt a bit of unfinished business waiting there. And Silas. His best worker, like Seth Jefferson before him, had been taken from him. He didn't like it then. He didn't like it now. For as long as Silas had been in jail, French had been thinking about the episode. He knew the reputation of the banker's daughter. He wasn't surprised that she had been at a waterfront tavern. He had talked with Silas's gaming friends. He knew without any doubt it had been a frame-up. But why?

It had been so public, no one could hope to blackmail the banker concerning his wayward daughter. And an insignificant, poor, black dock worker? No, it had to be part of something else, something bigger. It took a sinister mind to understand another sinister mind.

It was cloudy, humid, windless. Jeb sat in his office. He poured himself a tumbler of whisky and scanned the shipping orders in front of him. Silas was a part of some plan, a pawn, a victim... an order for cotton in New Orleans... payroll to sign... the banker's daughter had been the bait... a bigger scheme... a scheme to frame a black man...

He looked up from his desk as if the memory was real. *So you see, Jeb, we all have to work together to keep blacks in their place... underneath our boot!*

He had stood in this very office and delivered a heated Klan speech—a farmer in thick-soled, ugly boots.

Chapter 20

Chisolm Crossing

♦♦ ♦♦ ♦♦

*M*ail carriers, train porters, traveling salesmen, Aunt Mollie's best friend's third cousin near Greenville—by whatever means, whatever fashion, the story of the pretty Yankee schoolteacher making a school for blacks was passing along the veins of communication from Greenville to Vicksburg. Schools for blacks weren't novel this year of 1893, nor the moralizing temperance of Yankees, but the school at the Crossing was causing quite a stir, little ripples in a pond tucked away in western Mississippi. Where would the ripples lead to?

The old cotton warehouse, so dingy, so neglected, had undergone an amazing transformation over the hot summer. Citizens of the Crossing, whatever skin color, were spellbound. A skeleton of decay had evolved into a white frame structure, imposing for its fresh, bright whiteness. Impressive for the black lettering over the door, the four shiny windows on each side, the brass bell, the neat squares of zinnias and marigolds by the front steps. The three other Chisolm dwellings looked like shabby, embarrassed cousins in comparison.

Chisolm Crossing had the fame of Ford's Creek at its doorstep; now the school was becoming an attraction. Hopefully the fuss and fury would die down about the school just like the dust that rose on the wide, dry road, but for now it was the principal topic of conversation. Some white folk drove out from Greenville in their surreys to see the construction for themselves, pacified that at least the saws and hammers weren't ringing out on the Sabbath. Truth to tell, they glumly conceded, this black school was looking almost better than their own.

Chester Chisolm was not above gloating. He felt he'd "discovered" the pretty schoolteacher; they had a first-name friendship! Stuck-up Yankee? Not this one! The school was bringing in added business for the store, which pleased Matilda, but Chester found he was never tired of talking about Miss Alcott, or her plans and how he encouraged them, or how the building was really his, and on and on. Everyone who came into the store had a comment about the project. Chester quickly and firmly let them know that unfavorable comments weren't tolerated, and they could ride to Greenville to shop if they cared to.

It was a Friday evening in late August. The sky was rose-colored in a shadowy, gold-tinted sunset. One young woman stood alone in front of the school building, her apron stained, her hair straggled and loose, her hands clasped behind her, her face a mixture of eagerness and fatigue. It was still now. Only the sound of birds singing in the nearby pines could be heard, where moments earlier there had been the voices of six adults and one child as they stood and surveyed the school with great satisfaction. Meg would never forget young Micah Jefferson, taking her hand in his own and saying, "It's real! It's a real school for us!" He had been nurtured well from his parents' own enthusiasm.

Matilda and Chester had gone back to their home behind the store; Seth, Viney, Micah, and Amy had returned to Tanglewood. Meg was alone in the place she had chosen, now her home.

Come Monday morning, a bright new day, 8:00 A.M., the yard would be alive with the voices of children. A summer of planning and toil and hope would come down to that morning—a new beginning for Miss Meg Alcott, a new beginning for generations.

"Are you nervous, Meg?" Amy had asked before she left.

Meg sighed and then smiled. "Terrified!"

"You'll do fine. The children are going to love you, Meg." Softly, she had added, "Andy would be proud of you for what you're doing here."

This was one of the few times Amy had used Andy's name and not referred to him as "your brother." Meg did not fail to notice.

"I hope so," she answered just as softly. She did want to make Andy proud of her, no matter what her feelings for him right now.

Their eyes held a moment, then Amy continued.

"I'm going to miss you, Meg. My only comfort is knowing you're coming back to Tanglewood Friday nights for the weekends."

"I'll look forward to that. Tanglewood will be like an oasis for me!" She turned back to the building. "But I know staying here is the right thing to do. Folks around here would have always thought of me as the white Yankee who lives up in the rich mansion if I didn't live among them. It may be hard for them to accept me as it is. But we've made me a cozy apartment in the back room, haven't we?"

Amy nodded.

"I'll miss our talks together, Amy. I know I'll get lonely."

She didn't add that she might just be a bit fearful living alone on the edge of the clearing. A forest of pines might be cool, inviting, and fragrant in the daytime, but come nightfall it could be shadowy and full of imaginations. Still, Chester and Matilda were only a few hundred yards away. Could they hear her if she needed them during the deep of night? If she screamed? She drove the fears away quickly and smiled brightly.

"I promise to bring you lots of stories about my little scholars each Friday night, Amy!"

Meg watched her as she drove away to Tanglewood. Back to her little daughter, back to her lonely mansion. From what she had learned about

Jeb French, Meg was convinced Amy Cash was a young woman with a painful past. Hadn't her brother hurt her also? She couldn't sort through those feelings now.

It had given Meg real joy to know that white and black hands had gone into raising Chisolm Crossing School. Now the neat, plain little school was finished and ready for business.

"Chisolm Crossing School, Established 1893" was painted in black block letters above the green door. Meg stepped inside, greeted by the smell of fresh paint and new lumber. She took one final look around the schoolroom in the fading light—her schoolroom.

Victorian America had made little imprint on the rural schoolhouse. Further west, school was still held in the dark cavelike soddie. Most often the schools had but one room. So it was with Chisolm Crossing School. Meg had brought the deliberate stamp of the little frame school she had been raised in and taught in to this school. Perhaps it was a lack of imagination, yet it was all she knew, and she hoped it was more than adequate.

As she gazed at the room, she saw rows of smooth wooden benches with tables in front of them, enough to seat 30 pupils. She chewed her lip in concern. What if more children arrived than she had planned for? She and Chester had been over the list several times. She frowned at herself, nagging over a hundred little things already. What condition would she be in come Monday morning?

Each desk had a slate and and new chalk pencil, purchased by Meg from her own small savings. Perhaps later, by spring, some students would be ready for paper. An old bottle filled with water and plugged with a small rag rested by each slate for cleaning. Matilda had graciously provided these articles. Meg would not have her scholars spitting and wiping their slates with their sleeves!

A black stove stood in the center of the room, its pipe jutting upward. How cold could a Mississippi winter be, she wondered? Pegs had been driven in the wall by the door for caps, a bench constructed for dinner pails. Would the children bring nourishing noontime meals? A bucket and ladle lay ready on the bench for drinking.

At the front of the room sat her own golden-hued oak desk and chair her parents had freighted down. On the desk lay a neat stack of books. She eyed them critically. *McGuffey's Readers*, 12 copies, *Maury's Geography*, 5 copies, *Robinson's Mental Arithmetic*, 7 copies, *Kellog's Grammar*, 9 copies, *Chamber's History*, 2 copies. Clearly not enough texts for each child, but they would have to serve.

She looked down at her own leather journal, ready to receive the names of her students. Within the cover was an inscription. She closed her eyes a moment; she knew it by heart.

>A teacher affects eternity; he can never tell where his
>influence stops.
>
>—Henry Adams

A heady suggestion perhaps, yet it seemed to capture the essence of her responsibility.

Behind her desk hung a long blackboard and a small map of the United States. Somber portraits of Lincoln and Washington would look down on the scholars from the front of the room. Windows, just high enough that the smallest pupil must stretch on tiptoe, ran four along the eastern wall and four along the western wall. She was pleased with those windows; they changed the entire feeling of the old cotton warehouse. Chester and Seth had done a good job.

Her apartment was a little room at the back of the schoolhouse. It too had been fitted with a window. She could look out on the evergreens and cypress and watch the sunlight making beautiful patterns on the forest floor in the morning. The mahogany bed, chest of drawers, chair and table, small gas stove, and shelves, all simple yet elegant, had been given to her by Amy. A wedding-ring quilt for her bed from her mother, a few family pictures, her own personal library, a basket of shells she'd gathered from Mediterranean coasts, her jewelry box from the crew of the *Magnolia*, a silk fan from Paris, and a tea set from London completed the furnishings—this was home now.

Later that night, after a cold supper, Meg lay tensely in her bed, her window open to the orchestra of crickets, the solo of the owl, the scolding songs of birds. She lay there nearly an hour before she relaxed, before the surrounding darkness and quiet seemed less threatening and ominous.

How could she possibly go to sleep with so many thoughts running riot through her mind? She thought of young Micah again, so eager to learn. Yet these children had no background, no foundation for her to build upon. She'd never taught children who knew . . . nothing! Not a letter, or stroke of the pen, or number! A surge of panic filled her. These children were as clean, as unmarked, as the new slates in the schoolroom.

Finally her eyes grew heavy, Seth and Viney Jefferson the subject of her last conscious thoughts. Viney had impulsively hugged Meg, saying, "God bless you, Miss Alcott!"

They were excited about Chisolm Crossing School. This school was the culmination of their dreams and hopes. Was she a worthy keeper of those dreams?

"How do you plan to teach about the war, Miss Alcott?"

It was Saturday morning, and Colonel Higgins had come from Vicksburg to inspect Chisolm Crossing School. He stood in the square of sunshine from a window, his arms crossed, his eyes intent upon her. He was in his shirtsleeves, buttoned decorously to the collar and each cuff. He'd made the concession to remove his black broadcloth coat; she could imagine he'd make no others. She could also imagine him in the butternut uniform of the Confederacy 30 years earlier—younger, still stern, passionate for the cause of the South.

"Well, Colonel Higgins, I don't think my students will be ready for in-depth history lessons right away. I think basic reading and math will be our beginning point."

"But if the question is raised by one of your students?" he persisted.

"Then I will present the war as I did to my students in Illinois. We'll look at both sides, and the issues, and try to understand."

It sounded lame, and she knew it. This man's gray eyes were piercing, and she quelled under them. She would rather face the sarcasm of Matilda Chester, or the acid tongue of Abby Mayhew, or the scornful Dr. Browning.

She drew a deep breath, but he interrupted.

"I've examined you in spelling, reading, mental and practical math, geography, English and grammar, composition, U.S. history, and philosophy. Your scores were nearly perfect."

Was he praising her?

He sauntered around the room again, pausing at the sober portrait of Lincoln. Meg glanced out the window. She could see Chester nervously pacing the front porch of his store, pretending to sweep. He was clearly worried for her.

Higgins swung around. "You didn't use the black church for a school, Miss Alcott. May I ask why?"

"I thought of that, of course, and I'm sure the congregation would have been willing. Still I felt it was important to establish a separate schoolhouse . . . to make people feel I was in earnest, that I wouldn't leave easily."

There was the briefest hint of a smile in the superintendent's eyes. He drew on his coat slowly. Meg felt she could hardly breathe—this man had the final authority concerning her school.

"You've done a fine job with this building, Miss Alcott."

Her breath expelled loudly. "You really think so?"

He smiled at her childish eagerness and stepped closer. "I've been posturing with you, Miss Alcott. I had to."

"Sir?"

"I had to determine if you had the mettle to teach here. I discouraged you purposely to evaluate your commitment."

"But, why?"

"You're living in the South now, Miss Alcott. You must leave your Yankee notions at the state line. This is Mississippi."

"I know that."

His warm voice grew firm again. "You have heard of a Mississippi import called the Klan?"

"Yes, I've heard a little."

"All Mississippians are not like that, and I don't know the strength of the Klan here in Washington County. But county lines can be crossed pretty easy. You have chosen an enormously controversial task. I cannot predict how the whites will tolerate this school. I cannot say the Klan will ignore this threat."

Meg leaned wearily on the edge of her desk.

"Why must teaching children to read be considered a threat?"

"Ignorance always breeds fear. There is more than just the education of young minds to be done here." His voice softened. "You have all my support and encouragement. I can't tell you how all this will end, Miss Alcott. I only know you've made a good start."

First Day, Fall Term,
Chisolm Crossing School,
1893

There was no nervous laughter or shrill voices of little girls, or impromptu games of tag, or boys scuffling and shouting. There was none of that. It was quiet, deathly quiet, Meg thought to herself. From inside the schoolroom, she could hear only the birds, a dog barking in the distance, an occasional baby cry that was quickly silenced, and subdued, muffled voices.

She peeped out the window again, suddenly very nervous, very frightened, very intimidated. She felt weak with worry. Outside in the schoolyard, in the lovely morning sunshine, the children had gathered with their parents, standing in separate groups, tense and waiting. Some of these families she had met; some she had not. Yet every face was a stranger, a question mark.

Suddenly Chester was inside, his apron flapping in excitement.

"Meg? Meg! They've come! Just a standin' out there!"

"I know, Chester, I know!"

"What's the matter? Got the jitters?" He saw she was pale and trembling.

"Chester, suddenly I'm afraid. This is too big for me!"

"Not a thing too big when you got help. Look out there, Meg. See that little one there... that's how small this is, ain't big at all, not really."

His plump arm went around her. "Don't be afraid, Meg. Come and greet them."

She stood on the front steps, Chester beside her, smiling and benevolent. Oh, this dear little man was a strength to her!

She glanced at the groups scattered about the yard, perhaps 20 children in a quick count. They didn't know how to approach a school, didn't know the traditions, the customs. She felt a wave of shame and sorrow for these proud people.

She drew a deep breath, "Good morning! If you'll just line your children up in front of the door..."

His chocolate-brown skin glistened in the morning sunshine as he stood sweating in his overalls before her. He was nervous, yet he smiled as he laid a big hand on the head of the boy and girl in front of him. This was a family she had not met.

"This here's my boy and girl child, Miss..."

"Alcott."

"Miss Alcott."

"And you're?"

"Called Boon."

"Mr. Boon, I'm—"

"Oh, no, Miss 'Cott, just be Boon. Never had a mister in front."

"I see."

"My wife done taught 'em some letters and numbers."

"Oh, that's fine."

"But we're wantin' you to teach 'em the rest like."

"The rest?" Meg asked dully.

The big man nodded eagerly. "Just need to learn 'em everything else, ma'am."

Meg smiled nervously. *Everything else.* She glanced down at the two quiet children, immediately recognizing the boy named Tick. Their eyes told her they were as eager for their education as their father was. She extended her hand to the man.

"I feel very honored to teach your children, Mr....ah, Boon."

He took her hand awkwardly, lightly. He had never touched a white woman in all his 28 years.

"I look forward to meeting your wife, Boon. I'm sure she's done a fine job teaching your children."

His smile was wide. "She'd a come herself, she was wantin' to, but—" He stopped and the smile disappeared. He pushed the children forward. "She's a birthin' my new boy. I better get on home."

He turned, swung up on a mule, and was gone.

"Did your father mean your mother is having a baby this morning?"

The two heads bobbed vigorously. Meg drew another deep breath. Such a fertile place, this Chisolm Crossing!

"Well, you know my name is Miss Alcott. Can you tell me yours?"

"I'm Chessie," the little girl said eagerly, "and eight years old too!"

"I'm glad you've come to school, Chessie."

"Name's Tick, ma'am. I'm ten and my pa said to tell you I was to help you all I could with anything you need."

"Well that's very thoughtful of your father, Tick. I'm sure I'll need your help."

The children were still lining up very slowly, very quietly, pushed forward by their mothers. Their eyes were huge as they stared at her.

She took their names quickly as they filed in so solemnly and took their seats in the clean, new schoolhouse. But the mothers remained in a timid group at the bottom of the steps, nervous and shy.

"Oh...you needn't wait for your children. School will dismiss at 3:00. You can come for them then, or they can leave on their own."

"The kids are gonna be just fine, ladies, sure are," Chester echoed at her elbow.

They turned then, filing down the dusty road or swallowed into the cool, gray woods. Meg watched them. They were trusting her. She took a deep breath and entered the schoolhouse.

Her shoes made a hollow beat as she walked up the aisle to her desk. Only the sound of her shoes, and breathing; no other sound. She was counting quickly as she walked. She had taken down 22 names. Twenty-two. When she turned, there would be 44 eyes upon her!

When she faced them, she smiled bravely, still standing behind her desk and hoping that they could not see she was shaking. She would look them over quickly and let them look her over. Get acquainted there in the silence for a moment.

Ten boys, 12 girls. There were no economic levels here; they all dressed alike, as if they came from the same large family. The boys wore overalls, frayed and patched, shirtless. The little girls wore faded calico or dresses made from flour sacks. All the children were barefoot, and all looked at her with serious, expectant eyes.

She smiled and felt herself relax. "Good morning, children. I'm glad to see each of you."

"And we're surely glad to see you!" boomed Tick. There were shy giggles at this, a few smiles, movement at last.

"Thank you, Tick. Now, if you'll raise your hand when I call your name, I'd like you to tell me your age and whether you've ever had any schooling."

An hour later, she had some resemblance to a roll. It was a beginning point. She glanced over the list of names, some so different they seemed to jump out at her. Names like Tick, Chessie, Mary Rose and her younger sister Mary Sis, Temple and his little brother called True, and a slim girl of 12 called Faraway. Her oldest scholar was 14, the youngest, just turned six.

"This is a beginning for all of you, and a beginning for me. I've always thought the best way to begin the school day is with Scripture, reading from the Bible."

She picked up her own and began to read.

> *I will lift up mine eyes unto the hills,*
> *from whence cometh my help.*
> *My help cometh from the Lord,*
> *which made heaven and earth.*

A hand went up when she was finished.

"Do you suppose we'll be able to read like that someday, Miss Ma'am?" Faraway asked.

"Oh, yes, Faraway, I do. It will take work, but I know we can do it together."

"You sure read fine," the small boy named Ben added.

"Let me show you something." She went to the blackboard and printed a large *a*. "Reading is made up of words and words are made up of letters. The first letter is *a*. A makes the sound..."

The morning wore on, and reflecting later, Meg decided she had never had a more obedient and eager class. Would they stay so willing and pliable? They were like little cups waiting to be filled. Twenty-two children had watched her every move, hung onto every word. Of that 22, only six had any knowledge of numbers or letters. Only two had ever held a pencil or piece of chalk. When she thought of her well-supplied schoolhouse in Illinois or the pampered girls at Bishop's Villa, she felt her throat tighten. These children had nothing! No wonder they looked at her with such hope.

Then she led them out for a morning recess. Some boys ran and jumped, even hollered a bit, their pent-up energy at last breaking loose. She smiled; this was behavior she recognized.

The girls crowded around her, some bold enough to reach a hesitant finger to touch the fine fabric of her skirt.

"You're so...white," a nine-year-old named Mattie whispered in awe.

The other girls tensed for Meg's reaction.

Meg drew the little girl closer to her, taking the child's hand in her own. "Yes, I am very white. And your skin is so dark. Isn't it wonderful how God made us both so different and so much alike? Both of us have two legs and two arms, two eyes and a mouth."

"It's purely amazin'," she murmured. Meg resisted the impulse to laugh.

"Let me teach you a few games for recess," Meg offered.

She led the older children in Fox and Goose and the younger ones in Ring Around the Rosy. She had never imagined that she would ever teach at a school where she must teach recess! Back home there were jump rope and crack the whip, balls and tops, and crudely made but serviceable seesaws. In time, however, Meg would find that her children were not such blank slates as she thought them. They would bring their own unique experiences and traditions, their own style of fun, to their new school.

In the afternoon she read to them from *Anderson's Fairy Tales* and *Aesop's Fables*. They seemed to enjoy that. Their eyes lit up when she opened up a box of clay. Each child received a gray lump.

"Just like playin' in the mud," a young boy squealed.

"First I want you to shape your clay into the letter I showed you this morning. Does anyone remember the letter?"

A dozen wildly waving hands went up. *"A!"*

Meg could not help but laugh, so eager...

"After you shape the letter *a*, I want you to shape the clay into whatever you like."

Three o'clock came sooner than Meg expected. She had spoken to each child during the day, looked into each face. There were two sisters with crossed eyes, many children with bad teeth, some children who had been carefully scrubbed, some who had not. Meg's mind was in a spin with all the mental notes she was taking—supplies needed, ideas for teaching, impressions of individual children. She could see it would take some of the shier children time to accept her "whiteness."

The mothers who came for their children placed gifts on the school-house steps as a kind of offering—fresh greens, a crock of butter, a jar of buttermilk, a dish of raspberries, a chunk of home-cured ham. They were the most humbling and touching gifts Meg had ever received.

"Oh, really, you don't need—"

Chester nudged her. "Let 'em, Meg. They want to pay you in some way. If you refuse, you'll hurt 'em."

"Thank you all so much. Goodbye, children! Goodbye! I'll see you tomorrow!"

Then Tick and his little sister, Chessie, stood before her. Their young black faces were suddenly solemn. Chessie stretched out a handful of wild violets.

"They're beautiful, Chessie! Where did you find them?"

"Special place in the woods, that's all," Tick said proudly. "Wanted to tell ya, we all thought today was...a fine day, Miss Ma'am."

Meg smiled, controlling the tears that would come into her eyes.

"It was a fine day for me also. Goodbye."

The two turned and skipped down the lane toward home. Meg heard Tick's voice as he tossed his cap into the air, a commentary on the day, she thought.

"A fine day, yes, sir! World without end, amen and amen!"

"It was the best first day of school I've ever had!" Meg enthused over supper with the Chisolms. "No discipline problems at all!"

Chester patted her arm affectionately. "Didn't I tell ya?"

Matilda passed Meg a peach fritter, her voice skeptical.

"I wouldn't go celebrating quite so fast, Miss Alcott. I'd imagine the children were more spellbound than anything. Children are high-strung creatures, temperamental at times. You have 22 of them, remember, none of whom are accustomed to sitting on hard benches for six hours."

"I know," Meg said softly.

"Those children are eager now because their folks are. It's bound to wear off sooner or later. Then you'll have your hands full."

"Now, 'Tilda, don't go throwin' buckets—"

She ignored him. "What about Jacob Brown? He wasn't so eager and friendly, was he?"

"Never seen that child smile," Chester managed with a full mouth.

His wife snorted. "He's not a child much longer. Nearly as tall as a grown man."

"Skinny as a fence post too!" Chester said with equal vigor.

Meg finished her meal. "He was fine."

"Did he speak?" Matilda persisted.

"Only to give his name and age."

The truth was Meg had noticed the boy's rigid posture. It radiated sullenness. It was easy to notice him, so vivid a contrast from the friendly faces of the other children. He was the oldest child in her school; he might present some challenges.

She stood abruptly, unwilling to let Matilda Chisolm's gloomy prophecies infect her.

"I'm going to take a walk before it gets dark. It's so nice out this evening. Thank you for the meal, Mrs. Chisolm."

"Stick to the trails I've told ya 'bout," Chester warned. "We'll be lookin' for a light in your room just after dark, or I'll come for you."

Meg smiled and waved. It was just like having a father lay down a curfew!

She wanted to be outside in the gray dusk of evening. She wanted to be by Ford's Creek, to sit on the bank and listen to the water, to watch the fish jump. It would be a good place to sit and reflect, reminding her of Peppercreek back home. She would write her parents when she returned to her room and tell them all about her first day. She should write Andy, but she wouldn't...

The trail curved and stopped abruptly, sloping down to the bank, meeting the water's edge in a fringe of jade green grass. It was perfect. The setting sun was dimpling the water, making it hazy and tranquil, an angler's paradise. She closed her eyes, so thankful that her first day had gone so well.

She heard him before she saw him. He was whistling a tune that reminded her vaguely of a song the children had tried to teach her today. He stopped as if he'd run into a wall. The whistling ended; the guarded look came up instantly. Meg frowned inside herself. Here was the man to ruin the ending of her day, a man who could be as astringent as Matilda Chisolm. Well, she wouldn't let him!

"Good evening, Dr. Browning."

"Miss Alcott."

They gauged each other, let each sweep the other with their eyes, taking in details in one quick measure.

He looked like he'd been enjoying himself, Meg decided. His pole was resting over one shoulder, his creel basket slung over the other. A thin book was jammed in the belt of his pants and there was dirt on his shirtsleeves, grass stains on each knee. A very worn straw hat sat at a jaunty angle on his head. His face was tan, yet burnished like a peach on his cheekbones.

Miss Alcott looked like the exemplary schoolmarm in her dark serge skirt and white blouse. Her hair was still neatly coiled in a dark pompadour. She was very respectable looking, very competent, very... Yankee-ish.

"Any luck?" Meg asked cheerfully, pointing to his basket.

He shrugged. "A little. It's more for rest than sport."

Well, that was a beginning. He could be civil.

"And you?" he asked.

"Excuse me?"

"This was the first day of your school, wasn't it?"

"Oh, yes. It went very well."

He nodded absently, looking away. Could she draw him into further conversation? She felt so strengthened by her day she accepted the challenge.

"I had 22 students."

He did not miss the pleasure in her voice. He looked at her now as if seeing her for the first time. Such green eyes, such long lashes...

"I'm glad your first day went well, Miss Alcott. I hope they all go well and that your school is a success."

"Do you really?" she asked impulsively.

He smiled thinly then. "Yes, I do. I'm not as perverse as you think, Miss Alcott. I'm glad when other folks succeed at what they aim for."

"How long have you been practicing here, Dr. Browning?"

"Nearly ten years, in the spring."

"Your first practice?"

"Yes."

She sat down, hugging her knees, looking up at him, hoping for some odd reason that he would sit beside her.

"What made you choose Chisolm Crossing, if I might ask?"

"I was raised here. I know the area. I know the folks. Seemed the logical place to work."

Meg looked back across the water. She could sense him reluctant to talk about himself. She must move to something safer.

"It's a beautiful evening," she said softly.

"Yes, very beautiful," he agreed.

She could feel his eyes on her.

She turned back to him. "I see you've been reading while you fished. Let's see, surely not a medical journal from the size. Probably not a novel. Poetry perhaps?"

Her voice was light, and when she had started speaking she could see the promise of a smile in his eyes. He was finally relaxing. But it was a fleeting promise. His eyes grew instantly hard and cold.

"Not poetry, Miss Alcott. Never . . . that. Actually, it's a journal I keep for some foolish reason. I hope you don't read poetry in your classroom."

Was he joking? "Of course I'll read poetry. There are so many—"

He shifted his pole and basket. "I need to get home. Can you find your way back to the Crossing?" His voice was gentle, and somehow sad to Meg.

"Yes, I think so." What in the world had she said to cause such a reaction?

She followed his eyes as he watched the river, so silent and peaceful. "As you said, a very beautiful evening. Good night, Miss Alcott."

With another man, Meg would have felt the reference to the evening was really a reference to her. The intensity of his look, resting on her, seemed gentle, almost appreciative. She had wanted to keep him there, or have him offer to walk her home. She chided herself as she took the trail to the Crossing. This was a troubled man, not the sort you could flirt with, or even be cordial to! He didn't need or want her attention. He had rebuffed her attempt at friendliness. Well, she'd be careful to not try it again.

Barrett cleaned his fish in the moonlight just outside his back door. He needn't worry about the mess he was making; old fat cat would have it cleaned up to the last scale before he had his boots pulled off. But his thoughts were not on the fish, or the day fishing he had enjoyed so much. He was thinking of his irrational outburst against poetry. The schoolteacher must think him crazy!

Was the past forever going to haunt him? Make him do silly things like he had done this evening? He must somehow make up to the teacher for his rudeness, for politeness sake. He glanced around at the darkened hills, hoping she had made it back to the schoolhouse safely. He didn't like the thought of her walking the trails around the Crossing. Another time perhaps, but not lately. There was no predicting if Willet Keller or another Klansman would have a burst of independence. Maybe he could drop a hint to Chester. She would listen to him.

He had told her the evening was beautiful. On the walk home his stubbornness had been broken down. He must consider her. She was a part of that beautiful evening. She had made it lovelier.

Chapter 21

Greenville

♦♦ ♦♦ ♦♦

*T*he banker of Greenville was preparing to enjoy his dessert when the servant announced the sheriff. The banker did not care for the interruption; it seemed poor courtesy when a man was at his own table. It must be about the trial that had been set in Jackson. He gave his daughter a quick, dark look—this mess was her fault.

"I'll see him in the library," he told the servant.

But the sheriff stood in the dining room doorway, hat in hand, looking uncomfortable and apologetic.

"Good evening, sir," he said.

"Is it necessary to intrude upon a man's dinner hour, sheriff? This unpleasant business could surely wait, could it not?"

The sheriff looked confused. "Well, I . . . I was just coming because of the note, sir."

"The note?"

"Yes, sir, right here." He pulled a scrap of paper from his hat band. "Says to come to your home, urgently. One of your servants brought it. I came as quick as I could." He smiled boyishly then. "I was at my own dinner."

"I sent no message, sheriff," the banker said sourly.

"I did. I sent for the sheriff." It was the steady voice of the banker's daughter.

The banker's wife went to bed with a sudden headache. The banker stalked the library with a furious energy he hadn't felt in years as his daughter told the story to the sheriff. He was quietly seething, and thinking of the bold newspaper headlines that would sweep across the state. Now instead of having a daughter as a victim, he had a promiscuous child who had been in the wrong part of town late at night, a player in some mysterious setup. He felt humiliated.

While the sheriff was new to Greenville, he had studied the reports on the banker's daughter and the warehouse beating. He hated gossip and slander. His father had told him it was like putting your ear to the mouth of the devil himself. Such a chilling illustration had stayed with the sheriff all his 28 years. He didn't want any bias in any case, and he didn't want to hear anything about folks' reputations. He liked to see things with his own eyes, hear things with his own ears. He wanted facts, not implications or whispers.

The banker's daughter looked nothing like the talkative deputy had babbled to the sheriff about. Finally he had told the man to be quiet. Now as he sat there taking notes on this sad story, he felt this young woman was not the same woman that the deputy had cruelly maligned. She was not aggressive and gaudy. This young woman was calm, rational, meeting him eye to eye, speaking with almost no emotion.

But the new sheriff realized this *was* the woman with the tainted reputation. That would explain the sadness in her eyes, the pleading for him to understand what she couldn't express with words. She looked like one who was new and fresh in some way—and broken. He listened attentively, taking down the facts, but his eyes and ears were registering more. The angry father, the distant mother. This woman, who had been a girl not long ago, was starved for friendship and love. He nodded, posed a few questions, and wished he could tempt one small smile into her eyes.

The banker's daughter was relieved that the sheriff who had found her in the warehouse was on a leave of absence. She was grateful for this earnest young man who looked like a fresh-scrubbed farmboy. He was speaking kindly and gently, not accusing or implying.

"Just for the record, ma'am, so I have it straight. You're absolutely certain that the black man was not the man who beat you."

"I'm certain, sir."

He wished she felt comfortable enough to call him by his first name.

"The man who beat me was not drunk."

"And you did not clearly see the man who did beat you."

"No, sir, I couldn't identify him at all." She hesitated and cast a nervous glance at her pacing father. "Except that once when he raised his hand, in the streetlight that came from the warehouse door—"

"Excuse me, Miss, but wasn't it closed?"

"Not completely. Not while he was beating me. Only after, when the black man was pushed in. Anyway I saw . . . that he was . . . white."

The sheriff scratched his head.

"Then I'd say what we have here is . . . is . . ."

"A setup, a frame," she said easily.

"Yes, ma'am, exactly. Have any notions why someone would do that, Miss? Why they would set up you and this Silas fellow?"

"I've thought a lot about that, of course." She lowered her head, and the sheriff had the strongest urge to tilt her chin up and tell her not to worry, that things were going to be all right. He didn't, of course, what with professional objectivity and ethics and being nearly strangers and . . . her father in the room.

"But I was hoping you might," she continued.

He scratched his head and smiled.

"No, ma'am, not right off, I can't. Just ain't that smart."

She gave him a fleeting smile then, as if his reply had pleased her, and wondered what it would be like to have him call her by her first name. Her smile definitely pleased him.

"Well, that's about all, ma'am. If you'll just sign this statement to make it all legal and proper, I'll let you get back to your dinner."

"As if we could eat!" the banker said hotly across the room.

They ignored him. She was looking in her lap again; her bottom lip was trembling.

"I'm so sorry," the sheriff said suddenly and low enough for only her ears.

The tears slid down her cheeks at his words.

"I'll call Jackson, first thing in the morning," he continued.

"A telephone call? Couldn't you...go free him yourself?" she asked timidly.

"Do you want me to do that, Miss?"

She nodded. "You could convey my—"

"You'll not be apologizing to a nigger!" the banker roared. "I won't have it!"

She kept her eyes fastened on the sheriff's face.

"I could trust you to tell him..." She was close to sobbing now. "You could tell him how sorry I am."

"I'll go and tell him, Miss, you have my word."

The banker was looming over them now.

"Do you have any idea how foolish this is going to make me look?"

She stood up, wiping her tears. She was exhausted. All she wanted was the safety and quiet of her room.

"I only know that it's going to free a man, and how free I am now."

She looked at the sheriff. He smiled and nodded. She knew he understood. "Good night, sheriff, and thank you."

"So there he was...pacin' around like a...pit bull on a leash!"

"Son, don't talk with your mouth full."

The sheriff had found his parents still waiting up for him when he returned to the house they shared. His mother had fixed him a heaping plate of scrambled eggs. They listened to him as he detailed the hour spent at the banker's house. He was careful not to slander, but the hostile and unloving atmosphere of the home had shaken him.

"She sounds like a poor, pitiful girl," his mother said.

The sheriff nodded. "Well, she is, Ma. But I kinda think she has spirit underneath. You know, the good kind."

"Takes spirit or courage, or whatever you want to call it, to tell the world you made a mistake," his father added. "She could have saved face and let that black boy hang."

"Yeah, she's brave all right. Just wish her father could see that," the sheriff said slowly.

"You told her you would go to Jackson and free him yourself. Will you?" his mother asked, though, knowing her son, she knew the answer.

"I'll be there before sunup," the sheriff said bluntly.

His mother stood up. "I'm going to bed. You two can stay up and solve the world's problems."

The sheriff laid a hand on her arm. "Will ya pray for her, Ma?"

"Plan to."

The sheriff finished his late supper while his father watched and yawned. "One more question, son," he asked, with a sparkle in his eye.

The sheriff smiled. He knew the question because he knew his father. "Yeah, Pa, she's pretty."

He watched from the cover of trees at the side of the schoolhouse. He had a clear view of the schoolmarm's apartment window. Her lights were always off and her curtain prudently drawn by the time he took his nightly position. It was growing cooler at night, and he wondered how far into the winter he'd have to keep this vigil, how many nights he'd have to leave the warmth and comfort of his bed. He felt exhausted and nerve-racked already—what was a little more lost sleep? But it was worth it knowing the Yankee schoolmarm was completely ignorant of the ugly Klan messages. He smiled grimly in the dark stillness. If Miss Alcott knew what he was doing, would she be appropriately grateful or predictably aloof? If she caught him at this post for no reason that he could explain, she'd be highly indignant. *That* he was pretty certain about.

He was glad the Klan messenger was predictable. Every other night, just after midnight, Willet Keller rode quietly to the school. He always watched from a group of trees opposite the schoolhouse for a few moments to make certain no one was stirring. Neither the Chisolms nor the Yankee seemed to be night owls. Then he would sneak forward with commendable stealth and deposit his grisly warning. Willet Keller was just vain enough to think this nasty work could only be done by him alone. He did not trust anyone else to do his bidding. Like the doctor, he was losing his sleep to keep these appointments, but unlike the doctor, he did not mind at all.

Night before last it had been a dead skunk in the girl's privy with a very ugly note attached. Before that, a load of very fresh manure on the front steps. Barrett had a bit of labor to do each time and was climbing back into bed even more frayed, hoping Willet Keller would not get any more daring, original, or destructive. Evans had promised to take the vigil the night after next. Both men knew the course they had suggested wouldn't satisfy Keller and the others very much longer. The rumblings were getting louder.

This night it was a dozen slaughtered chickens staked and hung from trees. Keller rode off to his bed very pleased. The doctor watched, waited a few moments longer, heaved a very weary sigh, and went to work.

Martha Keller was a nervous woman. She had come to Chisolm's Mercantile with a full shopping list—and only one thing on her mind. Willet was at home with one thing on his mind and a nervousness born from expectant, excited energy. The Klan had met the night before in Keller's lower pasture. A huge, blazing bonfire had proclaimed that the Klan was about to ride. The Klan leader was finished with patience, finished with subtle steps of fear. The school at the Crossing had been open long enough. The state leadership had been ominously silent of late, and Keller was concerned that they would take some independent action. That would be too humiliating. The dramatic little incident that he planned would stir them up to some praise he was confident.

The farmer was not completely settled that the night army would actually torch the school. Perhaps a very frightening display for the Yankee would be persuasive enough. He wasn't squeamish about a little arson, however; he had done it before. Either way, he would not leave Chisolm Crossing School without a promise that the school would close and the teacher would leave Mississippi.

So Martha Keller came to the mercantile with a determination that matched her husband's. He had concealed nothing from her when he returned to the cabin flushed and drunken with power and Klan enthusiasm after the meeting.

"Willet?"

"Don't start sermonizing or frowning, woman!" he had nearly shouted. "You can't stop what's meant to be! Not you or anyone else!"

She kept her voice steady and even.

"What is meant to be, Willet?"

"The Klan will stomp out the nigger school, yes, ma'am! We ride tomorrow night!"

Mrs. Chisolm thought Martha Keller was more remote than usual. And absentminded this morning too. The store was full of shoppers, and the storekeeper's wife had little patience with a distracted, indecisive customer. So she bustled between the people in the store and gave the farmer's wife only occasional attention. She whispered to Chester as she passed him and rolled her eyes at Martha.

"Skittish this morning. Told me she needed two yards of coffee!

This alerted Chester. He began to watch her with the covertness of a skilled master. He noticed she went from one side of the store to the other, fingering things, examining things, consulting her paper, and putting nothing in her basket. She met his look a number of times. A stiff smile and betraying eyes.

"Yep, she's a little pig that wandered into the butcher shop..." he murmured to himself.

If she waited until the store was empty, she'd be obvious and exposed. If she approached him with customers all around, she ran the risk of being overheard. But it would be more natural that way. She took a deep breath and confronted him, speaking clearly.

"Will Jr. has a birthday coming up and's wanting a new hunting rifle. Will you please show me what you have in stock, Chester?"

"Be glad to, Martha. Right this way," he returned cheerfully.

He showed her several models. He described them expansively in his finest storekeeper's eloquence, and knew she didn't hear a word. *Something is on this woman's mind,* he decided. He was a kind man. He wanted to make it easier for her. He lowered his voice just a fraction. "Martha, you're not in the market for a new rifle, now, are you?"

"No, Chester, not really."

"Then how can I help you, Martha?"

She smoothed her list on the counter and studied it a moment with a frown.

She's trying to reach a decision...

"Is it about Willet?" he asked quietly.

Her eyes met his instantly. "I'm afraid, Mr. Chisolm."

"Now, Martha, you know it's Chester. Why are you afraid?"

"Willet. He..."

Suddenly she felt like she was going to cry. She knew what she must do was the right thing. But in spite of his blindness, she did love her husband.

"A problem with Willet?" Chester pressed.

"You're a friend to Miss Alcott," she said simply.

"Well, sure. Mighty fond of her, like a daughter to me. Is this about her?"

Martha nodded. He glanced down at the rifles. He couldn't get angry in front of this harassed woman. No matter what she said, he couldn't get angry. He suspected she got enough of that at home.

"Chester, the Klan... is very upset about the school."

A customer passed them.

"So you see, Martha, the Sterling is a fine rifle, but the Wesson is a better price. Either way your boy won't be disappointed."

He leaned forward slightly. "How upset, Martha?"

"Tonight," she said firmly. "Thank you for showing me the rifles, Chester. I'd best be finishing my shopping now." She turned and walked away.

"Thank you, Martha," Chester replied slowly.

Now that Chester Chisolm had been warned, he hardly knew what to do. Matilda showed an unexpected turn of confusion and uncertainty as well. They waited until the store was empty, then huddled together in the back room.

"Should we go tell her?" Matilda asked anxiously.

Chester shook his head. "No. What if Martha was wrong or they change their plans; she'd be worried for nothing. And here she's been thinkin' the Crossing was so friendly and all. Makes me riled up for sure at Willet and his low-down kind."

"We have to do something besides wring our hands and wag our tongues," Matilda pointed out in typical fashion.

Chester was pacing. "I know, I know. Could send Sawyer for the sheriff."

"Mr. Chisolm, I hardly think that man will be sympathetic. You know what kind of investigation he did on that beating case. Why, he may be a Klansman himself!"

"Matilda, you forget there's a new sheriff. We don't know what he's like. He's sworn to uphold the law, and this bunch will be lawbreakers like a pack of foxes in the henhouse! The very idea of Willet Keller trying to shut the school down and run Miss Alcott off! It's...it's..."

Chester was moving from fear to anger again. And right now, anger was so much easier to deal with.

"Now, Mr. Chisolm, calm down. Rational minds must prevail. Remember your heart."

It was not a prudent thing for the woman to say. It made Chester think of Barrett Browning. Barrett Browning, who had done nothing to help the school or be a gentleman to the schoolmarm. He gritted his teeth in a fresh wave of frustration.

"We could send word to Seth Jefferson and some of the others tonight to wait with us. If the Klan does come, we'll just step out and surprise 'em!"

Matilda Chisolm was alarmed. There was a grimness in her little man's words. There could be bloodshed. As much as she knew in her heart Chisolm Crossing School was needed, for a wavering moment she was regretting it. What was going to happen to their peaceful little community?

She spoke soothingly and managed a stiff little pat on his shoulder. "We'll keep our plans very quiet. We'll send Sawyer for the sheriff. We'll see if a few of the men who helped on the school will come and...and ...help."

Chester nodded and fervently hoped it would be a strong enough defense.

There were 20 riders of the Imperial Ku Klux Klan on a crisp, windless night. A full moon peaked behind a moving sea of clouds. A perfect night for such adventures. The Washington County Klan leader felt the turn-out with such short notice was respectable. They had assembled at Keller's, laughing and joking nervously, putting on their uniforms with undisguised pride. Most in the group were farmers and most found the night's plans the most exciting thing they'd been a part of in years. The night they burned down the school for darkies—it was something they could tell their grandkids.

Just before they rode off, a lone rider appeared on the road. It was a Klansman sent from the state leader. He had come to join them, and to carry back the results to the leadership.

"Am I not trusted?" Keller had snapped at the newcomer.

The man shrugged. "I'm just following orders, Keller," he replied in a bored voice.

"How did you learn of our ride?" Keller continued testily.

The new man leaned forward in his saddle. Every other Klansman gathered was listening as well. "Let's get going, Keller," he said tightly.

Keller cursed and turned his horse. He didn't like this new develop-ment at all.

Barrett Browning and Tom Evans rode at the back of the group. They had little chance to talk. They looked at each other in silence, knowing all their efforts had come to this fateful night. Tonight they would have to stand and reveal their identity and their true convictions. There was no point in talking, in planning, or in trying another coordinated action. The moment would come for both of them, and they would have to face it alone.

Nell Evans had watched her husband ride away with tears in her eyes. She didn't know if she would see him again. The young farmer felt strongly about the ugliness of the Klan and the purpose of the school. He would lay down his life if he had to. Nell Evans was praying for a miracle.

The doctor rode along toward the Crossing with a sort of cold detachment. Somewhere, somehow, he was watching himself moved like a chess piece across the board—coming closer and closer to capture. He could have used his medical duties as an excuse to be absent from the activities. But in his heart, he knew he couldn't do that. Yankee or not, he would not allow the teacher to be harmed.

Meg seemed to feel the heat from the torches before she actually saw them. She was pulled unwillingly from sleep, groggy, relaxed, and wondering what that strange, muted orange glow on her wall was. She opened her eyes and studied it, still dull from sleep. Then she heard a horse neigh and stomp. Then an eerie quietness.

Her heart began to thud as she crept across the floor and peeked past the curtain. She saw a dozen hooded riders, mounted in a half circle in front of the school. Meg felt an almost paralyzing terror. They were silent, staring at the building. She knew they were waiting for her.

She dressed quickly, though she shook uncontrollably. She cracked the door to the schoolroom. The walls were alive with the glow of dancing flames. The phantoms had invaded the building. It was the most dreadful moment of her life. They were going to burn her school-house. She glanced around quickly to see what she should grab and save. There was too much...and now, nothing mattered.

Then a commanding voice broke the stillness.

"Teacher! Teacher of a nigger school! The Klan wants to see you!"

She could hear the low murmur of laughter. She did not want to go out there like the victim of an inquisition. But she did not want to be indignantly dragged from the building before this tribunal. She stepped to the front door and opened it.

Tom Evans had positioned himself at the edge of the riders, between the store and the schoolhouse. The doctor sat mounted on the opposite side near the trees. Both men were like tightly pulled wires waiting to snap. At least they would have the advantage of surprise over Keller. Barrett nudged his horse forward when the door opened.

Meg felt very small and exposed facing the Klansmen. She bit her lip to keep from crying. She felt hatred radiating from them—felt as if she had stepped up to the yawning edge of hell, with a jury of demons waiting for her.

"Well, well, a pretty Yankee," the state leader's representative spoke up. "Sure did hate to wake you up. But the Ku Klux Klan has business with you."

Keller was highly incensed that this man was stealing his authority. He was glaring at him and being summarily ignored.

"You are very mistaken," Meg returned in a firm voice. "I have no business with a bunch of...of ruffians and criminals in white sheets!"

Barrett tensed. Just like a Yankee to scold a hot-tempered Klansman. The riders moved closer to the schoolmarm.

"I think you must still be asleep, lady. You don't understand. The Klan has decided to burn your school for niggers!"

Keller moved closer to the speaker and hissed, "I will talk to the Yankee!"

"You're not welcome here in Mississippi!" he yelled at Meg. "Go back home."

"I will stay just where I am!" she retorted.

Barrett could see in the torchlight that she was shaking. He was afraid she was going to faint. He felt an odd, fleeting stirring in his own atrophied heart and rode a few feet closer.

"You get out of here! All of you! You should be ashamed of your cruel, ugly ways!"

"I'm warnin' ya, Yankee teacher! You watch your mouth!" Keller spewed. "We could have burned down this building while you whimpered under your quilts!"

Meg stumbled backward at the force of his venom. An arm reached out and steadied her. She glanced at the ungloved hand—slender fingers, blunt-cut nails, red-blond hair on the back of the hand . . . and a gold ring with a medical insignia. She felt herself go shockingly weak. She looked up at the white hood.

Barrett felt her hatred piercing the cloth, ripping away his mask with a fury. She jerked her hand away as if he had touched her with his torch.

"Go away! Go . . . all of you!" she screamed hysterically.

Keller rode closer. A shot rang out in the clarity of the night.

Chester Chisolm had been very disappointed when Sawyer returned from Greenville with the news the sheriff had gone to Jackson on business. Matilda was disgusted.

"And what's the good of a sheriff, if he's not around when you need him, I would like to know!"

But Chester's disappointment evaporated when he stepped from the side of the darkened mercantile. Suddenly *he* felt like a sheriff with a tin badge on his chest, facing the town desperados at the end of the street. And it didn't hurt the little man to have a small army beside him.

Seth Jefferson was looking very tall, strong, and resolute beside Chester. Sixteen black men were flanked beside him, all neighbors, all with children at the school that was threatened. They were equally grim. On the opposite side of Chester stood Walter Hudson and his two stout sons. They could not conceal the thirst for a fight on their young faces. A handful of other white men who had either worked on the school or come from curiosity had joined Chester. On the front porch a group of women had gathered. Matilda stood in the forefront with the solemn face of a woman not to be trifled with. She held a kerosene lamp high, boldly challenging with her eyes any Klansmen who would look her way. Few dared.

The Klansmen were now eyeing Keller nervously. The state leader's man had become mute.

"This is none of your concern, Chester!" Keller bluffed in a hollow voice.

Chester smiled indulgently and leaned on his rifle.

"It is my concern when someone is threatening my personal property. I reckon it's my business then."

Keller cursed. "This is county land, little fat man. It's a public school!"

"Ain't deeded it to the county yet," Chester continued smoothly. "So, I reckon it's you and yours, Will, that ain't welcome on it."

The Klansmen's agitation grew noticeably. It was an ominous thing to have the leader so openly and brazenly identified. It made them feel transparent. Here were some of their neighbors, men and woman they worked with and traded with challenging them. Suddenly this little squabble over a school for darkies seemed less important. Here were folks they had to live by.

Willet was furious—and wanting to lash out at somebody or something. He could feel the loyalty of the group slipping away. He was losing his power. And the Klan leader in Jackson would surely know all about this over his morning cup of coffee.

"You going to leave peaceably, Keller? The school is going to stay open for the children for a long, long time. You and your kind might as well get used to that fact. We'll be forgiving of your frightening the teacher and being so rude. Ya'll go on home and go to bed." Chester's voice was as mild as if he had spoken to a child.

The riders were turning their horses around, and heading down the darkened road. Only Keller and two others remained.

"I don't want your forgiveness!" he screamed. He leaned toward Meg and spit at her feet. Evans had anticipated the wrath of the Klan leader. His horse pushed Willet's back.

"Turn on back, Willet. It's over. And if you don't, I won't lift a hand if this crowd comes at you," Evans said in a low, seething voice.

Keller turned abruptly and lashed his horse down the road. The last two Klansmen trailed behind him.

And Barrett Browning could feel the burning eyes of the schoolmarm on his back.

The rain brought a temporary relief from the heat. But it made the streets of Jackson sloughs in some places, especially in front of the squatty county jail. The sheriff of Greenville felt like the mud was up to his knees as he waded to the front door. He was assaulted by a multitude of unpleasant smells. But not fatigue or hunger, mud or bad odors was going to keep him from his task. There was a young woman in Greenville depending on him.

He presented the facts and sworn statement to the jailer and sheriff of Jackson. The news was stunning. He watched as the official paperwork was completed.

"You can go on back to Greenville; we'll take care of things now," the Jackson officer said moodily. This new turn of events was not going to sit well with the public no matter where their sentiment lay—either an innocent man had been held for nearly four months or a black was going to be turned loose on a suspicious populace.

Silas was released and almost stumbled out the door with shock. The Greenville sheriff carefully steered him to a boarding house to get him fed, cleaned up, and returned to his family. The sheriff felt bad for the bewildered young man. He felt obligated to help him.

"You going to be all right, Silas?"

"Yes, sir, I reckon."

"You know how to find your family?" the sheriff pressed.

Silas shrugged. "Ain't sure. They was run off from home when I got into trouble, last I heard."

"I'll try to help you find them."

Silas finally smiled, as if he had stepped from darkness to light. The pit had given up its captive.

"Why are you smiling, Silas?" the sheriff asked kindly.

Silas looked at him. "Just thinkin' what Preacher Dilling said one of the days he came and talked with me."

The sheriff of Greenville was curious.

"What did he say, Silas?"

Silas turned his face up to the sky that was clearing and nearly shouted. "He said, 'Remember, Silas, the truth will set you free!'"

Jeb French had what he considered a brilliant idea. He would ride out to the Crossing and pay a visit to the Yankee schoolmarm. He hadn't seen her since the time at Mim's, when she had arrogantly snubbed him. It couldn't hurt to try again. Perhaps hidden underneath that cool exterior was a woman who thrilled to the chase. And it would give him an opportunity to hear about Amy Cash.

Willet Keller felt as if the unshakable grip of madness had seized him. But he didn't care. He was beyond caring about much of anything except his own disgrace. He had ridden from the Crossing that night to Greenville. He could not go home to bed as the smiling merchant had suggested. Instead he went to a waterfront tavern and got very drunk.

He could not face the disgust or pity of his family, the humiliation in front of his neighbors. By now everyone would have heard: Willet Keller and the Klan had been downed by a pudgy, moon-faced storekeeper and his little assembly of darkies. It was absurd! He took another drink. He was unwashed, unshaven, red-eyed, and menacing when he

left the tavern at sunrise. It was Chester Chisolm's fault. He would
pay.

Barrett knew it was foolish to go to the mercantile that morning. If
Miss Alcott were present, he could expect her look of loathing. But he
had to know if he had been recognized beyond the schoolteacher. In a
way it didn't matter; who was going to believe his motives? The Yankee?
Or Chester, who had become so obviously disappointed in him?

Chisolm Crossing

The mercantile at Chisolm Crossing should have been doing brisk
business, considering the place was fuller than it had ever been at one
time. But few people were shopping. Most were listening, loafing, and
talking about the night's drama. Martha Keller had slipped in looking
grieved and fragile. The crowd became instantly silent. She came to
stand before Chester.

"Have you seen Willet?" she asked in a strained whisper.

"No, Martha, not since . . . I'm sorry."

She nodded. She turned and faced the crowd, her neighbors. She had
no pride left. "Have any of you seen my husband? Please tell me. He
didn't come home last night."

No one said a word. She headed for the door, but Nell Evans passed
the baby to her husband and followed the woman outside.

Meg was wanting to slip away to the quiet of her apartment 30
minutes later. She felt exhausted. She had spent most of the morning
talking with parents and those gathered in the store, answering questions as if she were a celebrity. Meg hadn't wanted to talk; last night was
still too vivid and ugly. She wasn't sure when she would sleep through a
night without waking in fear. She had talked with Amy on the phone and
assured her of her safety. Now Tom Evans had come up to her.

"Miss Alcott, you needn't worry about the Klan bothering you or
your school. I'm sure last night will pretty much break up the Klan
around here."

"I hope so," she agreed softly. Then she remembered the note in her
buggy, and an idea sparked in her mind. "It was you who wrote the note,
wasn't it, Mr. Evans?"

He looked a bit sheepish. "Please call me Tom, and yes, ma'am, it was
me. I . . . I tried to help you in my own way. Now Nell and I can help you
however you need."

He was being as mysterious as his note had been, but she did not
pursue it. She knew now that the doctor had not left the message, no, of
course he hadn't.

"Thank you, Mr. Evans," she smiled tiredly.

The crowd began to thin. Meg turned to Chester and Matilda.

"I think I'll throw a few things in a bag and go to Tanglewood for the night."

"I'd be glad to escort you, Miss Alcott."

She turned reluctantly. Jeb French had stepped up behind her, smiling as he always did when he saw her.

"Hello, Mr. French."

"Mornin', Jeb," Chester broke in with false heartiness. "What brings you to the Crossin'?"

"The lovely Miss Alcott, of course."

"Thank you for your offer, Mr. French. However, I'd prefer to ride alone."

The embarrassed silence was broken by the entrance of the Greenville sheriff. He introduced himself politely.

"Had a message when I got in from Jackson that I was needed quick at Chisolm Crossing," he explained.

"I'm Chester. I sent for ya," the storekeeper said as he extended his beefy paw.

"You missed the need we had for you," Matilda briskly informed the young man.

"Oh?"

"Had a visit from the KKK last night," Chester said. "They came to burn the school."

"Well, I see it's still standin'. Anyone hurt?"

"Nope. Besides Miss Alcott being terrorized and a crowd of us losin' some beauty sleep, not a hair on a head was harmed!" Chester beamed proudly.

"Well, I'm glad to hear that. Do you feel like it's taken care of? The Klan I mean. Will they come back?"

Tom Evans spoke up. "They won't come back, sheriff."

"Well, I do apologize for not being able to be here."

Matilda and Chester exchanged a look. Here was an ally!

"Perhaps you folks could help me out a little."

"We are always willing to be of service to the law," Matilda said virtuously.

"Well, you see, I'm trying to locate a family that used to live around here. A man was released from jail and can't find his family."

He had their total attention. Matilda was not one for formality.

"Who was released from jail, sheriff?"

The sheriff gave the name. "He's from this area, isn't he? Told me the Klan ran his family off when the trouble started."

"Silas is out of jail?" Jeb French asked as he pushed forward.

The sheriff nodded. "The young woman in Greenville mistakenly identified him."

"Well, I'll be a kitty cat's kissin' cousin!" Chester exclaimed.

"I'm Jeb French. I employed Silas."

"Then you'll be glad—" the sheriff began. But a voice from outside stopped them all. The drama was not quite over.

"Chester!"

Willet Keller was staggering across the dirt yard in front of the store.

"Sheriff, here's a man who can tell you more about that night in Greenville with Silas," French said smoothly.

"Oh, really? Who is this?" the sheriff asked.

"Willet Keller," Matilda said dryly. "I guess we found him."

Keller had gone to his home. He had frantically dug out the pistol buried in a drawer. Then he had claimed a fresh mule and rode through the woods to the Crossing.

Chester, Matilda, the Yankee, Evans, French, a man he did not know—he took them all in, in one swift glance. They must have been putting all the pieces together against him. He leaned heavily against the doorframe.

"Willet, this is the sheriff. He's here to tell us Silas is out of jail."

Meg was not watching Keller; she was watching French, who had spoken. His face was arrogant and cruel. He was purposely taunting this already broken man.

So, they knew! They knew all about it! The entire plot to strengthen the Klan through the banker's daughter and the black man. He drew the pistol out quickly.

"You!" he slurred drunkenly. "All ... of you ... did this!"

"Mr. Keller, put that gun down," the sheriff responded calmly. He was the only calm one. Even Matilda was speechless.

"Don't be a fool!" French spoke up savagely.

Chester was sweating like the proverbial pig in the summer sun.

"Mr. Keller, come on now. We'll talk this over," the sheriff continued.

"Put your gun down, Will. Martha is at home worryin' over you." It was the unruffled voice of the doctor.

Keller was startled and frightened by the voice at his back. In his drunken fury, he did not care who it was.

Keller swung around wildly and fired. The last thing Barrett heard was the schoolmarm's scream.

The trees raised leafless arms. Meg now had to light a fire each morning in the coal stove before school to take the chill off the big room. School had been in session nearly three months. Life at the Crossing was slow-paced and predictable again. Chester was laughing with the customers, and Matilda was bossing. The steady calm after the storm had settled on the rural community.

Willet Keller was in jail—an odd twist to his hopes and dreams. Matilda and Chester hired Martha to help in the store. The Evanses helped her with the farm work.

The doctor had finally recuperated from his arm wound. With a brief word to Chester he had slipped away on a deep-sea fishing vacation. A doctor friend took his cases.

And Meg Alcott was again feeling the joy that she had first felt when she came to this place. The fear was gone at night. She was enjoying her students tremendously. But sometimes as she graded papers in the evenings or went walking through the woods, she thought of Dr. Barrett Browning. She felt again the shock that he had been a part of the Klan. Knowing Amy's friendship, she had said nothing to her about seeing him that night. But it didn't make sense. For all his abrasiveness he didn't seem capable of Klan meanness. And she thought of the words she had heard Tom Evans say in the store when Barrett had fallen under Keller's gun. The big farmer had cradled the doctor's head in his lap.

"Don't give up, Barrett! Our side won. We got our miracle!"

Chapter 22

Tanglewood

♦♦ ♦♦ ♦♦

*M*elanie Cash loved to play with Gideon and Micah Jefferson. They were her only playmates. She was older than Gideon, so he was her little boy. Micah was older than her so he was the father. This seemed perfectly plausible and logical in her mind, and even if it wasn't, what did that really matter in the world of pretend? Gideon allowed her to mother him, and he adored her. Micah took the responsible, protecting role of an older brother. And now that Viney was growing bigger with another child, well, Melanie Cash was hoping she would soon have a little sister!

Amy was reading to her daughter before bedtime. It was their favorite time together—with Melanie warm and sweet-smelling from her bath, cozy and quiet. But it was always a time that made Amy feel the void of a man, a father to carry Melanie on his shoulders and comb the tangles from her wet hair. And a man for her, to smile into her eyes when Melanie said something funny. How long would it be before the face she always put to that man would belong to someone real—flesh and blood and not a dream of the past?

"Mama, will Miss Viney have her baby soon?" Melanie asked from her bed.

"No, not for several months."

"Will Gideon and Micah share her with me?"

Amy smiled. "I'm sure they will. But how do you know it's going to be a she?"

Melanie smiled as if that were a silly question.

"Because I want it to be. Mama, I wish you were having the baby. But . . . we need a daddy first."

"That's right, sweetheart."

Amy knew what was coming. These questions were a trial. She ran an estate. She made decisions. She was raising a child. But she was unprepared for all the questions she knew her daughter was bound to put to her.

"I'd like to have a daddy, wouldn't you?" the little girl asked.

Amy felt tears pool in her eyes, though she struggled against them.

"Yes, Melanie, I would . . . someday."

"What about Dr. Browning? He's very nice, isn't he? He doesn't have a mama does he?"

"No, he isn't married, Mel, but we're just good friends."

"But he could be a daddy. He looks lonely too."

Amy took her daughter's hand in hers.

"Do I look lonely, Melanie? Because you know, you make Mama very happy."

"You look sad sometimes. Mama, couldn't I pray for a daddy for us?"

Amy returned to the library where Meg was mending. Meg heard her enter, but did not look up.

"I've just realized why I've always disliked sewing. It's so boring!"

Amy sat down, leaned back in her chair, and closed her eyes.

"Amy? You all right? Is Mel in bed?"

"She's fine. She's asleep."

Meg waited. She could see Amy was upset.

"Melanie told me she would like a daddy, so she could have a brother or sister," Amy said softly.

Andy Alcott was instantly between them, unspoken, but vivid in their minds. Meg wasn't sure what to say.

"Children have a way of being very direct, you know. Just last week Chessie Boon asked me during reading why I didn't have a m-a-n. She asked me that right after she successfully spelled *man*."

Amy smiled; Meg was lightening the mood.

"Melanie thought Dr. Browning would be a suitable candidate for a father," Amy continued.

Meg looked at her lap. Amy Cash was such a tease, always bringing up the doctor as if he were destined for significance in her life!

Amy leaned forward in her chair, her eyes suddenly sad and concerned. "Meg, Barrett is an old friend."

Meg nodded.

"He thinks you find his company disagreeable," she said bluntly.

Meg became very fascinated with her very boring sewing. They *had* been talking about her!

"Do you, Meg? Do you dislike him that strongly?"

"I don't dislike him...strongly. I hardly know the man."

"But do you even dislike him a little bit?" Amy pressed gently.

They smiled at each other then.

"Now, Amy..."

"Well, Meg..."

"All right, I do think he's...he's cold and acts superior. I know what you're thinking, that I've been acting cold and superior to him."

"Like I told you after the first time you met him, I think you misjudged him. I know it's easy to do that with someone. I was...guilty of it once myself."

Mrs. Cash was hesitating, and Meg was intrigued.

"With whom?" she asked carefully.

Amy did not look away from Meg's probing look.

"With Andy."

"You misjudged *him*?"

A dozen thoughts flooded her mind, but she kept them reined in. Amy's courage failed her; she did not want to say more. She could not predict how Meg would react. Talking about Barrett was safer.

"Anyway, Meg, Barrett is a very kind man and I—"

"Amy, are you trying to play matchmaker? You keep trying to promote the man!" Meg laughed.

"No, I'm not. I just wanted you both to feel more comfortable around each other."

Meg stood up and went to the window. She stood there thinking for a quiet interval.

"Meg, are you angry at Barrett for some reason?"

Meg sat down facing Amy. "In the fall, when we had the trouble with the Klan..."

"Yes, go on."

"That night when they came to burn the school...Barrett was there."

Meg could still hear the hissing of the torches and feel the hand that had reached out to her—the hand of a hooded rider.

"Well, Chester needed everyone's help. What was wrong with Barrett's being there?"

"No, Amy," Meg said softly. "He wasn't there with Chester. He was... one of the Klansmen."

"What?"

Meg explained quickly, and Amy Cash was stunned.

"No, Meg, it couldn't have been Barrett! You had to have seen the wrong ring."

Meg shook her head. "I had seen it the day he delivered Mim's baby and after that. It's the same ring."

"Well, maybe someone else has the same kind of ring."

"I know his...hands, Amy. I've really looked at them."

It was a confession full of implication, and Meg blushed from it. But Amy seemed not to notice.

"Meg, this doesn't make sense. He doesn't hate black people. He works for them. He helped build Seth's new shop!"

"I know it doesn't make sense right away, but it's true. He was there that night."

"There has to be an explanation, a reason," Amy murmured.

"Amy, listen. He never worked on the school last summer, even though Chester asked him several times. He discouraged me from ever opening the school in the first place. He got angry one evening when I said I would teach poetry! He has always dropped Yankee remarks."

Amy had to admit that was true.

"The only explanation I can come up with is he was a part of the Klan and trying to stop the school because of me!"

"Meg, no, that can't be true."

"Amy, you said he thinks I despise him. Well, he despises me!"

"I'll ask him. We're friends. I'll just ask him."

"No, Amy, please don't do that! He'll hate me even more for telling you."

"Meg, I can't come up with a reason why he was there that night, but I will. I know he doesn't hate you. Quite the opposite, I think."

Meg reddened. "What do you mean by that?"

"I think Dr. Barrett Browning is uncomfortable around you because he finds you attractive."

"Mrs. Cash, you are ridiculous."

Amy smiled. "Time will tell, Miss Alcott."

Amy went to bed with her thoughts and emotions in a tangle. There was the sweet face of Melanie, hoping for a father, her own near confession about Andy, and then this revelation about her friend, Barrett. Why *would* he have ridden with the Klan?

She could not make sense of it; she was too tired. She fell asleep and dreamed of a beautiful ship with three figures on the deck.

Meg was in a bedroom down the hall, having her own battle with insomnia. So Amy had misjudged her brother. How? And what had happened when she grew to understand him? She hoped Amy was not hurting about Barrett's involvement with the Klan. She had not meant to spite him, or hurt the friendship between the two. And *did* the doctor find her attractive?

The next bright Saturday morning, Meg Alcott took Melanie Cash out for a drive in the buggy. When noon approached and Melanie said she was hungry, Meg turned to Greenville with decision. She had hesitated only a moment; she did not want to encounter Jeb French like she always seemed to do when she was away from the Crossing. But if she did, she would simply and firmly tell him she was not interested in any kind of relationship with him. He would finally have to understand that.

But she was also determined that her "niece" must not be tucked away at Tanglewood like some hothouse flower. It was a well-meaning, if arrogant, intention on Meg's part. Amy's isolation was unhealthy enough. Meg did not want to see the same thing happen to Melanie.

She glanced down at the little girl sitting on the edge of the smooth leather seat beside her. Her hands were clasped; her eyes bright with excitement.

"What do you think, Melanie? Lunch in Greenville with ice cream for dessert?"

Melanie nodded eagerly, then sobered. "You don't think Mama will mind, do you?"

"No, of course not."

"Any flavor?" Melanie asked.

"Any flavor!"

They ate in Greenville with pleasure, and no sight of Jeb French.

"Can't we ride longer, Aunt Meg? Do we have to go back yet?"

"All right. We'll take some of the pretty roads around the Crossing."

They drove for over an hour along the peaceful roads around the Crossing. They saw no one, only meandering cows and scolding crows and swift, shy cottontails. Wild, untidy trees arched the grass-rutted paths, making fragrant tunnels full of singing birds.

"These are like roads...to other worlds!" Melanie exclaimed with delight.

But she grew warm and drowsy. She laid her head on Meg's lap and was soon asleep. Meg glanced down at her; she was a sweet, loving child. Meg was pleased Melanie had taken to calling her "Aunt Meg." She wasn't sure how Amy felt about it. Meg had been guarded with the child at first. She represented... No, Meg had reprimanded herself severely. Melanie was Melanie. She represented nothing; she was innocent. And with her brown, silky hair, slender face, and blue eyes, Meg was convinced the child was growing more and more to look like Andy Alcott.

She was about to turn back to Tanglewood when she spotted the road that led to Abby Mayhew's. She groaned and pulled the buggy to a stop. Melanie did not stir. She debated with herself. Here was an opportunity, a lovely day, to make this much-needed call. She had been putting it off long enough. She wanted to, but wouldn't, ask Viney to accompany her. She must face this challenge alone. But today? Now?

She glanced down at Melanie. No, it wouldn't be a good idea to go when Melanie was along. What if the black woman was just as nasty as she had been on the previous visit? She started to turn the buggy away. "You are a coward!" she whispered harshly to herself. She glanced again at the sleeping girl. Perhaps the child's presence would serve as a restraint on the woman. She might even manage a touch of friendliness. Meg turned down the lane with a sigh.

Abby Mayhew's husband had left her two years earlier. For two years, she had been clawing out an existence for herself and her three children. It was a hard, demanding, tireless, colorless life. And she could see no hope of it changing. So she'd given up all hope.

She had not forgotten the visit of the white lady. She chuckled sometimes as she remembered it. She hadn't really meant to be mean, but it was . . . amusing to make people quake a little, especially someone who knew absolutely nothing about a barren life. Maybe the virtuous-looking white lady had learned her lesson!

Abby was in her meager garden pulling weeds when the Tanglewood buggy rolled up. The emotionless mask she wore concealed her surprise. She stood up, completely unembarrassed at her appearance. Her cheap calico dress hung like a shapeless sack. She was sweating, dusty, and barefoot. Let the white lady take a long look, she thought bitterly.

"Good afternoon, Mrs. Mayhew," Meg said easily.

Abby said nothing. She took a dipper from a bucket and gave herself a long drink. Then she looked up at Meg, still mute, still just as defiant in her posture.

Well, so far, it's just like last time, Meg thought angrily to herself. She took a deep breath.

"I came back Mrs. Mayhew to . . ." She stopped. She must be honest. "Mrs. Mayhew, I really didn't want to come here this morning. But—"

"Why did you then? Sure didn't send you an invite or nothin'," Abby snapped irritably.

"I came because I've been praying about . . . you. And I felt like the Lord wanted me to come."

There she had said it! She steeled herself for the scathing retort. But Abby Mayhew was just watching her.

"You see, I was afraid of you," Meg continued. "That's why I really didn't want to come."

"Still?" the woman asked bluntly.

Meg clutched the reins tighter. This woman made her feel like a trembling schoolgirl! Another deep breath.

"No," she said firmly. "I'm not afraid of you now. Your unfriendliness is just a bit intimidating though."

Meg gambled with total frankness. Abby was tempted to smile. She didn't know what intimidating meant, but the white lady was a curious one for sure. And the honesty had faintly touched the calloused heart.

"Well, ain't no reason for ya to be scared. I ain't wanted in Mississippi or any other state for murderin' skinny white women!"

Meg was surprised; then she burst out laughing. Only then did she see that Abby Mayhew's eyes were a shade less frigid, her posture less defensive.

Her laughter woke Melanie. The little girl sat up, rubbing her eyes "Are we home, Aunt Meg?"

"No, Mel, we came visiting. This is Mrs. Mayhew."

Abby's eyes raked over the little girl, then back to Meg.

"She yours?"

"This is my niece, Melanie Cash."

Melanie was staring as brazenly as the woman had. This was the tallest black woman she had ever seen. She didn't look friendly like

Viney Jefferson. But Melanie was far more intrigued than frightened, especially when the three children came crowding around their mother. She perked up and leaned forward.

"Are these your children?"

Abby was visibly surprised at the question from the white child in the spotless pinafore.

"They are."

"Micah and Gideon are my best friends at home, next to Mama."

Wordlessly, Melanie climbed from the buggy. She smoothed her dress carefully—then reached her small hand out to the three wide-eyed children. Her smile was shy. "Wanna hold my doll? She's kinda sleepy."

Abby was too stunned to speak.

"You two thirsty?" she asked suddenly.

"I am," Melanie chirped.

"Go fetch a cup," Abby ordered a child. "A clean one."

The child brought back a chipped enamel cup. Abby's eyes challenged them. Would they dare to drink? But they did without hesitation.

"Mrs. Mayhew, will you reconsider letting your oldest daughter come to the school at Chisolm Crossing?"

"No, I won't."

"But why?"

"Told ya. Wouldn't do 'em a bit of good."

"Well, do you think it would do them a bit of harm?"

"Don't know about that."

"If they stay home and receive no education they have very few chances of improving their lives. And I think that is exactly what you would like for them."

"Said it before, and I'll say it plainer now—always will be whites pushin' black folks down and takin' away their chances. Seen it happen too many times not to believe."

"I'm sure you have. And you're right. But only partly so. You can see the color of my skin. Why would I take the time and effort to teach if I was just planning to beat these little ones? Abby, I'm not alone."

It was hard to put into words all the racial complexities that had taken years to form. How could she erase years that this woman had hurt?

"What about the Klan?" Abby asked with weakened vehemence. "Heard they was roamin' around . . . seekin' who they could devour!"

"The Klan has not disturbed the school in over six months. I don't consider them a threat any longer."

They both turned to look across the flat dirt yard where four children were laughing. Melanie was leading them in a game.

Abby Mayhew was frustrated. She wasn't sure what to say. Her anger was like the ebb and flow of a tide.

"Mrs. Mayhew, please think about this. Come to the school any day that you choose. Bring your children, of course. I'll make a place for you at the back of the schoolroom so you can observe everything. At the end of the day, if you still don't want your children to come, I won't ever bother you about it again."

Abby's heart had been hurt and hardened for years. She could not change in one hour even if the white lady was honest and ... kind.

"I'll think about it."

The Tanglewood buggy was turned for home. Melanie waved enthusiastically from the seat until the Mayhew cabin was out of sight. Meg smiled and breathed a prayer of thanks, grateful she had taken Melanie Cash for a buggy ride.

Tanglewood

"Deep-sea fishing must agree with you," Amy smiled as she walked along the drive with Barrett. She had not seen him in several months.

"I think it was getting to sleep through the night that helped the most," he returned easily. "But the fishin' certainly didn't hurt."

The doctor did look healthier, tanned and rested. The shadows were gone from his eyes.

"And your arm?"

"Hurts if I work it too much. It's an excuse not to chop wood, but nothing serious." He looked down the drive, remembering that morning at the mercantile. "No false heroics intended, but I'm just glad I was there to stop Willet's foolishness and not someone else. He was pretty angry at Chester. If he'd have fired at such close range, Matilda would be a widow, I'm afraid."

Amy squeezed his arm. "Well, I think you are heroic. I'm so glad all the Klan business seems to be over. Meg says there hasn't been any trouble with them since that morning."

Barrett nodded but was silent.

"Since we're speaking of Meg—" Amy began.

Barrett chuckled. "Since *you* are speaking of her."

"All right, all right. I was thinking of calling you if you hadn't come out to check on Mary's arthritis."

He raised an eyebrow.

"I'm worried about Meg. She has a serious-sounding cough. She was here last weekend and sounds terrible. She said she usually gets it in the winter, but hasn't had it in the last few years. I think she's working too hard."

Amy waited for the doctor to comment. But the man was absorbed in the cinch on his horse.

"Well, Barrett, are you going to go see her?"

He sighed. "Amy, I usually don't go until I'm called."

"Well, she won't call you! She's stubborn!" Amy said with exasperation.

He returned to the cinch. He was suddenly angry.

"I know she won't, Amy. But I can't barge into the schoolhouse and demand she let me listen to her lungs!"

"I know."

"She despises me, Amy! I'm not about to go to her when I haven't been asked."

Amy was shocked by his words, his tone. She stepped closer and met his eyes. "Barrett, Meg doesn't despise you. Why would you think that?"

Barrett dug his hands deeply into his pockets. He felt vulnerable before Amy Cash.

"I'm inexperienced with women—no sister or wife," he said slowly.

They both knew the significance of the omission. He had not said mother.

"I'm awkward when I don't mean to be. I'm a bachelor, Amy, with lots of rough edges."

Her voice was gentle. "You're not with me."

"We've known each other for years. We're friends."

"And I value that, Barrett, or else I couldn't speak so bluntly. I'm only asking you to go see Meg in a professional way. But Barrett, you and Meg *could* be friends."

"Amy, I know a look of contempt when I see one."

"Barrett, I think you both have gotten off on the wrong foot with each other, and I hate to see that."

"She's your friend," he replied crisply. "And I'm glad for you, Amy. Well, I have four more calls to make."

He climbed onto his horse. Amy was looking up with such hurt in her eyes that he regretted his sharpness.

"Amy, look, I'm sorry. If she's really needing to see a doctor, have her go to Dr. Mills in Greenville. He's very good."

He waved and rode off. She watched him until he was out of sight, and wondered how long he would hold a wall around his heart.

Chisolm Crossing

It had been a very long day for the teacher. Actually, Meg felt it had been one entire week rolled into one day. The children had been full of energy, with little interest for studies. The schoolroom had been unusually noisy. A baseball thrown at recess had shattered a window of the mercantile. That interruption had cost over an hour and fortified the scholars with more distraction. One little girl had tried to bite her seatmate. The young girl called Faraway had been in tears all day for no reason that Meg could discover. By 3:00 Meg's head was pounding as she reevaluated the teaching profession. In 30 more minutes the schoolday would be over, and she could go collapse on her bed.

One last calamity crowned the day. Jacob had been unusually belligerent. His scowl had been darker, his muttered threats to his classmates more frequent. Meg stepped into her apartment to take an aspirin. Before she could take it, however, the little girls in the primer class were screaming.

"His head!"

"Blood!"

"Teacher! Teacher!"

Meg hurried back into the schoolroom. The children were gathered around ten-year-old David. He was stretched out on the floor, a gash bleeding freely on his forehead. Meg quickly applied a compress.

"What happened?" she demanded with a sharpness her students had not heard before.

No one spoke. But their eyes were eloquent. They were afraid. Tick stooped down. "He was pushed, Miss Ma'am."

"By whom?"

Her eyes lifted to find Jacob smirking at her from across the room. He was alone and defiant. And very obvious. She hadn't the strength to confront him now.

"Shall I go fetch the doc?" Micah asked.

"No, Micah, I think I can handle this," she replied briskly. "Children, quickly gather up your things. School is dismissed early today. David will be fine. Tick, could you get him a cup of water, please?"

Jacob flung the door open, and the children slowly filed out.

"How are you feeling, David?" she asked.

"Head don't hurt too bad, Miss 'Cott, but the room is kinda spinnin'."

Meg was alarmed. Micah leaned down again, confidential and quiet.

"Sure is a lot of blood, ain't it? Want I should fetch Doc? He's over at the mercantile; I seen him go in."

"No! No, Micah, it really isn't necessary. I'm sorry. I don't know, do you think you should? Hand me that other rag, will you?"

But one of the children had already run to the store, and now the doctor was entering the schoolhouse. Meg did not look up when she heard him, but she did notice the calm, casual tone of his voice.

"All right, kids, no point in hanging around. David's going to be fine. School's out."

"Micah and Tick? Thank you for your help. I'll see you tomorrow."

The schoolroom was silent. Barrett bent over the boy and went to work. He told him about his fishing trip as if they were alone. He worked carefully. Meg found herself drawn against her will to watching his hands. Hands that were skilled and gentle. The ring flashed in the sunlight.

"There," he announced at last. "How does that feel, David?"

"Okay, Doc."

"Let's get him sitting up." It was the first thing he had said to the schoolmarm.

"Dizzy?" Barrett asked.

"Not much. Think I'm gonna make it, Doc."

Barrett smiled. "That's what I like to hear."

The schoolhouse door opened, and Chester's pink face popped in. "How's he doing?"

"He'll be all right," Barrett replied.

"I have to make a delivery. I'll give him a lift in my wagon," Chester offered.

"That's a fine idea, Ches." Barrett helped the boy stand.

Chester's face furrowed at the sight of Meg sitting disheveled and undignified on the floor. It was not a posture the Yankee schoolteacher often took. "You all right, Meg? You look kind of—"

"It's been a very long day, Chester. I have a terrible headache, and I'm not entirely certain if...if a Klansman came to me and wanted me to shut the school, I wouldn't do it!"

Barrett and Chester exchanged a look. "She didn't mean that," Chester hastily whispered to David as he backed out the door. Matilda had moods like this. They were dangerous.

Meg stood up, completely ignoring the doctor as he gathered up his tools very carefully and quietly. She slumped in a desk at the front and sunk her head in her arms.

He looked at her back and the skin above her collar. Even in that posture, she was very beautiful to him. Barrett straightened the desks and picked up the scattered books from the floor. He cleaned up the basin and the bloodied rags. He turned to leave without a word, but the schoolmarm broke into a spasm of coughing. He closed his eyes and hesitated. Amy Cash, he thought grimly, could not have orchestrated this better.

He should leave. She didn't want his help. She didn't like him. He knew she was in a sensitive mood and one wrong word on his part could cause her to dislike him even more. But he walked slowly, like one under a death sentence, and took a seat beside her.

"Miss Alcott?"

Her head came up. She was pale, and her eyes were rimmed in red. "Yes?"

He cleared his throat. This...woman! She had no generosity! She was determined to make everything hard for him.

"I couldn't help but notice your cough."

She looked away. Her voice was flat. "It's nothing."

"Well, you know, coughs are...in my line of work. Just like," he glanced around the room, "just like penmanship is in yours. So, I'd give your cough...about a D+."

He was inwardly pleased. Amy would be proud at his attempt at humor and charm. But Meg would not smile. She felt too horrible. She did not feel like fighting, but she did not feel like giving in...yet.

"Could I listen to your lungs, please?" he asked kindly.

She faced him. "Really, Dr. Browning, I'm grateful for your concern, and I thank you for coming to my rescue with David. I...I didn't handle it very well, I admit."

"You were handling it fine."

"Well, anyway, my cough is...nothing."

"You are needing to cough right now. I can hear it in your voice. But you don't want to do it in front of me. Now don't be childish!"

"I am not...I do not need...to..." She exploded in coughing.

When she composed herself, he was ready with his stethoscope.

"I assure you, Miss Alcott, this is not painful," he said with a straight face.

He had never been so close. With any and every other patient, listening to lungs was completely academic and routine. But the doctor did not feel academic being this close to the schoolmarm. Barrett was scolding himself in his thoughts. He dared not look at her face. He kept his eyes fastened on the smooth whiteness of her blouse above her lungs. But he could feel her breath and smell some faint floral scent from her skin.

"Breathe in. Now out. Again. Deeper, please."

"I can't...breathe any...deeper!" She was racked by coughing again.

She had looked at the gray that was beginning at his temples and the line of skin where his tan met his hair. For a very brief second, she wished she could lean against him and close her eyes.

He pulled away and looked into her face.

"Will you listen to me?" he asked softly.

She nodded, and he was very surprised.

"Tomorrow is Friday. Three days in bed might keep this from getting any more serious. Please note I said *might*. You must close the school and stay in bed."

"I can't close the school," she whispered hoarsely. She was close to tears.

"Miss Alcott, do you expect your students to come to school when they are ill?"

"No."

"Do you want them to come?"

"Of course not, but this is different."

"How is it different? Would you go to another doctor, if you will not trust me?"

"I ... trust you ... Dr. Browning ..." she replied tiredly.

She turned back away from him. He thought he was nothing but rough edges with women, but he knew enough to be silent and wait.

"I feel wretched!" she moaned without defense.

For a very brief moment, the doctor wanted to pull the patient into his arms.

"I want you to listen carefully. I'm going to Greenville for your medicine. I don't have what you need at my place. I'm going to tell Matilda to spread the word that school will be closed tomorrow. If I know her, she'll be over here in a flash with soup and a hot water bottle and lots of advice."

Meg smiled weakly. The doctor had received his fee.

"I want you to get into your bed and not get out till I check on you Sunday evening. All right?"

"How is your arm?" she asked impulsively.

"My arm? Oh, it's fine, thank you."

She nodded. "Well ..."

They were standing too close. The doctor stepped back.

"What do I owe you for this?" she asked.

She had mentioned his arm. She remembered everything. He wanted to tell her about his experience in the Klan. He didn't want her to hate him anymore.

"I'll send you a bill, sometime," he said lamely.

"Thank you, Dr. Browning." She turned and went to her room.

He rode to Greenville thinking over every detail of his time with her. And he diagnosed he was softening toward this Yankee woman, and he mustn't allow that anymore.

Chapter 23

New Orleans

◆◆ ◆◆ ◆◆

Dear Mama and Papa,

School has only been in session one term, but what a term it has been! There are some days I don't know whether to laugh or cry. But don't worry, there's steady Chester Chisolm (and even steadier Mrs. Chisolm!) to hold me up. Chester lifts my spirit and encourages me; Mrs. Chisolm gets "practical" if I seem too buoyant for her sensibilities.

While I've enjoyed this work, I've felt overwhelmed with the responsibility of 22 young minds depending on me.

I can't decide what bothers me more, the grinding poverty of these people or that there are so many needs among the children *and* adults who are hungry for education and opportunities— things I've always taken for granted. Your generation freed these people; can mine do less?

Let me tell you about some of my children and see if they aren't like some I had at Peppercreek. First there is an irrepressible ten-year-old named Tick Boon. (Now I know Tick is an unusual name, but it's been in his family since "we come up the James from Africa, Miss Ma'am. Ticking is from my Ma's side.") He has a favorite expression, "World without end, amen and amen." I suppose I should reprimand him for irreverence like Mrs. Chisolm suggests, but it just makes me smile. In this brief time of knowing him, I can see that his little boy heart is far from irreverence.

Chessie is Tick's eight-year-old sister. If I feel little arms around my neck or touching my hair or dress, I know it's Chessie. She says I'm whiter than cotton. There's Lucinda and Matilda, twin nine-year-olds. Beyond saying their names and smiling shyly, they have said little else. They just watch me with huge brown eyes. Jacob is their older brother, my oldest student. He's 14. He's managed to be courteously sullen the entire time school has been in session. He does every assignment I put him to, and does it well, but I can see his heart isn't in being here. He's a real challenge.

Annie, age ten, giggles and makes "sheep eyes" at the boys. Micah Jefferson will be the first to read fluently. He has devoured everything I've taught him. There is always one student in a class who seems to capture your heart. For me this term it is a chubby six-year-old, oddly christened "True." He brings me a gift every day, a colorful rock or flowers mostly. Finally, I have a 12-year-old named Faraway. She is as isolated as her name, taking little part in recess play.

There is a family of deaf-mutes named Tildy. I cannot yet decide what to do for them beyond learning sign language. No one else around here seems to notice or even care about their situation. Papa, you told me once I was a born reformer. Well, there's plenty to reform around here.

I can feel your prayers for me, and thank you for them.

All my love,
Meg

Andy Alcott carefully folded the letter his parents had enclosed with their own. It was a letter already six months old, one of the first Meg had written from her new home. He looked out across the quiet foredeck of the *Magnolia* a moment. He was oblivious to the laughter, the voices, the groan of the rigging, and the hiss of steam from the other ships berthed around his.

Meg had stayed in Mississippi and was actually teaching in Chisolm Crossing! He frowned, tucked the letter into his shirt pocket, then unfolded the letter he had read earlier, a letter from Meg herself, also outdated.

Andy had been disappointed at the small packet of letters awaiting him when the *Magnolia* docked in New Orleans earlier that day. With his crew off on shore leave, Andy had looked forward to the time alone to enjoy messages from his family. He had spent three frustrating months in the harbor at Nassau in the Bahamas under quarantine as yellow fever swept through the port city. Three months idle in the harbor. It had been hard on business and harder on a crew unaccustomed to such inactivity. *Magnolia Remembrance* had never been scrubbed so clean!

He opened the lilac-scented notepaper dated months before and began to read.

Dear Andy,

I arrived at Tanglewood this morning. I'm staying in one of the second-story bedrooms, very elegant and "Old Southern." It commands a nice view of the gardens. I find Tanglewood as lovely as you and Papa described. And very interesting. Mrs. Cash is not like I expected. She greeted me quite cordially, expressing interest in our family. I gave her

our condolences for Uncle Pat. Tanglewood is a very large
estate for a woman to manage alone, but she has a daughter
now to think of as well. Melanie will soon be two years old.
Motherhood seems agreeable to Amy Cash. She has invited
me to stay awhile, and I think I will.

Meg

If Andy had not known Meg's precise handwriting so well, he would
have thought someone else had penned the letter. It was so unlike his
sister. Always before her letters had been several pages long. This one
was a mere paragraph. Her letters had always flowed with descriptions,
jokes at herself, and personal reflections. A letter from Meg had been
the closest thing to a personal conversation.

This letter was so different, so clipped, factual, emotionless. And so
very different from the warm and personal missive she had recently
written to her parents. Why had she written him this way? Even in such
a brief note she sounded almost *offended* at him! Why?

Magnolia Remembrance would leave for an extended voyage in four
short days. With so much to do, he would have to compose a letter to
her while at sea. As he lay in his bunk later that night, he stared into the
darkness, unsoothed by the rhythm of the boat. He set aside in his mind
Meg's curtness. He would ponder that later.

Amy had a daughter. A part of Patrick Cash lived on...

Greenville

"This is a real pleasure, Miss Alcott."

Meg turned from the counter slowly, jolted by the deep, confident
voice close to her shoulder. French's voice always triggered instant
tenseness. Now here was the chance to keep her resolve.

"Good morning, Mr. French."

"I've been looking over my accounts all morning. As impressive as
they are, you're certainly a sight prettier."

His eyes appraised her, taking in every detail of her cream-colored
skirt and mint-shaded blouse.

"Come to Greenville for shopping?" he asked, smiling.

"Yes, for a few things."

In the awkward silence that followed, she heard them. Two women
shoppers at a near counter were huddled together, casting proud
glances her way. Though they were murmuring, their voices were loud
enough for Meg to hear.

"She keeps the nigger school... Yankee kind... Imagine!... Might
catch some of their diseases..."

"So how are things at Chisolm Crossing, Miss Alcott?" French asked loudly.

"Fine."

"How about some light refreshment over at the hotel dining room?"

"Thank you, but no. I need to be getting back."

"Well, I could ride along and keep you company," he returned smoothly.

"Perhaps another time."

"Maybe I'll drop by your school sometime. After all, my taxes go into the colored school."

He jerked his head toward the women shoppers. "That's what has most folks in a stir now, you understand."

"No, frankly, I don't."

French's smile widened; he'd be glad to explain something to the pretty Yankee.

"Lots of folks around Greenville are complaining about their taxes going to a colored school. They plain don't like that. They think it makes the state skimp on Greenville schools."

"The citizens of the Crossing are as entitled to a free education as the children of Greenville. That's the law. If the Greenville schools have a problem, I hardly think that can be laid at the Crossing's doorstep."

"Perhaps you should have gone into the law profession instead of teaching, Miss Alcott." He had hoped to flatter her.

"I'd better be going," she said briskly.

"I'm a bit discouraged, Miss Alcott," he pressed.

"Excuse me?"

"Do you have a fiancé or a sweetheart back home?"

Meg's voice was frigid. "No, I don't."

"Then a man might come courting if—"

"*If* he was a gentleman. Good day, Mr. French."

It was noontime, and Meg always liked to do something special for her students on Friday. Today, a beautiful early spring day, would be their first field trip. The children had laughed and clapped and hugged her when she told them they would carry their dinner pails into the woods for a picnic.

"While we walk, I want you to tell me everything you can identify."

"Iden...what?" asked little True, grabbing her hand before any of the little girls could.

"Tell me the names of things: plants, trees, animals. Tell me what you know about them."

"Will you read to us from the fairy tales after we eat?" Faraway asked.

Meg patted the basket she carried. "Indeed, I will. Now, off we go!"

They trooped single-file into the cool, shady glade, a procession of young voices raised in laughter and singing interspersed with boyish yells. Meg had never been happier.

Tick and Micah led them to the meadow where they had held their evangelistic meetings. Meg feigned surprise.

"This is perfect!"

After dinner Meg read to them, young Chessie drowsing in the sunshine splashed across her lap. She loved the way they listened with such rapt expressions. Teaching had never been easier. She knew that soon most of her children would be reading and doing simple arithmetic.

Later she let them pick flowers and play while she worked on her journal. It was growing fatter each day. She was taking notes about more than just academic concerns for her students and their families.

1. George's crossed eyes. Can I do anything? Dr. B?

2. Body odors. How do I be tactful?

3. Abby Mayhew still has not taken me up on observation suggestion. Should I approach her again? . . . Eeek!

4. Visit again with Mim soon.

5. Evidence of mice again! Need a cat.

6. Faraway. How can I reach her?

7. Jacob. Still so hostile.

She glanced up. Her oldest student was off by himself again, leaning against a tree, whittling on a stick. Even as he worked, his face was set in a scowl. Meg chewed the end of her pencil in frustration. She did feel a pang of disappointment that he was still as remote and unfriendly as he had been on the first day.

"Miss Ma'am! Look over here!" one of the children called.

It was a carefully woven bird's nest, cradled in the crook of a low-hanging tree branch. In it were three creamy yellow eggs. The children crowded around.

"Shall we take it back to the school, Miss Ma'am?" Temple asked.

"No, we'll leave it here. When we come back next week, they may be hatched. Isn't it lovely? Now, it's time to head back. Tell me what you've seen."

The schoolday was over and the schoolmarm was doing a little shopping in the mercantile. Meg was in no hurry as she made her purchases. She was in a lighthearted mood and regretting Chester was not around to appreciate it. After all, it had been a good day in the classroom and a beautiful early spring afternoon outside. She would not allow Matilda to dampen her spirits. She would "soar" for a while; reality was never far off.

Matilda Chisolm was frowning. Miss Alcott was acting almost giddy. Chester got in these moods sometimes—too often—and they could be so provoking. The older woman sighed and shook her head. Surely the schoolmarm was more decorous in her classroom. She was certainly unconventional in her teaching, Mrs. Chisolm had observed. Just last week Tom Evans had brought a bag of bleached white cow bones for the schoolhouse. Miss Alcott was teaching basic anatomy. Matilda had been mildly alarmed at the word. Wasn't that the study of the *body*? Her New England roots of modesty asserted themselves. Her concern turned to skepticism. Then Miss Alcott bought her entire supply of red and blue yarn!

"Blood veins, Mrs. Chisolm," Meg said. "Would you care to join us in our project?"

Matilda had puckered her mouth in a fashion Meg clearly recognized as an emphatic no. Miss Alcott might be becoming a shade too creative in her teaching. Bodies and blood veins...where might that lead? Reading and ciphering were the staple diet practical Matilda prescribed.

"It's a beautiful afternoon, isn't it, Mrs. Chisolm? Care to go for a walk with me? I'm hunting out bouquets."

"Thank you, Miss Alcott, but I do have a business to run," Matilda returned with mild disapproval.

Meg smiled. "Of course. Let's see, what else do I need?"

Matilda was attending a male shopper. He was slow and indecisive, the kind of customer Matilda always referred to her more equitable husband. When he finally left, she let out an exasperated sigh.

"Men!"

Meg had finished her shopping. "Are you a man-hater, Mrs. Chisolm?" she asked teasingly.

"No, of course not. I could not live with a creature I hated!"

"Of course...But are you a secret supporter of Susan B. Anthony?"

Matilda would suffer no joking. She rolled her eyes. If it wasn't Chester, it was Miss Alcott. Giddy she was today.

"No," she said patiently. "I am not a supporter of that Anthony woman. She is a troublemaker and very immodest in her language. I've seen her picture; her hats are heathenish as well!"

"I agree. I can't abide a woman in a heathenish hat."

"But I do find men generally rather useless," Matilda continued.

"Oh?"

"Think of the wars in this century alone, Miss Alcott. All led and promoted by men!"

"And statesmen of peace, and inventors, and ministers, and doctors who heal, and—" Meg said in defense.

"Only God heals, Miss Alcott," Matilda retorted with Puritan vigor.

Meg smiled. "Of course. Well, if you'll just add my purchases up."

But Matilda was finally caught up in the schoolmarm's teasing. She could play the little game too.

"Doctors *can* be useful on occasion," Matilda conceded.

"Yes, that's true."

"Some women find men an indispensable, even necessary commodity!" Matilda said.

"A commodity, hmm?"

"Yes," Matilda continued with a crusader's passion. "I have known women who felt they could not live without a man!"

Meg shook her head in shock at such a thing.

"They are weak and foolish if you ask me," Matilda persisted.

"Well, I'd better get going if I'm going to get a walk in before dark."

"Are you lonely, Miss Alcott?" Matilda pressed pointedly.

"You mean, am I a weak woman?"

Matilda's face was hawklike. They had finally arrived at the purpose of this discussion.

"I am very content, Mrs. Chisolm, without any . . . male commodity."

"Ah." Matilda was adding the purchases while her mind made other calculations. "There really are few unmarried men around the Crossing, even if you were—"

"Weak," Meg supplied gravely.

"Only one in fact, that I can think of. And *he's* very busy. Wouldn't have time to notice anyone—"

"Without a fever. Yes, well . . ." Meg could hardly keep from laughing. Matilda Chisolm was delightful in her own original way!

"Goodbye and thank you," Meg called over her shoulder. At the door she paused. She must have one final tease with a little scandal thrown in.

"I can't agree with you, Mrs. Chisolm, about men being completely useless. Just think, without them you and I wouldn't be here to enjoy this beautiful day!"

Meg cleared her throat nervously, glancing up at the slim teenager who stood before her. Matilda had spoken the truth, Jacob Brown wasn't far from young manhood.

"I asked you to stay after today, Jacob, because I think we need to talk. You don't want to be in school, do you?"

He inclined his head toward her. "I purely don't."

"May I ask why?"

His chin went up defiantly. "Don't care to be bossed by a white Yankee woman," he spit out savagely.

There it was, just as Meg had suspected.

"Oh. I see."

"I don't take bossin' from whites. Never have, never will."

"Do your parents make you come?"

"Pa said I was to or he'd put a strap to me. Not that I ain't big enough to take a lickin', but he promised me a new squirrel rifle if I finished out this term. Bet you think you got all the folks tied up in this school, but you ain't. There's folks who ain't coming 'cause they don't care for their little ones to be bossed by a white." He smiled, waiting for her reaction.

"I'm sorry to hear that, Jacob." She kept her gaze level, her voice firm. "You put the dead rats in the girls' privy. You smashed the bird's nest. You crush all the chalk pencils that you find. Then you hurt David. If his injury was any more severe I would have had to expel you.... Malicious things like that can't close this school, Jacob. They only hurt the children."

"Maybe something bigger then."

"I think you're too smart for that," she persuaded gently, though she felt anything but gentleness.

"You gonna tell my pa?"

"No, I hadn't planned to. I thought talking to you—"

"A lot of white folks still don't like this nigger school. Maybe they'll do something about it. Maybe the Klan will come again even."

Meg stood up then, clenching her hands behind her so that he couldn't see her anger. "Shame on you, Jacob Brown! To wish such a thing on your own people! That's nothing but selfishness on your part."

He was silent, focused on the edge of her desk. Was he beyond reasoning? Would she really have an enemy within her classroom? She took a deep breath and relaxed.

"You're reading very well. You—"

"Baby stuff!" he burst out hotly.

"Then I'll get you more difficult material. I wonder if you are able to put learning above your fears."

"Ain't afraid of nothing."

"In a way, you're afraid of me, Jacob."

His short laugh sounded hollow. "Now you're being foolish."

"You hate whites because you're afraid of them, because you don't really know them. Many whites have the same problem concerning people of color. I can help you."

"I don't want your help."

"If you're as smart as I think you are, you'll put your hatred aside and learn."

"I'll come here for Pa's sake, but you'll never make me like it! Never make me skunk up to you like those babies, Micah and Tick."

"No, I can't make you, Jacob. I'll see you tomorrow."

The door slammed, sending a shudder through the building, and a shudder through Meg Alcott.

From her teaching days in Peppercreek, Meg had come to the conclusion that you could tell something about a student's homelife by the contents of his dinner pail. As she sat in the shade of the giant oak, the children scattered around her, she could not help but notice their midday meal. It flamed the secret sorrow she had for them.

Usually they ate cold biscuits or cornbread, left over from the morning meal and sometimes seasoned with a slice of bacon or grease. Sometimes they brought fruit or berries, but rarely. Often there was a cold sweet potato, peeled like a banana, a boiled egg, or a piece of cold squirrel. Her own food turned dry and tasteless in her mouth. Nutrition! These children needed lessons in nutrition, that much was certain. There was only one person qualified and already trusted in the neighborhood. In her eagerness to help the children, she was willing to approach him.

"Dr. Browning!" she called out, hoping her voice sounded calm and casual.

She had waited till he left the porch of the mercantile and was about to ride off. It was twilight, and she'd been watching for him from her window, trying to build up her courage. She had not seen him more than in passing in the several months since he had treated her. He had been very professional, very thorough. She had thanked him with sincerity, but he had never sent his bill. She had been so proud to tell Amy, "I was very cordial to the doctor, Mrs. Cash. I can recall smiling at him at least once. I took all the awful medicine he gave me without complaint. I exhaled and inhaled with complete obedience."

But Amy knew for all of Meg's jesting, she was still holding the man at arm's length in her behavior. Was it only this Klan suspicion, or something more?

Meg knew Barrett often stopped at Chisolm's at dusk to lean on the front railing and jaw with Chester. But she also knew he came by less lately, and she knew why.

"Good evening, Miss Alcott."

She noticed immediately how weary he sounded. He gestured toward the store.

"Where are the Chisolms? Do you know?"

"They went to Vicksburg this afternoon."

"Oh..." His voice sighed like a moaning in the wind.

"I wonder if I could have a few moments of your time, Doctor."

He said nothing, merely waiting, his arm slung over the back of his horse.

"The children, my students, need some lessons in nutrition. Their dinners are dreadful! No vegetables. They need lessons in personal hygiene as well. I wonder if you would consider coming by the school, at your convenience of course, to give them some informal lessons. The children know and—"

His hand went out to her as if she had struck him. Only then did she see he was trembling.

"Are you all right, Barrett?"

She hadn't meant to use his given name; it had slipped out somehow. She hoped he hadn't noticed.

Yet his gaze was intense. She wished she could know his thoughts.

"I've had a long day...have a terrible backache..."

"I'm sorry. Is there anything I can do?" she asked softly.

His smile was weak. He would have liked to have been comforted just this once.

"Thank you, but no. Just need some sleep."

She had a sudden impulse to rub his neck, to try to ease his pain in some small way. Such a thought!

"I'll consider your proposal, Miss Alcott. But I think you should consider that such plans are often best begun with the parents. They may want you to stick strictly to the three r's. Folks' nutrition and hygiene are not easy to change. They may resent it and think it's Yankee foolishness."

"Do you think it's Yankee foolishness, Doctor?"

He peered at her critically. "I don't think you really want my opinions, Miss Alcott. They have inflamed you in the past. But no, I don't think it's foolishness."

His voice softened in a way she had not heard often.

"I think you are a very capable young woman."

Suddenly she wanted him to stay and say more, something more complimentary than that she was so capable. What was wrong with her! This man had been so antagonistic in the past.

He swung up on his mount.

"Young Temple and True won't be in your school in the morning, most likely. Their little sister was bitten by a rabid dog." His voice dropped, his chin sinking down to his chest. "I was too late...There'll be a funeral in a few days."

She felt her heart go out to him then, against her will. She wanted to say something, anything. Was he as alone and lonely as she had become? He was just as busy, just as dedicated to his work, just as involved in the simple lives of Chisolm Crossing—and longing for the connection to another heart—as she was.

"I'm so sorry. She was so...little."

"Turned two last week," he sighed wearily. "Good night, Miss Alcott."

Tanglewood

It was Sunday evening, and Amy Cash always felt her loneliness more acutely after Meg had spent the weekend with her. Meg brought stories of her students, jokes from Chester, immortal words of wisdom from Matilda. She brought herself, her friendship. Even with loving and caring for Melanie and the running of the estate, the mistress of Tanglewood could not ignore the isolation that hung over her like a shroud.

She had walked along the perimeter of the grounds, oblivious to the soft beauty of the evening, oblivious to the tread of a man stalking her. She thought of the quiet mansion, her reluctance to face another evening of reading or sewing or playing chess with Fenwick. She felt the grip of panic that her life had come to this point of desperate loneliness.

A hand grabbed her wrist tightly, swinging her around. She was too startled to scream. French twisted her arm to her back, holding her close. She could feel his hot breath on her face.

"Jeb! I'll scream. They'll hear me at the house."

He laid the handle of his riding whip against her throat.

"I wouldn't."

She averted her face from him as he pressed himself closer.

"Let me go, Jeb."

"I will when I'm ready. I used to think ice water ran through your cool veins, little sis. Seeing your brat now, I know better."

He waited for her to respond to his taunt, but she was silent.

"Poor ol' Patrick Cash. Thought he had such a proper young wife. Didn't know she'd play the harlot with his handsome young cousin."

Her face had gone white. "You've a filthy, filthy mind, Jeb Jackson French! You always have had. Your ma knew—"

She cried out as he tightened his grasp on her arm.

"See? Just like I thought. You're tart, Miss Amy, right down to the last bite. It's only a matter of time until I get what I want. We both know that."

His mouth was silenced as he found her neck. No amount of struggling could match his strength. She had learned that long ago.

"Let her go, Mr. French." It was a soothing voice, strangely calm.

French's head shot up; Seth Jefferson stood in the clearing.

But Amy breathed no easier. She knew what French could do to her. What would he do to her rescuer?

French shoved Amy roughly away.

"Well, well, well. Never paid you in full for leaving me like you did, Mr. Jefferson. No, I never did. Well, boy, accounts are past due."

The riding whip uncurled in an instant, like a flash, the strike of a snake. It lashed across Seth's throat, sending the black man to his knees.

Amy screamed, rushing to him as he sprawled forward.

French was on his horse. "Another time, little sis."

Chapter 24

Chisolm Crossing

♦♦ ♦♦ ♦♦

*N*ell Evans was closer to her in age than any woman Meg had met around the Crossing. She was friendly and gracious. She had begun to invite the schoolteacher to dinner. Afterward the three would push aside the dishes and play gin rummy, dominoes, or whist. Meg enjoyed the relaxing evenings. Tom's teasing reminded her of Andy.

"If Mrs. Chisolm knew we were playing cards, she'd be shocked and very disapproving," Meg smiled. "She calls them the devil's playthings."

"Your secret is safe with us," Tom said expansively as he dealt a fresh hand.

Nell was reflective. "Just think of how peaceful things are tonight. I'm so thankful that nightmare Klan business in the fall is over."

"Is Willet Keller still in jail?" Meg asked.

"It's such an odd case," Tom began slowly. "I don't think they quite know what to do with him. I've heard the Klan in Jackson is trying to say they never heard of him and the banker in Greenville just wants revenge for his daughter. Don't see how they can keep him locked up much longer since he can't identify who did beat the poor girl. Martha says he's a pretty broken man, though . . . Hate to see that . . . Willet was a decent farmer. He knew his business."

"I can imagine how agonized Martha is for him," Nell said. "When I think of how frightened I was when you would go to one of their meetings . . ." She shook her head at the memory. "She's a strong woman, though."

Tom was quick to cover his wife's accidental disclosure.

"Your play, Meg," he said easily.

But the schoolmarm had excellent hearing.

"Did you say Tom went to their meetings?"

"More coffee, Meg?" the farmer asked.

"What meeting, Nell?"

Tom was leaning across the table with unusual forwardness.

"Another piece of pie? . . . You pass or play, Meg?"

Meg laid her hand on his arm and gave him a captivating smile.

"No coffee, no cake, thank you. And why is your husband so frantic, Nell?"

"Tom? What? Oh . . ."

Husband and wife were looking at each other, trying to send signals through their looks.

"A meeting Tom went to?" Meg pressed without mercy.

Tom laid down his cards with a resigned sigh.

"Well, Tom, can't we tell her? I didn't know you felt..."

Tom shrugged. "I don't know, Nell. I guess since it's all over with it would be all right."

"Well, I don't want to pry," Meg allowed with mock nobility.

"It's just..." Tom began. "Oh, tell her if you want to, Nell."

"You two are torturing me with suspense!" Meg laughed.

Nell Evans leaned forward dramatically as if they could be overheard through the stout log walls.

"Tom joined the Klan last fall."

Meg felt like cold water had been dashed in her face. Had she heard right? First the doctor, now this easygoing farmer?

"You're joking," she said flatly.

Nell shook her head. "It was very serious at the time, believe me. I was so afraid that Willet or one of the others would find out the truth."

Meg looked at Tom. His face was calm and suddenly sad. She realized that not only must it be true, but it must have hurt him deeply to join.

"But why?"

The baby began to cry in the next room.

"Tom will explain it, even if you have to drag it out of him," she said as she left the room.

He cleared his throat nervously. "You see, I just couldn't think of any way to help stop the Klan from growing. To confuse it or break it up from the inside seemed like the only course. Like a mole in your garden, you know. It's unseen but doing lots of damage anyway."

"But Willet Keller believed you were sincere?"

"Yep. All I had to do was mouth off about blacks from time to time and he was satisfied."

"Were you there...that night?"

Tom's face softened. He patted her hand. "I was, Meg. And I sure felt bad about how frightening it must have been for you. I'm sorry about that part. If it had gotten worse before Chester and his crew stepped in, I would have done something. We weren't going to let them burn the schoolhouse, even if we had to take Willet and the rest of them on ourselves!"

"We?" Meg was confused. *Did he say we?*

Nell had reentered the room. She stood beside her husband, her arm affectionately around his shoulders. She was smiling with pride.

"I don't know what to say, Tom," Meg whispered. "I don't know how to thank you."

Tom shrugged again, but Nell would be his voice.

"You were very brave, Tom, even if you are modest," Nell said. "You both were."

"Both?" She *had* heard this time, and her heart was pounding.

Tom frowned. "Now, Nell honey, it ain't right to tell someone else's secrets."

"But Tom, you *both* were very brave."

"It was Dr. Browning," Meg said quietly.

They looked at each other, then nodded. Nell was warming to the subject, now that it was past.

"It was Barrett's plan from the beginning," Nell explained.

"He called us the mole brothers," Tom smiled.

"He decided the only way to know what the Klan was planning to do, or who they were planning to visit . . . or hurt, was to be a part of them," Nell explained.

"The picnic you had for the school opening?" Tom continued.

"Yes?"

"Willet was all for riding through and tearin' it up. Barrett talked him out of it."

"Tell her what Willet did instead," his wife insisted.

"Barrett and I suggested he just leave warnings to scare and discourage you." Tom went on to describe them all, every night, each one.

"But I never found those things," Meg whispered with growing pain.

Nell spoke up. "Barrett was closest to the school. He stayed up every night to wait for Keller to do his dirty work. Then he'd clean it up. Poor man, he was exhausted."

"He was determined you wouldn't find any of them, not one, not a trace," Tom concluded. "But it all ended . . . without anyone getting hurt too bad."

"Except that young girl in Greenville," Nell said sadly.

Meg had gone white. The Evanses exchanged a look. Miss Alcott looked like she was going to break down and sob.

"Meg? We didn't mean to upset you," Nell said gently.

"No, I'm so grateful you told me everything. I'm just shocked."

"You know, Meg, it might be better if you didn't let on to Barrett that you found out about this. He's kind of a private person," Tom said.

"No, I won't say a word."

When her students came to school the next day, they found their teacher very quiet and subdued. Some of them worried that she was feeling sick again. She looked as if she hadn't had much sleep. And to their very perceptive eyes, she looked like she'd been crying.

Tanglewood

"Will he be all right?" Amy asked, her voice as weak as she felt.

Barrett ran a weary hand through his hair.

"Seth is very fortunate. It's a bad cut, much deeper and it would have slashed his windpipe. As it is, he's lost enough blood to leave him very weak. He'll have a terribly sore throat for weeks. He needs bed rest for a few days."

Barrett came to sit opposite Amy in the subdued light of the library. "You're looking very pale and frightened, Amy."

"I'm tired, that's all." She could not meet his eyes lest he see the raw anger she could hardly control, the sickened feeling as she saw the whip uncurl again in her mind, the fear that she would forever be terrorized by Jeb French.

"Chester has some expressions for what you're saying and not saying, Mrs. Cash, but I won't be so impolite."

Her smile quivered.

"Tell me what happened, Amy. Who did this? Let me help you if I can."

Her hand went out to him in mute appeal.

"Please, Barrett. Please don't ask. Not tonight anyway. I have to think."

"Amy, it's clear to me something or someone is threatening you."

"Barrett, there's nothing you can do."

"I'll ride through the Crossing. Would you like me to stop and ask Miss Alcott to come?"

"No! No. Don't involve Meg. I'll be fine."

"I'll be back in the morning." He stood up. "Since you're not telling me anything, I'll be forced to draw my own conclusions, and forced to interfere in my own way."

Chisolm Crossing

Meg looked up from her desk, startled as the door banged open. She guessed one of her students had forgotten something. But it was not one of her students. Jeb Jackson French lounged in, smiling and twirling a smoldering cigar in his fingers. Meg knew her students had been gone just a few minutes, barely out of sight of the schoolhouse. She realized French must have been watching the building, and it gave her a very uneasy feeling.

"Afternoon, Miss Alcott." His voice was smooth.

"Hello, Mr. French."

He chuckled. "Ain't you Yanks a proper bunch? Told ya to call me Jeb Jackson like most folks do. Don't need any of this Mr. French stuff between us."

He was up to her desk now, smiling that confidential smile that Meg could only describe as leering.

She returned to shuffling books. "I'll have to ask you to put out your cigar, Mr. French," she said without raising her eyes. "I don't allow smoking in my schoolhouse."

French burst out laughing and ambled to the open window. He tossed out the offensive cigar casually. Then he crossed his arms, regarding her.

"Sure, and we don't want your little students to think their teacher lights up stogies after hours, do we?" He laughed again and selected a desk to perch on. His eyes roved over the room, and Meg wished desperately this man did not put her at such ill ease, and that she did not show it so obviously.

"So, this is a nigger schoolhouse. Never been in one before."

"Mr. French, I must ask you to refrain from using that term for colored people. I ask my students to try to use only proper English when they are in this building. Your term is as offensive as your cigar," she added impulsively.

His leering smile dropped just a fraction.

"I ain't one of your students now, am I?"

"No, certainly not."

"Besides there isn't anyone in here but you . . . and me. No one to hear what I say."

Meg stood up abruptly and began to clean the blackboard.

"Seems a shame to me you don't get a little nig—, pardon me, a little darky to do that for you," French continued.

Meg swung around, trying harder than she had ever done in her life to control her anger and the fear that threatened to make her voice tremble. "Was there some reason you stopped in, Mr. French?"

"I recall hearin' that this school was open to any adult to come and observe."

"School is not in session, sir, and you are not a member of the school board nor do you have a child enrolled here." Meg's voice was remarkably hard despite her nervousness.

"I guess it would be interestin' if I did have a brat here, wouldn't it, Miss Alcott?"

She crimsoned, and Jeb smiled broadly.

"Just don't understand you, Miss Alcott, sure don't. You're keeping a school for darkies when you could teach whites. Left your fancy home to try to teach darkies that ain't got half the brains as whites."

Suddenly Meg's anger drained away. This man's absurd arrogance could almost be amusing. She smiled.

"On what do you base your educational philosophy, Mr. French?"

He stopped smiling, considering her words. "Darkies are inferior, and that's just a plain fact everyone knows."

"Those *facts* as you call them, haven't been proved to me, Mr. French. Yet even if they were, all the more reason to patiently teach these children. Now, if you'll please excuse me, I do have some work to do."

She was dismissing him, but he didn't mind. He stood up and walked toward the desk.

"You've got your starch all up, don't ya?" he chuckled. "Makes the color come to those pretty cheeks. Such a shame, seems to me, darkies gettin' to look on such prettiness all day." He shook his head sadly.

"Look so fine in your yellow dress . . . little white buttons all down . . . the front."

He took a step closer, and Meg wondered if he couldn't hear her heart thudding in her chest.

The school door opened. Barrett Browning stood in the entrance.

French frowned and visibly stiffened. "Callin' on the schoolmarm, Doctor?" His voice was full of sarcasm.

"Hello, Jeb. Yes, I am calling on Miss Alcott," Barrett said as he came forward.

"Reckon' ya'll cotton to one and t'other, having the same view toward niggers."

French felt reckless with his recent triumph over Amy Cash. He knew this snobbish Yankee was never going to have anything to do with him, not willingly anyway. He could afford to be crude and blunt, until he chose to do the teaching to the schoolmarm.

Meg looked to Barrett to respond, but she could see nothing in his placid face. He was silent, apparently focused on the portrait of Washington on the eastern wall.

The silence lengthened, and French's face grew red. Mumbling and without a backward glance, he left the schoolhouse.

Meg sat down limply, burying her face in her hands and not half minding that the doctor could see her emotion.

"Are you all right, Miss Alcott?" he asked finally. The gentleness and concern in his voice made her meet his eyes.

She nodded. "Could you just open the windows wider for me?"

Barrett nodded and opened them all. "You're pale. Are you sure you're all right? I can come another time."

"I'm fine, really."

"I came about arranging the hygiene classes with you."

Meg brightened. "Are you serious?"

"Yes."

"But you said—"

"I said I'd think about it, which you obviously took as a no." He still was not smiling, but she could hear that his voice was lighter.

Meg smiled. "An old habit from my growing-up years, I suppose. When my folks said they'd think about something, it usually meant no. Still, your tone seemed to say no even if your words didn't. I won't look a gift horse in the mouth, though."

She smiled at him, into his eyes, hoping he would relax and smile back.

He bowed. "Do I take it that you're calling me a horse, Miss Alcott?"

There was a full measure of levity in his words now, and Meg laughed. "There may be similarities from time to time, Dr. Browning."

Finally he smiled, and Meg was again amazed at how it changed his face. She searched for the word to describe it. Softer, younger. His eyes for just a fraction of time did not look so guarded, so probing.

"Smiling is something you should do more often, Dr. Browning," Meg ventured recklessly. "A layman's opinion, of course."

His smile dropped instantly, and Meg could see she had somehow offended him. What an odd, inscrutable man! So different from her easygoing brothers or father. No, Dr. Barrett Browning was not like any man she had ever met.

She searched for something to say to take that look out of his eyes. "Mr. French has informed me that the citizens of Greenville are still complaining about this school and my teaching."

"Some perhaps. Surely you expected that."

"Well, yes."

"Don't take everything Jeb French says as gospel, Miss Alcott."

"I don't."

"But you'll remember I told you that you'd do the white community no favors by teaching their neighbors the three R's."

Meg temporarily forgot the doctor's protection and sacrifice as she remembered one of their first conversations, and darkened.

"Yes, Doctor, I remember your words quite vividly," she returned coolly.

Barrett knew she had become defensive and sighed.

"I've put you off again, Miss Alcott. Let's talk about something neutral like the hygiene classes, shall we?"

Matilda Chisolm stood at the window of her parlor, her hands clutched behind her, her thin lips puckered, her head slightly tilted in thought. She could see the children and Miss Alcott quite clearly as they played tag in the schoolyard. She was secretly very glad of this view and glad that Chester did not know she watched each recess with religious vigilance. The routine had started so that she could witness any crime of mischief among the children, any indiscretion or oddity by the schoolmarm.

She knew when Miss Alcott took her meals from the smoke that wafted from the stovepipe in the evening, and when she said her prayers and went to bed. Matilda Chisolm was pleased that Miss Alcott seemed to have respectable and approvable personal habits. No poetical night-owling by the Northern schoolmarm. Indeed, Matilda Chisolm kept Miss Alcott under something of a private microscope.

Matilda's recess-watching had subtly changed over the weeks, however. Unbidden, she would smile at some silliness of the children at play.

It was an expression that exercised muscles quite unused to work. Most often she watched expressionless, unaware of the soft tenderness that threatened to thaw her heart. The day that Chessie had come up howling in pain from a fall, Matilda had moved closer to the window, alarmed and indignant that the teacher seemed so slow in coming to the aid of the little girl.

Then one afternoon she had watched as the students said goodbye to Miss Alcott on the steps. They were crowding around her, laughing and patting her arm. One of the younger ones crept up shyly to her side and laid a chubby hand on the teacher's cheek. A little black hand on a smooth, young white cheek. She saw Meg lean down and hug the little girl, her face radiant.

Matilda had moved away from the window, half angry, half amused with herself for the tears that had formed in her eyes. She sat in her hard rocker, the old wood protesting at the ponderous load. She felt something stirring inside her, long held at bay, buried. What was happening in the little schoolhouse at the Crossing? And what was happening to Matilda Chisolm?

Meg knew Chester Chisolm was generous, big-hearted, and forgiving. But she also knew the little merchant had been hurt by the doctor's attitude concerning the school at Chisolm Crossing. It had puzzled him. How could anyone, except Willet Keller's kind, not be enthused with the pretty Yankee's ambitions? Meg knew Chester still spoke with the doctor when he came into the store; she had heard Chester's booming laugh. Yet it wasn't quite the same. Something Chester could not understand had come between the two. And Meg held the power to tear it down.

So on an evening when Chester had insisted she come for dinner, she told them. Matilda was so surprised, she had no immediate comment or retort.

"You mean he was *in* the Klan? He was there when they came to burn...Aw, Meg, are you certain of your facts?" Chester sputtered.

"Miss Alcott appears to be quite serious, Mr. Chisolm," Matilda answered. "Still, this is hard to believe."

"I know how you feel," Meg said, studying the table. "I was shocked too."

"He never gave a hint," Chester muttered. "And there I was railin' at him!" The storekeeper shook his head. "He's a far better friend than I deserve, for sure."

"Now, Mr. Chisolm, there is no call for despair. What's done is done. What the doctor did is very commendable—"

"Commendable, Matilda?" Chester burst out with intensity. "Commendable! Matilda, think of what could have happened to Barry if the rest of those ruffians had found out he was a spy! He was putting an awful lot on the line for the school!"

And me, Meg thought to herself. *He did it to protect me...*

"And to get shot in the arm for his efforts!" Chester moaned.

Meg had been shocked, then grieved about the doctor's service. This man she had so scorned...She felt small and parsimonious. Now there must be some truth to what she had said to Amy. He would despise her for how she had treated him.

"How can we make it up to the boy?" Chester was lamenting.

"Well, credit to his account in the store would hardly be sufficient," Matilda offered weakly.

Meg and Chester managed a brief look between them.

"Got to do something," Chester agreed.

"You both know him better than I do. If you think you should say something to him..." Meg said slowly.

"He'll be embarrassed," Chester spoke up. "But I have to figure a way to say something to him...Tell him how sorry I am."

"Yes, Mr. Chisolm, you are exactly right. We must *all* think of something," Matilda added. Her eyes met the schoolmarm's, and Meg found herself blushing.

For Chester the solution was as simple as his own nature. When Barrett entered the store on his next visit, Chester was the Chester of old—friendly, teasing, encouraging. But that was not enough. He felt deeply that he had wounded his friend the doctor. Never again would he treat a friend so cheaply.

Chester walked the doctor to the front porch of the store.

"Barry, I just want you to know...how awfully sorry I am. And I'm wantin' your forgiveness."

Barrett was amazed. Chester was in tears!

"Ches, what in the world are you talkin' about?"

"Just am sorry..."

"Have you been overcharging me or something?" Barrett smiled.

"Wish it was just that simple. I am sorry, so sorry Barrett..."

Somehow, then, Barrett knew, and a weight was lifted. "Just glad we're friends again, Ches."

He could hear recitations through the open window. He reined his horse to standstill and listened. In the clear morning air he could hear the alphabet recited in eager, childish voices. Barrett heard a giggle here, a softly spoken word of encouragement from the schoolmarm there. He glanced up. If Matilda Chisolm happened to be spying from a mercantile window, she would see him. The doctor didn't want her to see him. He didn't want her to start speculating too deeply with her feminine mind.

Barrett had not forgotten the mystery surrounding Seth Jefferson's injury or the fear in Amy's eyes. He had stopped often enough at Tanglewood to stir gossip, if only there had been close neighbors. He had talked to Fenwick and asked a few unobtrusive questions of Seth. It didn't take a detective to figure out who had attacked the big black man. Being from the Crossing himself, Barrett was familiar with the painful past of Amy Cash and the cunning disposition of her stepbrother, Jeb French. If French presented a danger to Amy, Barrett could not help but feel that the threat extended to the Yankee teacher. The threat the Klan had posed had been very real. Yet when Barrett considered Jeb Jackson French, he saw a far greater menace, for reasons he could not quite define if he'd been asked.

He returned his attention to the schoolhouse. It seemed one of the students had asked a question about the war between the states.

"Was any of your folks in the war, Miss Ma'am?"

"Well, Micah, my mother was a nurse, and my father was an aide to the president."

A silence.

"That ain't true!" came the heated and rebellious voice of Jacob Brown.

Meg took a calming breath. "I assure you it is, Jacob. I am not in the habit of telling lies."

Barrett smiled from his log perch. Miss Alcott had spoken with proper Yankee tartness.

"So your father knew him? Your father knew Abe Lincoln?"

"Yes, Annie. They worked together."

"Did you know him?" came a young voice.

"That would make Miss Ma'am as old as Granny!" Micah scoffed.

"No, the president was killed before I was born."

Barrett listened to the teacher as intently as the little scholars who leaned forward on their benches. He liked hearing about her family; he liked listening to her voice.

"Now I think we'd better get back to our spelling."

"Miss Ma'am, just one more question?" Tick asked.

Meg debated with herself. Tick was forever bringing her the most challenging questions. But her heart was soft toward him. He always looked to her with such appeal and affection.

"All right, Tick. What's your question?"

"Why do you suppose God made us different colors? Why not just all black or all white?"

Tick invited God into every discussion, simply and honestly. He thought God belonged in the schoolroom. If God had a portrait, He would have been right up there with Washington and Lincoln. Tick didn't know, and wouldn't have cared if he had known, about separation of church and state. His reasoning was simple: You couldn't learn much without learning first from the master teacher. Each trip to the meadow became a cathedral experience.

"That is a big question, Tick. Maybe it's because He wanted us to be more like Him. He wanted us to have big, loving hearts like He does. He wanted to help us learn to love and care for people that don't look like us. A person might not like someone from the North because of an idea they have. But it's each person's heart that matters. The thing to remember is we are all made in God's reflection."

"Is He black or white?" True asked impatiently.

"That is too big a question, True!" Meg said laughing. "Now we really must go to spelling."

"Miss Ma'am, will you come back next year? Some grown folks say you won't, say you'll go back North, say you'll leave us and there ain't no teacher black or white to take your place."

Barrett inched forward; he could not miss this answer.

She looked out at their expectant faces. They looked as solemn as they had that memorable first day. Suddenly she felt tears come to her eyes. They had become so dear to her, taking root in her heart when she hadn't noticed.

Their faces became alarmed. Miss Ma'am was crying.

"I won't leave you. This is my home now. You've all become very special to me."

A few of the children crowded up around her, hugging her.

Tick put a comforting arm around her. "Wouldn't want you to ever leave us, Miss Ma'am ... world without end, amen and amen!"

Barrett rode home, thoughts tumbling over themselves in his mind but one voice very clear, "I won't leave you. This is my home."

Amy had not been the least shocked when Meg explained about the doctor's role in the Klan.

"That is just like something Barrett would do," she said, smiling.

She did not continue to laud or promote him as Meg expected. She didn't mention the obvious fact that he had been almost chivalrous toward the schoolmarm. Meg was certain she must be thinking these things, but was too kind and generous to voice them.

They had popped a basket of popcorn over the library fire and played rummy. Meg kept Amy laughing with stories of her students and their rehearsals for their first school program.

"All their projects and alphabet prints are on display. And Micah will read the Twenty-third Psalm," Meg said with delight.

"He's only been reading since September!" Amy exclaimed.

Meg nodded. "I know. He's learned faster than any child I've ever taught before."

"What about Jacob? Still no improvement?"

"None. He's my first and foremost failure at Chisolm Crossing School."

"Now, Meg."

"No, it's true, Amy. Hatred radiates out of every pore on that child. I cannot find the key to Jacob Brown. Mrs. Chisolm—"

"The Crossing's only living almanac, medical guide, and teacher's reference book," Amy interrupted laughingly.

"Exactly. She says I should send him home, quote, 'in no uncertain terms with no return invitation.' I can't do that. The Browns want an education for Jacob as much as the Jeffersons or the Joneses do. Matilda says he's like his uncle."

Amy nodded. "Jonas Brown. He's sort of a Crossing legend. Backwoodsman type. Supposed to be violent," Amy supplemented.

"Matilda says Jacob is 'painted with the same brush as his uncle and make no mistake.' Matilda can be a real comfort sometimes! Anyway, I feel like I have a package just ready to explode in my classroom."

"A package! Your mail! I forgot!"

When the letter postmarked New Orleans had come to Tanglewood, Amy had known immediately it was from Andy. She had held the slim envelope in her hand, her mind returning effortlessly to those months Andy Alcott had been a guest of the Cash estate. The afternoon they had confronted each other in the stable was still vivid in her mind, an afternoon when so much had hung unspoken between them, things that could not be said. Or the night in the library when she had told him about her past. She saw again his eyes of compassion.

She had rebelled against falling in love with a man who was not her husband. But how could she not respond to one so gentle, one who had stirred her passions where Cash had not?

Meg took the letter from Amy wordlessly and absently, oblivious to Amy's searching, appealing eyes. She scanned the letter quickly and glanced up, finally realizing Amy was waiting.

"It's from Andy. I haven't heard from him in months. He's somewhere around South America."

"Isn't that where *Ivanhoe's Dream* sank?" Amy asked cautiously.

"Hmm? Oh, well, yes, but Andy's very careful. He's the captain and all that. He's doing fine."

Meg had been so involved in her work at Chisolm Crossing that the tension she felt toward Andy had been consistently and summarily dispatched to the back of her mind. Her disappointment in him was still sharp, and she did not know how to deal with it. It was a new and different thing between them. To confess and confront it would mean to accuse and condemn. She couldn't do that to him in person or in a letter even—only in her mind. The nagging thought that her accusations and condemnations were as wrong as what she suspected him of couldn't be faced either.

"He sounds lonely," Meg mused aloud.

"Everyone gets lonely sometimes," Amy replied softly.

The easiness and the humor of the evening was suddenly dispelled. Andy's letter had come between them. They both waited, silent. Would it open up what they had both kept closed with vigilance and effort?

Meg would not speak. She had grown very fond of Amy Cash. They were friends now. To speak of Andy could only bring censure, and she didn't want to do that.

Amy could not speak. Her gentleness, her modesty, and her sense of right were strongly ingrained. How could she admit she had fallen in love with a man who was not her husband?

Meg took her hand. "You should travel, Amy," she suggested impulsively. "You and Melanie. Go places, see things, perhaps meet someone . . ."

Amy gave a shaky laugh. "What about you?"

"Matilda Chisolm would be very pleased if I would remain a proper spinster schoolmarm, I'm sure. 'Men are generally weak and rather useless, Miss Alcott,'" Meg replied with a laugh.

"So you're going to please Mrs. Chisolm, hmm?" Amy taunted with a smile.

When Meg read the letter again in the privacy of her room, she found herself smiling at the last line Andy had penned.

"The tone of your last letter reminded me of a Peppercreek winter. What's up?"

Meg's smile faded. Caught in a web of her own making, she would keep silent.

Meg would not admit to herself that, like her students, she looked forward to Dr. Browning's Friday afternoon visits. She had not imagined that the children would enjoy them so, and that the doctor would be so different from what she had seen before. He was relaxed, answering all their questions patiently, kindly, and with a dose of humor.

During his first visit, she had gone to her room, assuming he would feel more comfortable if she were absent. She had hurried back into the classroom when she heard peals of childish laughter. Barrett was perched on the corner of the desk looking very silly. The children had taken a vow of silence and would not repeat the joke. Meg returned to her apartment suspecting she had been its subject.

Now each Friday she took special care over her appearance, freshening up just before his arrival. She had turned beet red when Chessie had innocently asked, "You prettyin' up for the Doc, Miss Ma'am?"

It was Friday afternoon when clouds suddenly darkened the classroom. Barrett quickly finished the lesson on nutrition.

"That's all for today, kids. Looks like a downpour is on the way."

Meg hurried forward, helping them with their jackets, pails, and books.

"All this talk 'bout food has just got me to nearly starvin'!" Toby exclaimed.

Everyone laughed. "Well, my ma was puttin' on stew when I left this morning," Micah said proudly. "There'll be vegetables and venison, so we'll be..."

"Well balanced," Barrett nodded. "You're a good listener, Micah."

"What will you be havin' tonight, Dr. B.?" Annie queried.

Barrett rubbed his chin. "Let's see. Probably a can of beans and a cup of coffee."

There was a collective hiss of disapproval.

"Doc, that's awful!"

"No nu...nu...nutritional nothing!"

"No nutritional value whatsoever!" True repeated proudly.

"Seems there is nothing wrong with my students' hearing or memories, Dr. Browning," Meg said laughing.

"Quite right, Miss Alcott. Now, off with you rascals."

"You should stay and eat supper with Miss Ma'am. She cooks fine," Chessie interrupted.

The other students agreed with this suggestion vigorously as they piled out the door.

"Off you go," Barrett spoke easily.

The schoolroom was quiet, and Meg felt very awkward.

"Well, I do have plenty. I mean, nothing elaborate but if you'd like to stay, Dr. Browning, it's the least I can do for the trouble you take for these Friday lessons."

Barrett studied the worn sole of his boot, struggling to hide his amusement. Not since their first meeting had he seen the formal Miss Alcott so nervous.

"You needn't feel an obligation to invite me, Miss Alcott." His mouth pulled at the corner, which she recognized as his effort to control a smile. "But I'd be delighted to dine with you."

As she made the simple supper preparations, Barrett sat at her desk reading a newspaper. He looked relaxed and perfectly at ease, as if he did this every day after his calls.

"If only your feet were propped up on my desk, this would be quite the domestic scene!" Meg called out as she passed the doorway with a steaming bowl in her hands.

She froze, horrified at what her impulsive words could suggest.

She hurried back to her stove, her face flaming. She did not know how the man in the next room struggled with the temptation to do what she had suggested. She almost hated going back into the schoolroom, and hoped the doctor had the decency to pretend as if he had not heard her.

The paper was before him, but Barret could hardly concentrate. He could not keep his mind on the facts and figures in black for thinking of the woman who moved in the adjoining room. He was surprised at her sudden cordiality. She had haughtily snubbed him at their first meetings, then scorned him for his Klan involvement. Now she was sitting down to dinner with him. He wondered if the voluble little storekeeper had been talking. The corners of his mouth turned up in a slight smile. What did this truce mean...to him?

They cleared off her desk, Barrett's face as bland as usual. They sat down, Meg trying very hard, and succeeding very little, in relaxing.

Barrett assumed a professional look and tone as he surveyed the meal. "All food groups included. I'm impressed."

Meg smiled her thanks. Barrett talked now, more than Meg would have imagined someone so normally sober and offensive could talk. Her nervousness turned to amazement. He seemed like someone different, very unlike the man she was so accustomed to sparring with. He talked about the parents of some of her students, giving Meg valuable insights into her children.

Then he shook his head and told Meg some lighter aspects of his work. She found herself laughing.

The clouds darkened the schoolroom, and Meg rose to light another lamp. When she sat back down, Barrett was quiet. He leaned back in his chair, his eyes resting on the table before him. Again that domestic feeling crowded into Meg's mind. She pushed the thought aside quickly, forcing animation that she did not feel into her voice.

"I hope everything was all right, Dr. Browning, and that you don't regret your supper of beans and coffee."

He looked up then—and looked at her too long.

"You are an excellent cook, Miss Alcott. I enjoyed the meal greatly."

"Thank you." Meg suddenly felt very nervous. He was looking so intent, so grim—the same way he usually looked. What had caused the change?

"Would you care for more tea?" she asked.

He was looking out the window now. "Thank you, no. I need to be going."

Yet he made no move. Finally, he said slowly, "Are you ever lonely, Miss Alcott?"

It was such an unexpected question. "Yes, sometimes. I keep busy though."

Meg was startled. His face was more than tired now, more than sad. It was a look of complete vulnerability.

"Are you?" she asked gently.

He did not meet her look. "Like you, my work keeps me busy."

When he did look, he could tell she was unsatisfied with his answer. He also knew for this rare and fleeting moment, they both had dropped their guard of antagonism.

"Yes, I get lonely."

Meg was grateful for the sudden, window-rattling peal of thunder. Instinctively they both stood and walked wordlessly to the window. The rain was coming down in heavy slashes. Meg stood with her arms around herself, feeling cold, and feeling the nearness of Barrett Browning.

"Thank you again for dinner," Barrett spoke in a low voice, still gazing out the window.

Meg said nothing. When he whirled around to face her a moment later, Meg could read in his face that he had been struggling with something and come to a decision.

He stepped closer, feeling as if he was being pulled forward by an unseen hand.

"You're...welcome...for dinner," Meg faltered nervously.

Another step.

"I...I'd better...go now." His voice had gone hoarse.

"Yes..."

A step closer, till there were no steps between them.

"Well, I'd better go," he repeated, as if an enchantment had addled his powers of conventional or creative speech.

"You'll get terribly wet," she whispered.

"Soaked."

He leaned over her now, his face buried in her hair, his arms going around her.

"I'm...leaving."

"Yes...I...suppose...you should."

"It's...late."

"Late..."

He was kissing her. She tightened her arms around him.

It was funny the things that raced through her mind when passion should have dominated. First, she was warm, deliciously warm. She was surprised at the firmness of his arms, the muscles as they tightened. She would have liked to spend more time feeling just his arms. Then there was the smell. He smelled of woodsmoke and pipesmoke and something medicinal that she couldn't identify.

Meg was glad it was raining, and glad now of Chessie's suggestion. She relaxed and stopped thinking, except one thought—that he would go on kissing her.

But he stopped and pulled away. She heard him sigh, a sad and reluctant sound. He shook his head gravely.

"I'm very sorry, Miss Alcott. I shouldn't have done that."

"You sound like you've just pronounced a fatal disease," she said in a shaky voice.

He glanced around for his bag and hat. "We were both lonely tonight."

Meg felt tears rising as she nodded to him.

She stood looking out the window for a very long time, unaware that her nearest neighbor was at her window as well, shaking her head grimly.

Chisolm Crossing
Fall, 1894

◆◆ ◆◆ ◆◆

*T*he schoolmarm was weeding the flower bed beside the schoolhouse. She could have done a multitude of other things on this first day back to the Crossing. Yet weeding was what she felt like doing; it gave her that feeling of really being home.

She'd spent several hours of the time talking with Chester and Matilda on the front steps of the mercantile. They had plenty to tell her in view of her near three-month absence. There had been a few births, a couple of accidents, and news of her students. Meg had wanted to hear it all. She was no longer the interloper, the newest resident of Chisolm Crossing. Things that happened, happened to people she knew and cared about. From all the world over, finally Meg Alcott had a place of belonging.

She was eager to unpack her trunk and sort through the new school supplies she had brought from Illinois. But that could wait until tomorrow. After all, school did not open for another week. School...her second year already! It had been 12 months since she stood in front of the new school with such expectation and hope. Every dream, every hope, had been more than met. The opposition hadn't succeeded in closing the school. The doors were open to receive children again.

Tonight she wanted to weed until the evening shadows made it impossible to see. Then she would go into her little apartment, brew some tea, and think. There was so much to think about; she could stay awake until sunrise.

The months Meg had spent at Peppercreek had been her first opportunity to be with Andy since their voyage together. A homecoming with all her family, a time of pleasure, yet it had been shadowed by the distance between her and Andy. Constraint replaced closeness.

They had talked and laughed. She had told him about her school and students, about the unyielding Jacob Brown, and about the sagacious Matilda Chisolm. She spoke lightly about Tanglewood and Amy Cash. With hawklike eyes, she waited for a response from him.

Meg could not picture Amy's daughter with her blue eyes, fair complexion, light brown halo of hair without thinking of Andy. And she could not think of Andy without a flash of anger. How could he neglect a growing daughter?

Then she had spent a week at Tanglewood with Amy and Melanie. Amy was glowing with high spirits. She had spent the summer at a rented cottage on the Carolina coast. She had introduced Melanie to the ocean and put away for a time the gloom and isolation of Tanglewood. Meg could clearly see that the time away had invigorated her and pushed away the loneliness so often in Amy's eyes.

Finally, she would turn over the conversation with Matilda in her mind. That alone would keep her awake most of the night. Chester had hugged her tightly and told her he missed her more than molasses on biscuits. Matilda had given her a tight-lipped smile and even allowed "they'd all be busier now, with Miss Alcott back. The store will surely suffer."

Chester and Meg had controlled their impulse to smile at this, passing an affectionate glance between them. As much as Meg felt for the big-hearted storekeeper, she felt a measure also for the store-keeper's wife. She suspected, too, that Matilda Chisolm had grudgingly made a place for her in her own heart.

"Luke Jones brought in a bag of hickory nuts this morning," Chester was saying. "Never seen such thick shells before. Must have been half an inch thick! Means we'll have a cold winter."

"I hardly think they were that thick," Matilda retorted tartly.

"Well, they were thick and . . . say, there's the doc! Howdy, Barrett!"

From the crossroads, a lone rider had approached. It was Barrett Browning. The doctor rode up but did not dismount.

Meg had spoken perhaps half a dozen words to this man in the months since their supper in the schoolroom. Mere words of greeting, nothing more. Meg lifted her eyes to him with difficulty. She hadn't seen him in months, and now he was here before her, looking fatigued and guarded as ever.

She could almost feel the piercing look of Matilda Chisolm on her neck.

"Hello, Miss Alcott," Barrett said with typical formality.

No suggestion that they had ever shared a kiss, a kiss that had burned between them like a flame—a flame so quickly ignited, so abruptly extinguished.

"Doctor."

"Meg got back this morning," Chester persisted. If only he could get these two to quit acting like third cousins once removed.

"Did you have a pleasant visit home?" Barrett asked.

"Yes, it was very nice, thank you."

Barrett turned his eyes away from her at last. He must economize his looking at her from now on. She seemed to get more lovely each time he saw her.

He made an impatient gesture with his hand. "Any mail for me, Ches?"

"Nope. Sit with us, Barry. It looks like you could use a cold drink and a handful of gingersnaps."

"Thanks, but I need to get home. I may have a surgery in the morning. Good night, folks."

They watched him ride away in silence.

"I don't recall ever seeing a man who looked more like he needed a wife. Works all hours, sleeps less. Heaven knows what he feeds himself," Matilda said with typical bluntness.

"Well, I never seen a man look more like he was trying to kill himself with work," Chester countered.

"Are you suggesting that death is preferable to having a wife?" Matilda pursued with petty annoyance.

Chester winked at Meg and yawned dramatically. "Only saying that in the Best Book it does say that in heaven there'll be no marrying or givin' in marriage."

Matilda leaned forward, her bun of gray hair punctuating her words. "And I suppose you take real comfort in that!"

Meg smothered a laugh and turned back to the woods that had swallowed the doctor up in its evening gloom. She would pull the Chisolms away from a possible feud.

"Chester, do you remember telling me when I first came here that Dr. Browning had his own personal devils?"

Chester rubbed his chin thoughtfully, not meeting Meg's eyes.

"I suppose I said something of that color. Meant only that his past troubles him."

Meg ignored his obvious reluctance. She was on the scent of something. "*What* about his past?"

Chester Chisolm did not want to deny Meg Alcott anything. He would reach for the moon if she asked him to. Yet Barrett was his friend too, and the man had a past guarded and buried like an ill-gotten treasure. Chester would feel like a traitor to speak of it. Still, it might breach this impasse between the schoolmarm and the doctor...

"Well—"

"Mr. Chisolm, why don't you go on to bed. Let me visit with Miss Alcott—alone." Matilda's voice was firm, broaching no argument.

Unexpectedly, Chester smiled. Yes, this wife of years did have a generous heart, well buried at most times and seasons... He hopped up eagerly. "A fine idea, 'Tilda, a fine idea. Glad you're back, Meg, sure am! Good night."

Meg waited. She had never spent much time alone with Matilda Chisolm. Matilda, however, was open and ready for business.

"You asked about the doctor," she began without preface.

"Yes, but I don't mean to pry, really."

"Oh, I don't know that a little prying isn't healthy from time to time. Sleeping with a troubled conscience can be a terrible thing. I never have that malady myself. But Mr. Chisolm can rest easy. I can tell you enough about Barrett Browning." The older woman paused and collected her thoughts, unseeing of the purple shadows that fringed the pines.

"His past is like a sickness. I suppose he's wise enough to see it, just too weak to treat it. Men can be so weak, you know."

"What is his past?" Meg asked softly.

Matilda was blunt. "His mother. I knew Elizabeth Browning, or knew of her. I don't suppose anyone really knew her. She was a Yank, a Northerner, and I will concede she was quite a beauty. She married Barrett's father sometime before the war. He brought her back to the Crossing, and she found it wholly unacceptable. She struck me as a flighty woman, unsuited to housekeeping or child-raising, and yes, I can judge such things.

"From remarks she dropped, it was evident she expected Barrett's father to greatly improve their station in life. Barrett's father was a farmer, and a good one, but there certainly wasn't enough profit to make them wealthy. I remember quite vividly Barrett's father coming here to shop while Elizabeth Browning stayed in the wagon and read novels and poetry." Matilda's voice dripped with scorn.

"Did you say poetry?" Meg asked.

"I did, Miss Alcott, poetry. When Frank Browning came home from the war, he wasn't well. Nothing that time and a proper home life wouldn't put right. Elizabeth hadn't the patience to wait, though. She left when a minstrel troupe from New York passed through Greenville. I am not gossiping, Miss Alcott," Matilda added spiritedly.

"I'm sure you're not, Mrs. Chisolm. Please go on."

"Barrett was devoted to them both. I can remember the look in his young eyes as he watched his mother go. He loved her very much."

"How old was he when she left?" Meg asked in choked voice.

"I'm sure he could tell you to the minute how old he was. I think he was around six."

"Six!" Meg exclaimed softly.

"But he grew up very fast after that. Took care of his father, who never recovered from Elizabeth's leaving."

Matilda pulled on a philosophical face. "Of course I maintain she hadn't enough character to be worth having around, but men can be so dependent. Frank never would say the woman wasn't fit to Barrett."

Meg was silent there on the step as the puzzle pieces began falling into place.

"Rightly or wrongly, Miss Alcott, Barrett Browning grew up having very little use for women in general and Yankee women in particular."

Meg cried that night, under the cover of darkness and the privacy of her room—cried for a little boy with a broken heart who had grown up too soon. And for the man who had "little use for women in general and Yankee women in particular."

With a new term beginning, Meg was as ambitious as ever. This year she hoped to include the parents of her students in her plans, to bring them together socially more often, and to find a place of beginning in their education. She invited Mim to the schoolhouse for tea one Saturday morning when school had been in session only a few weeks.

"So you see, Mim, I really do need your help. I have 30 students. I need an assistant."

The face could have been lovely if it had not been so beaten by fatigue and fear.

"Oh, Miss Alcott."

"Meg."

"Meg...I don't know nothin' 'bout being a..."

"A helper. Just help me with 30 eager, energetic little and not-so-little bodies. That's all. I'll do the teaching."

"What 'bout Susannah?"

"You'll bring her. We'll fix up a sort of nursery in my private room. You can feed and care for her when she needs you. I can even ask one of the older girls to watch her when you're busy. I'm sure they'll like that."

The bright look that had come quickly to Mim's face vanished. Her eyes dropped to the folded hands in her lap.

"I don't know, Miss Meg. Folks might not like that."

"Oh, their children won't suffer for a little babysitting."

"No, I mean Susannah's being as she is."

"Mim? I don't understand."

"Her color, Miss Meg. Her color. See, she ain't black, and she ain't white. She don't exactly have a fittin' in place." The loving hand smoothed the forehead of the sleeping child. "Times be hard for my little gal, but she's been a wrapped in prayer."

Meg swallowed against the indignation that rose in her throat. With effort she pushed the arrogant face of Jeb French from her mind.

"Mim, listen. If your neighbors see that I accept little Susannah, perhaps that will help them accept her also. She's just a child. Oh, Mim, please come and help me. Chester says he'll loan you a mule to ride back and forth on."

"Why are you helping me, Meg?" Mim asked with the shyness of a child.

"I want to, Mim."

"Think I could learn to read a bit by listenin' as I helped you?"

Meg's smile was wide. "I think you'll be reading by Christmas!"

Jacob Brown had not returned to Chisolm Crossing School when it
opened its doors for its second fall term. Let the babies go to the white
school. He had kept his part of the bargain with his father, and now a
new hunting rifle stood propped in the corner by his bed. He would stay
home and work the land beside his father, like a man should. When his
sisters brought home news about the school, he turned scornful. Yet
when they weren't looking, he devoured their readers.

Jacob Brown did not like to take orders from any white man. His
Uncle Jonas boasted that he never had. But the gold coins that Jeb
French flashed before him proved too strong a temptation. They would
get him more than just a rifle.

If only for a little while, he would do the white man's bidding. He
could do the spying, the watching—gladly in fact—against the proper
Yankee schoolteacher.

"Miss Ma'am! Miss Ma'am!"

Meg had lit her lamp and begun her supper when the insistent
knocking came to the schoolhouse door. She hurried to unlock it.

"Temple? What's the matter? Is it little True?"

The older boy stood hopping from one bare foot to the other on the
front steps, the night throwing on a blanket of early autumn chill.

"Yes, Ma'am. He's worse and callin' for ya, and Pa says if you wouldn't
mind comin'..."

"Yes, of course I'll come. Let me grab my cape."

Moonlight illuminated the flat schoolyard where Temple stood holding the reins of a horse.

"Doc is there already and sent ya his horse to ride," the boy explained.

Meg smiled to herself. Was Barrett thinking of her then, or was this
simply a gesture of common courtesy?

As she rode through the forest with Temple behind her, she could not
help but think of Barrett and what Matilda had told her months earlier. It
explained so much and made him vulnerable when he didn't even know
it. It had thawed the last defense in her heart.

She had seen him very infrequently, and very briefly, since that night
when Matilda opened up his past. They had resumed the Friday afternoon classes with Barrett acting thoroughly professional. He came at
the appointed time, not a moment earlier, and left exactly when the
children filed out. It was flagrantly obvious that the doctor was determined not to be alone with her.

A campaign then . . . with the strategy of a general. She would show him women could be faithful, devoted, vital—and that all Yankees weren't dishonest opportunists. She had heard enough from her father about those long-ago battles at Sharpsburg, Antietam, and Bull Run, to know a measure of military skill. So how formidable were the defenses of the heart?

"Kinda scary tonight," Temple said, pulling Meg's thoughts back to the mission at hand.

"Scary?"

"Spooky, Miss Ma'am. So full of shadows and trees a bendin' and the wind a moanin'."

Meg laughed. "Spooks are in your imagination, Temple. This is a beautiful night."

Neither would imagine that a figure treaded beside them in those shadows.

The cabin came into view with light streaming out the two small windows, the smoke a curling tendril from the rock chimney.

"Miss Ma'am, you think my little brother is gonna die?"

She squeezed his hand. "He is very sick. I don't know, Temple. We've been praying for him."

She was greeted by the strong smell of onions as she stepped into the cabin. An onion plaster had been made for the little boy whose lungs were so terribly congested and inflamed. Dr. Browning would be trying to work with the spirited opinions of Granny. She was not surprised that the common room was nearly filled; she had seen that before. Grand-parents, uncles hunched over by the fireplace, half a dozen children sprawled in sleep or playing quietly though it approached midnight, a huddle of women around True's mother. It was another tradition, like the onion plaster. She should not expect to find the doctor in a very congenial mood.

Barrett stood at the bed, True's thin wrist in his hand as he took his pulse. He gave Meg a cursory look, but no word.

"Little True, it's teacher. It's Miss Ma'am."

The eyes fluttered open and rested on her face.

"Miss Ma'am, am I that . . . late that you come . . . for me?"

She smiled. "Don't try to talk, True. I came to see you. I'm going to sit here by you while you rest and get better, all right?"

"Sure am hot. They won't let me take the covers off . . ."

He drifted back to sleep, and Meg turned to Barrett, her voice well lowered. "How high is his temperature?"

"One hundred and three."

She sponged his face and gave him drink for three hours with Barrett at her side, never saying a word.

"He's been sleeping for a while," she said glancing around the room where the family sprawled in exhaustion. "I'm going to step out and get some fresh air."

The moon was high in the quiet yard, the chill welcome after the smells and warmth of the cabin.

Barrett followed her.

"How is he doing?" Meg asked.

"Not as well as I'd like. He's had that high fever too long."

"Well, I can hardly think a cabin full of people is healthy! Aren't they at least concerned about contagion, or just peace and quiet for the patient? I don't see how his parents allow it."

"If the patient is going to die, they want to all be there to say goodbye."

"I'm sure that's little comfort to the patient, seeing them all gather! It's...it's morbid!"

He smiled a frigid smile. "A fitting word, Miss Alcott, but the facts remain, it's their custom."

"As the doctor you should do something. You should insist they leave. And that pipe smoke!"

His smile vanished. She was sounding like she had as Mim's midwife, accusing in her passion.

"It's enough they let me come, Miss Alcott, and that they don't just send for Granny and her ancient arts." His voice was acid. "You've charmed them. I don't have the skill and Yankee charm you have."

He was very tired and too nervous about losing this precious little boy to be either patient or diplomatic.

She flared then, wiping away in an instant any designs to win Barrett with gentleness and sweetness.

"You have no right to have this idea about me based on what you think I am! With your bigotry, you're no different from Jacob Brown!"

"*My* bigotry!" Barrett's voice was as chilly as the night air.

"Yes, your bigotry! I am who I am, Barrett Browning—not a Yankee woman first and a person second. I'm me, with all my flaws and imperfections. Me, Meg Alcott." She had worked herself into a finely controlled rage. "Despise me for something I've done or said, but not for where I'm from! Get rid of your expectations, Doctor; they are really wrong."

The word *expectation* sent something tolling in her memory, but she could not think of it now. She regretted her rage, regretted that she had spoken of his past so unlike she had intended. He would retreat even further now.

She stepped up to him. "I'm sorry I implied you weren't doing your job properly. I didn't mean that, Barrett."

His face was set like stone, his arms crossed. She searched his eyes for some response and found none. She returned to the cabin alone.

It was nearly noon of the following day when Meg left the cabin. True had improved. Barrett had managed a smile and said the boy would recover now.

Exhausted as she was, she felt like walking back to the Crossing in the crisp morning air. The woods were warm, fragrant, and peaceful.

"Are you following me, Doctor?" she asked coyly, when she heard him behind her. He was leading his horse.

"Yes, I am. I think you're foolish to walk when you can ride. You didn't get much sleep last night."

His voice held no edge, no bitterness. She smiled; perhaps he had forgiven her for her impulsive, heated words.

She waited until he came up to her. "I . . ." She tilted her head, looking up into the sunshine that reflected all around him. Her heart was pounding. He was looking at her very much like he had the stormy afternoon in the schoolhouse.

It had come to this moment.

"Why are you so angry with me, Barrett? I mean, before last night." She could see her words surprised him.

"Yes, I'm angry. Sometimes I feel I'm insanely angry."

"Don't follow me then. Let me go my way. Don't be concerned if I walk or ride."

He laughed. "Let you go your way, hmm?" He came to stand very close to her, within striking distance.

"Yes, let me go."

"If only I could, Miss Alcott."

His eyes went over her face with such tenderness, she felt as if he had caressed her.

"You came here," he said haltingly, "and have taken away any shred of peace I've ever had. You."

"How have I taken your peace, Barrett?"

He sighed deeply then, not meeting her eyes.

"I've fallen in love with you, against my will." He lifted his eyes. "I don't want to love you."

She stared into his blazing eyes and smiled weakly.

"I can be loyal, Barrett. I can love. I can . . ."

"Has Chester or Matilda been talking to you? Gossiping?" he said with a touch of the old stiffness.

"What does it matter, Barrett? I'm going now."

But he caught her arm, pulling her almost savagely into the tight circle of his arms. "Oh, Lord, help me," he whispered.

Spring, 1895

"Children, do you remember we were talking about the world and its shape the other day?"

Gathered around her, they nodded their heads eagerly. They were in the meadow for a Friday afternoon picnic. They called it their meadow and never tired of playing, and exploring, and learning in it.

"Tick drew a circle on the board to show you what I meant when I said the world was round. Chessie, you and Temple come here, please."

She opened the basket and pulled out an orange.

"Oooh. What is it?"

"It's called an orange. It's a fruit. Here." She placed one in each pair of open hands. "Feel the roundness. This is the shape of the world."

"There's one for each of you. I want you to thank Mrs. Chisolm when you go home today. She had them sent here from New Orleans for you."

They were speechless as they touched and smelled the fruit.

"Ain't God such a mighty thinkin' God, Miss Ma'am? He made this fruit and the world so much bigger and us all." Tick's face was solemn, and Meg knew the next words he would speak. "World without end, amen and amen!"

They all laughed then, delighted with the gift, delighted with all they were learning. Miss Alcott could put the world in their hands!

Micah and Tick had climbed a nearby tree to enjoy their fruit. From their branch they saw him first.

"There's the doc! There!"

Meg's head snapped up. At the edge of the clearing, Barrett sat on his horse. Clearly, he was watching them.

Even from the distance, he could hear her—not the words, but her tone. He would know her voice above a million others; he could hear it in the depths of his dreams. He had watched her brush back her hair . . . beautiful hands. One of the children had said something that made her laugh. She looked so young and at ease . . .

Across the meadow, their eyes met, pulled, and held. Meg didn't hear any of the little voices around her. She could hear only her own heartbeat, see only Barrett. It was as if he was waiting for her. She stood up.

"Stay here, children. I need to speak with Dr. Browning a moment."

A few exchanged puzzled glances; Miss Ma'am did have an odd look on her face!

Meg walked across the meadow directly to Barrett. She felt no hesitation or trepidation. He did not seem surprised to find her coming to him. They waited.

"How's Mrs. Morgan?" she asked softly.

"She's doing fine. Woke up about two this morning."

Silence again, yet they were locked in each other's eyes.

"You need to go home and get some sleep. You look exhausted." Her voice was embracing him.

"I'm on my way there now."

He leaned down to push aside the lock of hair that a breeze had ruffled across her forehead. She took his hand then and laid it against the warmth of her cheek.

He could say anything; he could say nothing at all. It didn't matter to Meg. Her heart was there plainly for him.

Then he pulled away, his eyes betraying no emotion, no reflection of feeling. He swallowed hard, wanting to say so much.

She smiled then, seeing his hesitation. It was a brilliant smile he wouldn't find easy to dismiss from his mind when he lay down to sleep. She was waiting for him to come to her when he could, when nothing else pulled him. She would wait.

Yet she couldn't suppress a last fling of feminine coquetry. "Pleasant dreams, Dr. Browning!" she called over her shoulder as she turned back to the children.

Chapter 26

The Mississippi River

♦♦ ♦♦ ♦♦

*I*ts history was a tarnished one, the mighty Mississippi. It could be tranquil, peaceful, and drifting, then terrifying and raging, eating away shorelines and sweeping away boundaries and life in an instant. Farms, landings, fields, forests, villages, and towns could disappear overnight.

A steamboat captain could never be certain the river he ran down would prove faithful on the return trip. New curves would appear, new sandbars and snags, new threats and dangers. Those who lived within a hundred miles lived with an eye to the river. Rains of any duration meant floods of proportion. The mighty Mississippi was like a slumbering giant, nothing to grow complacent or cynical about.

It had been docile too long. Now prolific rains from an unusual storm throughout the Midwest had swollen the river, engorging it until it looked like a pulsing vein ready to rupture.

Greenville

The waterfront street of Greenville was wrapped in a fog, a thick fog like wet, gray cotton. When it wasn't actually raining, as it had been for the last few weeks, the sun remained hidden behind a haze thick enough to cut. The work of the waterfront went on, the loading and unloading, the work and repairs on the ships themselves. Yet no ship left its berth until those times when the sun would penetrate and melt the thickness, especially since the river had risen four feet in the last month.

Bold as he was, Jacob Brown hurried his steps. He knew better than to be late for a meeting with the mighty Jeb French. The boy slipped into the inner office silently. He stood before French in a posture of defiance, though his insides churned. The man could get nasty, especially if he'd been drinking.

"You're late," French snapped from where he stood at the window.

Jacob smiled tightly. "Passed the clock in the other office, and it's five till. I'm not late."

French smiled then. Even if this was a darky, he was a shrewd one. "Well?"

"Nothing much going on."

"I don't pay you for nothing much."

Jacob took a deep, steadying breath. "School's out in one week. She's going to move to Tanglewood for the summer." He thrust his chin out. "Found out they're gonna travel together this summer."

French laughed. "A spinster schoolmarm and a widow off to see the sights, huh?"

He lit a fine cigar. "Doctor been around her lately?"

"Ain't seen 'em together alone since that time in the woods. Plain though."

"And just what's plain to you, Brown?"

Jacob was instantly regretful. He should stick to facts, not opinion. "She's sweet on the doc. Anyone can see that."

French regarded him with a sneer and silence.

"You'd find out more 'bout how she feels from Mim," Jacob burst out impulsively. "They talk all the time. Not 'bout school always."

The boy hesitated, suddenly uncertain, nervous, a thrust of conscience rising up.

French leaned forward with ferretlike eyes. "Yes?"

"Well, it's just that I heard 'em talkin' 'bout takin' Mim along on this summer trip. Ain't heard where."

French flipped a coin into the air, which Jacob deftly caught.

"Don't come back here unless I send for you or you have something better to tell me than this old lady gossip. Now get."

Jacob's nervousness disappeared, replaced by his seething hatred of this man.

Jeb French wanted Tanglewood. He had wanted Amy Cash even longer. Possessing Tanglewood would give him the status he had hungered for so long. He could become a powerful Southern landowner overnight. Taking the one guaranteed the other. Fear had worked in the past; it would work again.

New Orleans

Andy Alcott stood watching the crates of coffee beans being unloaded from the hold of the *Magnolia*. The brawny, sweating stevedores tossed the crates upward as if they were children's blocks.

Ben came to stand beside Andy. "The men are talking about the next trip. You haven't given anybody any clues about where the *Magnolia* is headed. They're gettin' kind of itchy about it."

Andy smiled. "I couldn't decide, but I have now. We've all been on voyage for over three years. I think it's time we put land under our feet for a while; let *Magnolia* rest."

Ben's grin was wide. "They'll be glad to hear that. Are you going home to Illinois?"

Andy leaned against the rail and shook his head. He had fought for peace and finally earned it.

"Nope, not Illinois just yet. I'm going to see my sister. I'm off to Mississippi!"

Chisolm Crossing

A room filled with 30 excited children was a testing situation for the best of teachers. With the close of school only two days away, Meg was beginning to think the very walls might burst with their young laughter and enthusiastic singing. She could not, and did not want, to harness their high spirits. She couldn't scold or frown—they made her join them in laughter at their very joy of living. They were affectionate and repaying her in riches she would not trade.

A young girl and boy were leading the class in a spelling bee as Mim helped them. Meg sat to the side of the class, smiling and encouraging, and sewing on a button that had flown from Temple's trousers in a fit of giggling. She was listening with half attention, called back immediately when a spelling was in question. She was thinking over the year that would conclude in two more days. Two years already...

This year had been a special one as she watched her students blossom as their learning increased. It was special because Mim had joined her. She looked at the woman across the room. She was leaning over a young speller with a smile. The shadows of fear and loneliness had faded from her brown eyes. She had purpose now. Meg could not imagine how she would have taught without the woman's aid. She had become invaluable. Meg smiled when she thought of some of her friends back home. They would be just a little surprised that Meg counted a poor black woman as one of her dearest friends. They had moved from mere acquaintances to friendship, laughing over the day or plotting some strategy together over a difficult aspect of teaching.

Mim understood the children. She shared the same humble, obscure past, with a colorless, limited future. She was like them too in that she had so little but had given so much. Meg was hoping Chisolm Crossing School was changing that. It had been a highlight of her year when Mim had learned to read. Meg would never forget that day. The woman's head was bent over a primer, her voice low and shy, stumbling, then triumphant!

"Bob...has...a...dog. His...name is...Tip. Tip is...a...big dog."

Mim had thrown her arms around Meg's neck and cried. A new world had opened up to her.

This year there had been no Klan threat, no murmurings from the white community. It had been of no small significance that when her students presented a Christmas play, half the audience was white. Granted most came from curiosity and the diversion on a Friday night, but they had come. They had sat in a school for black children and seemed not to notice, or at least care, that Mary and Joseph were black. Meg hadn't heard any cutting remarks or derisions. She would not forget Mrs. Chisolm's words when the play was over and the families were leaving the school. The storekeeper's wife had been surprised with the turnout as well. In the distance someone was singing a Christmas hymn.

"Churches can divide a community, a school can bring it together—even a black school. I would allow that you have worked a small miracle here, Miss Alcott."

A small miracle! It was the first real praise Meg could remember from this woman, who was very economical with her approval. But she valued the words as much as if they had come from Chester.

Meg glanced around the room. Maps, artwork, and penmanship lessons proudly decorated the walls. In one corner stood a grocery box fashioned into a mailbox. Meg wondered if this particular teaching tool had been a positive addition to her schoolroom. Mrs. Chisolm had been disdainful and snorted loudly, but her students had loved it.

"I want you to write any questions you may have concerning things in school that you are curious about. Anything that I can share with the class, and we can discuss together. You do not need to sign your names."

The box had been stuffed full the first Friday. Meg reached in blindly and selected three slips of paper.

"Do stars die in the morning?"

"Should I let a boy kiss me at recess?"

"Why do men get drunk at times?"

Meg had immediately regretted the project. She quickly substituted a replacement.

"This will be for those students who receive good marks on their spelling papers for three weeks in a row. I've talked with a teacher in Illinois at a school—"

"Over the phone?" Chessie asked in awe.

"Yes, Chessie. She teaches at the school where I used to teach. She and I have decided it would be a fun project for her students and my students to become pen pals. You would write letters to children your own age and they would write back."

"They white or black, Miss 'Cott?"

"Chessie, you need to raise your hand when you have a question. And they would be white children."

"They'll write us back!"

"Yes."

It was another, small, seemingly insignificant measure of healing between North and South.

There had been the usual leaven of trouble in the school, but it had generally been innocent mischief. She looked at the young boy in the third row. He felt her look and winked. She could not suppress a smile. Leonard had been her first and only attempt at paddling. He had been disruptive and disobedient all week long, and Meg's patience had worn very thin.

"I shall have to paddle you, Leonard, if you don't behave!"

The challenge was out of her mouth, too late to recall it. She must follow through, or lose respect.

She knew from old teaching journals that the paddling ability of a teacher was often considered more valuable to students' parents than academic credentials. It seemed barbaric and absurd to her sensibilities. If paddling strength measured a teacher's worthiness, then she had failed miserably. But now she must paddle Leonard as she had threatened.

The schoolroom was empty, save for the teacher and the victim. Leonard looked far more curious than repentant. Could the gentle Miss Ma'am really wallop like his pa?

"All right, Leonard . . ."

He had taken the swat, then stood up and smiled amiably at her.

"Don't believe you took the dust out of my britches with that one, Miss Ma'am," he said seriously.

She struggled to keep the stern look intact on her face. She never paddled Leonard again that year. She didn't need to.

"Miss 'Cott, Miss 'Cott!" An eager voice was pulling Meg from her daydreams. A dispute needed her attention. The spelling bee was almost finished.

"Yes, Joe?"

"True is taking too long to spell his word, and our team thinks he should have to sit down."

"Just am thinkin', Joe," the little boy sputtered.

"There is a time limit, True," Meg replied. "What is the word, Miss Mim?"

"Bacon, Miss Alcott."

"True, you know that word. I know you can spell it," Meg encouraged. The boy's face was a puzzle of concern.

"I do know it, Miss Ma'am. It's just slipped my mind."

"Well, go ahead and give it a quick try."

His tongue came out and investigated the sides of his face as his eyes searched the ceiling for inspiration.

"Oh, Miss Ma'am, I just can't seem to 'member it at all, for wantin' to eat on it!"

The class erupted in laughter. The door to the schoolhouse opened slowly. Abby Mayhew and her three children stood in the doorway. The room grew instantly quiet. Everyone knew the unsociable woman on sight. Every eye was on her.

Meg sighed. This woman had waited till the second school year was nearly over. A grudging, stingy gesture—but a beginning. Meg recovered from her surprise and hurried forward.

"Mrs. Mayhew, welcome to Chisolm Crossing School."

She watched from the steps until the last figure was out of sight. A group of her students waved wildly from the final curve in the road. She waved back, smiling, feeling tears come to her eyes. Her second year was over. She laughed to herself as she thought how naive she had been then to think the children knew nothing. They may have been blank slates in academics, but they overflowed in other lessons she had needed to learn.

On this last day she had passed out the little gift bags she made for them and made a little speech of how it had been a good year and they were wonderful students. They had come to trust her and returned her love in greater measure than she had given.

Her eyes embraced the class, the black faces turned to her with expectation.

"I thought when I came here two years ago that you needed me. I've found... I've found I needed all of you just as much."

Now the schoolhouse was silent. Mim came to stand beside her.

"Hard to believe the year is over," she said softly.

Meg nodded. "Teachers are supposed to be eager for summer recess, but I'm not. This year went too quickly."

"Think it will rain out our party in the meadow tomorrow?" Mim asked, for the early summer rain had become a near daily event.

Meg speculated on the tumble of deep blue clouds on the eastern horizon. If only they would wait until late tomorrow. The children were eager for the party to be held in the meadow.

Matilda came across from the mercantile, baby Susannah perched on her expansive hip. Meg smiled. She'd seen the merchant woman balance a 20-pound sack of flour in the same professional fashion. She was swept again with gratitude for this woman. Matilda had taken to watching Susannah when Mim became busy with the school. It had come to a climax when the toddler pulled over a bucket of coal dust on herself. Matilda had been indignant.

"Think what might have been the results if this had been a bucket of hot ashes. This is no place for a nursery, Miss Alcott. You teach; I will manage the health and safety of this child."

Mim could not conceal her alarm. Could this tart-tongued, brisk woman possibly be a fit caretaker for her child? But Meg had given her a reassuring smile and things had gone fine.

"Here's your gal, Mim. She's been full of ginger all day. Run me ragged...Absolutely into everything."

"I'm sorry, Mrs. Chisolm," Mim apologized quickly.

"Never mind; I managed to control her. She has a bit of a sniffle; keep her covered tonight," Matilda warned as she turned back to the store. She hesitated. "Since school is over . . . you can bring her by some days if she gets too much for you."

"Thank you, Mrs. Chisolm."

"You look pale and worn, Miss Alcott. I'd go to bed early if I were you," Matilda added with yet another burst of energy and purpose.

"Thank you, Mrs. Chisolm."

The two reentered the schoolhouse.

"I think Mrs. Chisolm has grown quite fond of Susannah," Meg said with a laugh.

"You think so?" Mim's voice held a hint of skepticism.

Meg lowered her voice. "Chester explained it to me. She's like a turtle. You know, shell on the outside, all soft inside."

Mim turned a look toward the mercantile, her eyes full of thought.

They finished working in the quiet, stacking schoolbooks and sweeping. Meg did not notice the anxious glances Mim was giving her.

"Meg?"

"Hmm?"

"I've been thinking about that summer trip, about Susannah and I going with you and Miss Amy."

"Yes?"

"It does sound nice, and I'm very grateful. I just don't think I can go."

Meg put down the duster. The old reluctance and fear was troubling Mim's eyes.

"What's changed your mind, Mim?"

"Nothing exactly . . ." Her voice trailed off as she wrung her hands.

"Mim? You know you'd be our guest. You wouldn't come as a servant."

"I know, Meg."

"Then what is it, Mim?"

"It would make it difficult for you and Miss Amy, traveling with a colored woman and . . . Susannah. Might cause a fuss somewhere."

"Who put these thoughts into your mind, Mim?" Meg asked gently, though she could feel anger rising in her.

Meg could not bring light to all the shadows in Mim's life. She suspected who was behind this new fear. Her fists clenched. She could teach Mim to read, stir her from her isolation, but there was one thread to the past she could not break. The name had never been spoken between them.

Mim's eyes filled with tears. "You're a friend to me, Meg, like I never had before. I'm afraid for you, Meg!" she burst out.

"Afraid for me? Why?"

"I want you to be careful. Go to Miss Amy's."

"Mim, someone is making *you* afraid. Is it Jeb French?"

Mim's eyes widened in answer. "Just be careful, Miss Alcott. Please be careful."

Meg's prayer was answered. The rain clouds remained a very real and promising threat, but no drops fell until the picnickers were beginning to disperse from the meadow. Meg was satisfied. The children and their parents seemed to have had a good time with the program, games, races, and food. Her students had covered her lap in homemade gifts; their parents spoke their gratitude warmly.

The children had felt it was only fitting that the doctor should be invited. He had been a teacher to them as well. Meg watched for him, disappointed when he did not show and relieved when he arrived at last. He smiled at her, laughed with Chester, and teased the children. Meg was surprised when he agreed to run the three-legged race with Tick. She had never seen him so relaxed. More than once she had glanced up to find him smiling at her, smiling into her eyes as if he knew a secret, smiling at her like a tender touch.

The clouds were boiling as if angry from the restraint of a mighty hand. The tempo of the wind increased, the sun was blotted out in a quickly dropping curtain of gray. The meadow was empty save for the Chisolms, Mim and Susannah, Meg, and Barrett. They were hurrying to clean up the final debris.

"Ches, you and Matilda go ahead and take Mim and Susannah back to your place before this wind gets worse and the rain starts. I'll take Miss Alcott home."

At his words, everyone turned to look at him in surprise.

Chester's eyebrows became gray, fuzzy arches. Matilda wore a bland expression.

"You sure, Barry?" Chester asked with suspicion. He could not have the doctor antagonizing the schoolmarm as he typically did.

Barrett leaned forward, meeting Chester eye to eye.

"I'm absolutely sure, Ches. I've never been more certain."

Chester smiled and chuckled, giving Barrett a hearty slap on the back. Meg felt herself crimson with embarrassment.

They were alone, and Meg felt very nervous. A guarded Barrett she was accustomed to, but this was a new Barrett.

"We'd better hustle or we'll get soaked. You don't mind me taking you home, do you, Miss Alcott?"

"No…"

He was helping her up onto his horse. "Actually I meant taking you to my home. For tea."

"...All right."

The same house, the same spareness, but there was a difference. This house was clean and tidy, with everything in its place. A small fire crackled in the fireplace; tea things sat on the table covered with linen. Meg could not help but look at Barrett, who waited beside her.

He had planned this.

He lifted one of the fine cups. "This belonged to my paternal grandmother. She brought it from Scotland."

"It's very lovely."

"Let me show you what I've been working on."

He took her hand without embarrassment and opened a door.

The screened porch that ran the length of the house had been cleaned and scrubbed and set to its proper purpose. It gave a sweeping view of the valley. Two polished rockers with spotless cushions rested there.

"Oh, Barrett, what a beautiful view!"

"It is beautiful, isn't it? You should see the sun come up in the morning."

His voice told her he was like an eager schoolboy, proud of his work, eager to please her. He was smiling and watching her.

Back inside Meg took in the main room with its wood floors, huge ceiling beams, and massive rock fireplace.

"This is a beautiful house, Barrett."

"Do you think so?" Again she detected that eagerness.

"Yes, I do. I love the rock and the wood. Did you build it?"

"My father and I. We worked on it over the years till...he quit. It was never really finished. He hadn't much drive to do it after my mother left."

She glanced up to gauge his face. No guard, no tension.

"Let me show you my workroom. It's not much."

The closed bedroom was opened. It too had been cleaned. Meg walked beside the tables and shelves silently. Here was Barrett's meticulous, professional side.

"A fine lab, Doctor," Meg said with an ease she did not feel.

"Ready for tea?" he asked cheerfully.

His hands were steady as he poured their tea. Hers were not. She searched for small talk.

"Chester says he's never seen so much rain in all his years here."

Barrett nodded. "More rain than I've ever seen."

"Could Ford's Creek flood?"

"I think it bears watching. Tanglewood is on higher ground. I think Greenville and the towns on the Miss are in more danger."

There was silence then, and the steady cadence of falling rain.

Barrett did not drink his tea. He had pulled a trunk beside them before the fire. He opened it, and for only a moment did Meg see him hesitate.

His voice was firm. "This belonged to my mother. These are her things. My father couldn't part with them, though they pained him to have them around."

He lifted out a silk fan and a shawl.

"Barrett, please, I know this is painful."

"It's all right, Meg." His eyes were tender, loving. "I wouldn't do this if you hadn't given me the courage to—if you weren't here with me."

He lifted out a stack of books, the smell of roses like a perfume around them. "She loved poetry. See? Elizabeth Barrett Browning was her favorite. Now you know how I come by my name."

He drew an ivory-colored wedding dress, a mirror, quilts, laces and ribbons, and a photograph from the chest.

"This is of my parents."

Meg looked a long time, neither she nor Barrett saying a word. Barrett resembled his father. The woman looked young and happy, a dutiful wife and mother. Meg laid the photograph down and looked long into Barrett's eyes.

Barrett pulled her to her feet.

"Meg, you told your students once it was the heart of a person that matters. I've seen your heart enough to know it's your heart I want in my life. Just you, Meg, forever."

She took his strong, gentle, skilled hands in hers.

"And it's my heart you have forever."

His kiss swept away any doubt and buried the past. For Barrett, Meg was a new beginning. And such a beginning...

The window was open. A light breeze that brought the clean scent of wet pine ruffled the lace curtains. Meg was very awake. The day, with the party in the meadow, had been a demanding one. But the evening at Barrett's had left her feeling weak.

Now she thought of the rock house a few miles north—and the man who lived there alone. She hadn't thought him attractive when she first saw him. He was barely civil when they met on Mim's threshold. He was arrogant and remote, a challenge to the open and friendly men she'd known all her life.

Yet he had defied her with his very differences. She did not think of his arrogance or remoteness now. She thought of him as attractive, lean, protective, and masculine. She thought of how her love had grown in those hours at his home as he tried to please her, as he trusted her with his past.

Her thoughts were on the man as he had held her in the firmness of his arms, his lips finding her eyes and the softness below her ear. The passion he had flamed would steal her sleep. His words had been soft as he murmured into her hair.

"It seems you fit just right in my arms, Meg, like you've always belonged here...just tardy coming."

She smiled in the darkness; he had not been without his humor when he delivered her to the schoolhouse door. He bent over her hand in a most dignified and Southern tradition. His lips were warm on her flesh.

"I do this to satisfy Chester and shock Matilda, who is surely posting vigil at her parlor window for the schoolmarm's safety."

"I suspect that the manner you kissed me in your home or in the forest would better satisfy Chester," Meg said teasingly.

His eyes were like living gems in the darkness.

"Don't tempt me, Miss Alcott. Good night."

She smelled smoke then, a thin acrid smell that drifted in through her window. Immediately the memory of Barrett Browning vanished. She tensed. She had smelled that smell before, the pungent odor of a cigar.

She crept from her bed along the floor to the window. Carefully, so she couldn't be seen, she peered out to see a small, vivid, glowing orange circle in the depths of the trees.

Jeb French was watching the schoolhouse.

Tanglewood

It was a fine morning for a tea party. The sky was clear, brushed in cerulean, a reprieve from the rains.

Meg, Amy, and young Melanie sat on the garden patio. Melanie was a quiet child, yet today she sparkled and giggled with the fine tea party her mama and Aunt Meg had laid for her. They indulged and delighted in her. No shadows would fill this day.

Melanie skipped off to show Fenwick and the cook the party dress that Meg had given her. Amy looked at her friend wistfully. Meg was radiating with happiness.

Over her teacup she smiled. "I'm sorry Barrett couldn't come."

Meg smiled that almost secretive smile of one in love, whose thoughts never stray far and turn effortlessly back to the beloved.

"He was sorry to miss it too, but young Jeff Taylor's arm had to be set."

"Meg, I'm so glad for you and Barrett. Glad you finally realized just how right I was about him!"

"You're not the only one. Chester is triumphant! He declares Barrett and I give new meaning to Appomattox!" she said laughingly.

Amy joined her. "And Matilda the sage? What does she say?"

"'A very practical decision, Miss Alcott.' Matilda can wipe away romance in very swift order!"

"Mama! Come help me try my dress on!" Melanie called from the library.

Left alone, Meg sat staring at the lush gardens of Tanglewood without seeing them. In her happiness with Barrett, Meg felt Amy's loneliness, her bleak future, even more sharply. A discreet cough from Fenwick returned her to the present. The servant's face wore an arch look.

"A caller has just arrived, Miss Alcott."

Andy stepped from around the butler. *Andy.*

She thought suddenly of that morning more than three years ago when he'd appeared in her Galveston classroom. She had thought him dead.

She saw now how deeply she had wounded him with her coldness. How foolish she'd been! Terribly, blindly foolish. Why had she let anything come between them?

He was standing there, hands thrust in his pockets, trying to be casual, but the smile he wore told her he was nervous. How was she going to welcome him? She walked forward and took his hands in hers.

"Hello, sis."

The tears came at the sound of her name so gently spoken from his lips.

"Andy...Andy, I don't deserve your forgiveness. I—" She was crying.

"Aw, Meg." He pulled her to him. "Meg, it doesn't matter. Whatever happened, it's all right now. Don't cry."

She pulled away. "If I don't explain, I'll be such a coward. I've asked the Lord to forgive me."

"And that's what matters most, Meg."

"Andy, you have a right to know what happened between us. It will sound so foolish...so ugly...to put into words." She took a deep breath.

"When I came to Tanglewood and found Amy so young, and when you hadn't told me what to expect, I drew all kinds of conclusions. I figured you must have fallen in love with her and felt very guilty about it. And when she heard you hadn't died on the *Ivanhoe,* well, I decided from her reaction that she had fallen in love with you too. Then I saw Melanie...I thought she was your child, Andy. Truth or not, I let that come between us...I was so disappointed...I'm sorry, Andy, so sorry."

She couldn't lift her eyes to him. A flat voice came from behind them, and they turned.

"You thought...Andy was Melanie's father?"

Amy stood in the shadow of the French doors, her hands clutched together, her face very pale.

"Amy, I—" Meg began, feeling as though this beautiful day was becoming the worst day of her life.

Amy took a step onto the patio, speaking more to herself than them. "That's why you always kept yourself . . . a little apart from me. The look I sometimes saw in your eyes. You thought I . . . I was just like the rumors Jeb started about me."

She sank down onto an iron bench. "Why didn't anyone believe me? Melanie was my cousin's baby, just as I said."

She covered her face, crying. Meg came to kneel before her.

"Amy, please . . . please listen. I know you have perfect reason to hate me. You heard what I said to Andy about how terribly foolish I was. Amy, even with what I thought, I couldn't help but grow to love you. Who you were kept pushing aside who I thought you were. Amy, you're the best friend I ever had. You're like a sister. I know I've wronged you. I'm so sorry. Please . . . please say you'll forgive me, Amy!"

A time of quietness, of hearts hurting—and hearts healing.

Amy flung her arms around the young woman sobbing in front of her. "Meg!"

She was wearing an apple green dress that he thought fit perfectly into the palette of garden brilliance around them. Her hair reminded him of golden wheat just before harvest, darker than he remembered. He suddenly remembered the first time he had seen her—when he thought her looks unremarkable. Had he been blind? This was the most beautiful woman he had ever seen. Four years of dreaming had blossomed into reality . . .

Amy had dried her tears. Meg had taken Melanie and left them alone.

He looked older and thinner, but the eyes were the same piercing blue, fastened on her with such intensity she blushed. If only she could delve into the depths of his thoughts.

"I went to the Crossing, and Mr. Chisolm told me Meg had moved here for the summer. I told you I'd never come back to Tanglewood . . . I hope you don't mind."

She tilted her head with a radiant smile.

"I don't mind at all."

The studio had not changed, except the artist was absent. Now there were no covered easels. Amy had proudly displayed every work of Patrick Cash. Yet one easel stood more prominently than the rest, capturing the eye when anyone entered the room.

Beautiful golds, roses, shades of blue and ivory filled the canvas. Amy sat on a bench in profile, an arbor of magnolia trees in full bloom around her.

Andy stepped forward. In the corner of the painting, near the edge of the painted garden, stood the figure of a man. A young man holding a sailor's cap and looking toward the woman. This was *Magnolia Remembrance*.

He closed his eyes. He could see the tender gaze of his great uncle in his mind. Amy came up behind him, watching him.

"I . . . didn't know," he whispered.

"I didn't either. I didn't see it until a few months after he was gone. I didn't have the strength to," Amy said softly.

"Amy, did he ever say . . ."

"No, not a word."

"I feel again like I betrayed him. Like he knew my feelings."

"Did you betray him, Andy?" Amy asked gently.

"I . . . fell in love with his wife."

"There was a great generosity in Patrick Cash, a generosity in heart for both of us. I've had a long time to think about that. You were honorable, Andy, and Cash knew that."

They were close enough to touch without touching, both afraid to make the first move.

"How do we begin, Amy Cash?" he asked tenderly.

Her smile came slowly. "We were enemies, then friends. That's a good starting place. From there . . ." Her words dangled in invitation.

Melanie Cash was sitting very prim and still as she regarded the stranger to Tanglewood. She watched him as he ate and talked and smiled at his sister and spoke with the doctor. The smile he gave her mother was different, but she was not quite sure in what way. It was something in his blue eyes. She thought he had a very kind face, as if he would understand her.

Andy Alcott was very aware of the young girl who watched him with her serious eyes. He smiled to himself; he could not remember ever being studied so intently before. He hadn't seen her smile a single time and she spoke only briefly when she was spoken to. He instinctively knew she was not the kind of child to force affection on, or talk down to.

They all went to the garden, and the stranger talked to the doctor about his ship. And the doctor talked about his deep-sea fishing trip. They both laughed a lot. And her mother and Aunt Meg smiled at each other a lot. She liked to listen to the stranger's laugh. She could tell when people really liked to laugh.

She was curled in Aunt Meg's lap when it came into her mind like the sputtering hiss of a just-lighted candle. Mr. Alcott hadn't said a word about having a mama. He was always on his boat. And there was the way he would glance at her mama—as if he were touching her with his eyes. Funny, but Aunt Meg and the doctor were doing the same thing.

She slid from her aunt's lap and stood soberly before her mama. She didn't mean to embarrass or scheme, but she couldn't wait till they had their bedtime chat. This was too important!

She waited till there was a lull in the conversation.

"Mama, I was thinking," she said eagerly.

"What, sweet?"

"Is . . . Could Mr. Alcott be the answer to my prayer?"

Amy pulled her daughter into the circle of her arms. She buried her face in the child's neck and cried with happiness.

Chapter 27

New York City

♦♦ ♦♦ ♦♦

*I*t was a balmy Saturday evening in New York City. The city was gearing up for a lively debate between the two major presidential candidates, William Jennings Bryan and William McKinley in a convention center in upper Manhattan. But for George St. John and the 22nd St. Players, that event was of no consequence at all. For them, the night meant only one thing—a performance at the Clarion Street Mission House. It wasn't a real theater of course, but St. John and Miss O'Hara had somehow transformed a portion of the dining hall into a respectable-looking stage. The chairs for the audience were in neat, semicircular rows. No, it was not in a real theater, but the cast had jitters that were as real as if they had been stepping in front of the house lights and orchestra pit at the best of Broadway. They were doing this performance with all their very best effort because of their affection and respect for Lilly O'Hara—and because the querulous face of St. John had allowed no complaint, no mutiny.

St. John had agreed to Miss O'Hara's plan for one simple reason. He could not resist her pleading green eyes. But he had not given in without a surplus of fussing.

"I don't know, Miss O'Hara... I don't know that it is dignified for our drama troupe to be performing in a mission house dining hall!"

"St. John, don't sound so pompous. You said we needed a good opportunity to perform without the scrutiny of the acting community and critics. You said we needed a large, varied audience. And," here she patted his shoulder affectionately, "you said we needed a place to rent very cheaply."

"I do not expect to be reminded of everything I've ever said, Miss O'Hara, like... like some annoying echo!" he said with petulance.

"Will you forgive me for remembering the words of the best drama coach in New York?" she asked as she batted her eyes outrageously.

Even at nearly 50 years of age, George St. John was capable of blushing. "Miss O'Hara, why is this little project so important to you?"

Lilly smiled. "St. John, this mission house has been my home since I came to New York. The staff has been my family. They took me in when I had next to nothing. They loved me with the love... of Christ. Now, I've moved and have my own apartment, but I still love to come here and visit the friends I've made, people as down and out as I was. I love to come here and hear the gospel." Her eyes filled with tears. "They have been... food and drink for me, St. John. Can you understand?

"This little play for the mission is a way of saying thank you in my own inadequate way. The people who come to the mission may never get to see a play in their life. This way they can see a performance by the 22nd St. Players, a premier thespian group, *and* hear a message of truth that they desperately need to hear...like I did."

St. John toyed with his watch chain for a long moment. He did not want to give in too quickly. He waved a finger in her face.

"Miss O'Hara, I feel like putty in your lovely hands!"

"Oh, St. John..."

The director did not wait behind the curtain or pace the makeshift backstage to watch the performance of his 22nd St. Players. He took a place at the very back of the dining hall in the shadows. The curtain opened; the play began. From this point he could still watch the audience with a well-trained eye. He was like a doctor looking for symptoms—laughter and tears at the correct places. He would weigh their applause in his mind as if they were the elite of New York's theater crowd.

The play had been in progress for ten minutes when a man slipped in beside St. John. The director was elated. He pumped the man's hand.

"You came!"

The man in the expensive suit smiled slightly.

"Of course. For an old friend, I came. If not, I would be eating oysters at Shellie's, then off to the 8:00—"

"Sshhh!" someone hissed from the back row.

St. John was immediately apologetic. "A barbaric crowd, pardon them."

"This is...a bit irregular, isn't it, St. John?" the man whispered. "Your group presenting a play at a mission house?"

"Never mind the environment, my dear friend. It is for the performance of a certain young woman that I have invited the best journalist and theater critic here tonight!"

"You always could pick the best oranges to swipe off the street carts when we were boys on Herring Avenue!...She on yet?"

St. John gave a low laugh. "You would know if she was on yet. In another moment. Be patient."

"All right, all right. But I have a dinner date at 8:30, so I can't stay for the whole thing. What did you say her name is?"

"Miss Lilly O'Hara!"

The gentlemen in the expensive suit and Manhattan sophistication did not make his dinner appointment. He forgot it completely. When the curtain was pulled and the audience stood clapping, he turned to St. John.

"Well?" the director drawled.

"To borrow the lingo of that rush up in the Klondike, St. John, you've struck gold!"

Sunday evening a light rain fell on the big city perched beside the Atlantic. A million lights were glowing through the wet, smoky vapor that hung over the city. The sky had no definition—it made the young woman who hurried along the sidewalks as quickly as she dared think it was melting. Her red hair made a vivid splash in the grayness.

She was like that everywhere she went, attracting attention by virtue of her friendly kindness, her charming Southern accent, her clean beauty, her effervescent laugh, and the quality of her voice in song. She was the kind of person who unconsciously drew a circle toward her.

She didn't get very wet in the block and a half from her small apartment to her destination. She entered the already crowded Italian restaurant. She sank into the chair at the table that had been lovingly reserved for her. She pulled a letter from her purse and began to reread it—though it was hardly quiet around her and the smell of pasta and bread was so distracting.

The big Italian was immediately looming over her.

"Not a book nor a script. A letter. . . . ah . . . from a young man, I would wager."

She looked up and laughed.

"You shouldn't wager, Valentino, but, yes, it is from a man."

"Have I met him? Forgive my boldness, but as you are fatherless in this vast city . . ." He shrugged and held out his hands.

"No, you haven't met him. He's a sea captain."

"Oh . . . that does not sound promising."

"Well, no. It is a friendship, you know."

Valentino raised an eyebrow, but was prudently silent.

"You haven't asked me how it went last night?" Lilly said easily.

"Could your performance have been less than magnificent?"

Lilly laughed. "Well, St. John was very pleased, and the audience seemed to like it."

"Of course!"

"St. John brought a critic. He was very kind also."

But her eyes traveled back to the letter with the New Orleans postmark. Valentino knew pasta; he also knew the troubled faces of women—he was raising six daughters.

"This letter," he pursued. "It makes you happy and sad at the same time?"

Valentino had been so accurate. A letter from Andy Alcott always made Lilly O'Hara happy—and sad.

But she managed a smile for the worried Italian.

"I am very happy just as I am, Valentino, and very ready for the finest lasagna in New York!"

She sang later, when the patrons asked her to, as they always did on Sunday evenings. Her voice was clearly heard on the gray, slick sidewalk outside—like a beacon.

Lilly O'Hara was singing. And she *was* very happy.

Greenville

The young sheriff of Greenville had become very frustrated with himself. He could not seem to think of a way to approach the banker's daughter without being forward and obvious. The only reason he could think of would be the beating. And he figured the young woman was more than ready to put that event firmly in the past. The sheriff would only be a reminder of it. Her father grew red-faced at the sight of the law officer—he represented the absurdity of the wretched affair. A local farmer was sitting in jail saying he had been a victim too. The banker of Greenville seriously considered looking for a bank in another city to preside over.

So the sheriff thought fleetingly of the young woman and decided they hadn't any possibilities.

He was going home from work, his mind on the petty details of his day, when he was struck with an unusual urge for ice cream. He altered his course and came to Greenville's candy and ice cream shop. The bell over the door jangled as he entered. He thought it sounded like an entire brass band. The customers were all in pairs, laughing, enjoying themselves, sharing the cold dessert. He felt awkward, large, out of place. He wanted to turn around, and forget this impulsive idea. Better to go home to a quiet—and predictable—dinner with his folks. Tonight was Thursday . . . Thursday was chops.

But he stood at the counter with his hands thrust into his pockets and a big frown on his face. The man and woman behind the counter waited for his order. Now it was really embarrassing. He had to make a choice from *three* flavors! He scratched his head while his frustration mounted. He felt like every eye in the store was on his back.

"Well, sir . . . Have you finally decided?"

"Ah . . . sure, vanilla."

"Vanilla, all right. One scoop or two?"

"One or two? Ah . . . chocolate, all right? Chocolate will be fine."

The man and the woman exchanged a look.

"Chocolate then, sir? One scoop or two?"

"Ah . . ." He was ready to turn and run.

"The strawberry is really your best choice," a sweet-sounding voice said at his elbow.

He turned slowly. He had heard that voice before. The banker's daughter was smiling at him.

"Strawberry?" he repeated to cover his great surprise and pleasure. She nodded.

"Strawberry then," he almost shouted with joy. "Two scoops. I mean, one scoop for me and one for the young lady."

She liked the way he said young lady. It made her feel like a treasure.

"I can buy my own," she began. "I only—"

"It's my pleasure to buy for you," he said quickly.

When they received their ice cream, they turned. There was one vacant table. Their eyes met. It was too loud, too open to prying eyes. He leaned forward slightly.

"The evenin' is sure pretty. Can we walk a ways?"

"I'd like that very much," she said softly.

They walked along the sidewalks in silence for a few long moments. She was the first to speak.

"Thank you."

"You're welcome."

She laughed. "Well, yes, for the ice cream, of course. But I meant more than that."

He kept walking. "I figured you did."

She stopped in her steps. "You did?"

"Your ice cream all right?"

"Yes, it's fine . . . You know that I was thanking you for . . . for going to Jackson and freeing that man, don't you? I started to come to your office half a dozen times, but . . ." She looked away from him a moment. "I've only started coming out lately . . . you know, in public. I felt like I was buried alive at home. But everybody on the streets stares, and whispers . . . things." Her voice dropped a fraction. "Some don't whisper. Anyway, I couldn't live afraid anymore. So, I come out, and they can stare all they want!"

"Glad you changed your mind," he said easily.

"Oh? Why?"

He crammed the cone into his mouth.

"'Cause I couldn't figure out a way to come see you," he confessed.

She had stopped walking again. Her voice was barely above a whisper. "Why did you want to come see me? Was it about the case?"

"No, I just wanted to come see *you*."

There on the streets of Greenville, they were alone, oblivious to anything else, suddenly drawn into each other's world—a world without threats or conditions.

"You are the kindest man I have ever met," she said impulsively.

His heart went out completely to her, never to come back.

"Don't know about that. Figure I'm the most fortunate man right now . . ." He scratched his head. "Hungry?"

She couldn't help but laugh at his boyishness.

"Hungry! We just had ice cream!"

"I know, but I haven't eaten supper yet. How would you like to come to supper with me somewhere? You name the place. If you're not hungry, well, I reckon you can watch me eat."

She laughed again. How could this near stranger make her feel so good about herself? She thought of all the eating places in Greenville. She would be recognized in any of the respectable places—and also at those of the lower world. She wouldn't go to the latter places, and she wasn't ready to face the former ones. She shook her head. "I can't think of any place. I'm sorry."

He smiled. He understood.

"Don't be sorry. I know this real nice place, real cozy. Nice owners too. They make great chops."

"Sounds wonderful, sheriff," she smiled.

Chisolm Crossing

He looked as dreary and forlorn and gray as the wet, dripping landscape. He was thin, his eyes circled, his skin an unhealthy yellow. He wore gray trousers and a shirt that had been white once. He was bareheaded and his thin, limp hair was even grayer than it had been six months earlier. But his dark eyes were alive, restless, darting.

The wagon had dropped him off seven miles from Chisolm Crossing. He would have to walk the remainder of the way home. He looked to have hardly enough strength for more than a dozen steps. He had shuffled along for an hour, resting beside the road and growing thirstier by the minute.

The sun came out and began to dry the land, and he felt himself growing weaker. He couldn't go on much farther. He looked around. He knew these woods that bordered the road he traveled. He had hunted them since he was a boy. He sighed wearily. He could crawl off into their cool, shadowy depths—and lie down and die. No one would find him until he was bones, a fitting end for Willet Keller, he mused. Bones. No more pain for Martha and his sons.

But he didn't even have the strength to crawl into the woods to bury himself. Instead he leaned against a cottonwood, and cried. He had cried a lot in the last six months. Cried till he didn't think there could be tears left. He didn't care if some neighbor happened by and saw ol' Willet Keller blubbering like a baby on the side of the road. Let them mock him; he didn't care anymore. When these fresh tears were gone, when he felt lightheaded, he called out in the morning stillness, three simple words.

"God...help...me..."

Like a spoiled, rebellious son who had run in every direction but that of his Father's outstretched arms, he finally turned to them, to the One who would love Willet Keller in spite of all his ugliness and sin. He leaned against the tree for an hour, growing weaker and talking silently to the One who would listen. After an hour he fell into a deep sleep.

Viney Jefferson did not look at her husband these last few months without letting her eyes rest on the red welt now growing fainter across his strong, black neck. He would always have a very visible scar there, a reminder...when Viney did not need a reminder. She would never forget the cries of pain from her tall husband or the sight of his bright red blood splashed on the tiles of Tanglewood's grand entrance. She would never forget the weeks when he could only drink nourishing broths. Nights when he was restless from the soreness. Nights when he finally slept with his hand stretched protectingly across her growing stomach, and her fingers resting like a feather touch across the angry red welt as she prayed for him. And nights when she cried for the fear of losing him.

It was so strange to them all. Moving from the Crossing where the touch of violence had not reached them, to Tanglewood, where it had struck them suddenly. And Jeb French, a free man with no punishment for his cruelty. Above the law? Viney wondered. "Vengeance is mine, sayeth the Lord," she would mutter through clenched teeth as she prepared a salve or broth or clean bandage for her husband. Yet Viney Jefferson took some unexplainable comfort in the thought that this act of French's was his final strike against Seth. Surely he had expelled his fury. They would not worry about him any longer.

And she could not think of the move to Tanglewood as a wrong move. Seth had assured her they had done the right thing, the best thing for their family. How many black men had the opportunity to rise above a meager lifestyle in rural Mississippi to become an equal partner in business? Now Seth and his sons had a future less bleak and narrow. Micah and Gideon were so happy in their new home and with their new friend, Melanie Cash. Viney had become devoted to Amy and was even finding humor in the proper butler with the strange accent!

On this bright morning, Viney felt no concern; Seth was at her side. They were cleaned and starched and visiting friends around the Crossing that they had not seen since they had moved. It was the middle of the afternoon when they began the return to Tanglewood.

"Look up ahead, Viney. Your eyes are better than mine. That a man layin' on the side of the road there?" Seth asked.

Viney peered forward with her sharp eyes. She laid a hand on her husband's arm. "Seth...Seth, it's Willet Keller."

She had not forgotten their last meeting.

"He dead, Daddy?" Micah chirped over their shoulder.

"Dead? He dead?" Gideon mimicked.

"Sit down both of you this minute! And hush. Hurry on by, Seth honey."

Seth turned and smiled at her. "Now, Viney darlin', you know I can't do that. Gotta see what the trouble is—"

"Seth, don't stop!" Her voice was sharp. "That man is trouble. Cut from the same cloth as Jeb French. Please pass on."

"Calm down, Viney. He don't look in the shape to harm a flea. 'Sides, we can't be passin' him like a Levite on the side of the road! Whoa, boys..."

Seth climbed down, and his shadow fell over the man slumped in the weeds.

"Been drinkin' probably," Viney whispered loudly. But Seth ignored her.

"Mr. Keller? Sir? You all right? Need some help, sir?"

Seth squatted down. The man did look near dead, but Seth could hear the farmer's ragged breath.

"Mr. Keller?"

The farmer stirred and moaned. He was reluctant to leave the pain-less peacefulness of his dreams. And such a strange dream. Not like any he had ever had. A hand reaching out to him, yet he could never quite reach it. Oh, but he wanted to reach it. If only he could, everything would be fine.

His eyes opened slowly. He was still so thirsty, so thirsty.

"Say there, Mr. Keller...You all right? Can I help you somehow?"

"A drink..."

Seth stepped back to the wagon. "He needs a drink. Hand me the jar, Viney."

Viney hesitated. She did not want to be like the Levite, but she was afraid. All she had to do was look at the brand above Seth's collar to see what men like Willet Keller were capable of.

"It ain't water he's a wantin', Seth."

Viney rarely heard Seth's firmest voice, especially toward her. When she did hear it, she knew wisely not to challenge it.

"The water, Viney."

He took the mason jar of cool water and bent down.

"Here you go, sir. Here's some water."

He had to hold the man's head to help him.

"Ah..." Keller lay back down. His eyes were finally focusing.

"Let me help you home, Mr. Keller," Seth offered gently.

"Yes...help..."

Seth stretched out his hand, and only then did Willet Keller see his skin clearly. Black. He moaned and closed his eyes. The dream was still in his mind. The hand in his dream that he wanted to reach, why hadn't he noticed before? It was... black.

Slowly, tiredly, he took the hand. Seth helped him to his feet.

"I'll take you home and go for the doc if your Mrs. is a wantin' me to," Seth continued.

Keller eyed the jar on the ground, the jar he had drunk from. It was half full and he was still very thirsty. He looked up—a black man, a black woman, and two black children were staring at him from a wagon.

"I need another drink."

"Sure, Mr. Keller, drink it all."

"Who are you?" Keller rasped.

"Name's Seth Jefferson, sir."

"Jefferson... Jefferson..." His mind was as enfeebled as his body had become.

"I'm a carpenter over at Tanglewood. Used to live at the Crossing."

Keller took another long drink. It was the best water he had ever tasted.

"I'll just help you up in the wagon and get you on home."

"Yes, home. And... thank you for the water."

Three days later, Willet Keller died in his sleep. Martha had been beside him, holding his hand, mingling her tears with his. She had listened to every broken word, each word that had pulled the strength from him, until there was none. And she bowed her head when he prayed and died in peace.

Chapter 28

Tanglewood

♦♦ ♦♦ ♦♦

*S*omething had snapped inside Jeb French when Jacob brought him the news that the schoolmarm's brother had returned. Restraint, caution, patience—all fled as his alarming temper mounted. He grabbed Jacob savagely by the collar and snarled his instructions.

French slipped through the garden doors into the Cash studio with the silence and stealth of a cat. The wolfhound lay panting by the open door, his appearance made larger by the half-light of evening.

He knew where all the principals in the drama were. He knew that the schoolmarm had gone to the Crossing. He knew that the Yankee sailor had taken Amy and Melanie for an evening drive. He calculated that any threat would turn the English butler babbling, pale, and weak-kneed.

The hand that seemed so casually thrust into his jacket pocket fingered the handle of a long-bladed knife, a cold reassurance at his fingertips should anyone intrude upon this little visit.

Boldly he switched on a lamp and began a relaxed stroll around the perimeter of the studio. The fine collection of Patrick Cash—he gave each painting a careful appraisal. *Magnolia Remembrance*. His stepsister looked so virtuous. He glanced at his pocket watch in curiosity more than concern.

The knife came out of its place and went to work with swiftness and zeal. Each canvas was slashed with a pleasure only Jeb French could enjoy. He hefted *Magnolia Remembrance* up, judging its weight, smiled, and slipped out into the night.

Chisolm Crossing

"Hello? Hello?"

The phone line sputtered and crackled as the storm increased.

"Can't hear ya!...Can't...huh?"

"Mr. Chisolm! This is...Alcott...at Tanglewood. Is Meg...you?"

"Huh?...I say this contraption is useless!" Chester fussed into the receiver, unreconciled to the purposes and profit of this modern invention. "Hollerin' into a box!...What's that?"

"Mr. Chisolm, keep Meg....in danger."

The line fizzled to an ignoble death.

"Who are you shouting at? How is a person supposed to rest?" Matilda called peevishly from the parlor sofa.

"Don't know who it was, but I reckon they'll call back when the line clears."

He went to the window. "'Course the line may not clear for a time with this storm." He shook his head soberly. "More rain. I don't see how the land can take much more soakin.'"

"It isn't the land to be so concerned over, Mr. Chisolm. It's the creeks and rivers," Matilda returned with spirit that no convalescence could quench entirely.

"I'm watchin' it for us, 'Tilda. Don't worry."

"I've been lying here for two days while Miss Alcott waited on me and the store hand and foot. It has not been an easy thing to endure."

Chester regarded his mate affectionately. "We got to learn to take just as we give, 'Tilda, hard as it is. Miss Alcott says she's enjoyed herself helpin' you, and I believe her. You need to slow down and rest. You go like a freight train all the time."

She felt a smile pulling at her mouth at his soft words, but she could not allow him the final say.

"I'll have plenty of time to rest when I have my burial finery on, Mr. Chisolm!"

"It was awful kind of Meg to come from Tanglewood to help us when you turned your ankle while I was gone to Vicksburg. I'd imagine she has a lot on her mind these days with her brother here and Barrett a courtin' her," Chester replied placidly.

"Is her light on?" Matilda asked.

Chester peered into the gloom. "Nope, all tucked in, safe and sound."

"She'll go back to Tanglewood tomorrow. I can more than manage."

Chester's smile dissolved as another blaze of lightning illuminated the purple heavens.

"She won't be going anywhere if this rain don't quit," he muttered.

Sometime after midnight the rain did stop. But it was only an interlude between dangers as towns along the upper Mississippi braced for terrible flooding.

Meg was awakened just before sunrise by knocking at her window. Pulled from a deep sleep, her heart was thudding with fear as she pulled on a robe.

In the gray, misty flush of dawn, Jacob Brown stood before her window.

"Jacob, you frightened me. Why didn't you come to the front door?"

He shrugged, and Meg could see in his face and posture his hostility toward her had not abated, though he had not been in her school for over a year.

"I came from Mim with a message for you."

"From Mim? What is it?"

"Coming by her cabin, she called to me and said I was to come for you—said she needed you quick."

"Did she seem ill, or was it for Susannah?"

She was not his schoolmistress anymore. She was a Yankee white woman, and he could be as rude as he liked.

"Ya heard what I said. She wants you to come quick—didn't bother to tell me why."

"All right. Thank you, Jacob."

Her voice was soothing; it made him hesitant. But for only an instant. Wordlessly he slipped back into the dripping forest.

Tanglewood

The vandalism and theft were not discovered at Tanglewood until the next day. Fenwick made the discovery and carried the news privately to Andy. It was difficult for the butler to make judgments on intangibles like feelings, but he made the assumption that the guest of Tanglewood was going to become the next master of Tanglewood . . . and he did hate to tell Mrs. Cash when the smile had come back to her eyes and the color to her cheeks.

"There's only one person who would do this," Amy whispered through her tears when Andy told her of the violence.

It was also evident to Andy he must hurry to Chisolm Crossing when the weather finally cleared. French was stalking them, and Meg was surely in danger. The attempt to warn her by phone had failed.

Amy clung to him without reserve. This was no time to be coy or timid about feelings. She needed him and wanted him. She need not face this threat alone.

Her face rested against his shoulder. "I'm afraid, Andy."

"Don't be, Amy. Everything's going to be all right. You're not to leave the house until I get back with Meg. Seth is here, and he has the pistol of Uncle Pat's. When I return, we'll send for the sheriff. I'll get the painting back. French will be brought to justice."

"I don't care about the painting! I'm worried about you and Meg. Jeb is dangerous, Andy. If he's been bold enough to come into my house, he won't stop at anything!"

He framed her face in his hands. "Years have passed, and oceans have separated us, Amy. But we're together now. The Lord has brought us together. He's in control . . . I'll be back for you."

Chisolm Crossing

The cabin stood silent in its remoteness as the first pale smudges of light penetrated the valley. Mim's cabin always seemed so separate and somber to Meg. She wished Mim could move closer to the Crossing.

Through the open door, she called, "Mim?"

Mim sat at the table. She did not look up when Meg first entered.

"Mim! You're all right! I was so worried when Jac—...Mim? Is it Susannah?"

Mim looked up then, her face tired but void of emotion, staring at Meg as if she were a stranger. A bruise was coming on her cheek, the blood drying on her lip.

"Mim..."

The cabin door swung slowly shut. Jeb stood there, unsmiling.

It was difficult, almost impossible, for Meg to quell the instant panic that rose in her. She felt the lightheadedness, the trembling of her nerves. She turned away from French; she would ignore him if she could. She pulled up a chair and took the black woman's hands.

They were icy.

"Now if only Mrs. Cash were here, our little missionary circle would be complete."

French's voice had always held mockery, but now it was chopped and steely.

Meg rubbed Mim's hands, not trusting her voice, yet hoping a measure of comfort could reach the frightened woman through her touch.

French came to stand beside them. Still Meg did not look at him. The leather handle of the riding crop forced her chin up, forced her to meet the gray hardness of his eyes.

"But Miss Amy won't be coming, will she, Miss Alcott? She's in your brother's arms." His words descended into a barrage of foulness and curses. "So here we are."

Meg's mind was racing. She must force herself to think calmly. French had lured her here. Jacob had brought the bait. Oh, Jacob. Her throat tightened. She had come without leaving a note. She had not disturbed the Chisolms because their lights were not yet on. No one knew where she was.

"You're not sayin' much, Miss Alcott." The handle gently stroked her throat. "Your tongue is usually so quick to be rude to me. What's the matter with you, schoolmarm? Hmm?"

"Mr. French..."

"Mr. French, what?"

"Please...please...leave."

"Leave? No, Miss Alcott—you just got here." He leaned forward, his eyes level with hers. "I can't have Amy. I'll take you, Miss Alcott—you."

"Jeb, please let her go." Mim's voice was a hoarse whisper.

French jerked Meg up harshly from her chair. He would dispel any illusions that he meant to be gentle.

"You just don't seem to be looking down your Yankee nose at me this fine morning."

He pulled her toward the doorway. "We're going to go for a little ride. Just you and me, Miss Alcott."

His back was turned as he pushed Meg into the yard, a moment long enough for Mim to uncoil like a spring and attack with the bravery of pent-up fear and anger. Her fingers clawed the back of his neck as she pulled at him.

"Run, Miss Meg! Run!"

French shoved Meg into the dirt yard, sending her sprawling. He swung around to Mim, his hand finding the Confederate pistol.

One shot—and silence.

Susannah began to whimper from inside the cabin.

Meg felt as if she had no strength to stand. Yet she must stand. She must ignore the roaring in her ears, the blackness that threatened to send her to the ground again.

French did not move as she staggered past him to Mim's still body. She cradled the woman's head in her lap. Mim...

Susannah's pitiful voice pulled her from the nightmare. The little girl sat in the bed, just awakened and rubbing her eyes. Meg moved to her. She could not walk properly.

"Get away from the brat. We're going now," Jeb commanded curtly from the doorway.

Meg swung around, tears blinding her.

"You're an animal, Jeb French! God forgive your evil soul!"

"There's that tongue. Now come on, or I'll make the brat quiet."

Meg sat before him on his huge horse as he plunged into the woods.

The group met on the steps of the school, grim-faced though the morning advertised fair and lovely weather. They had little concern for the weather, except that it was not raining. Andy felt almost overcome with panic to find Meg missing.

"Ain't like her not to leave a note," Chester said, pulling at his suspenders worriedly.

"Unless she left in a hurry for some reason. I've gone all over the schoolroom and her apartment and can't find a thing," Andy replied.

"Reckon she could have gone for a walk," Chester suggested.

Matilda cut him off briskly. "She wouldn't have gone for a walk. She'd have to be an ox to plow through this mud."

"Then where is she?" Chester's alarm was thinly disguised. Andy had told them about French.

"The man's lower than a snake's belly," the storekeeper asserted with asperity.

"An apt description," Matilda agreed.

Then Barrett rode into view. His body sagged with fatigue but was quickly transformed as Chester apprised him of the danger and Meg's disappearance.

"She wouldn't be headed for your place, would she?" Matilda asked without the usual thrust of implication.

"No, not this early. I've been in Greenville all night."

His face had gone gray. Meg...

Then a sound like a wounded animal reached them from the forest, a sobbing, panting sound. Jacob Brown came stumbling from the trees; Susannah hanging onto his neck.

Jacob had lingered in the shadows of Mim's cabin. He had felt the ages-old Judas stirrings as Meg entered the trap. What had French planned? Then the horror. What had he done?

Matilda reacted before any of the men, hobbling forward to take Susannah in her generous arms, cooing to her, turning wordlessly back to the store. Whatever had happened, the men would deal with it—she had work to do.

Jacob had fallen on his knees before them, his thin shoulders shaking with sobs.

Andy knelt beside him. "Son, it's all right now. You're safe. Can you tell us what happened?"

Jacob looked into the white face, into the kindest eyes he had ever seen. This man...perhaps this man would understand why he had done what he had done. Perhaps he could forgive him...

"He killed her."

The men were frozen by his words.

"Tell us," Andy returned calmly, though his mind was screaming.

"French...he shot Mim. He killed her. It's my fault."

"Miss Alcott, Jacob. Did you see her?" Chester nearly shouted.

"Yes, sir. She...I...he took Miss Ma'am off on his horse...into the forest."

Barrett was on his horse in one swift motion.

"Which way did they go from Mim's cabin?" There was a calm evenness to his voice.

"Toward Greenville."

"Greenville's going to flood. The towns all north are already flooding. They're moving people out."

"The sheriff?" Andy asked, feeling helpless.

"I doubt you could find him today. I'm going for Meg."

Barrett Browning had never killed before; he wondered if he could now. He had devoted his hands to saving life.

"Lord, help me, please. Help me find them. Keep Meg safe. Take this...I don't want to...kill...even Jeb French."

It was not difficult to follow French's tracks. Barrett could only hope French's horse was having as much trouble in this mud as his own. French was certainly taking Meg closer to disaster if they reached Greenville. He must reach them...

French had no plan when he left the cabin. Over all his cunning and shrewdness lay this blinding, brooding anger. Amy was gone, but he would not lose entirely. He would cause her pain again as he stole her friend. The Yankee would pay.

He directed the horse toward Greenville, ignorant of the danger, uncertain of what he would do when he reached his destination. He had planned for one of his ships to be in crew and ready to cast off. But to take the schoolmarm with him or humiliate her in the forest, he could not decide.

Meg's scream alerted Barrett that he was very close. He must choose his course of action very quickly. He knew that French was armed—and what he was capable of. Barrett slipped off his horse and ran forward, the wet leaves muffling his approach.

Jeb had decided. He did not want to risk entering Greenville with his prize. She would probably scream, and then he would have to kill her before a thousand eyes. He reined the horse, jumped off, and roughly pulled Meg to him.

"French, you can't get away with abduction and murder," Meg said with artificial firmness.

"I can and I am, Miss Alcott." He smiled. "And you're in no position to scold or threaten me. When I'm finished with you, I'll ride into Green-ville where my ship waits for me, ready right down to the luggage in my cabin. Can you guess what hangs over my bed, Yankee lady?"

Meg felt sick. *When I'm finished with you.* She looked away from French, praying.

He grasped her wrists tighter until she cried out in pain.

"I asked you a question!" he snarled.

"What?"

"A fine oil painting hangs over my bed, courtesy of Patrick Cash. I can fall asleep looking at little sis..." He laughed again.

"Magnolia Remembrance!" Meg gasped.

He smiled, so very pleased. "That's right."

He pulled her tighter until she screamed.

Barrett crept closer, waiting for the moment of best advantage.

With no weapon of his own, he must wait until Jeb's back was turned. When French bent over Meg to kiss her, Barrett lunged forward.

"Barrett!"

French swung around with the unleashed fury of a beast. They fell onto the ground in a death struggle.

"Barrett! He has a gun!" Meg screamed.

It seemed like hours to Meg when it was only minutes. The nightmare was growing worse.

French pulled the pistol from his pocket, but Barrett held his wrist in a vise grip. One last surge of strength and Barrett sent the gun spinning into the undergrowth. French hurled forward, staggering Barrett and kicking him in the jaw. The doctor sagged to his knees.

French shook his mane of hair as if to clear his mind, blood streaming from his nose and mouth. His eyes narrowed on Meg for just an instant. Then he mounted his horse and was gone.

She was on the ground beside Barrett, crying with the broken-heartedness and fear of the last few hours.

His hand rested on her cheek, scanning her eyes.

"You're all right. You're safe now," he soothed.

"Oh, Barrett!...Mim...Barrett, hold me!"

He closed his eyes. To love someone like this...to be loved...

Lord, thank You...just thank You...

They stayed there until Meg grew calm, and the forest grew warmer with the rising sun.

"Barrett, he kicked you. Are you all right?" She leaned forward and kissed the angry red mark across his jaw.

He gave her a wobbly smile, and reached into his mouth and laid a tooth in his palm.

"French just took care of my toothache, that's all."

Greenville

"You can't be serious, French!"

"Do I look like I'm joking?" French's voice was severe.

"But listen to the river! It's roaring. It's suicide to take a ship out now."

French withdrew another pistol from his coat and leveled it at the seaman. "It's certain death for you, Captain, if you don't. Now shove off. We're going to New Orleans."

Chisolm Crossing

Chisolm's Mercantile did not open its doors for business that day. Matilda hardly noticed and certainly did not object. She was brewing what seemed like a gallon of cocoa, refilling cups, hovering over Meg in the best mother-hen style.

Barrett had brought Meg back to the store rather than venture the ride to Tanglewood. She had fainted in the circle of his arms on the ride home, and the doctor knew he must get her quiet, safe, and warm before she went into shock. They had laid her in the parlor.

She could manage only a weak smile for the three anxious men who gathered around her. They talked in low voices.

Then a child's cry brought them back to the youngest victim of the morning's tragedy. Susannah was waking, sipping greedily from the cup of warm milk that Matilda held for her.

All eyes rested on her. Mim's child...

Meg had forgotten her for just a moment in the relief of being in Barrett's arms. Little Susannah, motherless. She cried out, and Barrett held her.

"Meg, she's going to be all right. And Jacob, Meg. Jacob wants to come talk with you when you're ready for him."

Then Matilda spoke. There was a quality in her voice that Meg had never heard before. She sounded humble, appealing, tender.

"Meg, I know Mim was your friend, I do know that. And I know you have a generous heart. I can easily guess what you'll want to do with this little one."

She stroked the soft brown curls as Susannah snuggled against her.

"But you have a chance for...for little ones of your own. I don't."

She hesitated. They were all staring at her so. Chester's eyes were about to bulge out. She took a deep breath and returned to the brisk tone they all knew well.

"I know it's absurd to think of at my age, but the fact remains—"

"What are you sayin', 'Tilda?" Chester gasped.

"I'm trying to say, Mr. Chisolm, that we should keep Susannah for our girl."

Chester was clearly stunned. Had Matilda ever acted so...so un-Matilda-ish?

"But like you said, 'Tilda, our age! And there could be, well, problems about her color. I mean, not that I mind myself, but..."

It had been years, decades, since Chester Chisolm had seen his wife moved to tears. But they came now, slow tracks down full cheeks—and a voice, joyful.

"Those things do not concern me, Chester. I love this girl!"

Meg felt listless and apathetic as she packed up her bags to return to Tanglewood. It was odd how sorrow and joy could compete in her emotions on this clear morning. All she really wanted to do was revel in the love she had found with Barrett Browning. She wanted to think of every detail of a future with him. At long last, she had found a love that was right; there would be no more tragedies of the heart.

But she could not ignore the pain of Mim's death. Jeb French had been a thief in many ways. And now Mim would not be there in the fall to learn and share.

The school door opened, and the doctor stuck his head in.

"Miss Al—," Barrett laughed at himself. "Meg?"

Meg came into the schoolroom.

"Miss Alcott? Aren't we past such formality, Dr. Browning?"

He took her hand. He was so glad to see her. It seemed like days, when it had been only eight hours.

"Yes, I suppose we are." He stood close to her. "How is it you are more beautiful this morning than you were last night?"

She smiled.

His finger traced her cheek. "You've been crying."

She shrugged and lowered her head. She shyly fingered the fabric of his shirt.

"Barrett, I hurt to think of Mim. I . . . I'm in there packing, and I can't help but think of her . . . how thrilled she was learning to read . . ."

She looked up at him. "She was my friend. She thought I was an angel."

"I'm sorry, Meg. I wish French could have been stopped," he said gently.

He held her until she pulled away and gave him a faint smile.

"Off on a call?" she asked.

He loved the question. She was making a place in his life.

"I'll be gone till late this afternoon, at least," he said. "Off to Greenville," he added mysteriously.

If the jewelry store in Greenville could not satisfy him, he would go farther.

She slipped her arms around his neck. "All right; I'll wait for you before I go to Tanglewood. That way I can give you a kiss without tears."

"I am not complaining," he said, tasting the salt on her cheek and on her lips, "about anything, Meg."

There was a firm knock on the schoolhouse door. They pulled apart.

Barrett frowned. "Must be Matilda. She must have seen me come in and thinks we've been in here alone too long."

But it wasn't Matilda Chisolm. Abby Mayhew and her children had returned to Chisolm Crossing School.

Barrett quickly said goodbye and left the two women staring at each other.

Meg eyed the tall black woman with obvious reluctance. She didn't feel up to any verbal sparring or debate. She sat down at a desk.

"Good morning, Mrs. Mayhew."

Abby Mayhew had not been around very many white women in her life. And then, it was mostly at a distance. She saw the little merchant's wife more than any other. White or black, she knew the schoolteacher looked tired, sad, and certainly not as cheerful as usual. She looked brittle, and Abby was suspecting the reason. It surprised her. It was that suspicion, and something else she could not explain, that had kept her awake all the night before.

She had fed her children in the morning, bathed, and started to Chisolm Crossing School. She wasn't sure how she was going to say what had come into her mind. This time, Abby Mayhew was feeling nervous.

Meg wanted a short interview.

"We really didn't get a chance to talk those two days you came to school, and then so much...happened. Is that what you have come to talk about, Mrs. Mayhew?"

"Can I sit down?" she asked.

"Oh, yes, of course. I'm sorry."

Abby took a chair and looked ridiculously bent in the small seat. But Meg hardly noticed. She was noticing Abby's subdued manner.

"I didn't come to talk about them two days I come to school. Not exactly."

"Oh?"

Abby toyed with one of her children's braids and averted her eyes. This was going to be more difficult than she had thought. Perhaps she should just leave.

"I heard...about Mim," she said finally.

She looked up. The schoolteacher was looking at her clenched hands on the desk in front of her.

Meg wished this woman had chosen another day to visit. And had not spoken her friend's name. It poked at her composure. She didn't know what to say.

"Did you have a specific reason for coming today, Mrs. Mayhew? You see, I have some packing to do."

"You leavin'?" Abby asked in alarm.

"For the summer."

"Comin' back in the fall to teach?"

"Yes." Meg stood up.

"I...was sorry to hear about Mim," Abby continued.

Meg was growing confused and frustrated. Why had this woman come to talk about Mim? She could not hold them back. Her tears spilled over—and won Abby Mayhew.

"She was my friend, Mrs. Mayhew," she said simply.

Abby nodded. "That's why I come...in a way."

"Excuse me? I don't understand."

"I's sorry 'bout Mim...really was. And I got to thinkin'...after I come those two days here...and seen..."

Meg was shocked. Abby Mayhew was acting shy!

"I wondered. I thought maybe...you might...I would like to be what Mim...was. What she did here at the school. I want to work with you and maybe...learn to read. Thought maybe you might take me."

Meg slipped back to her seat in surprise. This woman, so hostile, so abrasive and rough—not like the gentle Mim. No, she couldn't do it. She couldn't take her for an aide. It wouldn't work. She shouldn't be expected to help everyone that came along. It wouldn't work. She would say no. She would.

"I think that is a wonderful idea, Mrs. Mayhew. I would love to have you work with me in the fall."

The black woman did not smile—yet.

"Reckon you could call me Abby."

The roads were deeply rutted from the rains, muddy bogs in some places. So Andy Alcott drove the carriage south from Tanglewood toward Vicksburg, where the land gently sloped upward and was drier and firmer. The rains had generated an explosive growth in the vegetation of the countryside—flowers both in gardens and the wild, hedges, shrubs, and fruit trees formed vibrant tableaus of color.

Amy was surprised when Andy pulled into the very center of an unfenced field. The yellow green grasses came to the wheels of the buggy. It was as if they were alone in the vastness of an ocean. It dawned on her then—this was the closest thing Andy could find to imitate the unique quiet of an ocean expanse. She smiled to herself, pleased that she had understood his intentions. But it didn't make her any less nervous.

They had said no more than half a dozen commonplace words since they had said goodbye to Melanie and rode away from the mansion. Now, they sat in an ocean of grass—unheard and unseen, safe from any prying eyes or curious ears.

Andy Alcott had not been detailed in his plans for coming to Mississippi, beyond seeing Meg and figuring out what had happened between

them. He had hoped they could return to the closeness they had once
shared. Now that had been done. But he knew to come see his sister
would be to see the mistress of Tanglewood as well. Just to see her once
more, then leave. He dare not hope or plan or dream for more. He had
seen *Magnolia Remembrance,* and found the blessing from his gracious
cousin that he needed. He found a little girl with questioning eyes, a girl
praying for a father. He found a young woman as beautiful as he knew
she was—with nothing between them. He came to Tanglewood and
found more than he expected.

He still didn't know how to begin, what to say exactly. Finally he
turned to her. "Amy, could you tell me about the years since I left
Tanglewood?"

She began slowly and uncertainly. But as she spoke, she opened up.
She told him everything, like turning pages in a treasured book. She told
him of the fire, and rebuilding the shop, and of Cash's death. She told
him of the night Jeb French had brazenly come to Tanglewood and what
she had done.

Her eyes brightened when she talked of Melanie coming into her life.
She talked about the little girl for a long time. She wanted Andy to know,
for many reasons—and one she would not allow her mind to dwell on.
She stopped only once to ask a question.

"We know who Meg thought Melanie's father was," she said without
bitterness. "What did you think?"

He didn't want to hurt her, but he knew she wanted the truth.

"I thought since Meg hadn't bothered to tell me what you had said
about your cousin, there was only one conclusion."

A silence there in their ocean of grass.

"You thought Cash was her father," Amy said softly.

He nodded. But Patrick Cash was gone now. She resumed her narrative: the Klan activity, Seth and Viney moving to Tanglewood, and
French's attack on the carpenter.

Suddenly Andy didn't want to talk about Cash or French or Meg or
Melanie. He wanted to know Amy's feelings, what she held inside.

"We've been separated a long time . . . a lot has happened," he said
slowly.

"Yes, and God has been good to me through all of it."

"And to me. It's been a long journey."

He took a deep breath. "Amy, I don't want to journey alone anymore.
You're the piece that will make me whole. For all these years I tried to
put you as far out of my mind as I put miles between us. It didn't work.
And I see why now. His timing was perfect, not mine."

He slipped his hands around hers. "Amy Cash," he whispered,
though he could not be heard for miles, "here and now, I'm asking you
to marry me. I don't want any more time or miles between us. I want to
love you for the rest of my life."

"No more time, no more miles between us, Andy," she smiled through her tears.

Their first kiss, there in their ocean of grass, held a beginning, a seal, a promise—and for the mistress of Tanglewood who had lost faith in dreams, the sweetest reality.

The opal shimmering light where, like a spilled pot of gold, the sun had begun its descent defined the low mountains in shades of deep purple against water-color blue. Cottonwoods with slender, graceful spines, and silvery green leaves silently danced in a twilight unbroken except for the sound of a mockingbird in an ageless song.

Andy stood on the front steps of Tanglewood mansion. He turned from it when he heard the step behind him. It was Meg.

"Barrett's just off the phone with the sheriff, who's been on the phone with someone downriver. Jeb French was found this morning, drowned. His boat is at the bottom of the river. That means *Magnolia Remembrance* is gone. I'm sorry, Andy; I know you would have liked to have had Cash's last painting. It was a masterpiece!"

His arm went around her shoulders, his eyes sweeping the land, his mind full of Amy and Melanie, and of the happiness and love that his sister had found.

"It's all right about the painting, Meg. It's lost, but look what we have here, look at the masterpiece God has made for us. Think of what remains..."

For I know the thoughts
that I think toward you, sayeth the Lord,
thoughts of peace, and not of evil,
to give you an expected end.

—Jeremiah 29:11

Mississippi, 1950

♦♦ ♦♦ ♦♦

*T*he young reporter was nibbling on finger sandwiches with little interest. She was bored and wishing the editor had given this assignment to another staffer. Covering anniversaries or grand openings was pretty tame copy. She would have liked something a bit more challenging and exciting, like a courtroom drama or political scandal. Something like the Senate investigation of communism up in D.C. Now that would be an assignment!

Apparently her editor didn't think she was ready for the tough stuff. So here she was strolling around on the emerald green lawns of this college, half listening to the speeches of the alumni, waiting to scribble down a few lines to make a decent byline. Then she could leave. The crowd was bigger than she expected. One of the staff estimated there were close to 800 gathered. Eight hundred staff, faculty, students, graduates, and family. A Bible college for blacks, celebrating its fiftieth anniversary. She yawned.

She could see a handful of whites like herself. They were like specks in a sea of ebony. She knew some of her friends would have balked at this assignment. Americans were still having trouble living peacefully beside each other.

She left the assembly and ambled around to the back of the big redbrick building. She would get an interview with a dean or someone in a little while. First, she'd see the rose garden that was locally famous. It wasn't difficult to find. It was not hard to see this had been an impressive antebellum mansion in its prime. She found a stone bench in the shade of a huge magnolia and sat down, slipped off one of her pumps then the other, and rubbed her feet. It was pretty here, and quiet for a change.

Then came a slow, shuffling step, and an old black man appeared on the gravel path. He leaned heavily on a cane. She heard his wheezing before she actually saw him.

He stopped when he saw her. She held her breath. She suddenly felt like a naughty girl caught somewhere she shouldn't have been. His eyes looked huge behind the thick bifocals. He finally smiled.

"You like it here? Smell good?"

"Yes, it's very nice."

She started to slip her shoes back on and gather up her things.

He eased himself down to the bench opposite her.

"Don't need to put your shoes on; I don't mind. You got pretty white feet."

He chuckled at that, and she felt a little nervous. He was dressed in worn khakis, a faded flannel shirt, an old silk vest. He looked too warm to the young woman.

"So...do you work here?" she asked to fill the silence and because he was staring at her.

It was an absurd question, she realized. *He's at least 70!*

He nodded at something private and smiled again.

"Been keepin' this garden a long time. Years, yes, ma'am."

"You're a gardener? Retired?"

He nodded again. "Who are you? Why aren't you 'round front with the rest?"

"No, I'm not a student. I'm a reporter for the *Greenville Daily Dispatch.* I'm covering the anniversary...50 years, you know."

"Oh?" he quipped and smiled at his own humor. But she didn't understand.

"You're a newspaperwoman, hmm. Is there a story back here in the rose garden?"

She really didn't understand his humor. She felt a little nettled.

"No, I'm just waiting for an interview, that's all."

He nodded in a slow, deliberate way that she already recognized as a personal habit with him.

"So maybe you could interview me," he suggested with a trace of shyness.

A decrepit old gardener! She almost laughed out loud.

"Well, I—"

"Go on now. I've been here awhile. Maybe I can tell you something they can't." He jerked his head toward the house.

She couldn't see his eyes sparkling behind the thick lenses.

"Well, really, I—"

"I took over caring for these roses a long time ago. In fact the lady of the house, the mistress, she showed me herself before she left."

"Oh, really," the reporter returned with little interest.

"Yep, she showed me all about roses. She was a fine woman, yes, ma'am."

The reporter scanned her scanty notes. She would humor the old fella. "Let's see. That would be..."

She had no ideas, but she must look professional.

"Mrs. Amy Cash," he supplied proudly.

"Cash? No, I think the name...somewhere...Alcott."

"No, ma'am," he persisted. "You've got the facts wrong. Her name was Cash first."

"Cash." She printed carefully. "Then she became Alcott?"

"Yep."

"She was a...black woman. My notes—"

He burst out laughing, a laugh from the depths of his old soul.

"Black like me? Oh, no, ma'am. She was white as you!"

"Now look, my notes—"

"Do you want the truth, the story, or not?" he asked with a bit of spice.

"Well—"

"'Course you do. You can get the facts, the black and white from folks out front, but I can add the color, see? Now you ask the questions, and I'll tell you all I can about Magnolia College."

She sighed. She'd run into a poor old gardener with visions of grandeur!

"All right, all right. Amy Cash Alcott. Who was she?"

"Wife of Patrick Cash, then wife of Andy Alcott. This land, all these acres, have been in the Cash name since the late 1700s. It was a cotton plantation for years. One of the richest in the state. Bet you didn't know what they called it when Pat Cash became the master when he came back from the war."

"No, I don't."

"He named it Tanglewood, and so it was until it became Magnolia Bible College. Think of that, ma'am; first it was a cotton plantation that worked hundreds of slaves, then it became a college for blacks! Ain't that somethin'?" His old face was illuminated.

She tapped her pen on her chin. Well, that certainly was an interesting angle. "All right then. The Cashes, or Alcotts rather, were white, and they sold it to the founders to make a college for blacks."

Well, that would certainly raise some eyebrows among her readers!

He laughed his deep laugh again. "No, ma'am. Mr. Andy and Miss Amy gave Tanglewood to one man."

He picked at a thread on his sweater, suddenly becoming subdued.

"Gave it all to him," he murmured.

The change in his manner pricked her reporter's instinct. And here she had been thinking what he said was true.

"They *gave* him a huge plantation? Gave it to him? Why?"

Still, he did not lift his eyes. He fingered a thin white scar that barely showed above the collar of his shirt.

"'Cause they was that kind of folks. Too many memories and all..."

"That's it? You expect me to believe they just gave away this land that had been in the family for decades?"

He nodded. She tried again.

"All right, who did they *give* Mag—Tanglewood to?"

He sighed wearily. Maybe he wasn't up to this after all.

"A fella, Seth Jefferson. Just a fella. Is he in your notes?"

"No, he isn't, and you know he isn't. None of this is. Who is Mr. Seth Jefferson?"

"Well, he would be hard to describe exactly. First he was a share-cropper, then he worked at a warehouse in Greenville. Then he became a carpenter here at Tanglewood."

She wrote fast...a sharecropper, warehouse worker, carpenter—and finally the last master of Tanglewood. Where were the academic credentials to begin a college?

"Now, let me get this straight. These wealthy landowners *gave* their plantation to...to a carpenter! You expect me to believe that?"

He shrugged and smiled. "A real story, ain't it, ma'am?"

"Yes, it's a story all right. Let's see. Let's just fill in a few more details. What year was it that this Jefferson fellow was given Tanglewood?"

"1899," he stated simply.

He knew she did not believe him, and at his age he expected as much.

"I don't know why I'm asking you this, but whose plan was it to make Tanglewood a Bible college? The Alcotts'?"

"Well, not exactly. They agreed to it, thought it was a fine plan. But it was mostly Mr. Jefferson's idea. And that of his wife and two sons."

"Hmm...So he made it a college."

"A Bible college," he corrected gently. "A place for young and even old black folks to come and learn the Word, then go out and preach it. We send out more preachers each year than any other Bible college in the state," he beamed proudly.

"We?"

He jabbed his cane toward the building. "Magnolia Bible College."

"Why was it named Magnolia? I'm sure you can tell me that. Why not Alcott or even Jefferson College?"

Her voice was tinged with skepticism.

"Well, magnolias are a pretty fact around here, sure you noticed, ma'am."

"The college was named for a tree?"

He chuckled. "You'll make a fine reporter someday, ma'am."

But she did not bristle this time. The old man was wearing her down.

"It was called Magnolia for a painting called *Magnolia Remembrance*. Miss Amy thought of that. For...memories..."

"Magnolia Remembrance."

"Some things aren't easy to explain, ma'am."

"*Magnolia Remembrance* sounds very romantic. Can you give me more details?"

"Oh, it's a long story, that one is," he admitted slowly.

"Well, I'm in no hurry. I have all afternoon."

She was hooked now.

He smiled. A nice, warm smile, she finally noticed.

"If you walk back behind the dormitories a ways you'll see the rock foundations of some slave cabins. They left them there, like a reminder. That building they made into a car shed used to be the carpenter's shop." His face grew troubled a moment. "The first one was burned one night."

"Was burned? How?"

But he waved his hand at her as if to brush aside an unpleasant memory. "If you keep walkin' behind them new buildings you'll find the family cemetery. They didn't move it in all these years. All them Cashes still lyin' there."

He rubbed his chin thoughtfully, the humor rising in him again.

"'Course I hope they ain't still a lyin' there. Do hope they've moved on...least ways in spirit!"

He slapped his knee as he laughed. She joined him this time. At last she understood.

"About the cemetery?" she prompted.

"Cemetery? Oh, there's a stone there. *Magnolia Remembrance* is carved on the last line...like a tribute."

"Whose stone?"

"Mr. Patrick Cash. I worked for him years ago. Did I tell you that already?"

"Do you mind if I ask you how old you are?"

"Don't mind at all. Bible says gray hairs are a crown. I'm 96 last spring."

"Ninety-six!" Yet she had come to the place where she believed every word he said. "I thought you were about 70!"

"Well, that's fine. Viney always thought I was a handsome man, she surely did. Do you want to know my secret?"

She leaned forward. This old man was delightful!

"Prayer. Yes, ma'am. Prayer at the beginnin' and at the endin' and a lot of hard work in between."

They heard steps on the path then. Someone was coming. The old man frowned. "She found me. She'll be sayin' it's time to take my nap. You watch and see if she don't say that. You'd think at 96 I'd be too old for naps!"

He was a petulant little boy again.

"Now about what you've told me. Were you...?" She quickly calculated in her mind, "were you alive during the Civil War?"

He grimaced. "Is that what they're callin' it these days? Didn't seem too civil to me, no, ma'am. I was a boy when the states fought."

"Can you tell me about *Magnolia Remembrance* and the college if I come back here sometime?" she asked eagerly.

He stood up stiffly. She came to him. She gave him her hand. She had never touched black flesh before.

"It's been a real pleasure for me talking to you...*sir.* Thank you."

"And for me." He bowed over her hand with touching gallantry.

Then a woman appeared, dressed in nurse's whites.

"There you are, Mr. Jefferson. Just where I thought you'd be. It's time for your nap."

She watched him go, hobbling along, leaning on the nurse.

Then a door opened in the young reporter's mind. Mr. Jefferson...

She had just interviewed a sharecropper, a laborer, a carpenter, and the former president of Magnolia Bible College!

She'd be sure to thank her editor for the afternoon's assignment when she got back to town. Yes, ma'am!

Afterword

It was about 20 years ago. I was in junior high school. (To save time and sacrifice vanity, I'm *just* 34.) My brother, Jim, and I were taking a short trip together. It was spring break, and we headed for the Texas coast to camp on the beach. Time has stolen most of that memory, except that on the second night, about 2:00 A.M., a strong Gulf breeze flattened our tent on top of us. In the gale, we couldn't get it back up, so we crawled into our sand-filled clothes and started the six-hour trip back home.

That was the way things were for us—we shared lots of fun and laughter. We laughed over silly, odd, ridiculous things. No sister ever had a better brother. Fifteen years have passed since a humid August night when the policeman came to our door and told us Jim was gone.

My real desire in writing *The Masterpiece*, besides creating an entertaining historical novel, was to paint a picture of the importance of family relationships free of bitterness and estrangement. I hope Meg and Andy did just that.

To those readers who picked up *The Masterpiece* because of *The Tapestry*, you have my gratitude. I take the trust between us seriously, and for however many books, I hope my writing will be an enjoyment and blessing to you.

The Alcott Legacy continues in the final book of this trilogy (expected release, 1995). Think of the young girl in the prologue. Who is she? (I think that's called a teaser...)

What is written without effort,
is often read without pleasure.

To your reading pleasure,
MaryAnn Minatra

The
Alcott Legacy
begins in

The Tapestry

From Tennessee battlefields to the White House itself, this sweeping Civil War epic traces the lives of two brothers—linked only by a broken locket—the people who loved them, and the triumph of faithful prayer.

Ethan Alcott could not ignore the war any longer. His family could do the praying—he was going to fight. Chosen as President Lincoln's personal aide and bodyguard, the young captain quickly finds himself drawn in to the swirling intrigue of Washington politics. Then tragedy strikes. Broken and ashamed, Ethan must come to terms with his pride and his guilt, foes stronger than the Confederate army.

Follow Ethan and the woman he loves as strong cords of faith and hope are beautifully woven in *The Tapestry.*

Harvest House Publishers

For the Best in Inspirational Fiction

RUTH LIVINGSTON HILL CLASSICS

Bright Conquest
The Homecoming (mass paper)
The South Wind Blew Softly (mass paper)

June Masters Bacher
PIONEER ROMANCE NOVELS

Series 1

1. Love Is a Gentle
   Stranger
2. Love's Silent Song
3. Diary of a Loving Heart

4. Love Leads Home
5. Love Follows the Heart
6. Love's Enduring Hope

Series 2

1. Journey to Love
2. Dreams Beyond
   Tomorrow
3. Seasons of Love

4. My Heart's Desire
5. The Heart Remembers
6. From This Time Forth

Series 3

1. Love's Soft Whisper
2. Love's Beautiful Dream
3. When Hearts Awaken

4. Another Spring
5. When Morning Comes Again
6. Gently Love Beckons

HEARTLAND HERITAGE SERIES

No Time for Tears
Songs in the Whirlwind
Where Lies Our Hope
Return to the Heartland

Lori Wick
A PLACE CALLED HOME SERIES
A Place Called Home
A Song for Silas
The Long Road Home
A Gathering of Memories

THE CALIFORNIANS
Whatever Tomorrow Brings
As Time Goes By
Sean Donovan
Donovan's Daughter

THE KENSINGTON CHRONICLES
The Hawk and the Jewel
Wings of the Morning
Who Brings Forth the Wind (Fall 1994)

MaryAnn Minatra
THE ALCOTT LEGACY
The Tapestry
The Masterpiece

Ellen Traylor
BIBLICAL NOVELS
Esther
Joseph (mass paper)
Moses
Joshua
Samson

Other Romance Novels
The Hills of God, *Wiggin*